CATHY WOODMAN

Follow Me Home

arrow books

Published by Arrow Books, 2014

2 4 6 8 10 9 7 5 3

Copyright © Cathy Woodman, 2014

First published in Great Britain in 2014 by Century

Arrow Books
Random House, 20 Vauxhall Bridge Road,
London SW1V 2SA

www.randomhouse.co.uk

Addresses for companies within The Random House Group Limited can be found at: www.randomhouse.co.uk/offices.htm

The Random House Group Limited Reg. No. 954009

A CIP catalogue record for this book is available from the British Library

ISBN 9780099584926

he Random House Group Limited supports the Forest Stewardship Council® (FSC®), the leading international forest-certification organisation. Our books carrying the FSC label are printed on FSC®-certified paper. FSC is the only forest-certification scheme supported by the leading environmental organisations, including Greenpeace. Our paper procurement policy can be found at: www.randomhouse.co.uk/environment

Typeset by SX Composing DTP, Rayleigh, Essex
Printed and bound by CPI Group (UK) Ltd, Croydon, CR0 4YY

To Charlotte and Millie

Acknowledgements

I should like to thank Laura Langrigg at MBA Literary Agents, and Gillian Holmes and the team at Random House for their enthusiasm and support.

For their patience and help while I've been writing *Follow Me Home*, I'd like to thank my friends and family, especially Tamsin and Will.

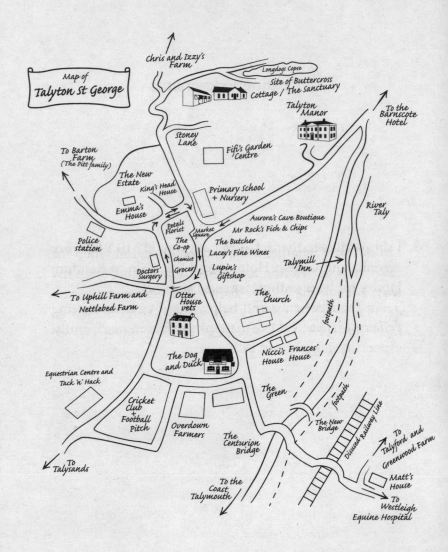

Map of
Talyton St George

Chris and Izzy's Farm

Longdogs Copse

Site of Buttercross Cottage / The Sanctuary

Talyton Manor

To the Barnscote Hotel

Stoney Lane

Fifi's Garden Centre

To Barton Farm (The Pitt family)

The New Estate

King's Head House

Emma's House

Primary School + Nursery

Petals Florist

Market Square

Aurora's Cave Boutique

Mr Rock's Fish & Chips

The Butcher

Lacey's Fine Wines

River Taly

The Co-op

chemist Grocer

Lupin's Giftshop

Talymill Inn

Police station

Doctors Surgery

Otter House vets

The Church

footpath

To Uphill Farm and Nettlebed Farm

The Dog and Duck

Nicci's House

Frances' House

Equestrian Centre and Tack 'n' Hack

Cricket Club + Football Pitch

Overdown Farmers

The Green

footpath

Disused Railway Line

The New Bridge

To Talyford and Greenwood Farm

The Centurion Bridge

Matt's House

To Talysands

To the Coast, Talymouth

To Westleigh Equine Hospital

CHAPTER ONE

Special Delivery

I'm not sure whether to be excited or scared when the call I've been waiting for comes at last, but I'm on my way. I leave the Village News, the newsagent's, and drive through the empty streets of Talyton St George on a cold February afternoon with the sleet pelting against the windscreen and the antique streetlamps dancing reflections on the puddles. I pass King's Head House, and Petals, with its colourful window display of flowers, before turning right at Mr Rock's fish and chip shop and Lacey's Fine Wines. Mrs Dyer, the butcher's wife is walking, or – it would be more accurate to say – is being walked by her giant dog that reminds me of Scooby-Doo. I wave, but with two hands on the lead, she can only nod back as the dog tows her out of the churchyard towards home.

I switch the heating up and continue out of town, following the signs for Talyford and beyond, where

1

torrents of orange water rush down the sandy banks dotted with bushes and bare-rooted trees on both sides of the road, and flood across the lane on the way to Greenwood Farm.

My mobile rings – I answer it on the hands-free.

'Zara, when are you going to get here?' Murray, the father-to-be, is panicking.

'I won't be long. Two minutes max,' I say calmly, although my heart is beginning to beat faster. 'How is she doing?'

'I reckon she's about to drop,' Murray says in a broad Devon accent as his wife utters a high-pitched wail in the background.

'Why didn't you get in touch earlier?' I ask him.

'Emily didn't want to bother you too soon.'

'It's my job. I'm supposed to be there.' My fingers tighten on the steering wheel. 'How often are the contractions coming now?'

'Since her waters broke, every three or four minutes. I don't know. I've lost count.' Briefly, he recovers his sense of humour. 'I never thought I'd hear myself say this, but I can't wait for you to turn up.'

I smile to myself. In Murray's opinion, I spend far too much time with Emily.

'Murray, calm down, will you? We always thought it would be quicker this time.' I try to reassure him. I wouldn't mind betting that Emily's in transition at least, which means this baby will soon be here. I hope I'm not going to miss out. 'I'll be with you at any minute. Tell her to remember to breathe,' I add lightly.

'I heard that. I am bloody breathing,' I hear Emily

2

yell back before the mobile signal cuts out. Emily never swears. I put my foot down, speeding up along the lane before slowing and turning into the driveway just after the leaping deer that Murray created from brushwood last summer and placed by the gate to mark the farm entrance. I pull in off the muddy track into the yard and park between a tractor and a pick-up in front of the cob and thatch farmhouse where the door is open and the lights are on. I grab my bag and trolley from the back of the car and head inside, leaving my shoes on the mat in the hall and checking in the mirror above the table that I've remembered to tie my hair back. I straighten my uniform too, navy trousers and a royal blue top with our midwifery team logo, Topaz, embroidered onto it.

'What kept you?' Murray, Emily's husband of five years, pops his head around the living-room door. He's thirty-three, two years older than me and Emily, and six foot four tall with a freckled complexion, a mop of curly red hair and hazel eyes. 'Seriously, I've never been so pleased to see you, Zara. Come on in.'

I follow him into the room where the scent of lavender oil drifts through the air, displacing the smell of sheep and farmyard from my nostrils.

'I thought you were all for delivering this baby yourself,' I say, observing that he's had time to change out of his outdoor clothes into clean jeans and a chunky-knit sweater.

'I shouldn't joke about that. I thought I was going to have to.' He wipes his palms on his thighs. 'Where's Kelly? I thought she'd be here too.'

'She will be.' Kelly's my partner in our close-knit team of community midwives, and we usually attend a birth together, at least when delivery is imminent. 'She's coming from Talymouth, but the road's been blocked by a landslip. The last I heard she was stuck in traffic.' I make my way to the sofa where Emily is on her knees in a long grey T-shirt with her blonde hair loose around her shoulders. She rests her arms on the seat, rocking back and forth and biting into a cushion.

'Emily, how are you?' I kneel down beside her and she answers with a low moan. Her brow is beaded with sweat and her expression is pained. The lights flicker as if they're coming out in sympathy with her.

'How are you doing?' I repeat gently.

'How do you think?' She swears out loud and glares in my direction as if she blames me for putting her in this situation. I can see myself in her, in the deep blue of the eyes, the plumpness of the cheeks and the shape of the mouth. I can feel her pain as the contraction peaks and dies away once more, giving her a short respite during which time I make quick checks on her and the baby. Emily's fully dilated and the baby's heartbeat is strong and regular.

'It won't be long,' I say, smiling despite my anxiety because, although all my babies are precious, this one is a particularly special delivery.

Murray waits perched on the arm of the sofa while I stroke Emily's back. There is a stack of logs burning in the grate behind the fireguard, plastic sheets and blankets thrown over the sofa and sponges strewn across the carpet. A cross-eyed teddy bear looks down

4

from the mantelpiece in the direction of a wooden crate overflowing with toys, as if to say, put me away so I can have some peace and quiet, as Emily moans again with the onset of another contraction.

I check my fob watch. Where the hell is Kelly? I thought she'd have found an alternative route and be here by now. At this rate, I'll be catching Emily's baby single-handed. The realisation of what I've agreed to do suddenly hits me.

Emily had such a traumatic labour giving birth in hospital the first time around – I wasn't her midwife on that occasion – that she wanted a home birth and a better experience for her and the baby. She was reluctant to ask me initially, but I would have felt hurt if she'd asked anyone else. Emily's children are the closest I'll ever come to having children of my own.

'I want to push,' She says through gritted teeth.

'Go for it,' I say.

'I need something for the pain,' she goes on. 'I'd forgotten how bad it is. It hurts sooo much.' She gasps as she starts to bear down. 'I want the gas and air. Now!'

I set up the Entonox and hand her the mouthpiece, but she can't really concentrate any more.

'Do you want the music on, my darling?' Murray says.

'No thanks,' Emily says.

'Are you sure? I spent ages putting those tracks together.'

'I said no,' Emily snaps, and I'm glad because although my sister's taste in music under normal

5

circumstances is similar to mine, I wouldn't put it past her to have chosen something soothing like pan pipes. I have delivered so many babies to the sound of pan pipes, I never want to hear one again.

'Concentrate on your breathing,' I say. 'That way you'll get the full effect of the gas and air.'

There's a strong gust of wind, which rattles the windows and the lights go out, leaving us in near-darkness.

'Am I hallucinating, or has it just gone dark?' Emily says.

'It's a power cut,' Murray says. 'I expect the overhead power lines are down.'

'Have you got candles or torches?' I've never had to deliver a baby in the dark, and I don't want to start now.

'I'll get the candles,' says Emily, attempting to stand up.

'No, you won't,' I say firmly. 'You aren't going anywhere. Murray will get them.'

'Lewis has a couple of storm lanterns in the barn.'

'He'll need them for the ewes,' Emily says.

'I think our baby is more important, don't you?' Murray walks towards the door.

'Don't leave me, not when you got me into this state,' Emily shouts.

'I'm here. Emily, calm down,' I go on with sisterly impatience. 'Everything's going to be all right.'

Murray returns within five minutes.

'Let there be light.' He places a lantern on the side table before striking a match and lighting several

6

candles and tea-lights around the room, his presence seeming to enable Emily to regain her focus on the imminent birth of her baby.

'Let me check the baby's heartbeat again before the next contraction.'

'It feels like it's got hiccups,' Emily says, frowning, and I check with the Doppler. The baby's heart rate is slower than before.

'Something's wrong,' Emily goes on. 'I know it.'

'Baby's heart rate has dipped,' I say, as the lights flicker on and off again. 'It's getting a little stressed, that's all. It's perfectly normal.'

'It isn't. I can tell from your voice. Zara, you can't hide anything from me.'

'I'm not hiding anything.'

'You would tell me, wouldn't you?'

'Of course I would,' I say, lying through my teeth. 'Everything will be fine. All you have to do now is concentrate on pushing as hard as you can – between as well as during contractions.'

'Should I call somebody, Kelly or an ambulance?' Murray asks.

'I need you to help,' I say, knowing that by the time an ambulance reaches us, it will be too late. I have to help Emily get this baby out as soon as possible. I look towards Murray for help to get her into a better position so I can use suction to assist the delivery if necessary. Five minutes later, although it feels like much longer, the baby's heart rate comes back up, but then it begins to dip again. I'm more worried than (I hope) I am letting on.

'Come on, Emily. Push,' I urge her. 'Push as hard as you can.'

'Come on, love,' Murray joins in.

'I am pushing,' she says through gritted teeth as she bears down. 'I can't push any harder.'

Come on, baby, I say inwardly, wishing Kelly was here with me to make the decisions, because I'm wondering if I can trust myself, if – as my supervisor suggested – I'm too close to my sister to make rational decisions over her care. I thought I could do it. I really thought I could, but I'm beginning to have doubts and this is really the wrong time . . .

'I can't push any more . . . Emily moans as her body begins to relax, the contraction fading. 'I'm finished. I can't do this any more.'

'Don't waste your energy on talking.' Murray looks down at the marks on his arm where Emily has loosened her grip with her fingers. 'Come on, love, squeeze my hand, take another breath and push. You can do it.'

Emily grimaces and closes her eyes and pushes and I can see the top of the baby's head.

'Pant,' I tell her as I attach the ventouse and apply suction, explaining what I'm doing as I go along. The baby's head is swollen and ominously blue rather than purple. Birth can be – and usually is – a wonderful, positive experience for all concerned, but this one might be one of those occasions when it isn't. I ignore Murray's white face and focus on getting the baby out.

'Now push again. Harder than last time,' I urge her.

'I can't.' Emily seems exhausted, shattered by the

8

effort and shock of what has proved to be a rapid labour.

'You have to,' I say a little curtly, knowing what Emily doesn't, that the cord is loose around the baby's neck, but getting pinched as its shoulders pass along the birth canal, causing the baby's distress. 'Push as if your life depends on it. Emily, please, listen to me.'

'Oh no,' she wails. 'It's all going wrong like the last time.'

'Emily, just shut up! Trust me. One more push should do it.'

Emily succumbs to the next contraction and pushes and I'm waiting with bated breath when out comes the baby's head, then the shoulders, followed by the rest of its body and a gush of fluid. I catch her – it's a girl – in a towel and, watching her the whole time and praying for some sign of life, I place her on the mat on the side table in the fractured light of the storm lantern.

I rub her mottled skin, trying to stimulate her to breathe, while checking for a heartbeat – there is one bumping faintly beneath my fingertips – and fumbling for the Ambu bag on my trolley, as well as keeping an eye on the seconds that are ticking away all too quickly.

Just as I open my mouth to tell Murray to call an ambulance, the baby screws up her face and opens her mouth to take her first gulping breath, and a second and a third, before expanding her lungs to their full extent and letting out a pitiful cry, at which Emily cries with relief and exhaustion, and Murray cries, and I want to cry too, but I can't because I'm supposed to be the professional here.

At five minutes, the baby's Apgar score is up to seven from five and I'm happy to hand her still damp and covered in the vernix that looks like shea butter, over to Emily to meet her new daughter.

'Congratulations, you and Murray have the most beautiful baby girl.' It's what I say every time – some babies are more beautiful than others and this one is absolutely gorgeous. I can't wait to have a proper cuddle.

Emily sinks gingerly onto the sofa as she holds the baby to her breast.

'What's that lump on her head?' Murray asks.

'The chignon? It's from the suction cap I used to assist the delivery. Don't worry – it will go down within a couple of days.'

'Are you sure?' Murray says.

'It will be fine.'

'Only Lily had a mark on her head . . .' I notice how Murray swallows hard, keeping his eyes fixed on his new daughter. Emily reaches out and touches his arm.

'Oh, Murray, I'm so sorry,' she murmurs. 'I wish . . .'

'I know, love. Seeing this baby brings it all back, somehow.'

I stand back, a lump in my throat, as they recall the baby they lost.

'It was my fault,' Emily says.

'We've been through this over and over.' Murray's tone is rough with renewed grief. 'It was a risk we took for the farm, for our family. We'll never forget her, never stop loving her, but we have a new baby and Poppy to concentrate on now.'

'I know,' Emily sighs.

My heart goes out to them. Not only did Emily dismiss my advice, she trained as a nurse before she married Murray, so she should have known better than to work with the sheep while she was pregnant. She lost the baby through an infection caught from delivering lambs. This time, she's been ultra-careful.

She kisses her daughter before looking up at her husband. 'Thank you, darling. I'm sorry I yelled at you.'

'It's all right,' he says ruefully. 'You bit me the last time. This time, you cut off the circulation to my hand. I can still feel the pins and needles.'

'That's good, then – that means your hand isn't going to fall off.' Emily turns to me. 'Thanks, sis. I couldn't have got through it without you.'

'Thank you for asking me to be here,' I say in return, my eyes burning with tears of relief and happiness. 'I wouldn't have missed it for the world.'

'Baby, say hello to your Auntie Zara.'

'Hello, niece.' I reach out and touch the baby's cheek. With Murray's hair and Emily's nose, she's a real cutie. Silently, in the flickering candlelight, I wish her a long and happy life. 'I wonder what Poppy is going to make of her new baby sister,' I begin, after I've taken photos of the three of them together.

'I dread to think,' Emily says with a small smile. 'I hope Mum's convinced her to give the baby a chance. I'm afraid she's going to be really jealous. She's been an only child for four years. It's going to be hard for her to adjust.'

'I'll get the phone,' Murray says. 'We'd better not keep your mum and grandmother in suspense any longer. As soon as you've let them know, I'll call my side of the family and give them the news.'

'Gran's been calling all day. If you look at my phone, you'll find hundreds of voicemail messages.' Emily smiles. 'Zara, can you put her out of her misery? I'm not sure I have the energy left to speak to her right now.'

'One of us will bring her to see you,' I say, sympathetic to my sister's opinion, 'but we won't let her stay too long.' I know very well what she's like. There are times when she can't stop talking. I contact Kelly to let her know she isn't needed this time.

'I could have done with you here,' I tell her, explaining out of my sister's earshot what happened. 'I so nearly misjudged it . . . I'd never have forgiven myself—'

'It was a successful outcome, though,' Kelly points out. 'You should be proud of yourself. I wish I'd been there.'

'Have there been any other calls?' I ask. 'I haven't been answering my phone.'

'Just one, Celine, and I've sent her off to see the emergency doctor for antibiotics for a possible UTI.' I know Celine well – her pregnancies are never straightforward. 'Tell Emily I'll pop in for a cuddle when I'm passing. I'll see you at work tomorrow, Zara.'

'Unless another of our ladies decides to go into labour tonight.'

'All's peaceful, so I'm quietly optimistic that I'll be able to have dinner, take a bath and slip into my PJs without being disturbed.' Kelly is five years older than me, in her mid-thirties, with a husband and two kids. 'Bye, Zara.'

I wish her goodnight and wait for Mum who, in spite of the weather, turns up in less than twenty minutes, which means she must have driven like a demon taking the longer route to avoid the landslip. We've barely had time to boil the kettle on the range when she and my niece arrive, Poppy stumbling indoors, dressed in a red pinafore, woolly tights and shiny purple wellies, and carrying a fluffy black and white toy cat.

'Mummy's had the baby,' Murray says, gathering her up, wellies and all, into his arms and resting her on his hip.

'We heard her crying all the way from Talymouth.' Mum smiles warmly. She's almost sixty and wrapped up in a grey turtleneck sweater, flowing lilac cardigan and wide-legged trousers in an attempt to disguise the fact that, like me, she's a few pounds overweight. She tucks a curl of her bob of ash-blonde hair behind her ear.

'We didn't hear her.' Poppy frowns and shakes her golden ringlets of hair. 'I didn't hear a baby.'

'Oh, you are wearing your grandma out with all your arguing, Poppy. Emily, you are such a clever daughter.' Mum moves across to the sofa and embraces my sister and the baby and I feel a sharp pain in my chest, a pang of love and envy combined.

'Where's Dad?' Emily asks.

'He's coming up to see you all later. He's been held up in that traffic coming back from the cash-and-carry, and I told him I couldn't wait a moment longer to see the baby. It's been the longest nine months ever. Now Poppy, come and see your new sister. Have you got her present, the one you're going to give her to welcome her into the world?' Mum continues.

Murray holds Poppy so she can see the baby up close, but Poppy isn't impressed.

'Mummy, I don't want a sister.' She clutches the toy cat to her face.

'I thought you'd be pleased,' Murray says. 'You said you didn't want a brother.'

'I want a kitten.'

Murray laughs. 'You know Mummy can't have kittens.'

'Or a snake. Mummy, send it back. Put it back in your tummy.'

'Mummy can't do that.' Mum reaches up to stroke Poppy's head. 'There isn't room for her any more.'

'You must give her away. Auntie Zara hasn't got a baby. She can have her.'

'Auntie Zara doesn't want a baby at the moment.' My sister looks at me, her expression one of apology, knowing how much I wanted a baby with Paul. 'Besides, Daddy and I wouldn't dream of sending the new baby – or you for that matter – to someone else. We're going to be one big happy family now.'

'No,' Poppy squeals.

'Pops, give the toy to your baby sister,' Murray says.

'Nooooo!' Still hanging onto the cat, Poppy sticks

14

her fingers in her ears and starts kicking out at her dad. Murray puts her down and she collapses onto her bottom, crying inconsolably.

'Leave her for a minute,' Murray says when I move to comfort her. 'She'll calm down.'

I wish them luck, I think. They'll be needing a visit from Supernanny before they know it.

'Have you decided on a name?' I ask.

'We were going to ask Poppy to help choose,' Emily says, 'but considering the circumstances, I think it's better that we don't. I can't imagine what she'd call the baby.'

'I can,' Murray says dryly. 'I'd lay bets on a particular bodily function.'

'Well, I still like Daisy,' Emily says.

'I'm not so sure about that one,' Murray responds. 'It's the kind of name you'd give to a dog.'

'She looks like a Daisy,' Emily says, looking wistfully at her husband.

'I thought we'd decided on Esther for a girl.'

Emily tips her head to one side. 'Oh, Murray, please . . .'

He smiles and sighs, 'Anything for you, my darling. I suppose Daisy isn't too bad, as it goes.' I think Murray's so relieved that both mum and baby are well, that he'd agree to anything right now.

'I think it's the perfect name for a wonderful new grandchild,' Mum says. 'Poppy, come with me and we'll phone Great Grandma to tell her the good news.'

'Bad news,' Poppy interrupts. She scrambles up

from the floor, runs to her mother and clambers onto the bed before trying to whop the baby with the cat. Murray restrains her.

'Come here, Poppy,' Mum says. 'You can help me cook the tea for everyone. What did we buy at the butcher's?'

'Sausages,' Poppy says, more cheerfully.

'Come on then. Hurry up. I expect Zara has things to do here.'

'I want Daddy to come with me,' Poppy insists, but Mum takes her firmly by the hand and almost drags her away.

'Sometimes Poppy makes me wonder why we went ahead and had another one,' Murray sighs.

Emily reaches out her hand to him. 'She'll come round eventually.'

'Let me recheck Daisy, then you can give her a cuddle while I have a look at you, Emily. You're going to need a couple of stitches this time.'

'Do you really think I'm going to let you sew me up by candlelight?' She says lightly.

'It'll be okay, I promise. Unless you'd prefer me to call Kelly and ask her to do it.'

'No, let's get this over with.'

Later, after Dad arrives to greet the baby, Emily insists on taking Daisy downstairs to the warmth of the kitchen where we sit at the table by candlelight while Mum dishes up sausages, boiled potatoes, carrots and lumpy gravy, evidence that the cooking gene skipped a generation in our family. Emily perches on a cushion while the baby feeds at her breast. Poppy is now more curious than antagonistic as regards her new sister, especially since Murray has run through a long list of reasons why a sister is better than a kitten. Poppy seems pleased that the baby will have nappies, whereas a kitten would have to have a litter tray, or 'stinky box', as her dad describes it.

While we're chatting, the temporary shepherd who's filling in for Emily strolls into the kitchen from the utility room at the side. His brown hair is windswept and his face clothed in stubble. In his early twenties, he's tall and incredibly fit, in more ways than one, and he's wearing a beanie hat, a tatty waxed jacket, moleskin trousers and workman's boots. He carries a tiny lamb with a speckled face tucked under one arm and I can't help thinking how cute the pair of them look as he walks across the kitchen tiles leaving a trail of muddy footprints.

'Hey, Lewis, leave your boots at the door,' Emily scolds. 'How many times?'

'I'm sorry. I'll mop up.' He looks a little sheepish as he unlaces his boots with one hand, keeping the lamb close to his chest with the other, and removes them, scattering straw from his socks. 'I'll sweep first,' he adds with a rueful smile.

'This is a house, not a barn, in case you hadn't noticed,' Emily goes on lightly.

Lewis stops and stares. 'The baby – she's arrived! That was quick.'

'Meet Daisy,' Emily says as Lewis looks away awkwardly, having perhaps just realised my sister is breastfeeding.

'Congratulations,' Lewis says. 'That's great. How are you, Emily?'

'Well, thank you. It was so much better than the last time,' Emily looks towards me with a smile on her lips, 'thanks to my lovely midwife. This is Zara, my twin.'

'We've met briefly,' Lewis says.

I smile, meeting his gaze. Lewis has been working at the farm for about a month now and we've said hello two or three times when I've been up to see Emily for her antenatal checks and have brought Gran to visit her. I touch my face – it's burning, and not because I'm sitting close to the range.

'What's up with the lamb?' Murray asks as Lewis kicks a cardboard box out from under the oak table and pops the lamb into it, where it lies tucked up and shivering, its coat damp and curly.

'This is one of triplets and the others are pushing it out,' Lewis starts. 'I've tried putting it with another ewe who has a singleton, but she isn't having any of it. It's a bit of a wuss. I hope you don't mind me bringing it indoors, but it's getting cold and I can't use the heat lamps while the electricity's off.'

'Come on in,' Murray says dryly. 'Oh, I see you already have.'

Lewis grins. 'Would you like to feed this one, Poppy?'

'Yes, please.' Poppy's face glows as she plonks herself down beside the box.

Lewis warms a baby's bottle from the fridge in hot water on the range before testing the temperature on his wrist and handing it over to Poppy with instructions.

The lamb bleats plaintively – there is no other way to describe it – and waggles its tail as it feeds and butts its nose against the teat of the bottle, dripping milk over Poppy's fingers. She licks it off.

'Poppy, I don't think you're supposed to do that,' I say.

'It's nice,' she says, doing it again.

'Let the lamb have it, please.' Murray rolls his eyes.

'It's attention-seeking,' Mum comments. 'She's bound to feel insecure.'

The lamb drains about half the milk and Lewis takes the bottle back.

'Thank you. Are you going to stay up to give her another feed later?'

'Yes, please,' she smiles, grabbing the opportunity to have a pet, even if it is only transitory, and maybe recognising a kindred spirit in the lamb that has been cast aside by its siblings.

'Oh, don't encourage her,' Emily groans.

'I don't think it matters what time Poppy goes to bed tonight,' Mum says. 'None of you will sleep.'

'I'm going to.' Murray yawns. 'It's been a long day.'

'Hey, what about me?' Emily gives him a gentle prod.

'There's some dinner if you'd like it, Lewis,' Mum says.

'And a glass of champagne to wet the baby's head,' Murray adds.

'Thanks for the offer, but there's another ewe about to lamb. I need to get back out there.'

'I must get going too,' I say, feeling ridiculously

disappointed that he has to leave so soon. 'Gran will be wondering where I am.'

'I'll fetch her up here tomorrow, if that's all right,' Mum says. 'Dad can cover a couple of hours in the shop, can't you, Jim?'

My father grimaces at the thought, but says he'll do it.

'I'll be back tomorrow for a home visit.' I watch Murray at his wife's side, the baby feeding at her breast and Poppy bouncing up and down on his knee and the pang of envy I felt earlier grows into a heavy ache in my chest. I love my sister and her family. I just wish I had one of my own. I almost did. I was this close with Paul and then my dream gradually unravelled.

Back in my car, I check my mobile to see if Paul's tried to get hold of me. He sent the last text three days ago, just to say hi, check I'm okay and ask if Emily had had her baby yet. I've texted him twice since. I touch the screen to bring up his number to call him, change my mind and drop the phone into my bag. What is that phrase Gran uses sometimes? Out of sight, out of mind.

CHAPTER TWO

Sherbet Lemons and Mint Humbugs

On the Tuesday morning a week after Daisy's birth, I wake up in the flat above the newsagent's, shower and grab a piece of toast and butter as I'm getting ready for work. It's dark outside and when I look out of the kitchen window across the street, listening to the purr of the ancient fridge, I can see the roofs of the buildings opposite sparkling with frost. Ron's float pulls up outside to deliver the milk.

I eat a second piece of toast, a cereal bar and a packet of smoky bacon crisps before I head downstairs past the green, pink and gold wallpaper that harks back to the 1980s, looking out for the elderly tabby cat that has taken offence to me living here.

At the bottom of the stairs, I walk along the corridor, past the cuckoo clock and through the multi-coloured plastic strips of the fly curtain which hangs across the doorway into the shop, where I find my flatmate wobbling precariously on top of a set of wooden steps beside the display of old-fashioned sweets, the ones you buy from jars by weight and scooped into paper bags.

'Good morning, Gran,' I say. 'Are you sure that's a good idea?'

'Zara, dear, have you seen your granddad?' Gran asks without answering my question. She clutches a jar of sherbet lemons to her chest. Her silver hair is swept back from her face and she wears small gold hoop earrings, a black dress, pink cardigan, black tights and purple slippers, and most remarkably, she is almost as round and cuddly as she is tall. I'm five foot four and the top of her head just reaches my shoulder – when we're standing on the same level, that is.

'Please get down. Let me do that.'

Only last week, I found her on a stepladder, hanging a Union Jack in the window to complete her new display of patriotic red, white and blue china, which Uncle Nobby, who's actually my great uncle, bought at a knock-off price from some anonymous bloke at the Dog and Duck, and sold on to her. It's no wonder it was cheap – it looks cheap and it is cheap, but Gran insists there's no money in newspapers any more and she has to stock anything that sells, which means the place is looking more like a bric-a-brac stall than a newsagent's. She hasn't sold a single piece of china yet, but people do come in for sweets, lottery tickets, scratch-cards and cigarettes, and – most of all – to pass the time of day.

'You promised me you'd keep your feet on the ground,' I remind her.

'I'm fine,' she says brightly. 'Please don't keep treating me like I'm some old biddy. Haven't you heard that eighty's the new twenty-five?'

'I think you're rather exaggerating.' I can't help smiling as I make my way between the counter and the newspapers that are still stacked on the floor when they should be on the shelves or in the bag for the paper boy by now.

'Not at all.' Gran tips her head slowly to one side. 'You sound just like your mum. It's time you started going out again and having some fun, my lover.' She calls everyone 'my lover' – it's a Devonian thing.

'I do go out, although you're right, I'm struggling to remember when I could say I last had fun. Does mine and Claire's attempt at Zumba count?'

'If it made you laugh and made your heart beat faster, then yes.'

'It did. We were hysterical, shimmying and shaking our booty, and bumping into each other.' The steps rock and Gran wobbles. 'Please get down. Here.' I reach up for the jar and place it next to the aniseed balls by the till before taking her hand and helping her down to safety. 'Those papers should be sorted by now, shouldn't they?'

'I know, but I've lost your granddad and I don't like to start the day without him.'

'Let me do the papers and then I'll help you look for him. He can't have gone far.'

'You mustn't make yourself late for work. Those babies won't wait.'

'None of my ladies are due during the next week

– not that you can rely on due dates. I have a couple of antenatal checks, a clinic and a visit to the farm today, so I can spare a few minutes.' I pause for a moment. 'Are you sure you haven't left him upstairs like you did the other day?'

Gran looks at me, her forehead crinkled and pale, and not for the first time, I wonder how much longer she will cope with running the shop and what will happen when she can't.

'I'll check,' she begins, but I go for her, looking in the living room, where every surface is filled with Gran's ever-expanding herd of porcelain horses, and in her room, where Norris, the tabby cat, is lying curled up on a pillow on the bed. Keeping a close watch on Norris as a bloodcurdling growl crescendoes in his throat, I pick up the photo from the bedside cabinet and run for it before he can launch one of his full-scale attacks, which usually ends with me being scratched to pieces and on antibiotics. He's drawn blood four times so far, and I've no intention of letting him have a fifth attempt. I don't know what it is about animals; they always seem to go for me.

Halfway down the stairs, I glance at my granddad's whiskery smile in the picture as he and Gran stand arm-in-arm with the snow-covered Alps behind them on what was their last trip together to celebrate their sixtieth birthdays. Granddad passed away four years later when I was fourteen. Emily and I spent a lot of time with him, and I'll never forget how we'd sit on the counter after school while he fed us sweets until we felt sick.

'Thank you, Zara.' Gran kisses the photo when I hand it over. Her eyes are soft with love and affection and I think back to Paul and our wedding vows. Our marriage didn't last, despite my best intentions, whereas Gran still thinks of herself as Granddad's wife.

'One day I'll forget my head.' She places the picture in front of the mint humbugs. 'Where is that boy?'

'He's here.' James, the paper boy, is outside the shop, leaning his bike against the lamppost.

'He looks as if his mother never feeds him,' Gran observes. 'He's such a stringy bean.'

'Shh,' I say, as the door opens and the bell jangles, announcing his arrival, stamping his feet and shaking the rain from his hair. He's tall and skinny for thirteen, with dark-rimmed glasses and braces on his teeth. His fingers are blue with cold.

'Hi, James. I'm afraid we're running a little behind.' I grab the list and a pen from behind the till and start making my way through the papers, scribbling house numbers onto the top right-hand corners with black pen, and wondering how there can be so many people left who don't read the news on the Internet. I fold the papers over and hand them to James to pack.

'Don't dawdle,' Gran says. 'I'll make sure your envelope is waiting for you when you get back.'

'Thank you, Mrs Witheridge,' James says, weighed down by the fluorescent yellow bag slung over his shoulder.

I check the time. I've really got to go. 'See you later, Gran. Promise me, no more mountaineering.'

'Have a good day, Zara,' she says, not promising anything. 'Give little Daisy a hug from me and tell Poppy I'll see her soon.'

'Will do.' I check my mobile for messages on the way to the surgery, which is a short walk away. I don't take my car unless I'm going out on my rounds or down to the centre in Talymouth.

Ben, or Dr Mackie to the older generation of Talyton St George, holds the door open for me as I enter the surgery. He's wearing his check shirt, jacket and tie, and looking very much the country GP.

'Morning,' he says in a low voice, as though he's about to deliver bad news to a patient. He is very reserved, well-respected in Talyton St George, and a good doctor, but I can't say I really know him in the same way I know Nicci, the other GP in the practice. Ben is married to Emma, one of the Otter House vets, and has twin daughters, Elena and Lydia. 'How are you today, Zara?'

'I'm well, thank you,' I respond.

'I wish everyone I met on a daily basis could say that,' and I smile even though it must be the hundredth time that I've heard him crack that joke. He has a crooked nose from playing rugby, but from the look of his growing waistline, his days as a sportsman have long gone. He scratches at the stubble at the side of his head – the rest of his scalp is bald, his hair having long gone too. 'The twins have brought some friends back from nursery.'

'That's nice,' I say, confused.

'Head-lice,' he adds in explanation.

'Oh, I see.' And I find myself scratching my head at the thought.

'I dropped by to check on Emily and her new baby the other night. I hear all went well, thanks to our wonderful midwife. Good job, Zara.'

I thank him and he disappears into his consulting room, leaving me with Janet, the receptionist.

'Have you seen Claire?' I ask her.

'Not yet,' Janet says.

'How long do you think it will be before she mentions the W-word?'

Janet smiles behind the lock of lank, mousy hair she holds across her mouth. She's very quiet for a receptionist; that's probably why Ben chose her, recognising a calm, kindred spirit. 'About a minute?'

'I'm guessing ten seconds.'

Claire is the practice nurse and one of my best friends – I've known her since we were at school. We took our A Levels in the sixth form and went off to do our degrees, hers with my sister in nursing and mine in midwifery, and we've ended up working from the same surgery.

'I'm here.' Claire rushes into reception in her bright magenta uniform. She runs her fingers through her hair, which is currently dark brown at the roots and copper at the tips, while I start counting down the seconds. 'What a nightmare! I overslept,' she explains. 'Kev switched the alarm off before he left for an early shift.' Kevin's the local policeman and Claire's fiancé. 'Sometimes I could kill him, the dopey sod. He's doing a spell in Traffic, but I can't see how he'll ever catch anyone. Hey, I need to talk to you about the bridesmaids' dresses.'

'Ten seconds. I was right,' I say, laughing.

'What are you going on about?' Claire frowns.

'Janet and I were guessing how long it would be before you mentioned something related to the W-word.'

Claire chuckles. 'I don't talk about it that much . . . Do I?'

'I don't think a minute goes by without you mentioning it.'

'I can't help it. It isn't long until the wedding and there's so much to do.' Claire hardly stops to draw breath. 'Anyway, I've seen these amazing gowns in petrol blue.'

'Are you sure you want blue?'

'You don't like the idea?'

'I thought you wanted the bridesmaids in pink.'

'I did, but the blue will have much more impact. You will look amazing, I promise.' Claire changes the subject. 'Are you up for the weigh-in at fat club tonight? I thought we'd go to the pub afterwards for a white wine soda – to celebrate, or drown our sorrows.'

'I'm sorry, I can't make tonight,' I say quickly. 'I've had a fat week. Living with my gran is no good for the diet.'

'Oh Zara.' Claire sounds disappointed. 'I'm relying on you to keep me motivated.'

'Next week, I promise.' We've been on a mission to lose weight and live healthily for the past six months, joining a slimming group as part of the build-up to the wedding. I check my weight on the scales here at the practice while awaiting my first appointment, grimacing as I take off a few pounds to account for my clothes and breakfast. I'm a size sixteen to my sister's ten or twelve and for a health professional I'm not setting a very good example.

I have a few notes from Nicci who has seen Rosie, a teenager, for a pregnancy test that turned out be positive. She's approximately nine weeks gone and has a supportive mother, but there's no mention of the baby's dad, apart from the fact he's eighteen years old. Janet has arranged for a twelve-week scan and has entered the booking-in appointment in my diary.

I call Rosie, who's accompanied by an older woman, through to the nurse's room.

'Come in.' She's only seventeen, and who knows how she will cope, but I don't judge. People have sex and contraceptive accidents can happen to anyone. They are part of life and there have been many times when I've wished one had happened to me.

'Can Mum stay?' Rosie asks as the woman with her introduces herself.

'If you'd like her to. Pull up another chair, Michelle.' I've already read the notes, but I take another look. 'So you're nine weeks pregnant, Rosie?'

'I think so.' She's slim and has her hair in a sleek dark bob that suits her elfin features. 'I'm not sure exactly, but I've missed my period twice. The first time I thought it was due to stress – I've been doing my mocks.'

'She's supposed to be doing her exams in May,' her mother says.

'There's no reason why you can't carry on as planned,' I say, keeping my focus on Rosie. 'When you have your scan, we can check the baby's healthy and see if the measurements tie in with your dates.'

'I'm living with my parents for now.' Rosie bites her lip when I ask about her home address.

'What do you mean, for now?' her mother says.

'You know Dad's threatening to kick me out.'

'Of course he isn't. He's upset, that's all. He'll come round. I'll make sure he does, anyway.'

'Are you planning to continue with your studies when the baby comes?' I ask tentatively.

'No,' Rosie says at the same time as her mother says, 'Yes, of course you are, and I'll look after the little one while you go to uni.'

'Mum, it's my baby. I'm going to look after it.' Rosie strokes her flat belly. Her complexion is pale beneath a layer of orange foundation and fake tan and her eyes are dark with exhaustion and mascara. She's wearing a top which reveals more than a hint of bra strap, and a pair of the shortest shorts I've ever seen over a pair of thick tights, and wedges.

'You'll soon discover you can't do everything,' her mother says. 'You think this will be so easy.'

Rosie rolls her eyes. 'You managed to look after a baby.'

'I know, but it was different for me. I was a lot older and I was married.'

'Don't keep going on about how I'm going to be

a single parent. It's happened. I'm pregnant and I'm going to have this baby and I'm not going to let you hijack it. Get over it.' Rosie stares resentfully at the floor.

I don't say anything, but I think I understand both Rosie's determination to stand on her own two feet, and her mum's disappointment and concern for her daughter's future.

I check Rosie's blood pressure and take a blood sample.

'I want a homebirth,' she announces when I'm filling in the request form for the lab.

'It's a little early to think about that,' I point out.

'I have thought about it, and I don't want to go to hospital. I hate hospitals. And I've read up on it on the Internet and I'm entitled to a homebirth as long as it's safe for the baby.'

She knows her own mind, I think good-humouredly as I suggest we get on with testing the urine sample she's brought in with her, and do a physical examination.

'Mum, I want you to wait outside now,' she says firmly.

'I want to be here. You shouldn't have to go through any of this on your own.'

'I'm not on my own. I have Zara here. Please, this is private.' She pauses. 'I haven't taken my clothes off in front of you since I was three. Go away!'

Reluctantly, Michelle gathers up the coats and bag and leaves the room.

Rosie breathes a sigh of relief. 'OMG, she drives me mad,' she groans.

'She wants the best for you and the baby.'

'Yeah.' She bites her lip. 'I've been lucky – Dad went ballistic when he found and Mum wasn't happy but she's calmed down now.'

'So, was this pregnancy planned?' There's a question on my booking-in sheet about asking the pregnant woman if she's ever had fertility problems – I skip it when Rosie confirms she fell pregnant while on the Pill.

'I tried the implant,' she says, 'but I didn't get on with it. Don't start going on at me about . . .' she raises her hands and holds her forefingers and middle fingers straight like rabbit's ears, bending them to indicate inverted commas, 'the options. I want this baby more than anything.' Her eyes grow bright with sudden tears. 'It's been awful. My mum told the dad's mum that she'd make sure I got rid of the baby, and when I said I wasn't going to get rid of it, she told her she wouldn't let the dad or his family have any contact with the baby.'

'It must be very difficult for you,' I say. 'The last thing you need is to be in the middle of a family feud. You must let me know if you want any support.'

It's a personal and sensitive question, but I ask her if the baby's father is supportive of the pregnancy.

Rosie falls silent for a while before responding: 'My boyfriend ended it when I told him.'

'I'm sorry.' I try to put myself in the place of an eighteen-year-old boy who's just been told his girlfriend is pregnant. I can imagine his sense of panic and fear of responsibility.

'He can do what he likes. I don't care any more,' Rosie says, but it's clear from the vehemence of her denial that she does.

'I understand that it's tough now but, for what it's worth, think about keeping him in the loop about what's going on. You never know when you might need each other – not as boyfriend and girlfriend, but as parents.'

'Mum says I shouldn't have anything to do with him.' She smiles suddenly. 'Not that I've ever taken any notice of what my parents say.'

'Let's concentrate on you and the baby. You two are VIPs. If you'd like to make your way over to the scales we'll check your weight, height and the size of your bump. Do you have a bump yet?'

She looks down. 'Not yet, but my boobs are killing me.'

'That's perfectly normal,' I say, as I put on gloves to test the urine sample that Rosie's brought along with her. That's all normal too, apart from some grit at the bottom of the pot. I take a closer look – yes, I'm a midwife, it's what I do – and find that it's green and sparkly. 'All is well with the sample, except for the fact that you seem to be passing glitter,' I say, amused.

Rosie blushes. 'I've got my Christmas knickers on. Mum said I should wear decent underwear for my appointment.'

'My gran says I should wear clean pants at all times, in case I end up in A&E.'

Rosie smiles for a second time.

'Here's my phone number.' I hand her one of my

cards. 'If you ever need to talk, or have anything you want to ask me, no matter how stupid it seems, call me.'

'Thank you. You're pretty cool for . . . an older person.'

'Thanks, but I'm not that old,' I say dryly.

'What I mean is that I'm glad you're going to be my midwife.'

'That's good, because we're going to be seeing quite a lot of each other in the next few months. I'll see you at the next appointment. Make sure you bring the pics from the scan with you when you get them – I can't wait to see this baby of yours.'

'I will,' she says, getting up. 'Goodbye.'

Having seen Rosie and completed six more antenatal checks, I spend some time at the Midwifery Centre in Talymouth catching up with phone calls and paperwork before I head out on my rounds, visiting three mums and their newborn babies before going up to the farm.

It's gone three and growing dark and I'm running a little late. I call Emily on the hands-free, but the mobile battery's flat and then the car starts to pull to one side and I just know I'm going to have to stop. I pull in tight to the hedge along the lane to inspect the damage, a nail driven deep into the tread of one of the front tyres, which is completely flat. I try pumping the tyre up, but it deflates instantly. I start to change the wheel, but when I try to loosen the nuts, they won't budge, so there's only one thing for it. I'll have to walk the mile or so to the farmhouse, see Daisy and Emily and borrow a longer spanner from Murray. It isn't great. It's freezing, I'm allergic to exercise, and I should be sitting in the warm, cuddling my baby niece.

When I begin to make my descent on the other side of the hill, a black pick-up comes rattling along with its headlamps cutting swathes of light through the shadows, but although I'm hoping for a lift, I don't think the driver sees me, because it keeps coming, forcing me to step onto the verge where I trip, lose my balance and land on my bottom in the mud. The driver stops and reverses back up as I'm pinching myself to check that I'm still alive.

'What the . . .?' I catch the gleam of a pair of eyes and the chiselled outline of a jaw with a dimple on the chin as a man leans out of the window. 'What do you think you're doing, Emily? It's dark. I didn't see you until the last minute.'

'I'm sorry,' I stammer, completely shaken up as I regain my feet.

'You nearly gave me a heart attack.'

'I'm on my way to the farm to visit Emily and the baby. My car has a puncture and I can't undo the nuts to change the wheel.' The garage in Talyton must have done them up too tightly. I move closer. 'Hello, Lewis.'

'You aren't Emily? You're Emily's sister, Zara, the midwife.' The driver's voice softens. 'I couldn't understand how she could have got down here so quickly, seeing I've just left her up at the farm. I thought I was hallucinating. Look, I'll give you a lift then I'll come back and have a look at the tyre. Jump in.' Lewis leans across and opens the passenger door for me. Not one, but two collie dogs with wild eyes and massive white teeth come piling towards me and my heart starts hammering furiously. I freeze.

'Thanks for the offer, but I'll walk,' I blurt out.

'You can't be serious? You'll either die from hypothermia or get run over. Get in!'

'Really, I'm fine.' My voice wobbles slightly.

'Am I going to have to get out, pick you up and throw you in the back like one of the ewes?'

I shake my head, even though the idea of Lewis manhandling me appeals far more than it should.

'Zara, I hate to ask, but are you completely mad?'

One of the dogs barks. I recoil.

'I don't do dogs – they make me nervous,' I say. 'I know, it's pathetic, isn't it?'

'Not really,' Lewis says, sounding unconvinced. 'Let me put the dogs in the back. Wait by the tree.' He jumps out, sticks his fingers in his mouth and whistles, at which the dogs follow him round to the rear of the vehicle. 'Jump in,' he calls, and I'm not sure if he's talking to me or the dogs, but I get in anyway, sliding into the passenger seat.

'They can't get you now,' Lewis says in a teasing voice as he gets back in and turns on the engine. 'Not that they would,' he adds quickly, perhaps noticing the look of horror on my face. 'They are the softest creatures on earth.' He goes on to apologise for the smell of wet dog, sheep and straw as we roar off up the hill. 'I had a ewe in the back earlier.'

'Oh?' I'm not sure how to respond. 'If you don't mind me saying, that sounds a bit weird.'

He grins. 'I could have found a better way to put that, if I'd realised how your mind works. Give us your key.'

'What for?'

'So I can change that wheel while you're with Emily and the baby. You're looking worried. Are you afraid I'll steal your car, or something?'

'Well, I hardly know you,' I say archly.

'We can soon fix that. Come on, give me the key.'

I drop it into his outstretched hand.

'Thank you,' he says as we reach the farm and pull into the yard.

'No, thank *you*. If you hadn't turned up, I'd still be walking down the lane in the dark.' I hesitate, my hand on the door-handle.

'You can get out now. You have reached your destination,' he continues, speaking like a sat nav.

'The dogs . . .?'

'They won't come after you. I promise.' He clears his throat. 'Um, Zara . . .'

'Yes?' I catch my breath, distracted by the sight of his face in the beam of the outside light on the barn. He is completely and utterly gorgeous and I'm reluctant to tear myself away as he continues, 'I'll catch up with you later, I hope.'

'Thanks again.' I find myself hoping the very same as I walk quickly up to the house, keeping an eye over my shoulder for the dogs who are watching me with their mouths open and tongues hanging out, from the back of the pick-up.

'Hi Emily, how are you?' I slip my muddy shoes

37

off in the hall. The door is unlocked – my sister never bothers with security, whereas Murray is obsessed with locking up his tractors and other equipment.

'Well, thank you.' Emily appears in the doorway to the living room in her leggings and sweatshirt, the first time I've seen her dressed in anything but her pyjamas since Daisy was born. 'I'm a bit sore, that's all.'

It's surprising how quickly a mum forgets the pain of labour, I think, and lucky for the future of the human race that they do.

'I can tell you I feel a whole lot better than I did this time last week, though. Come on through.' Emily glances at my trousers. 'What happened to you?'

'I thought it was a nice day for a walk in the country,' I say ironically. 'Actually, I had to leave the car down the lane with a puncture. Lewis gave me a lift.'

'Murray can fix it.'

'It's all right. Lewis is already on the case.'

'He's lovely, isn't he?'

'He's definitely fit,' I say.

'He's single too.'

'And?' I face my twin, mirroring the way she stands square to me with her arms folded. 'Emily, don't waste your time matchmaking. I've only just met the guy and, even if he was the most perfect man ever, it would never work – he's too young for me.'

'He's twenty-three, not some teenage toy-boy.'

'And he won't hang around here for long,' I go on. Murray's only given him a temporary contract. 'How's Daisy?'

'I'd forgotten you're working,' Emily says. 'Daisy's

asleep.' She shows me into the living room where the baby lies snug beneath a blanket, her wavy red locks peeking out from beneath the woolly hat that Gran knitted. Her hands are curled into small fists up by her ears, and covered with white mitts to stop her scratching her face with her tiny fingernails.

'Where's Poppy?'

'She's in her room, having a nap. The baby's keeping her awake all night too. I really don't know if it's possible, but it's as if she belongs to some alien nocturnal species. I don't remember Poppy being like this.'

'I think she was.'

'I was going to give her a full bath, not just top and tail her, but I don't like to disturb her. Do you really have to wake her up?'

'I let her sleep last time. I really should do the heel prick test today. Oh, let's let sleeping babies lie for now. Can I get you anything, Emily? Tea, or a milkshake? Toast?'

When I return from the kitchen with tea and toast, Poppy is coming down the stairs with the toy cat under one arm and bumping a kid's travel case in Barbie pink down behind her.

'Hello.' I block her progress towards the front door. 'Are you going somewhere?'

She looks at me through her curly fringe. 'I'm going to live with Grandma.'

'I think you'd better let Mummy know,' I say, diverting her to the living room. 'Look who I've found, Emily.'

39

'Poppy, I thought you were asleep.'

'I'm going to live with Grandma,' she repeats.

'Oh no, you can't do that,' Emily says. 'We need you here. Your baby sister needs you. Poppy, I want you to be as quiet as a library full of church mice because Daisy's asleep and I want her to stay that way, please.'

'I hate my baby sister.' Poppy explodes with red-faced rage and rushes over to the Moses basket and pulls Daisy's blanket off. I've never seen Emily move so fast, but she fails to intercept her and Daisy wakes up, fills her lungs and screams. Emily scoops her up and hugs her to her breast, while holding Poppy to her waist and shrugging with despair.

'I don't know what to do,' Emily says once we've calmed Poppy down with a bowl of ice cream and chocolate sauce, and helped her unpack.

'Give it time,' I say when we're sitting down at last.

'It would have been easier for them to have been twins, like us,' Emily observes. 'We have a really special bond.'

'We still fought when we were younger.'

'We didn't.'

'Oh yes, we did.'

'I know . . .' Emily sighs as I check Daisy over and weigh her. 'Sisters. Who'd have them?'

'Hello,' Murray says, walking into the room with a sack of potatoes in his arms. 'I've got your keys, Zara. Your car's ready in the yard. Lewis says to apologise for not having time to valet it.'

'Where is Lewis?' Emily pauses from stroking

40

Daisy's hair. 'He could have handed the keys over himself.' She glances at me and I know exactly what she's trying to achieve. It won't work, though. Lewis isn't my type, although I would admit that I'm slightly disappointed not to have seen him again to thank him in person, not for any other reason. I look away, picking an imaginary hair from my top to hide the blush that is spreading across my cheeks.

'He's taking a ewe over to Talyton Manor for a Caesar,' Murray says. 'One of the vets is waiting for him.'

'Oh, Murray, not another one,' Emily says, looking concerned. 'We can't really afford it.'

'It's the way it is. It has to be done. You have good days and bad days. That's farming for you. Here, Zara. Catch!' Murray throws me the keys and, to my surprise, because I've never been good at ball games, I catch them.

Emily claps and Poppy joins in. 'That's the first time you've caught anything more than a cold. Have you been practising for Claire's wedding?'

'What do you mean?'

'Catching the bouquet. She mentioned it to me when she came up to see me and Daisy.'

'Emily, what are you like?' I say, appalled. 'I've been married before, remember? I've been there, got the T-shirt . . . Never again!'

'Don't be silly. Think of what you had with Paul as a trial run.'

'I'll see you soon,' I say, changing the subject. 'I must go.'

'Give our love to Gran,' Emily says. 'I'll pop in and see her when I'm in Talyton tomorrow, if I can get the three of us out and dressed.'

'Will do.' I smile. 'I hope she's been behaving herself.'

'You sound like me talking about Poppy,' Emily observes. 'I thought she was supposed to be looking after you.'

'We look after each other. Thank Lewis for me, won't you? Tell him I'm sorry I missed him.'

I drive home with the rich aroma of sheep and dog in my nostrils, and when I check for the source of the smell, I find Lewis's coat on the back seat of my car. I pick it up and take it indoors, leaving it on the counter while I greet my grandmother.

'I thought I heard someone rummaging around in the shop,' she says.

'It was me – I couldn't resist a quarter of fizzy cola bottles.'

'I hope they aren't going to ruin your appetite.'

'Gran, they won't. I'm thirty-one, not thirteen.'

'Sometimes I think we should have a guard dog,' she says. 'That way I'd feel more secure.'

'I'm here now. I'll keep you safe.' Gran knows that if she ever decided to bring a dog to live here, I would have to move out.

I call Emily for Lewis's mobile number. Poppy is bawling in the background so we don't get to chat. I text Lewis to say I'll bring his coat back to the farm ASAP, but he's on his way back from the vet's, so he arranges to drop by to collect it.

I don't know why, but I run upstairs to brush my

hair and change into jeans and a long cream jumper with a belt around the middle, before he turns up.

'You look nice, dear. Who's the lucky young gentleman?' Gran says. 'There must be one.'

'I always change out of my uniform when I get home.'

'Yes, into your sweat top and jogging bottoms.' Gran's like a dog with a bone. 'Will he want tea?' She means dinner. 'There's plenty in the pot.'

'He won't be stopping. He left his coat on the back seat of my car by mistake.'

'If you say so,' Gran says, and she makes an excuse to be downstairs when Lewis arrives, unbolting the door to let him in and accompanying him to the counter.

'Thank you for fixing Zara's car, my lover. Your coat's just there.'

'Let me get it,' Lewis says. 'It's a bit of a health hazard.'

'How can we thank you?' Gran asks. 'Zara, offer the young man some sweets.'

'No, I'm fine.' Lewis stands by the counter, hugging his coat, apparently struck down by an uncharacteristic attack of shyness in front of my grandmother.

'Gran, I think I can smell something burning,' I say, wishing she'd leave us alone for a few minutes.

'Me too,' she says with a wicked glint in her eye. 'The fires of passion.'

'Gran! I mean you could just check . . . upstairs.'

'In a mo,' she says brightly, apparently having no intention of making herself scarce.

'How is the ewe you took to the vet?' I ask eventually.

'She's good, thanks. She's in the back of the pick-up with her lambs. Come and see them.'

'You stay here, Gran. It's too cold for you outside,' I say quickly, before following Lewis out onto the pavement where the pick-up is parked on the double yellow lines. In the back, one of the woolliest sheep I've ever seen lies propped on her brisket in the corner. She's panting so fast she looks as if she's having a panic attack.

'Mum's a bit stressed, not surprisingly,' Lewis observes. He reaches over and lifts the lid on a big plastic crate. 'Here are her babies.'

I move closer, brushing up against his arm, to peer inside, where there are three lambs curled up together.

'Ah, she's had triplets,' I say, captivated, until an icy blast whisks along the street, making me shiver.

'I would offer you my coat,' Lewis says hesitantly.

'That's kind of you, but . . .'

'You don't want to smell of sheep for the next week,' Lewis interrupts. 'How about sharing some body heat instead?' He turns his head and gives me the most wicked grin. 'I seem to have plenty to spare at this minute.'

'What are you saying?' I gasp.

'Oh god, I'm sorry. I hope I haven't offended you.' He steps away from me. 'It's just that with you standing so close . . . What I'm trying to say is that you have quite an effect on me, and that's a compliment. It wasn't supposed to come across as creepy.'

'No offence taken, Lewis.' I can't help giggling at his reaction. 'It's rather flattering to find out that I have this effect on you, but I won't take up your offer right now.'

'Maybe another time,' he says with a chuckle.

'Maybe,' I flirt back. 'I'd better go back indoors.'

'And I'd better get these little guys back to their nice warm barn,' Lewis sighs. 'I hope to see you again very soon. Goodnight, Zara.'

'Goodnight.' I return to the shop and lock up, turning to find Gran at my shoulder. 'Gran, you made me jump – and thanks a lot for being so embarrassing.'

'It's a pleasure,' she says with glee. 'That Lewis, he's nothing like Paul.'

'What does that have to do with anything?'

'Don't tell me it hasn't crossed your mind? He's devilishly handsome. If I was sixty years younger . . .'

She might be teasing me, but she has touched a nerve because it's true. It's the first time a man has caught my eye since Paul, unless you include Leonardo DiCaprio and Henry Cavill, but I don't think they count. It's odd because I haven't looked at a man in that way, let alone flirted with one, for quite a while. I must be getting my mojo back.

CHAPTER THREE

Love Me, Love My Dogs

It's Mother's Day in the middle of March and Gran is in the kitchen baking, the buttery aroma of choux pastry in the oven filling the air while I help out in the shop for a while. We're open for the morning only on Sundays in the winter, all day in the summer.

The initial rush for the Sunday newspapers to go with coffee and breakfast has subsided and it isn't exactly busy when Mrs Dyer turns up. She's in her fifties and well-built, her arms bulging through the sleeves of a long grey cardigan.

'You're looking well, Zara.' She smiles, appearing slightly embarrassed. 'I am talking to Zara, aren't I? Not Emily? I've always got you two in a muddle.'

'I'm Zara.' I almost add, the fat one. 'Thank you.' I go on, eternally amazed that people seem surprised to find me on my feet. Divorce isn't an illness and neither is being single.

'I've heard all about you moving in with your gran and I think it's wonderful.'

I realise I haven't had the chance to speak to Mrs Dyer since I moved in four months ago, partly because I'm not keen on her enormous dog, and partly because the dog won't stand still for long enough for her to hold a conversation anyway.

'It's so sad about you and Paul going your separate ways.'

'It was for the best. We're still friends.'

'I couldn't be friends with my old man if we divorced.'

'Everyone's different,' I say, not wanting to be drawn into gossip. Paul and I were happy together to begin with, but when we decided to try for a baby, our failure to conceive gradually strangled the life out of our marriage.

'Have a lovely day,' I say. 'Don't forget your paper.' I slide it across the counter.

'I don't suppose I'll have time to read it, but it's handy for all sorts: lining the floor when Nero comes in from muddy walks, and putting the shine on the shop windows.'

I smile to myself as she leaves, and watch her unclipping the dog's lead from the ring outside, freeing him up to tow her back across the road. Gran and I could write a book on 101 uses for a Sunday newspaper.

A car with yellow and green markings and 'Community Paramedic' along the side pulls up next and my heart misses a beat, a reflex reaction that I cannot suppress or explain.

47

'Hello, Zara.' My ex-husband steps inside and the door swings closed behind him. Paul is thirty-five, four years my senior, and what Murray describes somewhat scathingly as a raving metrosexual. He's looking good with his short brown hair waxed into position and his clean-shaven complexion smooth and shiny with moisturiser. 'How are you?' He walks around the counter and embraces me, kissing my cheeks. I like it. I miss being close to someone. I miss the physical contact.

'I'm well. How about you?' I say, stepping back.

'Great, thanks. I came in the other day.'

'Gran didn't mention it.' I'm a little surprised by her omission. I thought she told me everything.

'And you, Zara, didn't let me know about the big family news. I had to hear about Emily's baby from Rosemary,' he goes on, using my grandmother's Christian name. He looks a little hurt that I didn't get in touch, but not as hurt as I feel that the subject of babies has come up between us. 'A little sister for Poppy.'

That's right. Twist the knife. I don't say anything but my expression must have told it all, because Paul apologises. 'That was insensitive of me.'

'It's okay.' I watch him pick up a packet of mints and place them on the counter.

'I'm sorry, Zara. I didn't realise you still felt so strongly—'

'Paul, I don't want to talk about it,' I interrupt.

'We've been through such a lot together,' he goes on.

I don't respond – if I'm honest, I think Paul went through an awful lot on his own. Towards the end of

48

our marriage he withdrew from me, taking on different shifts at work which didn't coincide with mine so he didn't have to talk to me and let me know how he was feeling.

'Friends?' he says gently.

'Of course we're friends.' How could we not be when we were engaged for three years and married for seven? I met Paul, my first proper boyfriend, when I was starting my degree in midwifery. I was young and naïve. He was mature, sophisticated and heroic, and I couldn't believe he was interested in me. Within six months of meeting, I accepted his proposal of marriage.

'We must go out for that meal sometime. It would be good to catch up properly. I feel like I've hardly seen you.'

'Same here.' I gaze at him, finding myself less able to read him than I used to. Does he mean that in a just-friends way, or has he really missed me? 'Let me know your shifts and we'll go out for lunch or dinner.'

'Soon,' he says, taking his shopping.

'Soon,' I echo as I watch him go.

'What did you say that for?' Gran grumbles from behind me.

'Were you deliberately listening to that conversation? It was kind of private. Gran, why didn't you tell me Paul had been into the shop?' I turn to face her as she wanders in through the fly curtain, the plastic strips clattering softly as they fall back into place. Now I know why she keeps it up all year round even when there are no flies. It's to provide her with cover.

'Because out of sight is out of mind. It's time you forgot about Paul and moved on with your life.'

'He's a friend,' I point out.

'And ex-husband. What are his motives for popping up every five minutes, texting you and book-facing you all the time?'

'It's called Facebook.'

'It doesn't matter what it is. What matters is that he makes you unhappy.' Before I can open my mouth to argue, Gran continues, 'I've seen your face when you look at your mobile and find you haven't had a text from him for two or three days. I can't help worrying that you're still in love with him.'

'I'm not. At least, I don't think I am. I mean, when I see him, I find myself remembering the good times, and it makes me feel a little sad, that's all.'

Gran shakes her head as if she doesn't believe me, but how can she possibly know how I feel about Paul when I don't know myself? Can I honestly state that I no longer love him and that I've moved on? Perhaps now I'm getting my mojo back, it's time I thought about dating again, maybe having a light-hearted fling to take my mind off him and help me get back to my old self. I could do with having some passion and excitement in my life.

'Look at the time,' Gran exclaims. 'You go on up to the farm and help Emily get dinner on.' She means lunch. 'I love Sunday dinners with the family.'

'Mum's picking you up at one.'

'There's no need to keep reminding me. Go on, off you go.'

50

I take the profiteroles, still warm in a tin, plus a pot of cream and chocolate for the sauce, up to the farm, where Emily, dressed in trackies, is frantically trying to peel potatoes with Daisy in one arm and Poppy 'helping'. She smiles wearily and I wonder if we should all have descended on her like this so soon after she's given birth. It's only been a couple of weeks, after all.

Poppy stands on a chair and drops peeled potatoes into a saucepan on the floor from a great height.

'Splosh.' She grins at me through her curls when I walk in. 'I'm making a mess.'

'So I see. Emily, let me have the peeler.'

'Oh no, you can spend some quality time with Daisy.' She hands me the baby who takes one look at me and bursts into tears.

'Oh, Daisy,' I coo as I hold her close. 'That's no way to greet your auntie.'

'She's teething unusually early, just like Poppy did,' Emily explains. 'Actually, she's driving me mad because I can't put her down and I've got all these veg to prepare. I feel like I'm having a meltdown.'

'Mum said we should have had lunch with her and Dad at their house. It's too much for you.' I rock Daisy gently, wiping her cheek with the corner of her blanket. 'There, there, that's better.'

'Are you talking to me or Daisy?' Emily chuckles in spite of everything. 'OMG, I'm cackling like a mad-woman. Poppy, can you leave that now and feed the lamb instead? There's a bottle in the fridge. He can have it cold. Remember to use Larry's bottle, not Daisy's this time.'

51

Poppy clambers down from the chair, hauls the fridge door open and stares at the array of bottles on the shelf.

'Which one, Mummy?'

'That one with the blue top.'

'Which blue top?'

'There is only one.' Emily runs wet hands through her hair as I take the bottle out for Poppy. 'Sometimes I think it's easier to do everything yourself.'

Poppy heads out to the utility room to feed the lamb, which I notice is confined to an area penned off with crates and boxes.

'Can't he go back outside with the others?' I ask, looking out through the rear window across the lawn where the daffodils are on the verge of flowering, and the buds are beginning to appear on the fruit trees. Beyond, the first batch of lambs are gambolling in the field with their mothers.

'Murray's gone soft and said he can stay here as Poppy's pet until it's time for him to go off for you-know-what . . .'

I make Emily sit down with Daisy while I finish the potatoes and bring them to the boil for a few minutes before draining them, scoring the tops and placing them in a tray of hot oil then into the oven. I try not to think about the cute little lamb that Lewis carried in under his arm going off to become some other family's Sunday roast.

'What next?' I ask.

'Cabbage and carrots, and Yorkshire pudding.'

I prepare the rest of the main course before counting

out the place settings for the table with Poppy. We make it seven, but Emily disagrees.

'You need one extra, Poppy,' she says. 'How many does that make?'

Poppy counts laboriously on her fingers before coming up with eight.

'Clever girl,' Emily says fondly before looking straight at me. 'Lewis is joining us. He wasn't doing anything else so I thought, why not? He's always asking when you're coming up to the farm so he can hang around and make sheep's eyes at you, Zara.'

'He doesn't?' A fork thuds against the table as I lose my grip.

'Why is your face red, Auntie Zara?' says Poppy.

'Because it's getting hot in here.'

'Oh,' she says.

'Emily, this thing about Lewis is in your imagination.'

'Is it really?' My sister raises one eyebrow.

'Well, the other night when he picked up his coat, it felt like he was chatting me up,' I admit.

'There you go then.'

'He's very outgoing. Flirting seems to come naturally to him. I expect he's the same with everyone.'

'Yes, he's a young lad, but give him a chance,' Emily sighs.

'We hardly know each other and yes, he is attractive.' I'm being economical with the truth here. If he really wanted to start something with me, I don't think I could resist. In fact, I wouldn't. 'But I'm a few years older than him and there's no way he'll ever be interested in me.'

'Why not?'

I shrug.

'You're always putting yourself down. Paul has a lot to answer for. He really rocked your confidence.'

'He did not.'

'There you go, defending him again. He could be pretty sharp with you about your looks and your weight. You are beautiful, and it's time you remembered that. Men like women who like themselves.' Emily grins. 'Lecture over. Let the onslaught begin.'

The onslaught – consisting of Murray, Lewis, and Mum and Dad, who bring Gran with them – begins an hour later when they descend on the kitchen.

'There's a seating plan,' Emily says as Dad carves the joint and I drain the carrots, sending up a cloud of steam, at which my father has to remove his glasses and wipe them on the sleeve of his golf sweater, flashing the gold ring on his little finger at the same time. I don't ask, but I can't help wondering if he's dyed what's left of his hair – it seems a darker, bluer grey than when I last saw him.

'Since when?' Murray walks through from the utility room, leaving brown prints on a white towel as he dries his hands.

'I thought Gran and Zara would sit on either side of Lewis to mix up the conversation a bit. I don't want you and him talking sheep all day.'

'It isn't every day I get to sit down beside a nice young man,' Gran pipes up as she rocks Daisy rather violently in her arms.

'Don't let her have any more sherry, Emily,' Mum

whispers as she straps the booster cushion to Poppy's chair.

'I heard that. There's nothing wrong with my hearing. And I've had one glass, that's all, and it was no more than a thimbleful.'

The sherry continues to flow – for Gran, anyway – and so does the conversation as we settle down to eat. I pick at a carrot. Sitting beside Lewis is somewhat distracting, and I seem to have lost my appetite. I find myself casting glances his way, wondering if Emily could possibly be right, that he does fancy me just a little.

'You and Zara must have quite a lot in common, Lewis, seeing you're both involved in making deliveries,' Emily begins.

'It's a bit different dealing with people rather than sheep,' I point out.

'Yes, none of my sheep think they're too posh to push,' Lewis says.

'I can't imagine you have many worrying about their bikini lines when they have to have C-sections either,' I say, smiling.

'Please don't start, Zara,' my mother interrupts. 'I know it's perfectly normal to you, but I don't want to hear any gory talk of blood and afterbirth while we're eating.'

'I did have someone make a smoothie out of their placenta recently,' I say, winding her up.

'Don't upset your mother,' Dad says.

'I've heard that one before, sis. Haven't you got any new stories?'

'One of my ladies who has piercings in various places on her body told me she was scared of needles, and when I took a blood, she fainted.'

'That's pretty tame,' Emily says.

'Anyone for ketchup?' Murray asks.

'Me, Daddy,' Poppy says, putting her hand up.

'You don't have to put your hand up, darling,' Mum says. 'You aren't at nursery now.'

'What's the magic word?' Murray asks.

'Which? Oh, I know.' Poppy's hand is in the air again as she goes on, 'Please.'

Murray fetches the ketchup for Poppy, who promptly squeezes out most of the bottle onto her plate; we continue to eat until Gran excuses herself to go and powder her nose.

'She means she's going for a wee,' Poppy announces.

'I'm sorry. You can't do anything discreetly with a four year old in the house,' Emily says.

'Poppy tells it like it is.' Lewis smiles at me and my heart lurches.

'So how is Gran really, Zara?' Mum asks once she's left the room. 'I can never get any sense out of her.'

'She's all right,' I say.

'Well, I worry about her. I don't like her working like this at her age. She can't go on for ever.'

'It feels like she's going to,' Dad grimaces, the lines at the side of his mouth deepening and his whiskery brows twitching.

'Your father has a bad back from sitting in a car day in, day out for all those years, and he could really do without the runs to the cash and carry,' Mum says.

'That's true,' Dad agrees, and the realisation that, although he's nowhere nearly as old as Gran, he is sixty-eight, comes with a jolt to me. I suppose he should be enjoying retirement, playing golf and spending time with his grandchildren, not running around after my grandmother.

'If she sold the shop,' Mum continues, 'she'd have more than enough money to live by the sea, with some left over.'

'It's a dying business,' Dad adds. 'The Village News is losing money and that can't continue for much longer.'

'Because you can see Sarah's inheritance disappearing,' Gran interrupts as she walks back into the kitchen. 'Jim's always wanted to get his hands on my money.'

'You know that isn't true.' My father is genuinely upset.

'What are you doing, creeping up on us like that?' says Mum crossly.

'I thought I heard my name being mentioned in vain, so I listened behind the door – it's a bad habit of mine. I know you're talking about me. If you have something to say, you can say it in front of me to my face. I'm not stupid. I'm perfectly compost mentis.' Gran pauses. 'I will not leave the shop until I'm carried out in a box. I promised your granddad I'd look after it for him.'

'Nobody's interfering,' I say. 'Mum's only trying to help. She's right in a way. You should be enjoying a slower pace of life, not sorting newspapers at six o'clock in the morning.'

'Why?' Gran frowns. 'I enjoy it.'

'You could take it easier, though. You could take up a new hobby – gardening, for instance.'

'What on earth would I want to do that for? I don't need to grow tomatoes when there's a greengrocer just down the road. And why on earth would I go and live anywhere else when all my old friends are in Talyton St George...or dead?' she adds, matter-of-factly.

'Gran,' I say, 'I wish you wouldn't talk about dying like that.'

'Death is part of life. Birth is the capital letter at the beginning of a sentence, death is the full stop. That's how I see it.' Her tone hardens. 'I'm not going into a home by the sea. I won't go and live in a home anywhere. They're for old people.'

'Sarah and I went to have a look around the one in Talymouth a couple of weeks ago,' my father says tactlessly.

'It was so different from what we expected,' Mum says, 'wasn't it, Jim?'

I'm not sure which of us is most upset, me or Gran, at this discussion of her future.

'I don't think this is any of your business – it's up to Gran what she does.' I give my mother a look which means 'shut up and not in front of Lewis', but she's on a mission. I glance towards Emily who shakes her head. Nothing is going to stop her.

'It was light and modern and it didn't smell. Every room had en-suite facilities and the food options included pasta and Thai curry.'

'Curry? I've never had a curry in my life and I don't intend to start now,' Gran says.

'You'd have access to Wi-fi and multichannel TV.'

'Why on earth would Gran want Wi-fi?' Emily exclaims. 'She hasn't got a computer.'

'I might want to get myself on the Interweb one day, but not in an old people's home, thank you very much,' Gran cuts in. 'I have a smartphone.'

'You haven't learned to drive it yet,' I say.

'I can make a phone call and text. That's all I need.' Gran turns from me to my parents. 'I don't want to hear any more about it. If you like this home so much, then go and live there yourselves. Zara, I'd like you to give me a lift back to the shop this afternoon, please.' Gran might have had the final word on the matter for now, but I'm afraid this is probably just the beginning.

'That's no problem.' I smile to break the tension, adding lightly, 'I'm going that way myself.'

'Daddy, I bored,' Poppy says, and Murray jumps at an excuse to leave the table. He looks towards Lewis.

'Why don't you take Zara up to the lambing shed?'

'You two really know how to show a girl a good time,' Emily says with a mock sigh.

'Can I come?' Poppy asks, and I'm just about to say 'why not?' when Emily interrupts.

'You and Daddy are going to change Daisy's nappy and then you can play.'

'How about a game of hide and seek?' Murray says lightly.

'Without the seek part,' Emily says.

59

'What are you saying, Mummy?' Poppy asks, kneeling up on her chair.

'Oh, nothing,' Emily giggles. 'This is Mummy and Daddy stuff. Don't worry about it.'

'Zara, I'd be happy to show you around,' Lewis says shyly. 'I've left the dogs in the annexe.'

'Thank you.' Any excuse to get away from my parents and grandmother, find out more about him, and – a tiny shiver of anticipation runs down my spine – enjoy some more light-hearted flirting, if I'm lucky.

CHAPTER FOUR

Shepherd's Delight

'I'm sorry about my family,' I say to Lewis as I tramp across to the lambing shed in one of Emily's old coats and a pair of her boots. 'That was really cringeworthy.'

'Isn't that what families are for – to embarrass each other?' He grins. 'Come on. I could use the skills of a country midwife.' As soon as he pushes the barn door open, the sheep start bleating.

'They think I'm going to feed them.' He closes the door behind us. 'Oh, there's someone in trouble.' He steps over one of the hurdles that keep the sheep confined in small groups and approaches the ewe which is standing panting in the corner.

'I should have come out here between courses.' Swearing, Lewis gets down with the ewe, then turns back to me. 'Would you mind hanging on to this one?'

I clamber into the pen and cross the straw, kneeling

down beside the ewe, rather gingerly because the straw isn't completely clean.

'I'm sorry, I should have asked you if you'd mind. I just assumed . . .'

'I've seen Emily lamb a ewe before, but I haven't a clue what I'm doing here. They're so woolly I can hardly tell which end is which.'

'If you push her into the corner and keep your knee pressed against her shoulder, she can't run away. Put her in a headlock if that's easier.'

I gaze at the ewe. From the look in her eyes, I'd say she was in agony.

'The poor lamb,' I say gently.

'This is the ewe. The lamb's in there,' Lewis says, smiling and pointing to the ewe's belly. 'I can usually lamb them myself, but this one's a really twitchy character.'

'It seems odd to describe sheep as having character. I always thought they were pretty much the same, a bit dense. That's what Murray always tells me, anyway.' I struggle to keep the ewe still – she's much stronger than I imagined – and I find that I have to get up close and personal with my arm around her neck and my weight pushing her against the hurdle.

'They're all different. You get to know them individually when you're with them all day. They're quite bright too – they recognise the members of their own flock. Some are bold; others shy and retiring, like me.' Lewis's tone is teasing as he squirts some lubricant from a bottle onto his gloved hands and starts examining the ewe. 'The lamb's breech. I need

62

to push it back in and catch the back legs so they come out before the tail, but there isn't much room in here.' The ewe groans and strains as if in agreement and, a few minutes later, Lewis delivers a wet lamb onto the straw.

'Is it breathing?' I ask anxiously, caught up in the drama.

Lewis picks it up by the hind legs and swings it back and forth to drain any fluid from its lungs before he lays it down again and rubs its chest vigorously with a handful of straw. He pauses and, seconds later, the lamb lifts its head and looks around, trembling as if it's just woken from a deep sleep.

'You can let her go now, Zara.'

I release the ewe, which turns and bleats at her baby, nudging it and licking its face. Lewis squats to check the umbilical stump and spray it with purple spray, and I find my eyes drawn to a lightly tanned band of muscular loin.

He looks up and raises one eyebrow. Blushing at being caught out, I try to cover it up.

'Don't you get cold?' I stammer. 'I mean, you're out here and it's freezing and you aren't wearing a coat and . . .' I stop abruptly, feeling like a complete idiot.

'And I'm wearing low-rise jeans,' he finishes for me. 'I'm used to working outdoors. I don't feel the cold.' Chuckling, he stands up and pulls his sweater down.

'What next?' I ask.

'What would you do?' he says.

'Weigh and measure the baby, check mum's comfortable and make sure breastfeeding is established.' I smile. 'Sometimes I have to pick dad off the floor too.'

'We don't normally weigh and measure, but I do need to make sure the lamb feeds before I leave them to it.' Lewis reaches for my hand and pulls me up, holding onto my hand a few seconds longer than necessary.

'You'd make a good shepherdess, like your sister. You have small hands.'

'It's good to know I have that option, but I'm not planning to change careers any time soon,' I say.

'What made you go into midwifery?' he asks as we watch the lamb struggle to its feet.

'I wanted to do something practical and make a difference to people's lives. Emily went into nursing and I didn't want to do exactly the same as my twin, so I chose midwifery. I did a degree and qualified –' I pause – 'rather a long time ago.'

'I finished my degree two summers ago.'

'I didn't think you needed a degree to be a shepherd.'

Lewis smiles again. 'You don't. I did a degree in Agriculture in general. I'm a townie really, but I've always wanted to be a farmer. We used to go on holiday to a farm in north Devon every summer and all I wanted to do was work with the animals. At first, I was allowed to collect the eggs from the chickens and muck out the horse, and later I graduated to milking the cows. I loved it. I couldn't get enough of it, so in the end I went to work there most holidays before I went to college to do my degree. My parents didn't approve. They wanted me to go and do something more conventional in their eyes, engineering or law. My dad's an electrical engineer and Mum's a solicitor.'

'Where do they live?'

'Just outside Birmingham.'

'You haven't got a Brummie accent.'

'My parents haven't either. I speak proper-like,' he says, faking a Devon accent.

'Do you have any brothers or sisters?'

'A younger brother, Connor. He's doing a degree in Media Studies. I'm not sure my parents approve of that, either, but he keeps telling them they'll change their minds when he's directing films in Hollywood. It's good to have dreams.' Lewis fiddles with a piece of straw as the lamb wobbles up to his mother and nudges up between her front legs. 'You won't find what you're looking for there, matey.' He moves across to give the lamb a helping hand, lowering him onto the straw close to the ewe's udder where he latches on to drink, wagging his tail.

'What's your dream?' I ask.

He thinks for a moment. 'To have a flock of my own and maybe some land. And my dogs. Oh, and a wife and kids, although I haven't got a girlfriend at the moment and don't anticipate getting married until I'm at least thirty, because I want to have a lot more fun before I settle down. Not much to ask,' he adds ironically.

'I shouldn't hurry into marriage if I were you,' I say ruefully. 'I did and it was a mistake.'

'Emily told me you were divorced. I'm sorry.'

'It's all right.' I change the subject. 'How long have you had your dogs?'

'Since they were pups. Mick and Miley are working collies.'

'Miley?' I interrupt. 'Is that after Miley Cyrus?'

'No, it's because she can run for miles. I trained them both from scratch. They work with the sheep and compete at trials. I love my dogs. I wouldn't be without them. What happened to put you off them? You seem genuinely frightened.' He smiles again. 'You really did seem to prefer the idea of suicide to getting into the pick-up with the dogs the other night.'

'Uncle Nobby's terrier used to lie in front of the fire with its ears going pink and stinky, and farting with as much gusto as my uncle does – not endearing traits – and then one day, when I was ten, he bit me.' I shudder as I recall the small bundle of teeth and muscle and wiry coat turning on me and grabbing me by the ankle, hanging on while I screamed for help. 'The pain! I've never felt anything like it. Uncle Nobby hit him with a poker, making him let go for just long enough for me to shut myself in the bathroom where I fainted, banged my head on the side of the bath and knocked myself out.'

'Why did he go for you?' Lewis asks.

'You aren't one of those people who always blames the victim, not the dog, are you?' I say suspiciously.

'There's usually a reason for a dog to turn.'

'This one growled and barked at everyone apart from Uncle Nobby, but I don't know why he suddenly turned on me. Maybe I took him by surprise or got a bit too close, I don't know.' I shrug. 'Anyway, he made me wary of dogs. I still have the scars.

'Even now, if I see someone walking their dog, I'll cross the road to avoid them.' I smile ruefully. 'I don't know what it is about me and animals. My gran's cat wants to kill me.'

'What happened to your uncle's dog?'

'He couldn't bring himself to have him put down. The rest of the family weren't happy: they cut him off for a few years until the dog died a natural death. I'm glad, though, because I would have felt guilty somehow. I wasn't looking for revenge.'

'It must be hard for you. You must come up against dogs when you're doing house calls.'

'I let everyone know so they can keep them away. There was an issue when one of my mums-to-be wanted their pet present at the birth, but she saw sense in the end.'

'What do you do when you go out for a walk? There are hundreds of dogs around here – I've never seen so many.'

'I don't do much walking.' I glance down at my figure. 'Can't you tell?' I say lightly, trying to make a joke of it. Inside, though, I'm cringing. What a stupid thing to say. Emily's right – men love women who love themselves, and it isn't attractive to tell everyone how you feel too fat, even if it's true. Why does it matter, anyway? I gaze at Lewis – he's hot. Oh, yes, seriously hot.

Don't go there, Zara, I tell myself. There is no point

for many reasons, but now I look at Lewis properly, I find that I can't remember a single one.

'So it wouldn't be any good me asking you out for a walk along the river for a drink at the pub,' he says, 'or a wander along the beach?'

'I'm all right on the beach in summer when dogs are banned.'

'I won't be here in the summer,' he says lightly. 'Have you had any support to overcome your fear of dogs?'

'I had some counselling afterwards, but it didn't help.'

How would you feel if I brought Mick over here on a lead right now?'

'Panicky. A little sick.'

'I don't want to put you under any pressure, but Mick's a good boy. He'd never hurt you, I promise. I don't have to bring him right up to you, just as close as you can bear.'

'Are you planning to desensitise me? I'm not sure how that works. You're a shepherd, not a psychiatrist.'

'I know, but I was just thinking it might help, and just maybe we could go for a walk on the beach together before I move on to my next job, wherever that will be.'

I gaze at him. His expression is serious, and I think he's trying to be helpful, not angling for a date, because if it was a date, why not go somewhere dog-free – to the pub or to see a film?

'I don't feel as if I'm missing out, you know,' I say, trying to put him off in his quest to prove to me that a dog can really be both man and woman's best friend, but then as he shrugs his shoulders, I change my mind. If he's right and Mick can help me overcome my wariness of dogs, it would be worth having a go. I'd love to be able to walk down the road without crossing over to the other side to avoid Mrs Dyer or Wendy, the dog-fosterer, or Aurora from the boutique, and their dogs. I'd like to be able to spend time on the Green, not necessarily walking, but sitting in the sunshine watching the world go by, or reading a book, without worrying that a dog will approach.

'Oh go on then, I'll do it. Let's see what happens. Go and get him and I'll see how I feel.'

'Are you sure?'

'I'm sure.'

'All right, but don't scream or Mick will be more scared of you than you are of him.' Lewis grins. 'I'm joking, Zara. I'll bring him on a lead and stand in the doorway over there. I promise I won't go any further than you want me to . . .'

Is he talking about the dog, or do his words have an entirely different meaning? Or am I attaching too much significance to everything he says because on some level I want him to find me irresistible?

'You wait there. I'll go and get him.' Lewis disappears before I have a chance to change my mind.

I move to the corner of the pen nearest the door, figuring that I'll have at least one hurdle and a bale of straw as a barrier between me and the dog. A small pulse of apprehension begins to throb at my temple. What am I doing? Why have I agreed to put myself through this? I wipe my palms on Emily's coat as I listen for Lewis's footsteps. All too soon he's back with the black and white collie with the brown eyes, which is now on a rope lead. He stops in the doorway to the barn, at which some of the sheep look up and start off on another round of bleating and shifting around in the pens.

'Mick, sit,' Lewis says. The dog obeys, his gaze fixed on his master's face. 'How are you feeling, Zara?'

'Okay,' I say hesitantly. The dog yawns, revealing his tongue and teeth. 'That's close enough.' The dog stands up. I take a step back.

'He can't do anything. I've got him.' Lewis shows me the end of the rope in his hand to prove it. 'His overwhelming instinct is to round up sheep, but I can stop him in his tracks with a single whistle. Trust me.'

'Believe me, I'm trying to.'

'He'd lick you to death.' Lewis bends down and ruffles the dog's hair. 'Maybe that wasn't the best way to put it.' When he straightens, he moves a little closer with the dog at his side. 'How does that feel?'

'Not so bad,' I say, forcing myself to stand my ground. Mick can't get me. He's the other side of the hurdle and there's something in the way his master stands so tall and calm that inspires confidence. 'Thanks, Lewis.'

'We haven't finished yet.' He chuckles as he takes another short step closer. 'I know what you're doing, but I'm not going to put him away yet. Mick is the best dog in the world – apologies to Miley – and I'd like you to see how wonderful he is.' Keeping on my side of the dog, he brings Mick right up to the hurdle. I take another step back, but there's a sheep in my way.

'That's making my heart beat faster,' I say, touching

my throat as I try to make light of the fact that I'm really scared now.

'That's what all the girls say,' Lewis teases.

'Not you, the dog,' I point out.

'Oh? I guess I'll just have to try harder.' Lewis kneels down in the straw to face me, hugging the dog who sits between his thighs. 'See if you can walk across to us.' I shuffle one step forwards. Mick cocks his head to one side. 'When you approach a dog, use their name and speak to them.'

'How?'

'Nicely.'

'What do I say?'

'You can say what you like, as long as you say something.'

'Mick, it's great to meet you.' I suppress a sudden urge to giggle because it seems so ridiculous trying to make conversation with a dog, especially when I'm trying to be cool and completely amazing in front of Lewis. 'What do I do now? Ask him what he thinks about the weather?'

'That's better. You're beginning to relax. Come in a bit closer.'

Before I know it, I'm within arm's reach of the hurdle, with Lewis and the dog on the other side.

'You see, it's easy.'

'It is for you.' I feel rather silly talking to the top of Lewis's head, so I perch on the corner of the bale of straw.

'Would you like to stroke him?' Lewis asks eventually.

'I don't think so.' I gaze at Mick. I thought stroking

71

a dog was supposed to lower your blood pressure, but the very idea sends mine rocketing. 'I'm not that brave.'

Lewis rubs the dog's ears and sighs. 'She doesn't like you, Mick.'

'It isn't personal. I don't like dogs and that's all there is to it.'

'He isn't just a dog though, is he? He's an individual. He's his own person.' Lewis pauses. 'That's what I really want to show you. Dogs are all different, like people and sheep, and some of them are more lovable than others.' He looks at me, his eyes twinkling with humour, as if he's trying to tell me he's one of the more lovable people in the world, and I'm so absorbed in him that I don't notice until afterwards that he's slid the hurdle along with one hand so there's nothing between me and the dog. Lewis curves his arm around the dog's chest, keeping him back. 'Are you sure you wouldn't like to stroke him? He's like a teddy bear, aren't you?' Lewis plants a kiss on the top of Mick's head. Yes, he actually kisses his dog.

'Uncle Nobby didn't kiss his dog,' I observe. 'He reeked of fags and rotten teeth, for a start.'

'Poor dog. Mick doesn't smell much, just vaguely doggy. He wants to say "hi" to you.'

'Hi, Mick.' To my amazement the dog draws back his lips and pricks his ears. 'He's smiling at me. Is he smiling?'

'Here, hold out your hand.'

Slowly, I reach out until my fingers are within inches of Mick's nostrils. Suddenly, his tongue darts out and touches my skin. I pull back. Lewis laughs. I can feel the heat rushing to my cheeks as the dog looks at me with a quizzical expression, as if he's both surprised and a little offended by my reaction.

'You can stroke him now, Zara.'

'I can't,' is my immediate reaction, but I realise he's right. This is a different situation, a different dog, and I'm apprehensive maybe, but not scared. I reach out my hand again and touch the top of Mick's head. Breathe, I tell myself as my body tenses. It's fine. His coat is soft and silky and his skin warm as he leans into my hand, apparently enjoying the contact.

'You're such a lucky boy, Mick,' Lewis says as I withdraw my hand. 'That was better than you were expecting, wasn't it?'

'I can't believe I just did that.'

'You should be proud of yourself. Mick likes you – look, he's wagging his tail.'

I smile with relief, wondering how Lewis feels about me exactly.

'Let me know when you want to see your therapist again. We're available for appointments any time.'

'I'd better go,' I say, reluctant to leave. 'Gran will be waiting for her lift home.'

'And I'd better do another round of the lambing pens.' Lewis stands up, brushes the straw from his jeans and holds the dog to one side so I can walk past. 'Keep in touch,' he calls after me as I stumble across the cobbles in the dusk.

'What are you smiling at?' Emily asks when I return to the farmhouse, where Gran is sitting in the living room with Daisy in her arms, while Poppy pretends to feed her toy cat Fluffy with sweets that Gran brought from the shop.

'Yes, what took you and the shepherd so long?' Gran joins in. 'You've missed out on the washing up and your mum and dad left ages ago.'

'I didn't realise it was so late. I helped with one of the ewes, saw a lamb being born and I actually stroked Lewis's dog. Can you believe that?'

'Are you sure it was just the dog?' Emily teases.

'Leave her alone. Look at the poor girl blushing.' Gran gives Daisy a big squeeze. 'Come on, you'd better have your beautiful baby back. We should be going home, Zara. It's time to leave your sister in peace.'

As we go, I notice Lewis watching, his figure silhouetted in the doorway to the lambing shed.

CHAPTER FIVE

For the Love of Dogs

That image of Lewis stays with me throughout a busy week. I hardly know him, yet I find myself wondering what he's up to and remembering the intimacy of the lambing shed, every word and gesture, his heart-stopping smile, his broad shoulders and the flash of his loins.

'You're late!' Claire says, joining me as I get out of my car in a car park in Talymouth on Thursday evening.

'I've just finished a handover. I've been at a house in Talysands all day, waiting to catch a baby. I like to stay if I can, but I think it's going to be a while yet.' I look down at my uniform. 'I'll get changed inside.' I grab my bag, with the sound of Justin Bieber's 'Baby' coming from inside it, as we walk across to the entrance of the leisure centre where the lights are blazing.

'Are you really going to answer that?' Claire asks.

'It's one of my ladies,' I say, taking out my mobile and squinting at it to check the caller ID.

'I don't understand why they think they can contact you at any time, day or night, even when you aren't on call.'

'I have to take this. I'll catch up with you in a sec.'

'I hope this isn't another excuse to avoid the scales,' Claire says, shaking her head.

I gesture to her to move on and return to my call.

'Hello, Celine. How are you?' I saw her this morning. She's a week past her due date and there was no sign of labour being imminent, but that isn't to say it mightn't have begun since. This is her third baby and she's desperate to 'pop it out', as she describes it, in time to fly out to Benidorm for her sister's wedding. 'How can I help?'

'I've been thinking about what you said and I've decided I'd like to be seduced tomorrow.'

'Seduced?' I can't help it. I try to stifle a laugh, but it sneaks out as a loud snort.

'Did I say seduced?' Celine giggles.

'You did.'

'Oh-mi-god. My baby brain . . . I mean induced. I'd like you to come and give me a brush to start things off. I've tried the curry and raspberry leaf.'

'I'll come over tomorrow at eleven and we'll decide what to do then.' I don't have the heart to tell her that it's a sweep, not a brush, to break the membranes and get labour started.

'Thank you so much. I'll get Scott to set up the pool. You're a star.'

'Come on, Zara,' Claire cuts in impatiently from beside me.

'I told you you didn't have to wait.'

'I'm not going to give you the option of getting out of it this time. We said we'd do fat club together. I have to fit into the dress – I'll be gutted if I'm not a size ten by September.' Claire slips her arm through mine. 'You might want to hurry – there's a dog over there and it's coming our way.'

I follow Claire's gaze towards the car park entrance, where an elderly man is pushing a terrier in a pram. I feel the familiar rush of panic and urge to take evasive action, but I recall Lewis and Mick. All dogs are different. I take a breath, force a smile, and walk without deviating from my path.

'What's happened to you?' Claire asks.

'Didn't Emily tell you about Lewis's treatment for my fear of dogs when you went to visit the baby?' Claire's been twice now.

'Well, she mentioned you were an awfully long time in the lambing shed, having some kind of therapy.' Claire grins, making me realise that Emily has done a lot more than mention it.

'It was perfectly innocent. Lewis offered to help me, that's all, and it was great because I did actually manage to stroke one of his collies.'

'Is that a ewe-phemism? E-W-E, get it? I've never heard that one before.'

'Stop giggling. It isn't funny. What he did has really helped. Mick – that's Lewis's dog – is very sweet.'

'So is Lewis. I met him and he seems lovely. Emily

77

and I have plans for him to be your plus one for the wedding.'

'That's ridiculous and you know it.'

'I suppose it is rather far-fetched, seeing he'll have moved on by then,' she admits with a sigh of regret.

'It's a shame, because if he'd asked me to stroke him instead of the dog, I might just have said yes.'

'What did you just say?' Claire exclaims. 'Run that past me again.'

'You heard what I said.' I enter the leisure centre with a spring in my step. 'Come on, let's get this over with.'

I squeeze into my joggers and slip into a sweat top, although I have no intention of getting into a sweat, unlike the two svelte ladies I meet in the changing area. The room smells of chlorine and old shoes. I join Claire in the indoor tennis court where there's a set of scales in one corner, hidden by a screen. There's a table in front, which is laden with leaflets of recipes and dietary advice, and a banner with a slimming tip of the week, which is simply, 'Use a Smaller Plate. Eat Less!'

Dorien, the tall, slim yummy mummy who runs the club, escorts a smiling Claire from behind the screen. I don't need to ask.

'Ah, Zara, you can be next,' Dorien says. 'Are you a saint or a sinner? Let's find out, shall we?'

When I emerge from my turn on the scales, half afraid that Gok Wan will leap out and start pointing at my flabby bits, Claire asks me how I've done.

'Can't you tell from the despair that's etched on my

face?' I say mournfully. 'Two pounds this week. How about that?'

'Well done,' she says, touching my shoulder.

'I haven't lost it,' I explain. 'I've put it on.'

'Look on the bright side: the week before last you'd put on four. Never mind,' she says cheerily. 'I've lost enough for both of us.'

'I don't think that counts,' I say, smiling now. 'So what? I'll always be overweight. It's in my genes.' Inside, I know the truth, though – that I don't have the motivation, whereas Claire has the strapless ivory dress with beading, lace and an embroidered train. 'You can't afford to lose too much more. We don't want the bride to disappear altogether. Let's go to the pub.'

'So you can drown your sorrows in a Diet Coke?'

'Something like that.'

We head out through the leisure centre along the corridor past the pool.

'Watch out,' Claire catches my sleeve, 'it's Paul.' And he's coming straight towards us with a sports bag slung over his shoulder.

'Hello,' he says, greeting us both with an extravagant embrace. 'What are you two doing here?'

'We've been to the gym,' Claire says quickly. 'How about you?'

'I'm off to do some weights.' He flexes one arm, as if to show off his bicep. 'Any goss?'

'Not really,' Claire says. 'Come on, Zara.'

'Actually, I'd like a quick word with Zara. In private.'

I glance towards Claire, who gives me an almost imperceptible shake of the head.

'Two minutes.' Paul grabs my hand and takes me aside.

'I'll meet you at reception,' Claire says.

'She really doesn't like me, does she?' Paul says as we stand in the doorway to the pool.

'She thinks she's protecting me.' I pause and lower my eyes. 'I used to get upset when we met immediately after the break-up . . . Not any more. I'm kind of fine with it now,' I hasten to add. 'What did you want to say to me that you couldn't say in front of Claire?'

Paul clears his throat. 'There's something I want to tell you before anyone else does.'

I frown. 'Tell me what? You can tell me anything. You know that.'

'You're wonderful, Zara.' Paul gazes at me gently and my stomach lurches. I can't help my reaction. I don't like him all that much on occasions, but that doesn't mean I've been able to stop loving him. 'Sometimes I wonder why we got divorced.'

You divorced me, I want to say. It was your decision. I remember him telling me our marriage was over, that he wanted out. He came home after a long shift, sat me down and talked. I remember feeling as if I was collapsing, imploding from the inside out. I was hot, burning, my throat dry. My chest was throbbing as if it was about to rupture. The more Paul spoke, the more I tried to blot out his words until I couldn't hear, couldn't comprehend what he was saying. I cried. He cried. It was one of the worst days of my life. I bite my lip. What would Gran say? Don't keep going over old ground.

'Anyway,' Paul goes on after a pause, 'I wanted to tell you the other day in the shop, but I couldn't quite bring myself to. The truth is I've met someone and it's pretty serious.'

'You have a girlfriend?' The news comes as a shock to me.

'I'm sorry.' Paul's forehead is lined with concern.

'Why? Why apologise?'

'Because . . .' He shrugs.

'I'm pleased for you. Really.' It's an effort to force the words out. 'We knew we'd both move on eventually.'

'We?' he says. 'Have you?'

I shake my head.

'Aren't you going to ask me what she's like?'

'I'm sure she's perfect,' I say wryly. 'You've always had such good taste in women.'

He smiles, his male ego caressed and standing as tall as it can. He seems taller – either I've shrunk or . . .

'Are you wearing built-up shoes?'

'No,' he says.

'You liar.' I chuckle before growing serious again.

'I'm glad you're taking this so well.' Paul touches my arm. 'I thought you might be upset.'

'I'm fine,' I say, my voice sounding harsh. 'I don't mind you having a girlfriend. Please don't worry about me.'

'But I do. It's hard to stop worrying about someone when you used to be married to them.'

'Don't I know it.'

'Still friends?' he says.

'I'm not sure.'

The smug expression on Paul's face is replaced by consternation.

'What do you mean? You've just made out that you're cool with the situation. I don't see that this changes anything between us.'

'What about your girlfriend? What would she think of us keeping in touch?'

'She isn't the jealous type.'

'I don't think it's a good idea,' I say, trying to make the break between us, something I've wanted, but have been too much of a coward to do in the past, knowing that if I did, I'd be devastated. However, cutting all ties, although intensely painful, seems to be the only way for me to move forward in my life. I can't bear the thought of keeping seeing him, knowing he's with someone else. 'I wouldn't appreciate my boyfriend texting and phoning and dropping by to see his ex-wife all the time. It's quite a test for a new relationship.'

'Actually, it isn't that new,' he confesses. 'We've been dating for a while now.'

'And you never said, even though we're supposed to be such friends?' I'm angry now, resentful towards him for not mentioning his love interest before, and pretty furious with myself for letting it get to me. I turn away and start heading along the corridor.

'Where are you going?' Paul says, following.

'Claire's waiting.'

'I'll see you around then,' he calls after me.

'Goodbye,' I call back.

82

'What did he want?' Claire says when I catch up with her in reception. 'Hey, are you okay?'

'I will be,' I say, biting back tears. I tell her about the girlfriend.

'I'm so sorry.' Claire offers me a tissue. 'The bastard.'

'It was bound to happen, but I didn't think it would affect me like this. I wish I could say I don't care what he's doing and with whom, but I can't.'

'You don't want him back, do you?' Claire groans.

'No. No way, but I still have feelings for him.' I blow my nose loudly. 'I guess I always will.'

'That's because you will insist on this "let's stay mates" business.'

'I've told him I don't want to be friends any more.'

'Oh well done.' Claire pats my shoulder. 'If there's any time when you're tempted to change your mind about that, call me and I'll set you back on the right track.'

'Thank you.'

'You're bound to have moments of weakness. What you need is something, or rather some*one* special to help you move on, somebody to have fun with.'

'That's easier said than done, but if Paul's managed it, why shouldn't I?'

'Exactly,' Claire agrees, and we walk along the seafront in the sticky, salt-laden breeze that blows from the sea, and climb the steps to the top of the cliff. At the Talymouth Arms, we stop for drinks.

'Who is she then?' Claire asks, her curiosity piqued. 'What's she like?'

'I didn't ask.' I pay for a Diet Coke and a lime and soda at the bar and follow her past a couple of tables of evening drinkers towards the rear of the pub, which has dark oak beams across the ceiling and seafaring art on the walls.

'That's a pity,' she sighs. 'I'd like to know who would go out with Paul after what he put you through.'

'He isn't all bad. We weren't right for each other, simple as that.'

'Zara, you're too nice!'

'So how was your week?' I ask, finding seats in the corner close to the fireplace where a fresh log burns in the grate. 'I've hardly seen you.'

'The band's let us down, so Kev's trying to find another one – it's quite short notice and I so wanted the first one because they said they could play Eric Clapton's "In Your Father's Eyes", which we asked for especially. I don't know what we'll do.'

'Couldn't you have a DJ instead? Or choose a different song?'

'Oh no. I've pictured it all in my mind and it wouldn't be right without live music. I want our first dance as a married couple to be perfect. I have found the most amazing earrings, though – they'll go with the dress, everything.' Claire smiles. 'How about you? And I'm not asking about work.'

'I've done a couple of shifts for Gran, that's about it.'

'You really are going to have to get out more. When did you last go on a date?'

'I haven't, not since I started dating Paul. You know that.'

'Well,' she pulls her mobile from her bag, 'in anticipation of this moment—'

'What moment?' I interrupt.

'Your decision to forget about your ex and move on. Emily and I have mocked up a profile for you; it's all ready to upload to one of those free-to-join websites.'

'You haven't?' I exclaim.

'Look.' She shows me the screen. 'There you are.'

There's a photo of me, pinched from my Facebook page, and a whole lot of information. My personality is 'helpful', not 'passionate' or 'outgoing'.

'God, that makes me sound so boring!'

'The interesting part is designing your perfect man. You have to type in your preferences. Internet dating's great. Everyone's doing it and I want you to find someone to be your plus one at the wedding,' Claire says. 'The seating plan won't be right otherwise.'

'Look, it's going to take time for me to get over Paul. I'm not ready to rush headlong into another relationship, although the idea of some light-hearted dating seems quite appealing, so I doubt very much I'm going to be able to solve your dilemma with the seating plan,' I say, amused.

'You never know. Love moves in mysterious ways.' Claire swirls the ice cubes around in the bottom of her glass. 'I wasn't keen on Kevin when I first met him. He kind of wore me down.'

'That doesn't sound terribly romantic. I don't think I'd like that. If I were to go out with someone –' I almost say, Lewis, but stop myself just in time – 'he'd have to be funny, fit, and up for some hot and passionate . . .'

'Sex,' Claire adds for me.

'Thank you. I'd forgotten what it was,' I say. 'And that is a joke, by the way.'

'When I said Kevin wore me down, it was in the nicest possible way, all hearts and flowers, and constantly bombarding me with requests to go out with him.'

I humour her because I'm sure everyone has heard the story of how she and Kevin got together so many times that it's become legend.

'How many times was it before you said yes?' I ask.

'Twenty-one.'

'Couldn't he take a hint then?' I say, arching one eyebrow.

'I'm glad he didn't. He kept coming into the surgery: don't you remember how we used to joke that he was a hypochondriac?'

'Didn't he think he had a brain tumour at one time?'

'Oh yes, and asthma, irritable bowels and shingles.' Claire giggles.

After another hour chatting, we make a move, saying goodbye outside at the leisure centre before heading off in our separate cars. Claire disappears before I set out because another of my ladies is on the phone panicking that she hasn't got enough breast milk. I reassure her, promising I'll call in to see her and the baby in the morning in advance of going to induce Celine, and then I drive home, travelling via the narrow, twisty lane at the edge of the escarpment rather than the main road, because it's a shorter distance and my needle is in the red on the fuel gauge, and I really don't want to stop and buy petrol. It's very cold for the third week of March – minus one according to the thermometer on the dash – and darker than black, as my grandmother would say, without streetlamps or starlight.

As I begin the descent into Talyton St George, I catch sight of something at the side of the lane at the level of the bank, a pair of eyes reflecting the light from the headlamps. I slow to a stop, assuming it's a small deer or a fox about to cross, but there's something not quite right.

I pull in to take a closer look, only to find one of my least favourite animals dragging itself along on its belly and quivering with fear or cold, I'm not sure which. All I want to do is get out of here as fast as I can, but something – the look in the dog's eyes – stops me. I prepare to drive on and it slumps back into the grass, out of sight and out of mind.

Someone else will find it, I think, except . . . I gaze at the bare trees and the windblown hillside lit by the sweep of the headlamps. Who will find it until it's too late? I recall Mick's gentle, trusting nature. What if it was Mick? Would I even think of driving off if it was him in this situation?

Feeling slightly sick, I get out of the car and make my way to the verge. The dog utters a desperate whimper. I shine the flashlight on my mobile without getting too close, spotting a piece of rope, a noose digging into the dog's neck one end and the other tied around the nearest tree. I don't understand. Who would do such a thing?

'Oh, you poor thing.' I remember how Lewis told

me to speak nicely, but it isn't difficult this time. The words come naturally. 'You're frozen. Are you hurt? Look at your frosty whiskers.'

She – because I'm guessing she's a girl – lifts her head and whimpers again and my fear, the pricking of the hairs at the back of my neck and the rapid thudding of my pulse, is hounded out by a different emotion – compassion. The grey and white dog is long and lanky like a greyhound, and so thin I can see every bone along her spine.

'Now what am I going to do?' I could call Jack – he works for Animal Welfare – or the vet's surgery in Talyton, or Murray, or Lewis, even Paul at a push, but they could take a while to get here when I could take her straight to the vet myself.

'Now, what's happened to you, Frosty Whiskers?' I take a tentative step towards her, and another, and a twig snaps under my foot, making a noise like a gunshot. I force myself to squat down and hold out my hand, like Lewis showed me to with Mick, to let her smell my scent. She touches her nose to my skin, making me freeze. She seems to freeze too and I realise she's just as wary of me as I am of her. 'We're a right pair, aren't we?' I say, relaxing a little.

I kneel right down, oblivious to the cold, hard ground, and carefully loosen the rope noose, slipping it over the dog's head to release her and then, when she could have struggled up and run away, she pushes her head into my lap as if to say thank you.

'I'm going to make sure you're okay,' I tell her, and I pick her up awkwardly, like a first-time parent picking up their new-born, and carry her like I would a baby, albeit a skinny one with very long legs, to the car, where I place her on the back seat with my coat across her. I turn the heating up and drive into Talyton.

The lights are on at Otter House. I rush inside and ring the bell, bringing Maz, one of the vets, into reception. She's in her late thirties, tall and naturally slim.

'Hi,' she says, tying her pale blonde hair back with what looks like one of the postman's elastic bands. 'I wasn't expecting anyone else at this time of night . . . How can I help?'

'I'm Zara. I'm sorry, I should have called ahead, but I came across this dog and I didn't know what to do.'

Maz smiles. 'Slow down and start again from the beginning.'

'I was driving back from Talymouth when I found her tied to a tree. She's in the car.'

'Why don't you bring her straight in?'

'Actually, I wondered if you could come and get her. I was bitten by a dog when I was a kid.' I'm annoyed with myself for wimping out, but I'm feeling a bit wobbly now.

'I'll grab a muzzle just in case. Does she seem friendly?'

'She didn't try to bite me. She's sick, I think.'

'Oh, she is, the poor thing,' Maz says, when I open the car door for her. 'Let's get you indoors.' She carries the dog into the practice, where she rings the bell, summoning Izzy, the head nurse. I've met Izzy several times before at Greenwood Farm and Talyton's annual

Country Show – her husband is a sheep farmer and one of Murray's cousins. She's over forty, but looks younger with her cropped hair and freckles.

'Come through,' Maz says. 'I expect you'd like to see how the dog gets on.'

'I'm not sure,' I begin, but I go along with them anyway, not wanting the dog to think I've abandoned her in the same way that her owner has.

'Izzy, set up some warm IV fluids and a heat pad. Oh, and I could do with a stethoscope. I can't find mine.'

'You really should get one surgically implanted,' Izzy grumbles lightly as she marches ahead into what appears to be the animal version of a hospital prep room, complete with table and sink. It smells like a doctor's surgery – of scrub and surgical spirit. 'There it is, hanging from the hook where you left it.'

I smile to myself. I don't know what doctors and vets would do without us.

Soon Frosty, as I call her, is lying on the bench on a drip and with a blanket wrapped around her.

'Where did you say you found her?' Maz asks. 'This is a welfare case – the owner should be prosecuted for neglect.'

'If I had my way, I'd lock them up and throw away the key. Or worse,' Izzy adds darkly. 'There's no excuse for treating any animal in this way. It's appalling. Not only is she completely emaciated, she could have frozen to death. She would have, if you hadn't found her.'

'I don't recognise her. She isn't one of ours,' Maz

observes. 'I'll get Jack Miller in tomorrow morning. For now, we'll take some pictures and get a weight for her.'

At the mention of weight, I smile wryly to myself. The dog could really do with the extra pounds I've put on this past couple of weeks.

'She can't have been fed properly for a while,' Izzy says.

'We'll get some food into her when she's warmed up,' Maz says. 'Some of that new convalescent diet would suit her.'

'I don't understand how a human being can do this to an animal – and I don't even like dogs.' Aware of Izzy's sharp intake of breath, I soften my opinion. 'What I mean is, I'm not mad about dogs.' I pause, gazing at the raw gash made by the rope around Frosty's neck. 'Is that going to be all right?'

'It's the least of her problems at the moment,' Maz says. 'We'll clean it up and see what we can do, but her body's been starved of nutrients so it will take longer to heal than it would in a fit animal.'

'How old do you think she is?' I ask.

'I'd say about six to eight months, wouldn't you, Izzy?'

'I'd go for eight,' Izzy says.

'So she's still a puppy, really.'

'A teenager,' Maz smiles. 'Leave her with us – we'll look after her. And thanks for bringing her in. If it wasn't for you, she wouldn't have made it this far.'

'She is going to get better?'

'We'll have to wait and see if she makes a full

recovery. We don't know if she has any underlying health issues yet.'

I'm aware the dog's eyes are on me, as if she's trying to say something.

'You can stroke her,' Maz says. 'She could do with as much TLC as possible.'

I take a breath. The dog isn't going anywhere. What's the worst that could happen?

'She won't hurt you,' Izzy says. 'She seems like a real softie.'

Taking another deep breath, I tell myself to relax. I want to stroke the dog, to let her know I'm thinking of her and praying she'll be all right. Can I trust her? She seems to trust me. I let my fingers touch the top of her head and I can see her relax, the tension melting away. Her coat, which I thought would feel bristly, is smooth to the touch.

'What will happen to her if she does get better?' I swallow past a painful constriction in my throat at the thought of the alternative, which seems more likely the longer I look at her. She isn't just thin, she's a size zero.

'We'll keep her for as long as she needs medical attention, then she'll go to the Sanctuary where Talyton Animal Rescue will find a new home for her,' Maz says.

'You will let me know how she gets on.'

'Of course.'

'I could drop in tomorrow morning on my way to work.'

'Come in whenever you like. Someone will be here.'

Maz starts to organise a kennel for the dog, while Izzy heads out to find a camera to take photos as evidence, giving me a chance to talk without embarrassing myself in front of them.

'Good luck, Frosty,' I whisper. 'I hope you make it.'

'What did you call her?' I turn to find Maz looking in my direction. She grins. 'It's like a whispering gallery in here. You can hear everything.'

'I called her Frosty because she had frosty whiskers when I found her. It sounds a bit lame, doesn't it?'

'I quite like it. We'll call her Frosty then. We'll see you tomorrow. Can you see yourself out?'

'Yes, thanks.'

Back at the newsagent's, the lights are on in the flat and Gran is still up. She's nodded off in front of the television, with Granddad's photo in her lap and Norris lying across the back of the chair.

'Gran,' I call softly.

She starts. 'Oh, you gave me such a surprise. I don't think I'll ever get used to having a flatmate.'

'I'm sorry.' I touch her hand. Norris opens one eye and gives me a malevolent glare.

'Where have you been?'

I explain about the dog.

'And you're telling me you lifted it into your car and drove it to the vet's? I don't believe it.'

'I couldn't leave her there, could I? I'd never have forgiven myself if she'd frozen to death.'

'Perhaps you're over your fear of dogs, thanks to the shepherd.'

'I wouldn't go that far,' I say. 'She was so distressed I

could see past the fact that she was a dog, and recognise a creature – a person, even – who needed my help.'

'Well, I'm – what's the word?'

'Amazed?' I suggest.

'No, gob, gob-stoppered.'

'I think you mean gobsmacked.'

'That too. Can I tell everyone?'

'I don't know why you're asking, because you're going to tell everyone anyway,' I smile. 'I'm going to bed. Shouldn't you be on your way too?' I hesitate at the door. 'You're making me feel like I'm a lightweight.'

'A what?'

'Never mind.'

'Sometimes I think we speak different languages,' she says. 'You're right, though. I should turn in, but I haven't been sleeping too well since your mum and dad started talking about selling the shop and putting me in a home.'

'Don't worry about it. They can't make you do anything. Oh, one more thing,' I say, remembering. 'We saw Paul at the leisure centre. Did you know he has a girlfriend?'

'I heard a rumour, but that's all it was, so I didn't say anything. I'm sorry, but it's for the best. Now perhaps you'll see that there's no going back.'

'I knew there wasn't anyway.' I remove my scarf from around my neck.

'But in spite of that, you're still in love with the man.'

'Not "in love" as such.'

'I wish I could believe you.'

'And I wish you goodnight, Gran.'

'Goodnight.'

Dismissing any thoughts of my ex-husband, I go to bed, but I don't sleep for thinking about Frosty – what she must have gone through and whether or not she'll be alive in the morning.

CHAPTER SIX

Beyond the Call of Duty

When I turn up at Otter House the next morning, Jack Miller is in reception, dressed in a navy showerproof jacket, cargo trousers and boots with odd laces, one black and one tan. His hair is dark blond with natural highlights, and his cheeks are clothed in stubble. He's roughly the same age as me and married to one of mine and Emily's friends, Tessa.

Maz, who reminds me of how I look when I've been on my feet all night, invites us both through to the kennels to see the dog.

'So she's made it so far,' I say.

'More than that,' Maz smiles. 'She's on her feet.'

'Shouldn't that be on her paws?' Jack says cheerfully.

Frosty is bumping into the bars of her cage with a huge, lampshade-like Elizabethan collar around her neck.

'What's she wearing that for?' I ask, feeling more

upset than I thought I would be at seeing her confined.

'It's for her own good,' Maz says. 'She chewed through her drip tubing during the night.'

'I'm glad my ladies don't do that kind of thing.' Amused, I lean down towards the cage, but not too close. 'Hi, Frosty.' It takes her a few seconds to respond to my presence, but when she does, she gives a squeak of delight, which cuts through my wary reserve and brings tears springing to my eyes. As she wags her tail, repeatedly bashing the stainless steel walls of the cage, I swallow hard. She likes me. In spite of the cruel treatment she's received at somebody else's hands, she's prepared to give me the benefit of the doubt.

'She recognises you from last night,' Maz says. 'That's sweet.'

'I think she's trying to say "let me out of here".' Jack whistles through his teeth. 'She's one of the skinniest dogs I've ever seen.'

'She's had two small meals so far and she hasn't been sick. We'll keep feeding her little and often throughout the day.'

'I'll be looking for a prosecution under the Animal Welfare Act, but I'm not optimistic about the outcome,' Jack says. 'I don't suppose she's micro-chipped?'

'Dream on. We've checked and there's no ID. I've spoken to Alex about her.' Maz is married to Alex Fox-Gifford, who owns Talyton Manor vets, the local farm animal practice. 'He's seen a dog of this description, a lurcher/bull-terrier-cross type, once or twice when he's been riding his horse down by the river. She's a very distinctive dog. Someone must recognise her.'

'I'll make some enquiries,' Jack says. 'I'll start with Frank.'

'Frank Maddocks?' Maz exclaims. 'Wasn't he banned from keeping animals after the incident with the mare and foal?'

'He was, but he did a disappearing act a while ago. He's a hard man to keep track of.'

'I know of him.' Frank used to live in a mobile home on a site next to the industrial estate on the edge of Talyton St George, and he's been in and out of prison for various reasons. I made some antenatal and postnatal visits to a flat in Talymouth a few months ago, to Frank's elder son's girlfriend, who had a baby girl by C-section. Frank came to visit them, bearing armfuls of gifts. 'He didn't give me the impression he was a bad man.' In fact, I can hardly reconcile the image I have of the adoring granddad with a man who could starve and then abandon a dog like Frosty. I wasn't so sure about the son when I met him – he seemed as if he could have another side to him. 'So what happens next?' I continue. 'How long will Frosty stay here?'

'If she continues to improve as she is, she can go in three or four days – after the weekend, anyway.'

'Can I come in and see her again? I'll pay the bill, too.'

'Oh, you don't have to do that. Talyton Animal Rescue will fund her treatment – we charge cost price for waifs and strays. They'd appreciate a donation though, I'm sure. And you can drop by whenever you like, as long as you let us know when you're coming.'

I thank Maz and Jack and say one last goodbye to Frosty before I head off for work, picking up my car to visit Chloe who lives in a barn conversion near the Old Forge in Talyford. She's a high-flying lawyer and probably the most anxious first-time mum I've ever met. She opens the door to me in a blouse and pyjama bottoms. Her dark hair is long and lank, and I don't think she can have had a shower since she came out of hospital four days ago.

'Hello, Zara. I'm so relieved to see you – I'm very worried about Joshua. He's crying all the time – I don't think he's getting enough milk.'

I pause to listen, but I can't hear anything apart from the murmur of a radio somewhere in the house.

'Come in,' she goes on, and we chat over coffee and biscuits in the open-plan living area. I look out through the long windows at a herd of black and white cows at the end of the garden, and the Devon countryside beyond, while Joshua snores quietly in his Moses basket.

'How are you?' I ask eventually. 'How do you feel?'

'Exhausted,' she says flatly. I notice how she's chosen the chair facing away from the baby, as if she wants to ignore his existence. She continues, 'I didn't realise how hard this would be. I thought criminal law was challenging, but I find myself dreaming of being back in court, defending thugs and murderers.'

'Are you eating and drinking plenty? Does the baby latch onto the breast? Do you have any pain, cracked nipples or red patches?'

She shakes her head in answer to all my questions.

'Let's wake Joshua up and have a look at him.'

'Do we have to?' Chloe looks pale already, but her complexion blanches further at the suggestion.

'Yes, we do,' I say, in the positive, no-nonsense tone I adopt for these situations. 'Now, you pick him up and show me how you feed him.'

Chloe moves slowly across the room – she's had stitches – picks the baby up and shuffles back to the sofa, where she sits down, opens her blouse and cuddles the baby to her breast. He doesn't cry once throughout my visit. When he wakes, he opens his eyes, and looks around for a minute, his head wobbling about as his mum tries to support it.

'I'm afraid he'll hurt his neck,' she says, her voice wavering.

'Babies are pretty tough little things.' Chloe has lost her confidence since the birth. She wasn't like this at her antenatal checks, when she was excited and looking forward to being a mum. 'That's it. He's got it. He's latching on now and sucking.'

'But is he getting enough?' she wails. 'How do I know?' She glares down at her breasts. 'Why don't these things come with some kind of gauge?'

'You can tell because he's thriving. Look at those chubby cheeks.' I pause. 'Is Dominic taking paternity leave?'

'He's had to go back to work and my mum's gone home to Leicester. Dom doesn't like her staying with us.'

'That's a shame. Have you been out with your baby yet?'

'I thought I'd give it a couple of weeks yet. I'm not sure I can face getting everything together.'

'I'm going to ask Dr Mackie to visit you,' I decide. 'He can check on Joshua – that might help to put your mind at rest.'

'He came to see us two days ago.'

'I think he should come again. Ben can have a chat with you at the same time and then we can assess what help you might need.' I smile encouragingly, but she doesn't smile back. She's going to require a lot of support to get through what should be one of the happiest times of her life. Emily has the baby blues, whereas Chloe seems to be sinking into full-blown postnatal depression.

Back in the car, I call Ben and arrange for him to add her to his list of house calls for the afternoon before I go to Celine's to carry out a stretch and sweep in an attempt to induce labour.

'This baby is going to be overcooked by the time it makes an appearance,' Celine says ruefully. 'And my sister will be back from her bloody honeymoon,' she adds.

Blonde, with hair extensions, false nail and eyelashes, and a well-practised pout, Celine could have walked straight out of *TOWIE* – she even has the Essex accent, having moved to Devon a few years before with her husband, who works as a sales team leader for a company in Exeter.

They live on the new estate in a detached house that's been extended and revamped with the latest appliances, home cinema and hot tub, and every room has been painted in a different colour, every wall in a different shade, so it feels like a Dulux catalogue; but it's the kind of home that's always filled with the sound of laughter and children's voices – Celine's and other people's – and the scent of coffee and baking. Today I can smell cold curry too.

Celine shows me past the oil painting in the hall of her and her husband, who bears a passing resemblance to Keith Lemon, gazing into each other's eyes against the dramatic backdrop of dark skies and a stately home.

'I'm so glad you're here. Mum's here with the kids so we can go upstairs and you can get on with what you have to do.' Celine looks at my trolley bag. 'What's all that for?'

'Sometimes it's more comfortable if you have some gas and air for this procedure.'

She grimaces. 'I don't want it if it's going to hurt.'

'I thought you wanted to go to the wedding.'

'I do. Oh, all right. Let's get this over with.' I follow her up the stairs. 'We tried the curry and the you-know-what. We could hardly get it on for laughing. Ray said it was like having sex with a giant space hopper, even down to the colour. Look at me. I'm orange – something's gone wrong with the fake tan.' Soon Celine is roaring with laughter and I'm surprised her waters don't pop spontaneously. As it is, I have to do it for her.

'What happens next?' she says as she takes one last puff on the gas and air.

'We wait.'

It turns out that we don't have to wait for long. I

return with Kelly to check on Celine a few hours later and she's well on the way. Her baby boy is born at midnight.

I get to bed by two and I'm up again at six to help with the papers. After a morning in the shop, I check up on Frosty, who has made such a miraculous recovery from her ordeal that Maz wants to send her to the rescue centre on Monday. I volunteer to take Frosty there myself. Maz seems so pleased to have one thing less to arrange that I can't back out when I reconsider a couple of seconds later.

Next, I decide to go and see Emily at the farm. She's seemed a bit down the last couple of times I've spoken to her on the phone, and I'm worried that looking after Poppy – who has an increasing aversion to her baby sister – is too much for her.

'Isn't Murray about?' I say when I find her sitting in the living room in front of some television cookery show, with Daisy crying in the Moses basket and Poppy thumping around in a strop about running out of her favourite biscuits.

'He's working today.'

'Why don't we go out somewhere?'

'I'm not sure I can be bothered. It's a lovely offer, but it's a nightmare getting everyone ready.'

'I think it will cheer everyone up.' I look out at the rain. 'The weather's lousy and you're stuck indoors when we could be having cake or ice cream at the garden centre.'

'Can we, Auntie Zara?' says Poppy, immediately pricking up her ears. 'Can we have chocolate cake?'

'I expect so,' I smile. 'Why don't you find your coat and hat while I get Daisy ready? Emily, go and brush your hair. You look like you forgot this morning.'

'OMG, I did. I'm not sure I cleaned my teeth either.'

'Naughty Mummy,' Poppy scolds.

'Go on, both of you.' I pick Daisy out of the Moses basket, check her nappy and choose a knitted hat from the stack of woolly items that Gran, Murray's mother and the WI have presented to the baby since her arrival. 'What do you think of that one, niece-let?' I say lightly as Daisy continues to whimper, staring at me slightly boss-eyed. 'You remember me.' I slip the hat onto her head – it's bright pink and yellow – before holding her close and rocking her gently as I sing a rendition of 'If You Don't Know Me By Now . . .'

When I look up, I find Emily and Poppy and, worst of all, Lewis, huddled together in the doorway, laughing.

'I'm sorry to say that you aren't through to the next round,' my sister says.

'I disagree,' Lewis cuts in. 'In my opinion, Zara definitely has the X Factor.'

'So you'd put her through to boot camp, if only to give her the opportunity to learn to sing,' Emily jokes.

'Daisy likes it,' I point out, blushing. 'Look, she's stopped crying.'

'We're just off for a coffee,' Emily says. 'What was it you wanted, Lewis?'

'I saw Zara's car. I wanted to say hi, and well done for rescuing that dog.'

'You heard?'

'Emily told me. Your gran mentioned it too when I went into the shop.'

'Gran said you'd been in,' I say, and then it occurs to me that this could be divine intervention, a chance to spend some time alone with him. 'Look, I know it's a bit of a cheek and you have lots of other things to do, and I'm not sure your boss –' I glance towards Emily – 'will let you have the time off, but I offered to take the dog to the rescue centre on Monday.'

'You did what?' Emily exclaims. 'You're scared of dogs.'

'Thanks to Lewis, I feel a bit better about them.'

I notice how Emily raises one eyebrow. I'm not going to hear the end of this. She'll tease me without mercy.

'I was surprised when I heard you'd taken a dog to the vet by yourself,' Lewis says.

'I couldn't leave her there, could I?'

'I'm impressed.'

'It wasn't as hard as it sounds. I remembered Mick and how sweet he was, and saw how scared she was and how she was depending on me.' I pause. 'Anyway, Maz mentioned that they were really too busy to spare a member of staff to take the dog to the Sanctuary, so I kind of found myself offering. I feel responsible for her in a way, and I'd like to make sure she's okay, but she's rather lively now and I'm not sure I'll manage her.'

'I'll come with you,' Lewis says.

'Have you run that past your boss?' Emily interrupts.

'Well, no . . .'

'Don't look so worried. I'm sure Murray can spare you for a couple of hours.'

'Thanks, Emily. I'll drive, Zara. You can't possibly put a dog in the boot of your car with all your medical gear.'

'I was going to put her on the back seat.'

'She won't stay there, will she? You'd have to buy a travel harness. No, I'll take you.' Lewis gazes at me with a hint of mischief in his eyes and I blush again – furiously. 'I'll pick you up from yours on Monday – you say a time.'

'Nine thirty?'

'That's good for me. I'll see you then. Cheers everyone.'

'Bye-bye, Lewis,' Poppy says. 'Can I feed the lambs?'

'Perhaps when you get back if your mummy says it's okay.'

'It is,' Emily says, turning to me as Lewis heads back out to the yard, climbs up into the tractor and drives away through the driving rain. 'Larry has company. We have four orphan and rejected lambs now.' She grins. 'You didn't have to go to the trouble of rescuing an abandoned dog as an excuse to spend time with our shepherd.'

'I know.' I grin back at her. 'Let's go.'

I take Emily and the two girls to the garden centre on Stoney Lane. To Poppy it's like a treasure chest filled with all kinds of desirable items, from windmills on sticks to jolly red-faced gnomes who look as if they've been on the beer, to gaudy plastic ladybirds and frogs with solar lamps embedded in their heads, making them look like amphibious miners.

'I never thought I'd say this about Fifi's garden

centre, but I love it,' Emily says, choosing a pair of floral gardening gloves. 'Thanks for thinking of us and taking us out.'

I feel slightly guilty having been so consumed with my life – work and the shop – that I haven't made much time recently for my sister.

'Let's have coffee. Would you like to choose a piece of cake? Or ice cream?' I ask, trying to extricate a bright yellow plastic sunflower from Poppy's sticky grasp.

'I want it.' She stamps one foot to emphasise exactly how much.

'I think you should leave it with the others,' Emily says.

'Nooo!'

'There's only one left on the display – it will be lonely. We don't want that, do we?' I say, squatting down beside her.

'Oh?' she says. It's a tense moment as we – not just me and Emily, but everyone else in the garden centre – wait to see if she's going to explode again.

'Why don't you put this one back into the pot with the other one so they can live together happily ever after?'

'You put it back, Auntie Zara,' she says, suddenly pushing the sunflower into my hand.

'You're very good at this, Zara.' Emily swaps Daisy's car seat from one arm to the other. I'm laden with a mahussive changing bag, according to the principle of the smaller you are, the more kit you need.

In the restaurant, the first round of coffee and cake is on me. Daisy remains asleep and Poppy eats chocolate

107

cake and drinks squash before running off to play with the toys in the children's corner where we can keep an eye on her.

'I feel like I want to poke Daisy and wake her up so she sleeps at night. Murray says she'll be perfect for working shifts when she's older.'

'Maybe she'll be a midwife.'

'Murray wants her to be a farmer.'

'What about Poppy?'

'Oh, who knows?' Emily sighs. 'She's driving me mad. She hates the baby. I've spoken to the health visitor and we're doing everything she suggested and it isn't working. I don't know what I'm going to do.'

'She'll get over it. She's bound to be jealous at first. It's a big shock finding you're no longer the centre of attention at four. I see it all the time. You just have to be patient. I know Poppy's still very young, but can't you get her to think she's helping out more with Daisy?'

'I've done that, sent her on errands in the house to fetch a clean nappy or soother.' Emily smiles wryly. 'The last time I did that, she picked one off the floor and stuck it in Daisy's mouth. She knew it was wrong.'

'A few germs aren't going to hurt the baby, are they? I hope you don't mind me saying, but I think you're making too much of this. Daisy's growing so quickly, she'll soon be crawling, and before you know it she'll be toddling about. She'll seem much more fun to play with then. Why don't you let me and Gran have one of the girls for a day now and again?'

'Because you're both busy. It's a lovely offer, but I can cope.'

'Are you sure?'

'Of course I'm sure,' she says, with a hint of fire in her voice.

I change the subject, noticing that Poppy has returned, and is clinging onto Emily's arm. 'Shall we have another round of cake?'

Poppy has a healthy appetite, but mine seems to have disappeared. I'm going to see Lewis on Monday and, even though it's just because he's supposed to be helping me out with Frosty, I can hardly wait.

CHAPTER SEVEN

A Dog's Dinner

On the Monday morning, I'm showered and dressed and I've done the papers by the time James turns up to deliver them.

'You didn't have to do that, you know,' Gran says, placing two mugs of tea on the counter. 'Where are you off to today? You're looking . . .' she frowns as if struggling to find the right words, '. . . all glammed up. I love the nails.' She peers at my hands. 'What are those? Daisies?'

'Some kind of white flower, stencilled onto a blue background,' I say, showing them off. 'Would you like me to do yours sometime?'

'What would I want mine done for?' she says with a dismissive snort.

'Because you're green with envy,' I tease.

'Maybe I am,' she concedes.

'You can choose whatever theme you like. I'd like

to do it; we should have a girls' night in sometime.'

She smiles, making me wish I'd thought of it before.

'Anyway, where are you going?'

'I thought I'd told you that I'm taking Frosty to the Sanctuary with Lewis.' Gran looks at me blankly. She doesn't remember. 'Didn't you get Norris from there years ago?'

She remembers that.

'I took him as a kitten when Gloria Brimblecombe ran the rescue centre with Talyton Animal Rescue. Oh, it was a terrible place. The people were kind to the animals, but it was like they were in prison, waiting for someone to love them.'

'Please don't make me feel guilty.'

'I expect they'll find her a lovely home.' Gran rubs at her temple, leaving a red mark. 'You won't let them put me away, will you?'

'Why?' I try to make light of her concern. 'What have you done to deserve it, apart from overcharge for a few sweets?'

'I'm not talking about prison. I'm talking about your mum and dad plotting to put me in a home.'

'They won't make you. They can't force you to do anything.'

'They'll fix it so it looks as if I'm losing my marbles and then go for power of eternity.'

'You mean power of attorney.'

'Do I?' Gran bumbles on. 'You heard what they said. They've virtually chosen a place for me. I expect they've put a deposit on a room by now.'

'I don't believe they've gone that far.'

'Well, I want you to promise me that you won't let them cart me off to an old people's home. I couldn't bear to leave the shop – it's filled with memories.' Her voice is faint and her face etched with sadness. 'Promise me,' she repeats.

'I'm not sure I can do that . . .' I shrug. 'Things change.'

'Zara, I'm relying on you to do this for me,' she insists. 'There's no one else.'

How can I refuse her when she's been so good to me? Yes, I could just about have afforded to rent a place on my own, or I could have lived in Claire's spare room for a while, but it was Gran who suggested I move in with her so I could pay off my credit card bills and save some money – Paul and I had very little after the fertility treatment and the divorce – and she could spoil me.

'I promise,' I say eventually. 'Anyway, I don't know why we're worrying about this. There'll never be any need for you to move. You're fit and well, apart from the creaky knees, and I can look after you.'

'You can't look after me for ever. One day I might need a carer coming in.'

'Why?'

'When you meet someone special and move out,' Gran says quietly.

'If I do, they'll have to move in with us,' I suggest.

'So what happened to my other granddaughter, the one who said she wouldn't let anyone court her again? It doesn't have anything to do with Lewis, does it?' She reaches out and covers my hand with hers, smiling as she looks towards the door. 'Talk of the devil, here's your young man.'

'Let me go and grab my bag,' I say quickly, taking the opportunity to check my make-up and hair before returning downstairs in a pair of flats. I feel nervous and excited at the same time, keen to make a good impression.

'Your gran thinks I'm your young man,' Lewis grins. 'What have you been saying to her?'

'Nothing. I don't know where she's got that from,' I say, giving her a look. She's grinning too, her mouth a toothless cavern, making me realise this is part of her and Emily's plan to set me up, just that my sister is more subtle about it. 'Gran! Your teeth. I'll see you later.'

'Take as long as you like,' she says. 'I hope the dog is better – I'd quite like to have met her.'

'I'll take a picture to show you,' I say.

Lewis and I wait in reception at Otter House under the stern eye of Frances, the receptionist. She must be close to retirement by now, although her outfit is far from retiring. She's wearing a wig of spun candyfloss, pale orange rather than pink, glasses inlaid with crystals, a wedding ring, and an eye-catching lime and yellow tunic. A widow who lost her husband in a fishing accident, she's since remarried and is living in a house opposite the church.

'Frosty's ready for you.' Izzy calls us through to the consulting room, her eyes drawn to Lewis. 'He's lovely,' she says aside to me and I don't like to disillusion her. It's rather seductive, imagining I'm attached to such a gorgeous and young man. 'Are you going to take her on?'

'Izzy,' Maz warns as she joins us with Frosty at her side, 'I wish you wouldn't put pressure on people like that. Zara doesn't want a dog.'

'But it's like she found you,' Izzy says, as Frosty spots me and starts wagging her tail.

'I can't have a dog,' I say, fighting my instinct to kneel down and throw my arms around her. 'They aren't my thing.'

'But she's soooo sweet. Look at her.' Izzy holds out her hands. 'She wouldn't hurt a fly.'

Even if I did soften because she is cute and I feel safe here at the moment, I can't have her. 'I'm living with my gran – I don't think she and her old cat would cope.'

'Are you talking about Norris from the paper shop?' Izzy asks. 'He has a bit of a reputation. He left a couple of nasty souvenir scratches up our assistant's arm when he came in for a checkup recently.'

'I can't inflict a dog on Norris and Gran.' Heavy-hearted, I stroke Frosty's head. 'We'll take her on up to the Sanctuary.'

'It's very kind of you to offer.'

'It's the least I can do – you've been great.'

Izzy puts Frosty on a rope lead which makes me feel uncomfortable, worrying if wearing a noose around her neck will remind her of where she came from. I wish I'd thought to buy her a leather one from Overdown Farmers, or the garden centre, where they had some on display in the pet section yesterday.

114

Lewis takes Frosty outside while I'm saying goodbye to Maz, who is consoling Izzy as she sniffs into a tissue.

'Izzy gets too attached. She'll never change,' Maz says in explanation.

'I thought you were going to put her in the back,' I say, as Lewis encourages Frosty to jump onto the passenger seat next to me in the pick-up.

'It's safer to have her in the front where you can keep her under control.'

'Safer for whom?'

'The dog, of course. Oh, Zara, I'm teasing. She'll be fine – I have a way with dogs . . . and women, or so I've been told.'

I don't know what to say. 'Are you trying to chat me up?'

'Maybe.' As he reverses out of the car park, he slides his hand along the back of the seat behind me, a gesture that makes the hairs on my neck tingle with a desire to feel his touch on my skin.

'Do you know where you're going?' I sit with Frosty at my side, keeping an eye on her tongue and her big white teeth. Every so often, she presses against me and glances up, and I swear she's smiling.

'She thinks you're taking her somewhere exciting.'

'Thanks for that. Now I feel bad because she'll be disappointed.' I look at her brown eyes, the expectation and joy in her expression. How am I going to part with her? 'She'll think I'm abandoning her all over again.'

'She will,' Lewis agrees, and I wish he didn't. 'She's having a rough time of it, and who knows how long it will take for them to find her a new home? She's quite

115

cute, but she isn't the most appealing dog in the world. It could take months to find someone who falls in love with her.'

'Oh, please don't say that.'

'It's the truth.' I catch his eye as he glances towards me and I realise what he's up to.

'You're doing this deliberately, turning the emotional screw. That's so mean.'

'It's all in a good cause.'

'Everyone's having a go – first Izzy and now you.' This is the second time I've felt under pressure today. 'If you're thinking it will help me get over my fear of dogs, it's a step too far.'

'I wasn't just thinking of you. I was thinking about Frosty.'

'That's typical of you, putting the dog first,' I say brightly.

'What I'm saying is that you seem to have a bond with her already. She appears to have chosen you. I understand how you feel and I'm sorry for putting you on the spot like that. It isn't fair.' Lewis hesitates. 'She's only a pup so she'll have another twelve to fourteen years left in her and that's a massive commitment and not one that anyone should make lightly or in a hurry.'

'I know everyone wants the best for her, after all she's been through, and so do I, but I don't think living with a noxious old cat, an octogenarian and someone who isn't a natural dog-lover is the best for her.' The trouble is, though, I don't like the idea of just anyone having her. 'How about you?' I go on.

'Me? I can't take on another one. Mine have to work

for their living, while Frosty's the type that's more likely to chase sheep than round them up.'

Frosty snuggles up closer as we travel up a winding lane with grass growing along the middle, and even narrower than the one up to Greenwood Farm.

'I used to go to school with Tessa who runs the rescue centre for Talyton Animal Rescue. She's married to Jack, the Animal Welfare officer who's investigating Frosty's case. Jack's a bit of a hero.'

'In what way?' Lewis asks.

'Tessa was engaged to this guy, Nathan – none of us liked him. On the day of the wedding, Jack came into the church just as the vicar was at the part in the ceremony about does anyone have just cause or impediment?, and Jack said, yes, he did. Tessa ran outside, Nathan followed and talked her into going back in, but as they took their vows, she turned him down. It was such a shock, but she did the right thing. She trusted her instinct, and it turned out that not only had Nathan been cheating on her with her best friend, he was up to his ears in debt.

'Jack had always loved her. He waited, and then when she was free, they got together. It's very romantic. At least, I think so.' I shut up suddenly, carried away by the story. 'Most men say they have no interest in romance.'

'That's a sweeping generalisation. We aren't all the same.'

'Would you say you're a romantic, then?'

'You'll have to let me show you sometime,' he says, flashing me a smile which makes my pulse race and sends heat flooding through my body, to my cheeks and places I thought I'd forgotten about. Forget the romance, I tell myself. Lewis exudes masculinity and everything about him reminds me of sex.

We reach the Sanctuary and park in one of the bays in the tarmacked car park in front of a slate-grey bungalow with holly and beech growing around the outside. To our left is Longdogs Copse, and to the right is a small paddock divided into two with green electric fencing tape and pink posts. There are three skinny sheep in one side and a grey pony in the other. Beyond, there are some outbuildings, a barn open at one end, a cattery and a kennel block.

Keeping Frosty on the lead, I let her out of the pick-up, where she immediately tows me across to the hedge and starts sniffing.

'This way, Frosty.' I give a half-hearted tug on the rope.

'You see, she thinks she's going for a walk.' Lewis comes across and takes the rope from me. 'You have to be firm with her.' He gives the rope a tweak and Frosty trots along beside him to the bungalow where Tessa opens the door. She's one of those people who doesn't realise how beautiful she is; tall and slim with dark, almost black hair, full lips and sculpted cheekbones, like a Bond girl. Even in scruffy outdoor clothes and wellington boots, she looks amazing and, slightly annoyingly, she's warm and generous with it.

I introduce her to Lewis.

'How are you, Tessa?' I ask.

'I'm better than I was.'

'I'm sorry, I didn't know you'd been ill.' I frown.

'I wasn't ill. I had morning sickness.' She smiles. 'I still can't open a can of dog food without throwing up, but I've never been happier.'

'Congratulations. That's great news.' There's no hint of a pregnancy bump yet under her jacket, but she's looking suitably pale, with dark shadows beneath her eyes.

'I've got a booking-in appointment with you next week.' She turns to the dog. 'Who is this cutie here?'

'This is Frosty,' I say.

'It's Zara's idea of a name,' says Lewis.

'I like it. We have all sorts coming in here.' Tessa takes down a few details on a clipboard before showing us to the kennel block and opening the door. 'This is where she'll live until we find her a home.'

'How long do you think that will take?' I ask.

'It's hard to say. Our longest resident stayed for eighteen months.'

Lewis glances at me. 'Oh dear. You don't put them down, do you?'

'It's our policy not to, unless they turn out to be aggressive or have chronic medical conditions that can't be managed. We do our best.'

The kennels are purpose-built, clean and airy, but Gran is right. It's like a prison with concrete and bars and I can't bear it. There's a little old sausage dog with sad eyes in the corner of the first pen. I have to drag Frosty past him, her ears down and her tail tucked between her legs.

'She can have number seven,' Tessa says. 'If she's all

right with other dogs, we'll pair her up with one of the younger ones after a couple of days.'

I squat down beside Frosty, ready to remove the rope lead. She nudges my hand with her cold wet nose as if to say, please don't leave me here. My chest tightens and a tear springs to my eye and rolls down my cheek onto her fur. I can't do it to her. I can't leave her behind.

'Zara?' Lewis holds the kennel door open for me. 'You can let her off now.'

I shake my head. 'Nope. I'm going to take her home with me.' I stand up, embarrassed at my tears. 'I don't need a dog, but—'

'Everyone needs a dog,' Tessa interrupts.

'That's what I was trying to tell her on the way here. A dog is a man's – and woman's – best friend.' Lewis hesitates before reaching out and stroking my shoulder. 'What about what you said on the way here? What about the commitment and the time?'

'It's fine.' I look down at Frosty, who's looking back up at me with scared brown eyes. 'I'll do anything.'

'What about your gran? How will she take it?' Lewis asks.

'I guess I'm going to find out. That sounds bad, doesn't it, but I think she'll be pleased. She's always wanted a guard dog.'

'I'll have to ask you a few questions, make a home visit and get you to sign the adoption papers,' Tessa says, taking advantage of my change of mind. 'I can drop by this afternoon? You're still living above the shop, the newsagent's?'

We agree on a time and set off from the Sanctuary with Frosty perched on the seat between me and Lewis.

'I'm so sorry for wasting your time,' I say.

'It's no problem. I hope you're sure about this and you don't look back and feel you've been forced into it.'

'No one forces me into anything,' I say firmly. 'This is my decision. It might turn out to be the wrong one, but I'll have to deal with that if that's what happens.' I'm aware I'm sounding strong, but inside I'm wavering. Who do I think I am, imagining I'm a suitable owner for a dog like Frosty who's going to need extra-special care and understanding after weeks or months of abuse and neglect? She keeps flicking her ears in the breeze from the fan in the dashboard as she looks out of the window at the world going by. 'I want to ask you something. Promise me you won't laugh or make me feel like an idiot.'

'I'd never do that,' Lewis says, his expression serious. 'What is it?'

'I haven't a clue how to look after a dog properly.'

'I can help you out. It isn't rocket science.'

'What am I going to do if Gran doesn't want to give Frosty a home?'

'She gave you one,' he says light-heartedly.

'And what do you mean by that?' I say, flirting back. 'Are you implying I'm more trouble than a dog?'

'I reckon you could be. You do get yourself into odd situations – the flat tyre and finding Frosty. It doesn't happen to everyone.' Lewis parks outside the shop, and turns to face me, holding my gaze. The throbbing of the engine is joined by a pulsating ache of longing in my chest.

'Would you like to come in for coffee?' I ask, not wanting him to leave.

'I'd better go – my boss will be wondering where I am. Another time though.' He rubs the back of his neck. 'If you want any advice, you know where I am, any time. I'll text you later to find out how Tessa's visit went . . . If that's okay with you,' he adds in a low voice.

'Of course it's okay,' I say quickly, cringing when I realise how uncool that sounds.

'I'll be in touch then,' he says with a glint in his eye. 'Good luck!'

I watch him go, wondering if he's deliberately setting out to seduce me, before taking a deep breath and entering the shop with Frosty beside me, hoping that the sight of this poor skinny dog on a piece of frayed rope will be enough to convince Gran to let her stay.

'Before you ask,' Gran says sternly from behind the counter, 'the answer is no. It isn't because I don't feel sorry for her. It's because there isn't room for a dog under my roof.'

'But you said you would feel safer if you had a guard dog,' I say, disappointed at her reaction but as yet undeterred.

'Yes, a guard dog. What's a little scrap like that going to do if faced by a burglar?'

'She can bark as well as any dog. And she's got

some growing to do – upwards as well as outwards. I'm sorry for turning up like this without warning, but when I got to the Sanctuary, I couldn't do it.'

'You're too soft,' she says. 'How do you think you're going to look after a dog when you're out at work all hours?'

'I was hoping you might . . .' I say lamely, realising now how unfair I'm being, expecting her to care for a lively puppy.

'What about old Norris? Have you thought about his feelings? He had his nose put out of joint when you arrived. How will he feel about a dog at his age?'

'I didn't think,' I stammer. 'Look, I'll take her back.' It's going to kill me, I think, but better that than give my grandmother a hard time.

'Isn't there anyone else you know who could have her? The shepherd has dogs.'

'Lewis? I've already asked him.'

'Oh . . .' Some of the light goes out of her eyes. 'What about Poppy? She's desperate to have a pet.'

'Emily has enough to cope with at the moment. The last thing she needs is a dog.'

'Your mum and dad? They have time on their hands, time enough to go looking for a home for me.'

'A dog wouldn't fit into their lives – you know how they like to travel.'

The doorbell jangles.

'A customer for you,' I say, turning to find Tessa coming towards us.

'I was passing so I thought I'd drop by now,' she says. 'Is that okay?'

'I'm afraid not. I can't keep her after all.' I thrust the rope into Tessa's hands and, stifling a sob, rush along the hallway through the storeroom and outside into the tiny courtyard garden. What was I thinking? That Gran would welcome another waif and stray with open arms?

My mobile rings, interrupting my thoughts. It's Fiona, one of the other midwives on the team, wanting to know if I can sacrifice my day off to catch a baby.

'I wouldn't normally ask, but it's one of your mums, Sophie. She wanted to ring you, but couldn't pluck up the courage. She said she didn't want to bother you, so I said I'd do it instead!'

Sophie lost her eighteen-month-old child to meningitis not so long ago.

'She's asking for you. I said I'd speak to you on the off-chance,' Fiona continues.

'How far?'

'She's seven centimetres dilated and moving on nicely. I don't think she'll be much longer, but it doesn't matter if you're busy.'

'I'm not busy.' I look along the hallway where I can see Tessa and Gran involved in a conversation with Frosty sitting at their feet. 'I'll be with you in half an hour max. Tell her to wait for me.' I was at the birth of Sophie's first child, Toby, one of the happiest of occasions, and I promised her I'd do everything in my power to support her through this second labour. 'You're right,' I say, briefly rejoining Gran and Tessa to explain where I'm off to. 'How can I possibly look after a dog?'

'You go beyond the call of duty,' Gran says. 'This is supposed to be your day off.'

'I know.' I squat down, put my arms around Frosty's neck, all fear of her banished, and hug her goodbye. She turns her head and licks my nose.

'You'd never think my granddaughter used to be afraid of dogs,' Gran observes with pride in her voice.

'Good luck, Frosty Whiskers,' I mutter, straightening up and turning to Tessa. 'Thanks for this. I'm sorry for messing you around. I'll see you later, Gran.' I run upstairs, change into my uniform and drive to Sophie's home, a neat, three-bedroomed semi-detached house at the top of the new estate. The image of Frosty remains in my head and her unconditional love is etched on my heart, and I know I'm going to regret having to give her up for the rest of my life.

I knock on the door and Fiona, a bubbly redhead, lets me in. Married with three teenage children, she's been a midwife for twenty-five years now.

'Hello, Zara.' She lowers her voice. 'Sophie's a bit stressed and so is dad.'

I join them in the living room where Sophie's making waves in the birthing pool.

'I'm so happy you could make it.' She forces a smile and I take her outstretched hand.

'How are you doing?' I ask her. 'And you, Joe?' Joe is her husband; he's six foot four and a landscape designer.

'I'd forgotten how much it hurts,' Sophie says.

Joe doesn't say anything. I recall from the last time him being the strong, silent type.

125

'Joe, go and make Zara some tea,' Sophie says. 'And I'd like some music now – Adele's album.'

She squeezes my hand to help her through a contraction. Joe checks the water temperature, Fiona and I drink tea and Sophie wallows in the pool. It's very calm and both parents are more relaxed. The baby's heart rate is stable while Sophie's contractions are coming closer together and with increasing force.

'I'm ready to push,' she says suddenly.

'Do you want to stay in the pool to deliver?' I ask.

'Can I?' she says, glancing towards Fiona, who nods. 'If Zara's happy.'

'Would you like to catch your baby, Joe?' I go on.

'I'm not sure. I felt a bit faint the last time.' Joe looks up at the photos on the wall, at the pictures of Toby, a blond, blue-eyed boy like his mum, when he was first born and as he was growing up. There are none of him after he turned eighteen months old, though, and the house is bereft of the muddle I'd usually associate with a toddler's presence. There are reminders, a teddy bear on the windowsill and an album facing out on the bookshelf with *Toby* printed in gold lettering across the cream leather binding.

'I'll try,' Joe says gamely, moving to the edge of the pool to be with his wife.

Ten minutes later, the baby's head appears, and with one more push, it's out.

'There you are,' I say, supporting the baby in the water so that Joe can catch hold of her. He leans forwards and promptly blacks out, falling face down into the pool. Sophie screams. I lift the baby out, still attached by the

126

cord, while Fiona deals with the fainting father who, having hit the water, is coming round, gasping and shaking his head as he drags himself up to a sitting position.

The baby is wailing. I place her on Sophie's chest.

'Congratulations, you have a beautiful baby girl,' I say, smiling.

'Did you get that, Joe?' Sophie says, crying and laughing at the same time, while her husband sits on the floor, groaning, with his head between his knees. 'It's a girl.'

He looks up, slides closer to the pool and reaches across to his wife, putting his arms around her and the baby. 'I'm sorry for being such a wuss. I'm so proud of you.'

Later, Fiona and Sophie are with the baby in the living room and I'm clearing the mugs away in the kitchen where Joe joins me.

'A happy day,' I say.

'Yes, but we'll always be on edge after what happened to Toby.'

'I know.' I reach out and rub his arm as he continues, 'Every time she's sick with a temperature, a snuffle or a spot, we'll be at the hospital.'

'There will be good times, too.'

'I know. Thank you. You and Fiona have been wonderful. We couldn't have got through this without you.'

'Well, I'm glad you invited me to be a part of it,' I respond. 'Now, go and look after your wife and your new baby.'

'Will do,' he smiles.

I return home, leaving the family together to bond. Usually, after a birth, I'm walking on air, but this time, once the euphoria has worn off, I can't help thinking about Frosty and how she must be feeling shut up in one of the kennels at the Sanctuary. It's gone nine when I park the car and walk down the street to the shop, which is in darkness. I unlock the door, but the bolts are fastened on the inside and I can't get in. I ring the bell to attract Gran's attention, but she doesn't appear, which means I have to make my way around the rear of the shop and go through the gate into the garden and open the back door. I listen, hoping in vain to hear a dog's bark on the off-chance that a miracle has happened and Gran changed her mind about Frosty, but it was a long shot. There's no sound, apart from the television.

I head upstairs to the flat.

'Hi, I'm home.' I put my head around the living-room door. Gran is sitting there with Norris lying across the back of the chair and a grey and white dog stretched out in front of the gas fire. My pulse quickens with expectation. 'What's going on? Why is Frosty still here?'

Gran stabs a button on the remote, turning the television down.

'There's been a development. You say you like salad? There's lettuce in the fridge and a tin of tuna in the cupboard – I'm afraid the dog's had your dinner.'

Frosty jumps up and trots over to me, squeaking and

wagging her tail, sending two of Gran's china horses flying from the coffee table to the floor.

'Oh, look what you've done,' I say, hugging her.

'I know she's going to be trouble,' Gran grumbles lightly, 'but I thought we'd keep her anyway.'

'Gran, you're a star.'

'I know.'

'What made you change your mind?'

'When you left, she sat facing the door and didn't move until Ed from the ironmonger's came in to pay his bill, when she turned tail and hid under the counter. The look in her little eyes peering out from the dark broke my heart. How could I let her go?'

'What's that scratch on her nose?' I ask, noticing a fresh mark across her muzzle.

'Norris gave her a swipe when she tried to say hello to him. I've bathed it with cold tea.' Gran smiles fondly. 'I gave her a couple of digestive biscuits to cheer her up afterwards – she loves her home comforts.'

'I bet she does. Thank you.'

'It makes me happy,' she says. 'Just promise me you won't bring home any more waifs and strays, though. It's getting a little crowded.'

'At least she can earn her keep as our guard dog,' I point out, picking up the china horses, one of which is undamaged while the other has lost the tip of its tail.

'She's going to have to wash her ears out – she didn't move a muscle when you came in.'

'She was fast asleep. She must be exhausted. Give her a chance.'

'She needs rest and plenty of good food, then she'll

be ready for anything. Go on, I can see you're itching to let the shepherd know.'

'I'm not,' I argue, but she's right. I have my mobile in my hand ready to call him. I slip out to the kitchen to throw a tuna salad together, chatting to Lewis at the same time and listening to the rich tone of his voice; it reminds me of dark chocolate, molten and topped with cream.

'So you kept her? Oh, that's brilliant. You won't regret it, I promise you.'

'I'm not so sure about that,' I say, smiling. 'Gran's already given her my dinner.'

'You can always come and have dinner with me. Anytime. Like now?'

'It's a little late tonight, but thanks for the offer.'

'Another evening then?'

'Yes.' A pounding pulse of lust fills my ears, because if I joined Lewis for a meal, I'm not sure I'd be in a fit state to eat anything. 'Yes, that would be . . .' I don't know how to put it. The truth would sound completely over the top when I hardly know the guy, but 'lovely' seems inadequate. That's what it has to be, though. 'Lovely, thank you.'

'Let me know when you're free, Zara, and remember what I said – if you need any advice or moral support, you know where I am.'

I'm in need of some support for my morals right now. It's mad but Lewis makes me feel sick with longing and I'm more convinced than ever that he feels the same.

Later, when I'm in bed, with Frosty scrabbling frenziedly at the other side of the door, I recall his promise that I won't regret taking Frosty on. When I can take no more of her heart-rending whining, I get up with my duvet wrapped around my shoulders, and let her in, at which she jumps straight onto the end of the bed. After brief negotiations over sharing the space, I settle down with Frosty, who's like one of Gran's comforting hot-water bottles across my feet, but I still can't sleep for thinking about Lewis.

CHAPTER EIGHT

Cold Nose, Warm Heart

I am now officially a dog owner. I've joined the club. The dog walkers of Talyton St George smile and say hi, stopping to talk when they see us, but Frosty has other ideas, lunging and growling at every dog that comes within a few paces. Everyone with a canine connection has their own theory: she's young, she's finding her feet and she needs time to settle down after what she's been through. Lewis calls me to ask how we're getting on and I tell him we're good, thank you, and kick myself afterwards for not suggesting that we meet for a coffee and a chat.

Down on the Green, I decide to let Frosty off the lead so she can be just like all the other dogs. At first, she won't leave me as we stroll on towards the river, but as soon as she spots Aurora and her big black poodle, she charges up to it, barking and growling. The poodle sticks its nose in the air and trots along the path, but Frosty can't take the hint that the other dog isn't interested, and she continues to wreak havoc, running in circles until it finally snaps, at which she retreats briefly before diving in for another go.

Gasping for breath, I run to catch up.

'Frosty, you mustn't do that.' I'm beginning to feel like Emily must do with Poppy.

'You really should keep her on a lead,' Aurora says. She owns the fashion boutique in town and she's dressed like an advert for her clothes, as always, in a cool leather and hound's-tooth check jacket, short skirt and knee-high boots.

'I'm sorry,' I repeat, embarrassed. 'She wants to play, that's all.'

'She has a very funny way of showing it.' Aurora hesitates. 'I didn't know you had a dog, Zara.'

'She's new.' I make a grab for Frosty's collar, but she legs it again, this time heading for the main road.

'Frosty,' I yell in desperation, as I envisage my brief stint of dog ownership come to an abrupt and tragic end. 'Come back!'

My heart is in my mouth, but just as she reaches the exit onto the bridge, a small terrier comes running onto the Green. Frosty bowls it over, but it comes back for more. At first, they appear to be play-fighting, but the growling and snarling escalate until the terrier's owner goes in, pulls the dogs apart and drags Frosty across to me.

'You're lucky a) that the Bobster didn't bite your dog and b) that it didn't get onto the road and cause an accident.'

'I'm so sorry.' I'm also incredibly hot. I recognise the terrier's owner – it's Matt, Nicci's husband. Keeping my eyes on the ground, I clip the lead back onto Frosty's collar.

'She's in very poor condition – has she seen a vet?' Matt goes on.

'She's a rescue – we are trying to fatten her up.'

'I see. You know you really should take her to dog training or something.'

I feel really bad. I'm a rubbish mother, I think, looking down at Frosty and realising how some of my mums must feel about coping with a new baby, the doubts and insecurities.

'Thank you for the advice,' I mutter before moving on. 'Let's go home, Frosty. I don't know about you but I think I've had enough.' I wonder if I should contact Lewis for help, but I don't want to look like an idiot when I've been hoping that the next time I see him, I will be strolling across the fields with my dog at my heels or alert to the sound of my whistle. Looking after a dog can't be all that difficult. Uncle Nobby managed it, after all.

On the way back through the bottom of town, I run into Wendy, the dog-fosterer for Talyton Animal Rescue. She has five dogs swirling around on leads as she tries to pick up with a poo bag, a manoeuvre not helped by Frosty, who drags me into the melee.

'Do keep your dog under control,' Wendy says, red-faced and flustered. 'It's a lovely creature, I'm sure, but it really needs you to teach it some manners.'

'She isn't my dog, she belongs to a friend of mine.' I don't know why I say it. It just pops into my head.

Wendy frowns. 'When I went to pick up the paper, your gran told me she belongs to you.'

The lies dog owners tell! I'm even more embarrassed now that Wendy has caught me out. I don't know what to say.

'You should bring her to dog training. We have classes every weekday from seven in the hall at the school. The class you want is for our absolute beginners on a Thursday. Don't worry, Zara. We can train any dog. Our motto is, training is a walk in the park.'

I sign up straight away, intent on giving Frosty every chance of becoming the model canine citizen and hoping Claire will understand how much more important this is than the weekly weigh-ins at fat club. She doesn't, of course.

'You mean you're putting a dog before me and the wedding?' she exclaims when I call to tell her. 'You've gone a bit weird.'

'I can't help my busy social life.' I giggle. 'You should be happy for me. You're always telling me to get out more. Maybe I'll meet the man of my dreams at dog training.' I'm being flippant. At the moment, the man of my dreams is Lewis.

'You aren't going to be one of these people who can't think of anything else apart from their dogs, are you? I hope you aren't going to want to bring Frosty to the wedding.'

'She'd look so cute,' I say, picturing her outside the

church in the sunshine alongside the bride and groom. I continue through Claire's stunned silence. 'I'm winding you up. I'll have to find someone to dog-sit – Frosty hates being left even for a minute. If you shut her in, she whines and scratches the door.'

'Zara, you're mad,' Claire says. 'Now you have to worry about doggy day-care as well as everything else.'

'It's worth it, though – it's good to have something warm and furry in bed with me again.'

'Ugh, I don't want to know. Was Paul that furry?'

'He had hairy shoulders – he used to shave them.'

'That's disgusting. You really are better off without him.' Claire changes the subject. 'I'd better go. Ben wants a chaperone – for his peace of mind, not the patient's. I'll catch you later.'

Talyton's dog-training club meets in the school hall, which is used for various community events. It smells of cold dinners and plimsolls, and I feel like I'm about ten again. Frosty and I are in the class for absolute beginners with four other dogs and their owners. There's the tiniest Chihuahua dressed in a pink tutu, a wrinkled Shar-Pei with a studded harness, and two adolescent yellow Labradors. I can't believe my eyes and I don't think Frosty can either. I keep her in the corner of the hall as far away from her classmates as possible.

Wendy, dressed in a Puffa jacket, denim skirt and stout brown shoes, takes the class. She introduces herself as having been 'in dogs' all her life, picking hairs from her roll-neck sweater and discarding them where they float through the air and fall onto the wooden floor that's sticky with polish.

'Let me show you what you're aiming for with your dogs. Phil, our advanced trainer, is going to demonstrate a recall with the lovely Taser.'

Phil looks and sounds like he's ex-Forces. He's in his fifties, I'd guess, with lively eyebrows, a moustache, bulging muscles and a deep tan. He's dyed his hair one shade too dark to suit him and he wears combats and boots. Taser is a rangy black and tan German shepherd.

'Are you ready to do your thing?' Wendy asks Phil, her voice rising into a girlish giggle.

'You know me. I'm always ready for action.' He smiles as he looks along the line of dogs, his eyes for the owners, though, and I don't like it when he gazes at me, giving me a wink before moving on.

'Watch, listen and learn from an expert,' Wendy goes on.

'*The* expert,' Phil brags. 'They don't call me the Dogfather for nothing.' He marches Taser to the far end of the hall, gives him an almost imperceptible command to sit and leaves him to take up a position at the opposite end. I watch how Taser, his eyes fixed on his master, waits for his command, and I glance down at Frosty, who's more interested in having a good scratch at her ear.

Phil waits, as if to ramp up the tension, then releases the dog, but instead of trotting straight to him, Taser diverts to pick up some treats that someone has dropped on the floor, crunches them up and returns to his master to a ripple of amusement.

I notice how he grimaces as he lightly boxes Taser's ears.

'So you see, even a top dog can have an off day. Thank you. It's always a pleasure to watch you at work. Can I ask you to stay around for a while to answer any questions that our newbies might have about obedience?' Wendy beams around at us. 'Phil is a scout for our teams: agility, flyball, obedience and dance.'

I'm beginning to feel the pressure. I recall standing in this very hall in a white T-shirt and red shorts, and never being picked for the netball or rounders teams, because I was a 'big girl' even back then. I was always last, even though Emily, the skinny twin, did her best to persuade the captain to choose me next.

'I don't want to be in a team, Wendy,' I say, speaking out. 'All I want is to be able to walk down the street with Frosty on the lead without her lunging and barking at everyone. I don't want her to do doggie dancing – what if she has two left feet?' I look down and smile. 'She does have two left feet. How on earth can dogs dance? It's unnatural.'

Phil raises one eyebrow, making me feel as if I'm lacking ambition and inadequate.

'Let's wait and see if she has any aptitude,' Wendy says. 'It would be a shame to see talent go to waste.'

'Well said,' Phil agrees. 'Right, I'm going to watch you put these guys through their paces.'

'Let's make our introductions first,' Wendy says, and we have to say a little bit about ourselves and our dogs.

There's Baby, Candy, Craig and Alan – they're the dogs.

'I'm Zara and this is Frosty. I don't know exactly how old she is, about eight or ten months old, maybe. I found her tied to a tree.' I can't help it – the tears are back as I go on, 'I rescued her.'

Soon, we are walking in a circle with Wendy, Phil and Taser in the centre.

'Keep your dogs on a loose lead. Best foot forward. Make it loopy, Zara,' Wendy adds, as Frosty tows me around, intent on sniffing the bum of the Labrador in front.

'How can I?' I say, breathless. 'She just runs further and further ahead.'

'The more you pull, the more she pulls against you. Go loose, that's it.' Wendy smiles wryly. 'It's the owner who needs training, not the dog. That's always the way.'

I let the lead go slack and Frosty runs ahead and sticks her nose under the Labrador's tail. The Labrador promptly sits down, causing a traffic jam. It looks round at Frosty, a hurt expression on its face, but Frosty is glaring at Baby the Chihuahua, who's trotted into her and is tangling its lead around her back legs.

'Frosty, no,' I say, but it's too late. She pulls back, slips her collar and, to my horror, pounces on the Chihuahua and grabs her around the head.

'No!'

Phil dives in, extracting the little dog from Frosty's jaws and handing her to Wendy.

'I'm so sorry.' I want to cry, as Phil takes the collar from me and puts it around Frosty's neck, fastening it tightly with no thought for her wound.

'It's all right, no harm done,' Wendy says in a high-pitched tone, as she checks the little dog over, readjusts the tutu and hands her back to her owner, who is clearly trying, but struggling to be understanding.

'I don't like to condemn any dog,' the owner says, 'but is Frosty really ready for class?' Baby snuggles to her breast. 'It isn't fair that she should be allowed to bully the others.'

'I'm sorry,' I repeat.

'Let's give Frosty one more chance,' Wendy says. 'We gave Baby a chance when she pierced Candy's ear and she hasn't done it since. In fact, I think she has a good chance of winning this term's prize for the most improved.' Wendy tweaks Baby's tutu. 'Oh, you're such a little cutie, aren't you, darling?'

That seems to pacify Baby's owner for now.

'Wendy, you continue with the class,' Phil says. 'I'll take Zara and Frosty aside for some "one-on-one".'

'Oh, I don't think that's necessary,' Wendy says. 'I don't want to put you out at all.'

'I'm here.' He shrugs. 'I might as well make myself useful.'

'All right.' Wendy turns her attention to me. 'Zara, you can try the training techniques on your husband when you get home: reward the good behaviour and ignore the bad.'

'I haven't got a husband,' I say quietly. I thought Wendy would have known, being one of Gran's regulars, but she doesn't appear to be listening and I end up in the corner of the hall with Phil.

'We'll try "Sit",' he suggests.

'Frosty, sit,' I say, but she isn't listening, her gaze fixed on the Chihuahua across the room. I give a small tug on the lead to distract her. 'Sit.'

'I can't hear you.' Phil cups one ear. 'Listen up. Say Sssit, as an order not a question.'

I try again and Frosty jumps up, grinning as if to say, it's far too exciting here to sit down. I try to push her away.

'Look away from her,' Phil barks, and I wonder if I've put my child in the right school. Frosty is like a child, my baby. 'Come on, you stand like you've given in. Shoulders up, head back.'

To my shock, I feel his hand on my shoulder and slipping down to the small of my back, prodding me to straighten me up.

'Excuse me,' I say quietly to his moustache, which is like a bottlebrush perilously close to my face. 'Don't touch me.'

'Oh come on, it's all in a good cause.' His hand slides further down, and the next thing I know he's squeezing my buttock.

'Get off!' I squeal. 'I said, don't touch me!'

Silence falls. The rest of the class looks on, dogs and all.

'Is there a problem?' Wendy hastens over as Frosty growls and Phil steps back.

'No problem,' he says. 'Everything's cool. It's just a silly misunderstanding.'

'Yes, there is,' I contradict at the same time. 'Your expert can't keep his hands to himself.'

'I think you'd better leave, Zara,' Wendy says.

'Aren't you going to do something?'

Wendy glances towards Phil, a strange expression on her face, before turning back to me. 'I'm afraid I'm going to have to ask you to leave the class. Frosty is untrainable.'

I'm confused. 'I thought you said you could train any dog.'

'Not this one.' She shakes her head. 'She's a hopeless case.'

'So you're excluding her.'

'That's right. She's expelled.' I don't argue as Wendy sees Frosty and me off the premises. 'One thing,' she adds as we reach the school gates, 'you have to remember that men are very much like dogs. They aren't always in control of their natural urges.'

'You are hopelessly deluded,' I counter.

'Some people who come to dog training are grateful for some male attention.'

'You are! I can see that, but I'm not coming here to listen to you insult my beautiful dog and be groped by a dirty old perv. Goodnight.'

Back at home, Gran consoles us with tea and biscuits.

'It's funny how Frosty can sit now,' I say ruefully. 'She won't listen to a word I say when we're out and about.'

'She's a funny little thing,' Gran says. 'She doesn't bark when there's someone at the door, yet she barks at nothing in between times.'

It's beginning to sink in as the rain starts to pour down outside and the wind rattles at the windows that, by taking Frosty on, I may well have bitten off more than I can chew.

CHAPTER NINE

Being More Dog . . .

Our experience at dog training makes me wonder about hanging up the lead for good, but when I sit down and flick through the television channels looking for something to watch on a Saturday morning (I'm off today), I become aware of a cold wet nose nudging at my hand.

'Oh, do we have to?' I say with a deep sigh. 'I'm not sure I can stand the stress.'

Frosty nudges me again and whines and I can see I'll have no peace until I've taken her somewhere. The question is, where? We're no longer welcome on the Green and, even if I did decide to brazen it out, I think I'd be too embarrassed because everyone knows she's been expelled from dog training. I wonder about taking her to the beach, but there'll be lots of other dogs there, and then it occurs to me that I could take the car to the farm, park at the bottom of the lane and walk Frosty through the fields. Emily said it was all right with her and Murray, as long as I kept her on the lead because of the sheep – and, who knows, I might run into Lewis.

I feel a little awkward asking him for advice about training a delinquent dog, having turned down his offer of help before, thinking I could do it either by myself or with the assistance of Talyton's dog-training club.

I grab Frosty's extending lead, a couple of bags and a few liver treats to put in my pocket, slip into my wellies and go, leaving Gran gossiping happily in the shop.

'I'll see you later,' I call.

'You'll need your coat. It's mizzling out there.' She gives me half a wave before returning to her conversation.

It's the beginning of April and the skies are overcast, the mist and drizzle drifting across the hills, but there is a hint of sunshine trying to break through. Frosty is car-sick on the way to the farm, but she soon cheers up when we get going. We skirt the hedgerow of the first field, where the sheep are huddled together with their lambs, and drop down the hill into the covert of beech and hazel via a stile where I get into a bit of a tangle with some thorny brambles.

As I untangle Frosty's lead from the embrace of the triffids, I hear a whistle through the trees. Is it Murray or Lewis? My heart skips a beat as I catch sight of a pair of collies following a very modern shepherd across the field, with the sun's rays catching his hair, a crook in his hand and speaking on his mobile. The collies trot side by side with their heads lowered, their tongues out and the fur on their chests like rats' tails, dripping with mud. They are heading towards us, but I don't panic as I step out from the shade of the trees onto the grass. I let my lead go loopy as Wendy suggested at dog training and start to sing very quietly to help me relax so Frosty doesn't get wound up.

She's fine.

Until she spots the other dogs.

A growl builds in her throat, but the collies keep coming, and when Mick's a few feet away, Frosty lunges at him with a ferocious bark, at which Miley comes flying in and pounces on her, bowling her over and standing above her with her jaws around Frosty's neck.

Lewis lowers his mobile and whistles. Miley hesitates. He whistles again and Miley and Mick race across to him, turning and walking back towards us at his heels. I'm shaking and so is poor Frosty, but she doesn't give up. As Lewis reaches us, she lunges again, and I have to drag her back, hauling on the lead. She's strong and I haven't got a lot of grip on the wet grass, and I end up sitting right on my bottom, with Frosty between my legs, as the rain starts to fall once more.

Mick and Miley stare at us, Mick with his head tipped to one side as if he's finding the situation as funny as his owner is, and Miley looking down her nose. Lewis is almost bent double, laughing.

'It isn't that funny,' I say, taking his outstretched hand.

'I'm sorry, but it isn't often I have women falling at my feet. You know that's the second time you've landed on your backside – anyone would think you were throwing yourself at me,' he chuckles as he pulls me up and steadies me on the slope, grasping my arm at the same time.

'What if I am?' I say, taking advantage of the fact that he's maintaining his grip on me, and responding to his raised eyebrow with, 'Throwing myself at you, I mean?'

'Are you?' he says, with mock surprise, which suggests he knows very well how I feel about him.

'Maybe.'

'I thought you of all people would know their own mind. I mean, you're clever, confident and very attractive – the complete package, in fact.'

'That's very kind of you to say so,' I say lightly.

'Are you and Frosty all right?'

'We're okay, thanks.' I'm not sure which is more bruised, my pride or my bottom. 'I thought dog walking was supposed to be good for you.'

'It wasn't all Frosty's fault. Miley shouldn't have gone in to her like that. I don't know what got into her. She knows better.'

'Frosty wasn't exactly being friendly,' I say, feeling defeated.

'What are you doing up this way, anyway? I wasn't expecting to meet anyone.' Lewis holds my gaze and I can't help blushing. Does he realise that I came up here half hoping I'd see him? Does he see me as some crazy stalker? As I stand there, I become aware of the poo bag swinging from my fingers. It isn't a good look!

'I thought I'd go somewhere quiet. There are always too many dogs on the Green and down by the river.' I bite my lip. It's time I fessed up because I can't go on like this. 'Actually, this isn't working out between me and Frosty.'

'I've heard a few stories.'

'I can't manage her. I haven't a clue what I'm doing. I thought watching a couple of episodes of *It's Me or the Dog* would be enough, but she's too much for me. She's too energetic and naughty, and she just won't listen.' I start to cry because the idea of letting Frosty down, having gained her trust, is devastating. In fact, I can't help thinking it's worse breaking up with a dog than it is with a husband. 'I love her to pieces, but I can't keep her.'

'Hey, please don't cry.' Lewis reaches out and touches my face, wiping the tear from my cheek with a trailing finger. 'That's better. Why don't we go and sit in the pick-up? I have a flask of coffee.'

'What about the dogs?'

'The collies can mooch about. Frosty can sit in the cab with us.'

'She's muddy.'

Lewis grins. 'What's a little bit of mud between friends? Come on.'

A couple of minutes later and we're sitting in the front of the pick-up with the rain pouring down the windscreen. Frosty perches on an old coat on the seat between us. Lewis hands me a cup of coffee from a flask. I sip at it. It tastes metallic, but it's hot and vaguely comforting.

'I heard the dog training didn't go too well,' Lewis begins.

'Who told you that? Oh, don't tell me. Emily. She was in hysterics when I talked to her about it.'

'Well, it is quite funny. There can't be many dogs that get expelled from class. What did Frosty do, or not do, as the case may be?'

'I'm not sure whether it was me or the dog, actually, but Frosty kept distracting the other dogs and growling at them, and she wouldn't listen to any instructions, and then she grabbed the Chihuahua, the tiniest dog in the class. I assume it was because she didn't like its tutu.'

'I'm sorry, you've got me there.' Lewis scratches his head.

'The people at dog training are completely barking, so to speak. This dog was dressed in a pink tutu, can you believe it?'

'I don't understand it. I like my dogs to be dogs, if you know what I mean. My ex-girlfriend put a ribbon around Mick's neck once. He hated it. He was so embarrassed, he slunk away and hid under the bed.'

I find I don't like to think of Lewis, an ex-girlfriend and a bed in the same image. He's warm and disarmingly friendly, making me feel as if I could tell him everything – I correct myself, almost anything.

'A couple of days after, Wendy came into the shop and offered us a place on their remedial course, but the trainer is a right perv who kept staring at my . . .' My voice trails off, my face on fire.

'I can kind of understand where he's coming from,' Lewis says, amused. 'Not that I'm a pervert.'

'Anyway, Frosty didn't like him either, and he seems to be a bit of a bully.'

Lewis is scathing. 'It sounds like he practises the old-school style of dog training. Why don't you let me have a go?'

'I'm not sure that it's good for her – she gets stressed out. Why do I need to train her anyway? She's young yet.'

Lewis nods. 'She needs to be sociable and walk nicely on a lead, come to call, sit and stay. Mind you, I wonder if she's really capable of even that when she's pretty average, and definitely less able than the collies.'

'Are you saying she's thick?' I feel hurt on Frosty's behalf. Am I the only person in the world who has any faith in her?

'She is a little lacking in the IQ department, but that's not to say . . .' Lewis stops abruptly. 'I apologise. Being cutting about someone's dog is worse than being rude about their child. She'll have other qualities,' he goes on, trying to make amends. 'I'm sorry to have offended you. You'll never speak to me again,' he says glumly. 'Can I make it up to you?'

'It's Frosty you'll have to make it up to,' I say sharply. 'How can you judge her like that?'

'I'm trying to help.'

'I know. I'm sorry too.' I sit back with a sigh. 'It isn't just her behaviour out and about. It's how she is at home as well. She's so much like Poppy, out of control. She's wrecking Gran's flat. This morning, I had to hide a pair of her shoes because Frosty had chewed on the soles. Oh, it's okay, she has quite a few others, so she won't miss them in a hurry.'

'You should have come and found me before,' Lewis says softly. 'Look, it isn't raining as hard now. Why don't we take her out and see what we can do?'

We work with Frosty in the field while the collies watch from the back of the pick-up.

'If you are a nervous dog,' Lewis says, as I walk her up and down on the lead, 'every other dog you meet must feel like a threat, so you have to lunge and get your bark in first.'

'It's such a shame. Why do you think she's like this?'

'Because she had a bad start as a puppy. She had the wrong sort of discipline when she was young, if she had any at all. She isn't nasty.' Lewis holds out his hand. Frosty sniffs it, cowers, and wees on his boots. Chuckling, he takes the lead from me, our fingers touching and sending a shock of electricity through my arm. This is going to be interesting, I tell myself.

'It's no use scolding her because that will make her even more fearful.' Lewis walks along, and Frosty looks up at him. 'Good girl. Sit.' He pushes her bottom

151

down gently and gives her a treat before walking on once more. Miley doesn't like it. She starts barking, but Frosty ignores her.

'I'm not trying to find excuses for Frosty's behaviour, but I wonder if she might be deaf.' Lewis stops alongside me. 'She watches me, but she really doesn't listen.'

'Deaf?' I hadn't thought of that, but it makes sense. 'How can we test that theory?'

'We'll have to go somewhere quiet,' Lewis says, and I look away quickly, a flush of heat creeping up my neck and face. I wouldn't mind going somewhere quiet with Lewis, but he doesn't mean it in that way – at least I don't think so.

We walk back to the covert and in amongst the trees.

I smile. Alone in the wood with a gorgeous young shepherd? Who knows what could happen next? I picture him taking me in his arms and pulling me close.

'Right,' he says matter-of-factly. 'You take Frosty over to that tree, stand on the other side, let her on a long lead and I'll make some noise. We'll see what she does.'

At first Frosty doesn't want to stand behind the tree, preferring to follow the scent trail of a rabbit or squirrel, perhaps. Eventually I manage to wind her back in on the lead and perch on a damp log to wait, wanting to laugh because this is one of the most bizarre things I've ever done: a hearing test for a dog.

'Ready!' calls Lewis.

'Ready,' I call back.

First, Lewis calls Frosty by name, but she takes no notice.

'Nothing!' I shout back. When I thought she was answering to me calling her name, she must have been responding to other cues like my body language.

Lewis whistles as he does to his dogs, but Frosty takes no notice of that either.

Finally he rustles a plastic bag, the one I keep the liver treats in. If Frosty was going to hear something, she'd definitely hear that.

'Anything?' Lewis calls.

'No, nothing at all.' I straighten and walk back to join him, with Frosty tagging along behind. 'I'm sure you're right. She can't hear a thing.'

'Don't be upset,' Lewis says. 'It doesn't change anything. Frosty's still the same . . . person.'

'I suppose so.'

'You'll have to change your expectations for her, and the way you approach her training.' Lewis smiles and reaches out for my hand, taking it gently in his, giving it a gentle squeeze and letting it go again, a gesture that is both distracting and tantalising. 'I don't think it'll affect your relationship with her one bit. Let me know how the appointment with the vet goes.' He continues hesitantly, 'Perhaps I could help you out with the dog training another time?'

'Yes, I'd love that, thanks,' I say.

Lewis walks me back to the car and waits while I persuade Frosty to jump up onto the towel I've put across the back seat for her muddy paws, and clip her into her travel harness before I drive back to Talyton, hardly able to concentrate on the road. I don't know what's wrong with me. I can't get Lewis out of my head.

I make an appointment at Otter House vets where Maz, relying on a test very much like the one Lewis and I carried out, confirms that Frosty is deaf and that it isn't the end of the world. She has another client with a deaf dog, a white Boxer, and the owners have trained her to follow hand signals. There's nothing that can be done, no canine cochlear implants or hearing aids, so I just have to accept I have a dog with special needs. I can't let Frosty off the lead, although I can keep her on a long one, and Gran and I will have to put up with Frosty's fits of random barking because she probably can't hear herself. What's more, it doesn't matter which station we leave the radio on for her when she's home alone – it will make no difference to her level of anxiety because she can't hear it. And as for being a guard dog, she'll never make it.

A couple of days later, Lewis drops by the shop. 'You didn't call me and you haven't been up to the farm,' he says.

'I've been at work. I do have a job, you know.' I smile as he picks up a newspaper from the rack. 'Since when did you start buying a paper?'

He grins. 'I thought I'd buy a lottery ticket too.'

'You have to fill in a slip – they're over there.' I nod towards the Lotto stand. 'Wait a minute – you'll need one of these, too.' I take a biro from the drawer under the counter. 'People are always nicking the pens.' I pass it over to him, my fingers brushing his, or is it his fingers that are brushing mine? My cheeks grow hot, but I don't think he notices because he's filling in his numbers.

'You never know when you might get lucky.' Lewis hands me the slip and grins again, doubling my discomfort.

'Do you want one week or eight?'

'I'll have one week for now. I'd hope to get lucky before eight weeks are up.'

'In that case, I'd recommend you look at the lonely hearts page in the *Chronicle*,' I say cheekily, deciding to give as good as I get.

'I've already got my eye on someone.' He hands me the slip and I put it through the machine.

'And have they got their eye on you?' I ask.

'I'm not sure.'

The doorbell jangles – sometimes I hate that sound, and this is one of those occasions . . .

'Good morning, Zara.'

'Hello, Paul,' I say flatly.

'I'll catch you later,' Lewis says. 'Remember to call me to arrange a dog-training session. You will, won't you?'

'That would be great.' I notice how Paul hovers near the counter. 'How about we fix a time now? I'm free on Saturday afternoon.'

'I reckon Murray will be able to spare me for a couple of hours.'

'We'll say two o'clock then.'

'Aren't you going to introduce me?' Paul says, muscling in.

'This is Lewis, the shepherd who's working for Murray and Emily up at the farm.' I turn back to Lewis. 'This is Paul, my ex-husband, the one I told you about,' I go on, making it perfectly clear to both men that I have nothing to hide.

'How many husbands have you had? Only I was under the impression I was the only one,' Paul chuckles.

'Yes, and one was more than enough,' I say with mock weariness.

'Zara, could you do me a favour later?' Paul asks.

'That depends on what it is.' I wish he hadn't made that request in front of Lewis. It makes me feel awkward.

'My car's in the garage until tomorrow. I wondered if you could run me down to Talymouth later, any time, if you're going that way.'

'I wasn't, but I can.'

'That's great, thanks. I owe you.'

'Um, I'll see you at the weekend,' Lewis says. 'Bye. Good to meet you, Paul.'

'Is that your new bloke?' Paul asks as I watch Lewis go, driving away in the pick-up.

'No.' I bite my lip.

'But you'd like him to be,' Paul goes on. 'There's no need to be bashful about it. He seems nice enough, a bit of a country lad like Murray.'

'He isn't anything like Murray,' I say hotly.

'All right, keep your hair on.' Paul pays for a bottle

of water and bar of milk chocolate. 'I'll be back in an hour for that lift.'

On the Thursday evening, I go for my weigh-in with Claire. Mum and Dad take Gran up to the farm to see Emily and the children, so Frosty is home alone, apart from Norris – although he's so doddery, I'm not sure he counts.

At the leisure centre, I stand on the scales in front of Dorien, keeping my eyes closed.

'What is it? Don't spare me. I can take it.'

'It's good news.'

I wish she didn't sound quite so surprised, but then I haven't exactly been one of her star slimmers. 'You have lost –' there is a prolonged pause – 'five pounds since your last weigh-in.'

'Five pounds? Surely there's some mistake?'

'There's no mistake.'

I open my eyes and check the reading on the scales. It's true. I've lost weight! I can't believe it. Stepping off, I give Dorien a hug. 'Oh, thank you.'

'I knew it would work in the end. You just had to believe in yourself.'

I feel a bit of a fraud, though, because it had nothing to do with self-belief or counting carbs; it was all down to walking Frosty and the distraction of obsessing about one gorgeously fit shepherd. I can hardly stop thinking about him. The blood surges through my body as I picture him strolling through the fields with his dogs. I might as well have been dead or sleeping for the past few months. Meeting Lewis has brought me back to life.

'I think that makes you our Slimmer of the Month, which means you get a certificate of achievement,' Dorien says, bringing me back to earth. 'Well done.'

Claire isn't quite so enthusiastic about my mahussive weight loss. She was running late, held up at the practice, where a patient had to be sent by ambulance to hospital.

'You've done well, but don't lose too much more before the wedding – you can't afford to drop more than a dress size or we'll have to find you another bridesmaid's outfit.'

'I can't imagine I'm going to lose that much more,' I reassure her. 'Claire, you know your wedding list?'

'Which one?' she interrupts. 'I have at least six lists running at the moment, colour-coded and in duplicate. I've persuaded Kev to put them onto spreadsheets, but he doesn't have time to keep them updated. If anyone had told me in advance what planning a wedding was like, I'd never have got engaged. It's all so stressful.'

She doesn't mean it – she's desperate to get married.

'I'm talking about the list of presents. Is there anything you'd like, because I want to get you something really special?'

'That is one list I don't have. Kev and I have everything we need.'

'How about some contribution to the wedding?'

'Surprise me then, if you must.'

'You don't like surprises. You always have to be in control of everything.'

'It's great if it's a good surprise.'

I have an idea. Do I risk it, though?

Claire looks at her watch 'Shall we go to the pub?'

'We could wander along the seafront and buy an ice cream. I feel like I deserve one.'

'All right, but no ice cream,' Claire says. However, we have one each anyway, double scoops of strawberry that drip down the outside of the cones. I figure that having lost five pounds, I'd have to eat a whole vat of ice cream before I piled it all back on.

'So, have you got any gossip?' Claire asks as we sit on the sea wall, protecting the last of the ice creams from attacks by the seagulls that circle just above our heads, dive-bombing us now and again in a vain attempt to threaten us into dropping the cones.

'Not really. Lewis is going to help me train Frosty tomorrow afternoon.'

'Oh, wow! A date! Zara, that's—'

'It isn't a date,' I interrupt.

'Did he ask you or did you ask him?'

'I can't remember. He offered, I think, but it isn't a date,' I repeat.

'Why are you blushing then?'

'It's the light.' I nod towards the horizon, where the sun is falling through a pink sky.

'What are you going to wear?' Claire asks. 'You can't wear your dog-walking kit.'

'For the last time, this isn't a date.' I glance down and pick a piece of stray fluff from my linen trousers. 'I'm going to wear my new top, the one I ordered off the Internet last week.'

159

'That's better,' Claire smiles. 'What will you do with your hair?'

'Leave it down, I think.'

'This is so exciting. I can't wait to meet him.' She giggles. 'All right, I know, but he might ask you out.'

'Or I might ask him.'

The good feelings about our weight loss and Lewis don't last. When I return to the flat with Claire to continue the evening celebrating, Frosty is in the hall, wagging her tail.

'What's been going on?' I ask her, as she seems overly delighted to see me. 'Oh no, what's happened?' In the living room I find a vase of flowers strewn across the floor, the rug rumpled up and the floorboards scratched to bare wood and splinters. The sofa is completely wrecked, the upholstery torn and the stuffing eviscerated. 'Was this down to you?' I say crossly, and Frosty looks at me, all hurt, as if to say: would I do something like that? 'You can't pull the wool over my eyes, when there's all that fluffy stuff hanging out of your mouth.'

'She can't hear you,' Claire says. 'Why do you talk to her all the time?'

'I can't help it,' I smile in spite of everything.

'What are you going to do about the mess?'

'Well, it's cover up or fess up.'

'You didn't do it. The dog did.'

'This is Gran's flat – she won't let Frosty stay if she wrecks the place, and if Frosty goes, then I'll have to go too.' I cover my eyes briefly. 'Oh, this is a disaster. What is Gran going to say?'

Claire peeks around the corner of the curtain onto the street where a car is pulling up. 'I reckon you're just about to find out.'

'Quick, throw the rug over where she's scratched the floor.' I collect up the flowers and stick them back in the vase, which has a small crack through the rim. I grab the blanket which my grandmother uses to keep her knees warm and spread it across the sofa.

'That isn't going to work, is it?' Claire giggles.

'Gran, stay there,' I call, heading out to intercept her, but it's too late.

'Who isn't going to work?' she enquires, sticking her head around the door. 'Oh my goodness, we've been burgled.'

'I'm sorry, it was the dog. I'll pay for the damage. I'll buy a new sofa.'

'And what's to stop her doing it again?' Gran asks sternly. 'I don't think I can come back to this every time I go out and about.'

'I'll think of something. I'll stay in when you're out and vice versa.' I know as I say it that it's a mad idea, letting my life be run by a dog, but if that is what it takes to keep Frosty out of the Sanctuary, that is what I will do.

I notice how my grandmother's eyes twinkle with amusement.

'Don't panic, dear,' she says. 'I have no intention of sending Frosty away. In fact, I've been wanting a new sofa for a long time, but I haven't been able to afford one, so she's done me a favour, as long as you have the money. We can always go and look at something second-hand. There's an ad on the board in the shop window. That might do.'

I glance over Gran's shoulder. Claire is grinning as she pretends to mop her brow.

CHAPTER TEN

The Company of Animals

On Saturday, I help out in the shop for the morning before taking Frosty up to the farm to meet Lewis for dog training.

'Have a lovely time gallivanting with your young man,' Gran says with a twinkle in her eye.

'What young man? You must know something I don't,' I say lightly, relieved that she appears to have either forgiven or forgotten Frosty's antics from when we left her home alone the other night. I've ordered a replacement sofa and polished the floorboards, and spoken to Maz at length about the possibility of Frosty seeing a doggy psychologist after we've tried a course of canine calming capsules for her neurosis.

'Lewis. You're seeing quite a lot of him.' Less than I'd like, I muse as Gran continues, 'I'd like to come with you to the farm sometime. Those great-granddaughters of mine are growing up so quickly.'

'I'll take you up next time I go,' I say with a twinge of guilt. 'You could close the shop one lunchtime when I'm on a day off.'

'Oh no, I'm not sure I can do that. And anyway, I wouldn't want to be a gooseberry.'

'You wouldn't be. We call it a third wheel nowadays.'

'So you and Lewis are an item?'

'He's training Frosty, that's all.'

I drive up to Greenwood Farm and park in the yard, where the four orphan lambs are grazing on the verge, nibbling the grass down short to save Murray having to mow it. They are twice the size they were when I last saw them and their fleeces much woollier. Lewis comes bounding over, very much like a dog, as I get out of the car.

'Hello. Is Frosty ready for this?'

'How do you train a deaf dog? Any ideas?' I ask, releasing her from her harness and clipping on her lead before letting her out.

She leaps up at Lewis, wagging her tail and barking as if he's a long-lost friend. 'Where are Mick and Miley?'

'They're indoors. I thought I wouldn't complicate matters by bringing them along today. Would you like a drink or anything first?'

'No, thank you.' I'm definitely not hungry – seeing Lewis makes me lose my appetite completely. I'm afraid I'm becoming obsessed.

'Frosty!' Poppy, dressed in a vest, shorts and nothing on her feet, comes running out of the farmhouse, with Emily, who's carrying Daisy, close behind.

'I'm sorry.' She tries to grab Poppy's arm. 'She escaped. Please come here.'

'I want to give Frosty a hug,' Poppy wails.

'It's no problem, Emily,' I say.

'I don't want to hold you up.' Emily looks from me to Lewis and back again.

'You can come along with us, if you want to,' Lewis says. 'I don't mind.'

But I do, I think, and Emily knows it. 'No, we're going to do some shopping. Come on, Poppy.'

'I wanna stay at home,' Poppy complains.

'Another time,' Lewis says.

'Have fun,' Emily says. 'Catch up later.'

'I'm sure we will,' I say with a smile, knowing she'll interrogate me later.

Lewis and I take the dog along the side of the farmhouse, across the lawn and past the vegetable plot that's beginning to take shape for the summer. The rhubarb is spreading its leaves, encroaching on the bed of raspberry canes, and the deep red stalks of the ruby chard contrast with the runner bean seedlings that are beginning to curl around the frames that Emily has built from bamboo canes and baling twine.

'I don't know how your sister manages to do the garden with those two little ones,' Lewis says.

'She loves gardening. It's her escape. I expect she'll enter something for the show next month.'

'How about you?'

'Gardening?' I shake my head. 'I'm allergic to soil.'

'Are you really? I've never heard of that before.'

I giggle and then try to be serious again. I don't want him thinking I'm demented.

'I'm joking. Paul used to do the garden – not that there was much to do, just the lawns and a couple of pots.' Why did I do that? Why did I have to go and mention Paul?

'You seem very friendly with your ex-husband,' Lewis says tentatively.

'We're still on good terms, nothing more than that, though,' I add quickly.

'But you're happy to run him around when he asks?'

'Well, yes. He put me on the spot. I couldn't really say no, could I? And I'd have done it for any one of my friends.' I hesitate, wondering why I feel I have to be so defensive when there's nothing going on between me and Paul. 'Anyway, he has a girlfriend.'

'So why couldn't she have picked him up?'

'She was working.'

'It seems a bit of a cheek for him to ask you.'

'He did give me a bar of chocolate in return, and I wasn't busy,' I point out. 'Look, I've come out the other side of my divorce, and I never thought I'd say this, but I'm ready to move on now and have a bit of fun for a change.'

'Are you?' Lewis holds my gaze, a smile playing on his lips.

'Oh, I don't mean . . . I'm not coming on to you. Really.' I'm shot through with embarrassment.

'I wouldn't mind, an older woman and all that.'

'No, it's all right,' I say quickly. 'Let's just leave it at that. And, for the record, I'm not that old. Am I?' I hold up my hand. 'Let's not go there either.' I change the subject. 'Are you a gardener?'

'I'm not mad about it, but one day I'll rent a piece of land where I can keep sheep and grow a few plants.' Lewis smiles ruefully. 'I'll have to find a permanent job first, though, or win the lottery.'

We continue through the rickety wooden gate at the end of the garden, into the remains of an old orchard where the grass is rough and tufty, and a pair of moss-covered apple trees with gnarled trunks and leafy branches stand like old men propped on their walking sticks. Beyond is an open field, and in the distance the main road – carrying motorhomes and caravans to the coast – curves through the green meadows.

I take a deep breath, inhaling the scent of bruised grass, sheep and fresh air.

'It's a great view, isn't it?'

'It is from where I am,' Lewis says, standing at my shoulder.

I glance towards him. He's grinning. I grin back. He's definitely chatting me up, I think as he goes on, 'I love Devon. I didn't realise it held so many attractions.'

'I reckon we'd better make a start on this dog training,' I say archly.

'I think so too.'

And I wonder if he can read my mind, and hope he can't, because it isn't just Frosty who's imagining behaving badly at this minute.

'So, where do we start?' I ask.

'At the beginning.' Lewis reaches out for my hand and then, as if thinking better of it, withdraws. 'Let's go and sit down.' I follow him towards the apple trees where there's a fallen log. 'Will this do?'

I perch on the end. Lewis perches right next to me, so close that his thigh touches mine.

'The other end looks damp,' he says in a pitiful attempt at an explanation. Frosty sits down at his feet as he continues, 'I've been asking around about training a deaf dog, and it shouldn't be very different from training a hearing one. It's just a matter of communicating in an alternative language.'

'An adapted version of "dog", you mean? The problem is that I don't speak "dog". Frosty and I don't just speak in a different tongue; we might as well be from different planets.'

'That's why I have the pleasure of training both of you,' Lewis smiles. 'I know I can train the dog, but I'm not sure I can train the owner – that might take me a whole lot longer.' He gazes into my eyes and it's lucky I'm sitting down because my legs seem to dissolve at the thought that he's almost close enough to kiss me ...

'Dogs learn through repetition and respond to different cues, mostly based on body language, so you have to decide which cues to use, either sign language or the signals people use for obedience training. As Frosty's going to be on the lead, you'll need signals you can do one-handed.'

'That's going to take some doing. How am I going to handle a lead, poo bag and signal? That's going to cause some amusement down on the Green.'

Lewis moves a couple of feet away and sits down on the grass. Frosty joins him and I feel a twinge of envy that my dog appears to prefer his company to mine, and that he is stroking her when he could be stroking me. I'd roll over and let him caress my belly any time.

'What do you want to use as a "good dog" sign?' he asks, squinting in the sun.

'Let me think. How about thumbs up? One thumb.'

'Okay. What you need to do next is to get Frosty's attention.'

'How can I do that when she only has eyes for you?'

'You've got some treats with you?'

I nod.

'Use those.'

'What, you mean I should bribe her?'

'No, you use them as a lure to bring her to you and then I'll show you how to use them as a reward.'

I take a couple of treats from the bag in my pocket and move round to show them to Frosty, not letting her have them until she's at my feet, when she gobbles them up as if she's never been fed before, nipping my fingers in the process.

'Ouch.' I pull back.

'We're going to need a "be gentle" command too.'

'Okay, going back to the "good girl" – I mean "good dog" – command, what you do is give her the thumbs up, then the treat. Repeat that a few times.'

'How many times?' I interrupt.

'That depends on the dog. Mick would learn it the first time. I reckon it'll take Frosty, what, eight goes?'

'Your personal trainer is being very disparaging about you,' I tell her.

'Do it eight times, then give the sign and see what happens. If she looks for her treat, she's got it. Treat her and make a fuss of her when she does.'

Having got over my qualms about how embarrassing it is to be giving a dog the thumbs up, I show Frosty the signal and treat her eight times. Then I do the thumbs up again and wait. There's a long pause. At least, it seems very long to me, before Frosty gives me a nudge, as if to say: where's my treat?

'Good dog,' I say, giving her two and rubbing her ears.

'Give her the thumbs up,' Lewis says, 'she can't hear you.'

'OMG, I'm not very good at this,' I groan.

'I told you I was going to find it more difficult to train the owner,' Lewis teases.

'What next?'

'We'll give her a break, take her for a stroll around the field and then try the thumbs up again to check she's got it.'

We walk around the field along the hedge, where deep pink soldier buttons and white milkmaids grow in the bank among the brambles. Further along, a flock of sparrows fly out with a flurry of beating wings, landing in the elder blossom opposite.

'What about "No"? I'm going to need that one in the repertoire.'

'You could have two versions,' Lewis says. 'Shake your head and close your eyes briefly to break contact – you can use that for situations where she isn't doing what you want her to do – and an angry face when

170

there's an emergency. I'll have to get you to practise those.'

'I'm going to feel like a complete idiot,' I say, laughing.

'You won't worry after a while – it'll come naturally.'

We return to the trees and I walk Frosty past quietly on the lead. She isn't pulling or trying to run off, so I duck in front of her and give her the thumbs-up sign. She doesn't take any notice.

'That was rubbish,' I observe.

'It was. You need to be far more theatrical than that.'

I try again, making a dramatic thumbs up. This time, Frosty gets it and looks for the treat.

'That's great,' says Lewis, giving me a thumbs up in return. 'We'll finish there for today on a good note.'

'Oh?' I say, feeling deflated. 'Is that it then?'

'You shouldn't over-train a dog because they get bored. It's better that they co-operate because they want to please you. Not only that, we shouldn't leave it too long before we have another session.'

'Why is that?' I ask.

'Because, not only will it be good for Frosty, this is one shepherd who's looking for an excuse to see you again very soon, if you don't mind, that is.'

'Mind? Of course I don't mind. In fact, I'd love to see you again.' I can't help smiling – my cheeks ache. 'Can I tell everyone I have a personal dog trainer?'

'I shouldn't mention it to too many people – they'll all want one. Tomorrow?'

'I'm working tomorrow. How about the day after?'

171

He nods. 'Would you like coffee?' His mobile rings. 'I'm sorry – it's Murray.'

'Go ahead.'

Lewis apologises again when he finishes his conversation. 'I'm afraid the coffee will have to wait. Murray wants me to take a ewe over to Talyton Manor vets – sometimes I wish sheep weren't so needy, or that they could drive.'

'That's okay. I'll catch up with Emily. I'll see you soon.'

'Same time, same place,' Lewis adds. 'And make sure you practise. I'll know if you haven't.'

I pop in to the farmhouse for coffee with my sister and we sit in the kitchen, chatting.

'I can't wait to see what else Lewis can do—'

'I bet you can't,' Emily cuts in with a giggle.

'With Frosty,' I say, blushing.

'You haven't stopped talking about him.'

'Did you have fun at Mum and Dad's the other day?' I ask, changing the subject.

'I did, thank you. It was a relief to have some quality time with Daisy while Mum looked after Poppy. Daisy bit her big sister's finger at breakfast time – she only has a couple of stubs at the bottom, so it didn't really hurt. Anyway, Poppy says she was checking to see if she had any more teeth like I sometimes do – and now she wants Kev to come and arrest her.' I can hear the laughter bubbling up in Emily's voice and I'm glad she's feeling brighter.

'You're sounding like you're coping better,' I say. 'That's good.'

'I know. I feel more like myself. Poppy's still very hard work, but I am able to laugh about some of the things she does, rather than cry every time.' Emily pauses. 'So you'll be back to the farm very soon?'

'I'm bringing Frosty back the day after tomorrow,' I say, and my twin gives me a knowing smile that makes me blush for a second time.

When I return to Greenwood Farm two days later, Lewis is waiting for me, freshly shaven and dressed in jeans and a navy sweater with leather patches on the sleeves. He greets me with a kiss on the cheek – not a brief peck, but a lingering caress of his lips that ignites a flame of desire in my gut. I know it's ridiculous because I hardly know him, but it is there nonetheless and continues to burn as we revisit the field behind the farmhouse to continue with Frosty's training.

We practise the commands she learned on the first occasion, then move on to another set when Lewis decides that it's me who's in need of urgent training, not the dog.

'You aren't demonstrative enough,' he says, standing right in front of me.

'What do you mean?' I say, shakily.

'If you're going to give facial signals, you need to overemphasise them at first. Like this,' he adds, forcing a frown. 'Or this.' He raises one eyebrow independently of the other.

'What's that supposed to mean, apart from "I'm making myself look like a complete prat"?' I chuckle.

'That's better,' he grins. 'You do have a sense of humour . . . and you have the most amazing smile.'

'What's that saying? My gran uses it. Flattery will get you everywhere.'

'I think you mean flattery will get you nowhere, but I'm not complaining. Where's it getting me?'

I decide it's now or never. I'm risking rejection and hurt, but I'm pretty sure he likes me and it would be a shame not to find out if there can ever be anything between us because we're both too shy to ask. Holding his gaze, I reach out my hand. Lewis fumbles for my fingers and squeezes them tight, and my heart pounds.

'You must have some idea what's going on here,' I stammer. 'I mean, I really like you. You make me laugh.'

'I like you too,' he cuts in, smiling. 'Can't you tell?'

'I can't always be sure . . .'

'I think you're amazing, beautiful and funny –' Lewis lowers his voice – 'and I think you're really hot.'

'You're pretty hot too,' I say. I really fancy him and he fancies me too. I can't believe that I've thrown caution to the wind and admitted my feelings for him, but I feel liberated being with him, so very different from how I felt with Paul. 'So when is our next training session?'

'Well . . .' He pauses. 'We could go out later for something to eat.'

'I'm sorry, I can't. I'm going out with Claire.' It crosses my mind that I could cancel, but I can't do that to her. 'She's stressing out about her wedding,' I say in explanation. 'How about tomorrow after lunch?'

Lewis shakes his head. 'Murray and I are going off

to pick up some gear he bought cheap in a farm sale. I think it's an all-day job.'

'He's making you work seven days a week, even though lambing's over?'

'I need the money. The pick-up's due an MOT.' He moves closer and at the same time, he pulls me towards him and touches his forehead to mine. My pulse races because I know what is going to happen next. Guiding me back behind the hedge, away from prying eyes, he places his hands on my hips and pulls me tight against his muscular body.

'Oh, Zara,' he mutters, running his hand through my hair and twisting it through his fingers as he presses his lips to mine in a long, slow, lingering kiss.

I don't know how many minutes pass before I become aware of Frosty whining and straining at the lead wrapped around my wrist. I take a small step back.

'Frosty doesn't approve,' I say weakly.

'Does that bother you?' Lewis murmurs, his mouth brushing my cheek, a gesture that makes me melt.

'Strangely enough, my dog's opinion is suddenly much less important,' I say, kissing him back.

Eventually, he draws away slightly. 'I suppose we'd better save the rest for another time.'

'Do you think there'll be another time,' I say archly.

'There'd better be,' he says, giving me a quick hug. 'I suspected that kissing you would take my breath away.'

'You'd better be careful – it could be addictive.'

'We'll find out, I promise, but I think we'll stop there for now – I can see your sister peering around the curtains in one of the rooms upstairs.'

'I'd better go,' I say eventually.

'And I'd better put some hours in on the farm, otherwise Murray will be after me.'

We return to the farmyard where he collects Mick and Miley, and as I drive away with Frosty clipped safely onto the front seat, I notice how he gives me the thumbs up. I toot the horn and the orphan lambs scamper along the drive. I have to wait for Lewis to round them up and send them back.

Emily's on the mobile as soon as I arrive back at Gran's.

'How did it go then?'

'Frosty was a good girl.'

'And you? Were you a good girl too, Zara? Come on. Fess up.'

'There's nothing to say – you know exactly what happened because you were spying on us.'

'I just happened to look out of the window,' she admits. 'When are you seeing him again? You are seeing him again?'

'Yes, but it's just a bit of fun,' and that's what I tell Claire too when we meet up the same evening at the Talymill Inn to listen to the band she's thinking about having as her second choice for the evening do at the wedding.

'I've booked them already,' she explains as we make our way through the crowd with our drinks to the stage, where the band, a four-piece, are warming up. 'I

176

just want to make sure they're good enough.'

'Shouldn't Kev have some say in this?'

'He's at work. And he hasn't got a clue about weddings. He's all for having a Hogwarts-themed occasion.' She frowns. 'Do you think this is the right class of band for my special day?'

'I really don't know. If they can play the kind of music you want, then yes, they must be.'

'I'm not sure I like their image.'

'Oh, don't be so fussy. So what if the drummer looks a bit shaggy and the singer has rips in his jeans? My gran wouldn't approve – she'd want to give them a shave and sew up the holes – but it's the sound that counts. They're pretty popular.' I look around the room. 'It's packed tonight.'

Claire sips at her wine, apparently reassured.

'Did I tell you Lewis snogged me?'

Claire touches the tip of her finger to her chin. 'You know, I think you just might have mentioned it a couple of times since we arrived. Seriously, though, I'm really happy for you. It's time you had some fun after Paul and the divorce. Would you, you know, if he asked . . .?'

'We haven't even been on a proper date. In fact, we aren't dating.'

'But he kissed you . . .' Claire pauses as the band start playing an old Bon Jovi song, 'Livin' on a Prayer'. 'And you are going to see him again?'

'Yes, he kissed me.' My toes curl at the memory of how that made me feel. 'And I'm going to see him again, but not in a boyfriend-girlfriend kind of way.

I'm not looking for anything serious.' However, even as I say that, I know that if Lewis and I were alone and he kissed me again, it wouldn't necessarily stop there.

He calls me the following day, inviting me over for another training session because Murray didn't need him for the farm sale after all, but when I arrive, we walk the dogs for an hour or so and end up drinking tea in the annexe while Miley, Mick and Frosty mill around at our feet. Lewis shuts his dogs in the kitchen to give Frosty a chance to settle down, which she does, lying at my feet as I sit at one end of the sofa bed in the living area and Lewis sits at the other. At least, that's where he starts out. Gradually, though, he seems to shift towards me, until his thigh is touching mine, and then his arm is across the back of the sofa bed and his hand dropping down to my shoulder, his fingers tangling ever so gently in my hair.

I steal a glance towards him, breathing his heady, masculine scent of musk and aftershave.

'Do you want me to stop?' he whispers.

'Um, I don't know,' I mumble through the sound of the pulse that pumps at my eardrums. He's younger than me, yet he seems so much more experienced, and as his fingers caress my neck, I'm not sure I can, or want to resist. 'I don't normally do this kind of thing.'

'And what kind of thing is that?' he says, amused.

'Well, what I think you're suggesting . . . going to bed in the middle of the day with a man I hardly know for a bit of . . .'

'Fun,' he says. He leans closer and I can hear the catch in his voice when he goes on, 'I've been aching to make love to you.' As he presses his mouth to my ear, any remaining resistance I have disappears and I think, why not? Why not enjoy the moment? We're consenting adults, otherwise unattached, and I've never felt about anyone like I do about Lewis. I've never felt this urgency and passion.

Although we're having fun together, I find I can't help myself becoming emotionally involved, my feelings for him deepening each time we meet. It isn't what I planned and I don't seem to be able to do anything about it.

We catch up several times more over the next three weeks, snatching odd moments between his duties on the farm and my shifts, before the prospect of him leaving Talyton St George looms like a dark cloud on the horizon. One night I stay over. I wake the following morning and I'm lying in his arms on the sofa bed when he says, 'Can we meet up again soon? Tonight? I'll have to work late to make up my hours.'

'I'm on call Monday and Tuesday, so . . .' I hesitate. 'How about Friday? We're having a get-together with some friends. Me and Emily, that is.'

'Emily's already told me I'm coming along.'

'Has she? My sister is impossible.'

'My brother will be down too. He's finished his exams and he's dropping by on the way to Newquay for a few days' surfing. He'll be having fun while I'm milking cows in the wilds of Shropshire.'

'How long are you away for?'

'Just a month.'

'I'm going to miss you,' I say fondly.

'I'll see you on Friday,' he says, kissing me again, 'I'm not leaving until the Sunday morning, so we can have another training session with Frosty if we said Saturday at about two? After that, I'll be back for the Country Show. In the meantime, I reckon Murray won't miss me for another hour or so. What do you think?' As Lewis's fingertips trail across my cheek, down my neck and under the duvet, I find I can't think of anything at all.

CHAPTER ELEVEN

Top Dog

Friday night can't come soon enough, but when it does arrive and I'm ready to go out in a low-cut top and heels, I find Gran, looking lost and alone in the kitchen.

'Are you all right?' I call.

She looks up from where she's stirring some meaty concoction in a saucepan and gives me a small smile.

'What is that?' I ask, wrinkling my nose at the aroma of boiled cabbage and sage.

'Gravy for the stuffed hearts.'

'You have remembered I'm going out.'

'Of course I remember,' she says blithely. 'I've cooked one for me and one for the dog, and Norris likes a little cut up in his bowl. Have a lovely time, won't you?'

'I will.' I hesitate, finding myself torn between

going out with my sister and friends, and staying in with Gran. She hasn't lost any weight, but she looks more frail, and her hair, usually so neat, is like a bird's nest.

'Is your man-friend going to be there?' she asks.

I've given up trying to get through to her about the fact that Lewis isn't my boyfriend. Yes, we've slept together, but it isn't serious, and I really don't want to have to explain that to my grandmother when I can hardly explain it to myself. I don't do casual relationships. At least, I didn't before I met Lewis.

'He will be there, yes, and everyone else. How would you feel if I brought someone back to the flat? Not tonight,' I hasten to add. 'We didn't discuss that when I moved in.'

'How would you feel if I brought someone back?' she counters.

I take a step back, thrown by her comment.

'I don't know. I suppose I'd be . . .'

'Surprised?' she finishes for me.

'Well, that, and happy for you.'

She smiles again. 'There hasn't been anyone since your granddad, but I've had offers. I'm still a looker, apart from a few extra crinkles and grey hairs. You don't believe me, do you, Zara?'

'Well, enlighten me. Who was it, Gran? Who made you an offer?'

'Offers,' she says, with a gleam in her eye. 'There was one of Uncle Nobby's mates. I turned him down because he smelled of mothballs and flashed his Niagara at me.'

'Niagara?' I start laughing. 'I think you mean Viagra.'

'He kept his pills in his wallet. The other one was two summers ago. I suppose you could call it a holiday romance,' she goes on more seriously.

'You are a dark horse. I didn't have a clue.'

'It was something special, between the two of us. I didn't have to go telling everyone about it, putting it on Bookface or introducing him to my friends.'

'What was he like?'

'Like Mr Darcy – proud and handsome with a generous heart. John's wife died of cancer the year before and his daughter persuaded him to holiday in Devon with her and his grandchildren. He came into the shop every day for two weeks.'

'Was it very romantic?' I ask, as Gran gazes out of the window into the distance.

'He was charming. He brought me flowers and wrote me poetry, and he came up to the flat for tea. But nothing happened.'

'Don't go there. I don't need to know.'

'I did fall a little in love with him,' Gran says quietly. 'I sometimes wonder, what if? What if I'd been more forward like you young people seem to be nowadays? What if I'd invited him to come and stay for a weekend?'

'I didn't think you'd ever feel like that because . . . Well, you and Granddad were so close, I didn't imagine there could ever be anyone else.'

'Neither did I, but John was special, and when you've been alone for a long time, you realise that it could be your last chance of love. I just wasn't brave enough to take the next step. I didn't think I could be that lucky – to fall in love with two wonderful men.'

'Have you heard from him since?' I ask.

'He sent letters for a while and I wrote back, and then they stopped and I didn't like to chase it up in case . . . There could be lots of reasons why he gave up writing to me.'

I hear a car draw up outside and a toot on the horn.

'That'll be Emily.'

'Have fun.'

'I'll see you later.' I give her a hug. I don't acknowledge Frosty, who's hanging around at my feet, knowing full well I'm going out. It sounds mean, but Maz advised me to ignore her so she doesn't get so stressed about me leaving.

Emily is driving. Murray, Lewis and Lewis's brother are with her.

'Hi everyone.' I climb into the back of the Land Rover and squeeze up to sit beside Lewis – I think it's deliberate, I don't think he takes up that much room. He's wearing a white shirt, light sweater and gunmetal grey chinos, and smells of fresh aftershave, not sheep. I fasten the seatbelt, brushing his thigh at the same time.

'I'm sorry,' I say quickly.

Lewis chuckles.

'Hey, keep your hands off our shepherd,' Emily says, teasing.

'Emily! I'm trying to find the thingy for the seatbelt.'

'Is that a euphemism? I haven't heard it put like that before,' Murray laughs.

I'm going to kill my sister in a minute. I catch her glancing in the rear-view mirror and give her a look, just like my mum used to – and still does, occasionally, if we're doing something of which she disapproves.

While Emily and I are almost identical in appearance, Lewis and his brother are very different, and it's hard to imagine they're related. Connor is a couple of years younger. His face is smooth and boyish and his hair is long. He's wearing a hoodie, jeans and lashings of Lynx.

'Meet Zara,' Lewis says. 'Zara, Connor's hoping to catch some waves over the weekend before he goes down to Newquay to meet his surfing mates.'

'I can't wait,' Connor says.

'I wish I was a student again,' Lewis says.

'What do you do, Connor?' I ask.

'I'm studying for a degree in media studies. I want to get into directing.'

'You'll have to have a chat with Kev later. He's into directing too – traffic,' Murray says.

'Murray, what's up with you and all the witty banter?' Emily says.

'You've hardly let me out in the past couple of months.'

'Ha ha,' Emily says sarcastically. 'As if.'

We leave the Land Rover on the seafront at Talymouth, outside the Indian restaurant, Murray and Emily hanging back to search for Emily's mobile and lock up while the waves crash against the sea wall alongside us.

'It's a rough night,' Lewis observes.

'Great for surfing,' says Connor. 'I wish I'd brought my board along.'

'You have a one-track mind,' Lewis says.

'Not quite. There's surf, sand, sex . . . and more sex,' Connor laughs out loud as he mimics The Inbetweeners. 'Not necessarily in that order.'

'The others will be waiting,' I say, spotting Claire's car further down the seafront.

'Hurry up, you lot,' Claire yells from the door of the restaurant. 'Kev's almost finished the pickles, so you'd better get a move on if you're joining us.'

The interior of the restaurant is decorated with scarlet and gold wallpaper and dark wood. Tessa and Jack, Claire and Kev, Murray, Emily and Connor are already at a table with a stack of poppadums and pickles, and bottles of wine and Indian beer. Murray makes the rest of the introductions and Claire pats the chair beside her, inviting Lewis to sit there. I take the next seat along.

'Claire and Kev are getting married in September,' I say.

'There are one hundred and six days to go.' Claire checks her watch.

'I wish we hadn't had such a long engagement,' Kevin says. 'I don't know what we'll talk about after we get hitched. I'm an expert on biodegradable confetti and I know now that a favour isn't a good turn you do for a mate.'

186

Lewis glances at me and grins. I did warn him that the hot topic of conversation would inevitably be The Wedding.

We order food and drinks, while Emily calls Mum to check on the girls.

'Poppy won't go to bed,' she says when she comes off the phone.

'That's great news,' Murray says. 'The later she goes to sleep, the more likely she is to lie in tomorrow morning.'

'I don't know what we're going to do without you, Lewis,' Emily says. 'You've been amazing with the girls. Poppy loves your dogs. She's going to miss all three of you like mad.'

'I'll be back for shearing,' he says quickly.

'And the Country Show,' Murray cuts in. 'I'd like to see you knock Chris off his perch as reigning champion this year.'

'I'll make sure I get some practice in,' Lewis smiles.

'I'm glad I'm not helping out with the shearing this year,' Emily goes on, 'but there are times when I'd rather spend the day with the flock than with my little darlings.'

'Yep, Poppy bleats more than any sheep I've ever met.' Murray turns to Jack and Tessa. 'It's ironic, really. You can't wait for them to be born, and when they arrive you wish you could send them back. I love them dearly, but it's hard work being a parent.'

'Murray, don't put them off,' Emily says.

'It's a bit late now,' Jack says, reaching out towards Tessa, who takes his hand and guides it to touch her pregnancy bump.

'Don't let Zara start on the gruesome birth stories,' Emily warns.

'I won't, I promise.'

'What are you having to drink, Zara?' Lewis asks, his thigh pressed against mine.

'A fizzy water, thank you.'

'Are you sure you wouldn't like a glass of wine or something stronger?'

'Water's fine,' I say, thinking of my diet. 'I don't really drink.'

'You don't drink?' He seems surprised. 'Emily does.'

'She doesn't drink much. Alcohol doesn't really agree with me, but don't let me stop you.'

'Did you ever drink alcohol?'

'When I first started my training I used to go out with the other girls and drink too much – tequila, mainly.'

Gradually, Murray grows increasingly drunk in a cheerful way while Jack grows quiet. Claire is pretty sozzled, while Kev and Emily remain sober for the drive home. Connor and Lewis drink lager by the bottle, becoming ever louder, until Lewis eats one of the flowers from the vase on the table as a dare.

'Lewis, is that funny?' I ask lightly as he chews and splutters on a red rose.

'Funny?' Connor says. 'It's bloody hilarious.'

I have to force myself to bite my tongue as I clear up

the petals that are strewn across the tablecloth, with the waiter watching with a weary expression from the corner of the restaurant.

'My brother's mental,' Connor laughs. 'You can't take him anywhere.'

'You dared him to do that,' I say, embarrassed. 'Is he always like this?'

'When he's had a few.' Connor slaps him on the back. 'There's no need to be so uptight about it. We're just having a laugh.'

'Lighten up, Zara. Have some fun.' Lewis grabs his glass and drains it of beer, spilling half of it down his front before calling to the waiter for a refill. I know I'm used to being the sensible one and having to watch others making a fool of themselves when we're out partying, but I still find it embarrassing.

'We've only just started,' Connor says, encouraging him.

'Boys will be boys,' Claire sighs.

'I need a wee,' Emily says, coming to my rescue. 'You coming, sis?'

'Did we have to know the detail?' Murray groans.

'I spend too much time with Poppy,' Emily grins. 'Nothing fazes me. You'll find that out soon enough, Tessa. When I go to the doctor now, I walk in, pull my jeans straight down and jump on the couch.'

'I wish you'd do that for me,' Murray says hopefully.

'Maybe later,' she says, brushing her fingers through his hair as she leaves the table with me following along behind.

'It's going well, isn't it? Everyone seems to be enjoying themselves, some more than others,' Emily says from the cubicle in the Ladies.

'I don't know. Lewis and Connor are drunk – they're embarrassing.'

'I'm sorry, but in my opinion you're overreacting.'

'I don't think so,' I say, beginning to doubt myself as I look in the mirror over the sink.

'Murray is pissed, but I won't hold it against him. I'll have my vengeance tomorrow morning when he's begging me for a full English and paracetamol.'

'I really like him, but seeing him tonight makes me feel the age difference.' I hardly recognise the man who was walking through the meadow with me and Frosty the other day, and making love to me in his bed.

'He isn't going out with you, Zara.'

'I know, but I thought he liked me.' I don't tell my sister I've slept with him. 'I thought he'd have wanted to make a good impression.'

'In front of Claire and Tessa, you mean?'

'Well, yes.'

'Why are you bothered about what they think?'

'I wanted Claire to have a good opinion of him. I don't want her thinking he's a complete wanker.'

'It doesn't matter what anyone else thinks. It's what you think that counts.' Emily flushes the toilet. 'You aren't going to let your new love interest go down the pan over this.' She comes out of the cubicle, washes her hands and checks her make-up.

'You don't need any more,' I say, smiling weakly.

'You look as if Poppy's drawn on your face with her crayons.'

'Hey, what happened to the sisterhood?' Emily says. 'Do you think it's too much? Really?'

'No, it's fine, except I'm not sure I'd have gone for the red lip-liner or the metallic eye-shadow.' I dig in my bag for a tissue. 'It just needs toning down, that's all, like Connor and Lewis.'

'Come on, you wanted an opinion. Lewis is having a bit of fun, that's all.' She pauses, drying her hands. 'He's probably a bit nervous so he had a bit more on an empty stomach than he might have planned and it's gone straight to his head. He wouldn't mean to upset you. He's a lovely guy.'

'I thought he was.'

'You can't blame Lewis for how you feel.' Emily stares at me. 'It isn't his fault he doesn't know about Granddad.'

'He knows I don't drink.'

'But he doesn't know your reasons – at least, I'd hazard a guess that he doesn't. I certainly haven't talked to him about it.' Emily touches my arm. 'Don't overthink this. Put your smile back on and get out there. He'll be sober by lunchtime tomorrow when you're doing your dog training, or whatever it is. He's hardly stopped talking about it.'

Partially reassured, I return to the table, where Lewis has two mango and pistachio kulfis in front of him. He slides his arm clumsily around my back as I sit down again and gives me the biggest, most heart-melting smile and a belch of beery breath before he pushes one of the ice creams towards me.

'For you, Zara,' he says. 'Murray says I'm being a bit of a prat.'

'He's not wrong,' I mutter. 'But Emily says I'm overreacting, so I guess we're quits.'

He hands me a spoon.

Emily winks at me across the table while Jack asks me about Frosty, and Tessa and Emily talk about the best places to find nursery furniture, and Murray teases Kevin about how he'll soon be a dad. I wonder if Lewis and Connor are bored by this conversation.

'Wedding, honeymoon, baby, that's how it goes,' he chuckles.

'Oh no,' Claire says, 'I'm going to need at least a year to recover from organising the wedding.'

Eventually, we're ready to leave the restaurant. Emily and Murray go ahead to the car while I say goodnight to Claire. Connor and Lewis follow on some way behind, playing another game of dare with the waves, seeing who can get closest to the sea wall without being swamped. I turn to watch them messing about in the light of the streetlamps along the front.

'Lewis, you should have gone to Specsavers.' Connor staggers about.

'What do you mean?'

'If you fancy that. I can't see the attraction in a fat old divorcee who lives with her granny.'

'Connor, shut up and stop being a knob!' Lewis

shouts at him over the sound of the sea that seethes across the shingle. 'Zara is amazing – she's intelligent, kind and fit, most definitely fit.'

Although I'm incredibly hurt and offended by Connor's remarks, Lewis's compliments mollify me, and I manage a small smile to myself before Connor starts up again.

'What does Jade think? Does she know?' He moves up next to Lewis, his hands in his pockets. 'You haven't told her, have you? You really are a piece of—'

'I'm not with Jade,' Lewis counters. 'We're on a break.'

'Are you sure about that?'

What? I think. Does Connor mean what I think he does? I can't take any more. I scurry along the seafront, oblivious to the sea spray and the walls of water that crash and tumble away across the beach. Jade? I press my fist against my chest, fighting the unexpected pain. I mean, Lewis and I are supposed to be having a light-hearted fling – nothing serious – yet it hurts. The ex-girlfriend who apparently isn't quite such an ex as Lewis made out.

Wiping the sea spray from my eyes, I get into the Land Rover, choosing to sit next to Emily for the journey home.

'We'll let the three stooges sit in the back,' she says, as Connor and Lewis catch up. 'Would you like to come back to the farm for the night, Zara?'

I decline and Emily takes me back to Talyton where, outside the shop, I wish everyone goodnight.

Although it kills me to say it, I wish Connor a safe trip to Newquay and Lewis a good time in Shropshire.

'Aren't you bringing Frosty for dog training tomorrow?' Lewis asks quickly on realising what I've just said.

'No, I have things to do.'

'Oh, it would have been good to know before . . .'

'Hindsight is always a wonderful thing,' I say, unable to hide my sarcasm. 'Goodnight,' I repeat. What else is there to say?

I spend the following morning in the shop, trying to take my mind off what happened the night before. I'm upset – I've been sleeping with him for the last three weeks, after all, and now I've learned the hard way that I'm not cut out for a no-strings attached, friends-with-benefits arrangement. I'm usually level-headed and in control of my emotions, but clearly this fling with Lewis wasn't quite as light-hearted as I thought, on my part at least.

Pull yourself together, Zara, I tell myself.

I check my mobile for messages. Paul has texted to say, hi, u ok x.

In a moment of weakness, I text him back.

Not really x

At which Paul texts again, telling me to meet him in the café at the leisure centre tonight for a chat.

Should I go?

I text back my answer.

There's a voicemail from Lewis, three voicemails, in fact, and several texts, but as far as I'm concerned

194

there's nothing he can say to make it right. I should never have allowed myself to be seduced by his looks and his gentle manners. I don't like his immaturity and his lack of respect for me and his girlfriend, and my heart aches at the thought of how he couldn't bring himself to admit he was still going out with Jade while at the same time he was asking me about the status of my relationship with Paul.

I can't forgive his deception. If I'd known he was in a relationship, I would never have let him kiss me, or encouraged him in any way. It's so wrong.

'Zara, a penny for them.' Gran potters through to the counter with the pricing gun. 'You seem out of sorts.'

'I'm fine,' I say. 'I think the curry disagreed with me.'

'Are you still going dog training with Lewis today?'

How does she know, I think? How can she be so perceptive?

'Lewis is busy.'

'I see. That's a pity. You'll miss him, won't you?' she goes on.

'Gran! He's just a friend who's been helping me with the dog, that's all.'

'But you'll miss him all the same,' she insists, and grudgingly I admit that I'll miss him just a tiny bit because he's been so good with Frosty.

'Please don't go on about it.' I force a smile. 'I'm teaching Frosty the commands for "No" next.'

'You'd better show me what they are,' Gran says.

'Why?' I'm teasing. 'You never take any notice of anything I say.'

She looks confused. 'I want to know how to say no to Frosty.'

'Oh, never mind. Would you like a tea?'

Gran glances towards the door. 'You'd better make it for three. Here's Lewis. Why don't you take yours outside? I'll stay here.'

'What if he's here for a paper?'

'You know full well he isn't.' Gran stands as tall as she can and takes my place behind the counter, shoving me out. 'Hello, Lewis. It's lovely to see you.'

'And you, Mrs Witheridge.'

'Don't be silly. It's Rosemary to you. Zara was just about to make tea.'

'Thanks, but I can't stop for long.'

'Zara, you take Lewis outside. Frosty's in the garden, watching the birds with Norris.'

I bite my lip at her machinations. I have nothing to say to Lewis and I don't wish to listen to anything he has to say in return.

'Just a quick chat,' he says, as if he's reading my mind.

'Come through,' I say stiffly. I hold the curtain aside for him. 'Straight along the corridor, through the storeroom and out of the door at the end.' As we step into the light, I notice how he winces. 'Serves you right,' I comment as Frosty comes bounding up to greet him. 'I haven't done the "No" command yet,' I say as he tries to calm her down.

'Someone must have slipped a hangover into my

beer last night. I've been trying to get hold of you. Did you receive my messages?'

'Yes . . . Thank you,' I say.

'But you decided not to reply.' Lewis is on his knees, hugging Frosty as though for comfort. 'Look, I'm sorry for embarrassing you in front of your friends by getting wasted. There's nothing I can do to make amends for that, I can't undo it, but I can apologise and promise it won't happen again.'

'That's a ridiculous thing to say,' I point out, finding my voice. 'You can't promise anything of the sort.'

'Zara, I didn't realise it was such a big deal for you. Me and Connor, we like a drink when we're together. I should have thought, but I didn't. I wasn't counting—'

'It isn't that,' I interrupt.

'What is it then? I thought we were getting on so well.'

'It either doesn't bother you, or you don't remember.'

'Probably the latter,' he says lightly.

'It isn't funny.'

'I'm sorry,' he repeats. 'What was so awful that it made you change your mind about me?' Lewis stands up, going pale as he regains his balance. He smells of toothpaste and stale beer. He's tried to shave and missed some stubble on one cheek and nicked his chin, but I am not going to feel sorry for him when he brought this on himself.

'When were you going to tell me about Jade, your girlfriend?' I go on.

'I haven't got a girlfriend,' he stammers, 'not really.'

'So what is she? An imaginary woman? A fiancée? A wife?'

'Jade is real.' Lewis releases Frosty who is trying to escape his embrace. She tears free and joins me, sitting on my feet as if in sympathy. 'Oh god,' he sighs. 'I wish I'd told you before, I really do, but I thought—'

'That's bloody typical of a man. You thought you'd get away with it.'

'Well, yes, I did,' he says, his admission taking me by surprise. 'It isn't what you think. I met Jade before I left home for college.'

'Don't waste my time,' I cut in. 'Is she your girlfriend, or not?'

'She's my girlfriend,' he says quietly, 'but we've been more off than on, which is why she's never visited me while I've been at Greenwood Farm and why I've never talked about her.'

'You bastard! How can you do this to her, and to me?'

'Zara, Zara.' He touches my arm. 'That's why I didn't say anything. I knew it was wrong to kiss you while I still had any connection with Jade.'

'So you shouldn't have done it.' I'm furious.

'I couldn't resist . . .'

'Oh, here we go.' I fold my arms across my chest, determined not to let him back into my heart. 'I know what you're going to say. I'm a man, I can't fight my natural urges and all that.' I remember Phil at dog training and Wendy's excuses for his behaviour.

Lewis cocks one eyebrow. 'What are you talking about? What I mean is, I've been fighting my feelings

198

for you ever since the moment I first saw you getting out of your car to visit your sister. You took my breath away.'

'Is that supposed to make me feel better?' I say, because it only makes it worse, knowing that he really did fancy me – and at first sight.

'It was instant attraction on my side, and then, when I saw you again, I wanted to spend more time with you and get to know you. And we said we'd keep it casual and light, and fun, and that's when it gets complicated.'

'I can't see the difficulty,' I say stubbornly. 'You shouldn't have led me to believe you were free.' I don't say it, but the words echo hollowly inside my head, *You shouldn't have let me fall for you.*

'I know, but I wasn't sure you felt the same about me. You're older than me, more sophisticated. Why should you be interested in me, an itinerant farmworker, who has nothing to offer you except myself?'

'But you aren't free to offer anything.' I squeeze my arms tight. 'What does your girlfriend think about this? She doesn't know, does she? Of course she doesn't.'

'Jade and I have been mates for ages – we hook up now and again.'

'So you do this with every woman you meet?'

'Of course not. Since I met you, I've been intending to tell her that I wouldn't see her any more. I wanted to tell her face to face, not by phone or by text.'

'I don't care what you do. It's none of my business.' I recall, with a frisson of regret, the touch of his lips on mine.

'When we kissed,' Lewis goes on, 'I didn't plan that.

199

I thought I was in control. I thought I could hold back, but we were having such a good time and you were so close . . . I'm besotted with you.'

I gaze at him, my heart pounding and my throat dry.

'Why are you looking at me like that? You can't tell me you don't feel the same.' Lewis steps back, kicks over one of Gran's pots and swears. 'I'm sorry. I'll pay for a new one.'

'Don't bother,' I say, setting the clumps of tulips and yellow wallflowers upright and nudging the broken pieces of pot into a pile.

'I have to.' He bends down to help. 'I must.'

'Lewis, I really think you should go now, before you do any more damage. I'm not sure why you came here this morning.'

'Please listen.'

I've listened for long enough. I don't like liars.'

'I've arranged to meet Jade on my way to Shropshire – I was going to finish with her properly, face to face, and then, when I came back, ask you out. You see, I've been planning to do the right thing all along.'

'I'd be gutted if I was your girlfriend. That sounds so cold and calculating.'

'It isn't like that.' Lewis's face is etched with desperation, but I can't tell if it's genuine. 'As I've said, Jade and I have been on and off for ages. She's been out with other men, at least three that I know of.'

'And you? How many other women have you been out with?'

'I've had a couple of one-night stands when Jade and I were on a break.'

'You think I'll believe that now?'

'I don't see what the problem is. We were all consenting adults practising safe sex.'

'You're what me and my friends call a sleazebag. If I'd known, I'd never have encouraged you, let alone let you kiss me. Goodbye, Lewis.'

'Goodbye, Zara.' There's a catch in his throat. 'Is there any chance—?'

'Don't go there.' I hold my hand up.

'If you want any advice about Frosty, you can call me, or text, anything . . .'

'Thanks, but I won't.' I'm finding it difficult to dismiss him. He's certainly persistent, and it makes me think of Kev and how he wore Claire down until she agreed to go out with him – but that was different. Kev was a single man, and even if Lewis is telling the truth about his plan to finish with his girlfriend, how could I ever trust him? 'Now, please go.' I turn to pick up the pieces of flowerpot and drop them into the bin, the clattering masking the sound of his footsteps as he walks away, and then I fall to my knees and hold Frosty tight. 'I don't care if I never see that bastard again,' I tell her, and Frosty licks my nose.

'Lewis seemed upset,' Gran says when I return to the shop.

'I don't want to talk about it.'

'And I don't want to see you on your own when I'm gone.'

She says it so matter-of-factly that I burst into tears.

'It may have skipped your notice, but I am quite an elderly lady now. I'm not going to be around for ever.'

'Gran, please don't talk like that.'

'It's the truth. I'm tired, Zara. I have my good days and the not so good . . .'

It's as if Gran has opened the door into her future just a chink, and I take advantage of the opportunity to force it a little further.

'You see, you really should retire so you can have a rest and enjoy life before you go, if you're really that intent on dying on me that soon,' I say darkly.

'I do enjoy life. I make every day count and, as I've said before, why would I want to end up living in some old people's home? I don't think there's anywhere more lonely. I used to visit my friend in a home and she would sit in the lounge where no one spoke. The staff were all rushed off their feet so she didn't like to hold them up chatting, and the visitors fizzled out after a while. Anyway, what would happen to my customers? I'm a paper seller, shopkeeper and counsellor rolled into one.'

'Someone else will take on the shop.'

'You and Emily don't want it – you have your own lives. If I sell up, it will close. It will become a charity shop or computer repair place.' Gran clambers up the steps and brings down the jar of rainbow drops. Grunting with the effort, she unscrews the lid and pours out a generous heap onto the scales, before offering the bowl to me. We share them, taking fistfuls at a time.

'If it's true love, it's worth risking your heart for.' Gran pours out a second measure. 'Remember that.'

Regardless of what my grandmother says, I'm not prepared to risk my heart on Lewis, and one of her other favourite sayings applies better to my situation as the days pass by: out of sight, out of mind. I keep myself busy with work and continuing Frosty's training, so I can't dwell on what might have been.

CHAPTER TWELVE

Call the Midwife

Claire's birthday is at the beginning of June, two weeks after Lewis left for Shropshire, and Emily and I decide to take her for a picnic to celebrate. Okay, we know how to have a good time, I think wryly, and Claire would have preferred a night out, but Kev's taking her away for the weekend and we wanted to do something on the day of her birthday, not afterwards.

We walk along the riverbank in the sunshine. Claire is wearing shades, shorts and flip-flops, Emily a vest top, jeans and sandals, while I'm in a fitted T-shirt with 'Love Me, Love My Dog', across the front, jeans and trainers. As Gran said when the girls came to pick me and Frosty up, we are a motley crew.

I have Frosty on the lead, looking out as we go for other dogs. I've become an expert in tactical avoidance.

'You're going to have to hide in the bushes again,' Claire laughs as we spot Aurora and her poodle walking towards us. I make a beeline for the hedge alongside the old railway line, until we're down in a dip in the ground where Frosty can't see her. Claire and Emily join us.

'We'll have our picnic here.' Emily unrolls the picnic blanket and checks for sheep droppings before spreading it across the grass. Frosty assumes it's for her and promptly lies down in the middle.

'She's a bit of a princess,' Claire observes, sitting down and stroking her.

'Cake first?' Emily unpacks the basket.

'Why not?' I say. 'Here, give me the candles.'

Emily and I assemble the chocolate cake and arrange the candles. I light them and guard the flames from the breeze while we sing Happy Birthday.

'Frosty has her paws over her ears – even though she can't hear a thing.' Claire giggles and blows the candles out.

'You have made a wish, haven't you?' Emily says.

'You don't believe in magic, do you, Em?' Claire says.

'Poppy does,' she smiles, watching Claire take the knife and cut the cake into slices for practice for the wedding, of course.

'You have remembered to order the cake?' Emily asks.

'What a silly question, sis. I was there when we went to Jennie's to place the order and I know Claire's phoned to check on its progress at least three times since.'

'It isn't so silly. I was supposed to contact Jennie

about the cake topper last week.' Claire starts to hyperventilate. 'I know what I want now. What if she doesn't have time to organise it?'

'Calm down,' I say. 'You'll have a panic attack.'

'I need to call her.' Claire unzips her bag, looking for her mobile. 'I want a nurse and policeman, like me and Kev. You don't think that's too tacky, do you?'

'One day,' Emily says, 'when you've been married for as long as I have and you're changing nappies and reading endless bedtime stories, you'll hardly be able to remember the wedding ceremony, let alone the decorations on the cake. You'll look back and wonder what all the fuss was about.'

We eat all the wrong things in the wrong order, and soon the birthday girl is lying on her back in the sun and Emily is sitting against a tree stump while I lie on my front, propped up on my elbows, with Frosty belly-up alongside me.

The conversation inevitably drifts onto the topic of my love life, or lack of it, and Lewis.

'He'll be back in a couple of weeks for the Country Show. Have you spoken to him at all?' Emily asks me.

'He's texted me a couple of times about Frosty's training, and to tell me that the cows are sweet but not as endearing as the sheep.'

'Endearing!' Claire sits up. 'Is that what he said? You really are better off without him.'

'Our orphan lambs are quite endearing,' Emily says wistfully. 'I've grown quite fond of them.'

'That's because you're married to a sheep farmer,' Claire says.

'Did Lewis say anything else? Did he finish with his girlfriend?'

'He didn't – say anything, I mean.' I tear up a fistful of grass and throw it in the general direction of my troublesome twin. Subject closed.

'Have you seen Paul again?' Emily asks.

'He's dropped into the shop for bits and pieces, that's all.'

'That's good,' Claire says. 'It really wasn't wise of you to meet up with him that time.'

'It was –' I search for the right word, but can only come up with – 'nice.' We met at the leisure centre. Paul had just done a session in the gym. We sat in the café and chatted, and I asked him if his new girlfriend knew where he was and his eyes kind of widened and his pupils shrank. He stroked my hand and said he didn't want to upset her but, equally, he thought I could do with someone to talk to. 'It was my fault – as I've said before, I texted him in a moment of weakness.'

'Madness, more like,' Emily says. 'I can't believe you did that when you have us.'

'I know. It's ridiculous.' I imagined I'd pour my heart out to him, but when it came down to it, it felt wrong. I didn't stay for long, half an hour max. Paul said he wanted to see me again soon, but I said no. 'He's texted me a few times since to ask me out for a coffee.'

'Do you think he's worried that you're moving on?' Emily says.

'I can imagine him not liking the idea,' Claire says. 'Paul's always struck me as being quite controlling.

When you were married, it seemed as if he always wanted to know where you were and who you were with. We ended up seeing you less and less.'

'That comes with marriage. You have to balance your time between your husband and friends,' Emily points out.

'It doesn't matter now. I'm destined to remain single for the rest of my life. Cut me another piece of that cake, will you?'

'I will if your dog's left us any,' Claire exclaims, as Emily makes a grab for her collar, pulling her back.

'Oh, Frosty,' I scold, trying not to laugh at the same time because she's chomping on a mouthful of sponge, spilling crumbs. 'No!' I say, throwing myself into giving Frosty the angry face, at which Claire and Emily start laughing too, while Frosty looks on, licking her lips and the tip of her nose, completely oblivious of the message I'm trying to convey to her. I wish Lewis was here with us now for moral support and reassurance that I'm training Frosty in the right way. I wish too that he hadn't behaved as he did, letting me down, rounding up my dreams like sheep and tipping them off a cliff one by one. He is one bad shepherd but, the truth is, though I'd never admit it to anyone, I still can't stop thinking about him.

I can't help worrying about how I will feel when I see Lewis again because, no matter how much I try to avoid him on his return to Talyton St George for the shearing, I'm bound to run into him, either up at the farm, or walking the dog, or at the Country Show. Will

I be able to look at him as if he's nothing to me, or will my traitorous heart skip a beat? I've dealt with the anger and the sense of being seriously let down, even though it was partly my fault for putting myself in that situation, but have I banished the feelings I had for him?

On the morning of the show, which is held every year on the third Saturday in June, I sneak across the landing to collect the dog shampoo and towels from the airing cupboard, hoping Frosty won't notice, but she must have been watching me because I find her with her tail between her legs. She jams herself under Gran's armchair.

'Frosty,' I giggle. 'Out from there.' I hold a liver treat just in front of her nose, but out of reach so she has to wriggle on her belly to get it. I offer her another until she's out far enough for me to grab her and pick her up. 'Gotcha!'

When I stand her in the bath, she looks like the most depressed dog in the world, but under the hairdryer she lifts her lip in a lopsided smile, holds her tail in the air and arches her back for a scratch. I dry her, give her a brush and put on her smartest collar from her extensive wardrobe – she has almost as many collars now as I have shoes, and I put that down to Aurora's recent trick of displaying a model dog alongside the mannequin in her window and changing the dog's outfit and must-have collar every week or so.

I have given Frosty some intensive training sessions, involving the consumption of an inordinate number of liver treats, and she's finally beginning to focus on my commands and follow my lead to such an extent that I have managed to walk her down to the Green and pass several dogs, including Aurora's poodle, without Frosty causing a scene. She isn't keen on Mrs Dyer's Great Dane, but she's much more manageable.

I let Frosty out in the garden for five minutes before we go. Mistake. She comes in covered in dust and twigs.

'Have you been rolling in the grass?' She sits at my feet and gazes up at me as if to say, No. And I haven't got the heart to be cross with her. I attach her lead, pick up my bag and collect Gran's cake, which is in a tin on the counter in the shop.

'You know where you're taking it and how to set it up?' Gran says.

'To the WI tent. It goes on the white plate provided, making sure there are no crumbs. How many times have we been through this?'

'Enough, I hope,' she smiles. 'Don't let Frosty anywhere near that tin. The judge said there were hairs in my sponge last year, but I don't believe it. Someone made that up or planted them.'

'Oh, Gran, I doubt it.'

'You don't know what those people are like. They can be very spiteful.'

'They're competitive, but I really don't think they'd do anything like that.' I smile to myself. 'What colour were these hairs? Tabby, by any chance?' I say, thinking of Norris and how he sleeps curled up in the kitchen. I'm teasing, but Gran seems to be taking the perceived sabotage of last year's entry to the Best Victoria Sponge competition very seriously. There was a time when she would have shrugged it off, put it down to one of those things that happens and vowed to do better next time. 'Why don't you close just for today so you can bring the cake yourself?'

She is appalled. 'How can you suggest such a thing? Close the shop? Your granddad would turn in his grave.'

'The regulars have already been in for their papers and lottery tickets. I won't be able to watch over the cake all day because Poppy's taking Frosty in the Best Pet in Show class.'

'And you want to watch all those handsome young men shearing sheep,' Gran says with a wicked twinkle in her eye. 'Or one in particular, perhaps.' My face grows the colour of strawberry laces as she continues, 'I know you still think of him, and now maybe he's free . . .'

'Gran, were you listening? That day, when Lewis came round . . .'

'I popped upstairs and the window just happened to be open.'

'So you were. Great.' She might be forgetful at times, but she hasn't forgotten that.

'You go and enjoy yourself. I'll see you up at the farm for tea.'

Emily's invited us all for dinner. It's become a tradition since she married Murray.

'I'll pick you up on the way back from the show at about seven,' I remind her.

'Would you mind setting the alarm on my mobile? You know how dotty I am.'

I promise to text her instead.

At the showground, I park the car and meet up with Emily, Poppy and Daisy. Poppy looks after Frosty under Emily's watchful eye, while I head down to the WI tent, where the air is laden with the aroma of warm blackcurrants, roses and lavender. I remove the layers of greaseproof paper and string and place the cake on a white plate with Gran's entry slip alongside. My stomach growls at the smell and sight of it, a two-tier Victoria sponge with sticky strawberry jam running through the middle and a dusting of icing sugar across the top. I'd love to know how you qualify to be a judge.

I glance along the rows of trestle tables, laden with scones, chutneys and flower arrangements. There are decorated hats too, one of which has a set of handcuffs across the brim and a sign reading, 'Shades of Grey'. There is a small crowd gathered around it and what sounds like a heated debate over whether this display is crossing the boundaries of decency for Talyton's annual Country Show and the WI in particular.

Fifi Green, dressed in a blue polka-dot dress with a coordinating handbag and a white hat with blue silk flowers on the brim, is officiating the argument, a role she adopts naturally as the town's busybody, erstwhile lady mayoress and chair of the parish council.

'I don't see what's wrong with it,' says the contributor of the exhibit. It's Ally Jackson, roving reporter for the Talyton *Chronicle* and our newspaper boy's mother. She's carrying an orange satchel over one shoulder and wearing a green maxi dress. James is standing at the opposite end of the tent, as if he's trying to get as far away from her as possible. 'It meets the brief.'

'We've heard all about those books,' says a woman who stands with her friend in a bright yellow T-shirt reading 'Friends of Talyton Animal Rescue', 'and we think it's disgusting.'

'I've read them,' says Fifi, at which there's a collective gasp from the people in the tent.

'You've read them?'

'Well, dears, you can't make a judgement on something like that without experiencing it for yourself. The story wasn't as shocking as I expected from all the hype. I really don't think a set of handcuffs stuck to a hat is in any way inflammatory.'

'It demonstrates the oppression of women, the subjugation of female desire and the emphasis on male pleasure,' says the woman in the yellow T-shirt. 'Fifi, you are going to support us on this one?'

'I know we've sometimes struggled to maintain the moral standing of this town,' Fifi responds. 'However, I feel that this is a storm in a teacup and maybe we could do with "sexing things up", as they call it, for a change.'

'In that case, I'm withdrawing my entry from the show.'

'Joan, that's a bit hasty. You're in with a good chance with your flower arrangement. There are only three entries so far.'

'Is that all?' Joan appears to reconsider.

'Maybe it's better to make your point in a different

way,' Fifi suggests. 'By working from within, you can fight the oppression of women while we carry on and enjoy the rest of the day.'

I leave them to do just that, rejoining Poppy and Frosty outside the mini-arena that's marked out with string and straw bales for the Best Pet class. Somehow, Fifi is there too.

'She gets everywhere, that woman,' I say aside to Emily. 'She was in the WI tent discussing whether or not "Shades of Grey" was a suitable theme for a decorated hat.'

'I imagine she was disapproving.'

'She appeared to be quite open-minded. I think she has the potential to be a bit of a cougar.'

'I don't think so. Talking of cougars, though, don't you want to know how Lewis is?'

'Not really,' I say cheerfully, looking around at the fluttering flags and the flagpoles that gleam in the sunshine.

'I'm afraid you'll have to put up with his company tonight,' Emily says. 'I've invited him to the party. I couldn't *not* ask him, could I?'

'I suppose not. Would you mind if I opted out? I don't think I can face him.'

'You'll have to sometime. He's going to be around for a while.' She pauses. 'He's talked to me about the girlfriend.'

'You pumped him for info, you mean? I wish you'd left it alone.'

'It isn't as bad as you made out. Lewis and this girlfriend weren't really an item – he had to see her

214

to find out where they were at and tell her it was over for good.' When I don't respond, Emily continues, 'I believe him when he says he wasn't sure.'

'He might be able to pull the wool over your eyes – being a shepherd,' I say, trying to make light of my feelings, only to find they are still raw, in spite of the fact he's been away for a month. 'He can't do it to me.'

'That's because you're scared of being hurt again. He's finished with her.'

'I don't need to know.' I block my ears and say 'Na, na, na, na,' just like Poppy does when it's time for bed. Emily grabs me by the wrists and, laughing, pulls my hands away.

'Listen to your big sister for once.' (She's older than me by five minutes.) 'The first thing Lewis said when he turned up yesterday was, "How is Zara?" He adores you and I know, in spite of this little glitch, that you like him. Give him a chance.'

'Oh, I don't know,' I sigh.

'Yes, you do.' Emily gives me a dig in the ribs as she pulls the buggy in beside one of the bales and sits down. 'Are you going to supervise Poppy?'

'She won't let me. She wants to do it herself.' I squeeze in between Emily and another woman, who turns out to be one of my mums, with her child who is now three and a half.

'I'll never forget what you did for us, Zara.' She smiles from beneath the brim of a straw hat as she wipes the toddler's runny nose. 'Hopefully it won't be too long until we catch up with you again – we're trying for a brother or sister for Todd.'

I wish her luck and turn back to the ring.

'They're running late now. Who's judging?' Emily asks.

'It's Maz, the vet. Look.' Maz is at the entrance to the ring, fastening a judge's badge to the lapel of her jacket. 'How's she going to choose?'

The entrants file in with their pets – a giant rabbit on a harness and lead, a box filled with straw from which a ferret's head pops up and a cat hiding under a blanket in a basket. There's a snake wrapped like a scarf around a little boy's neck. Maz unwinds it pretty quickly and asks Fifi to hold one end while the boy holds the other. Fifi immediately declines and the boy's father, his arms covered with tattoos, helps out instead.

Three dogs follow. Mrs Dyer is supervising a teenage girl with her Great Dane, which is completely out of control, diving among the spectators to help himself to a hotdog, much to everyone's amusement. There are two more girls – in their early teens, I'd guess – with a scruffy black crossbred with a grey muzzle and grey rings around his eyes. A boy of about eighteen is bossing them around from the perimeter of the ring. I recognise him – he's called Adam and he's brother to the two girls. The third dog is Frosty, of course, and she's on her best behaviour, walking beside Poppy who's tripping over the lead in a red dress and sandals.

'How do you decide on which one is the best?' Emily continues. 'Is it the cutest or friendliest? Or the furriest or scaliest?'

216

'Poppy looks incredibly cute,' I say, as Frosty suddenly spots me in the crowd and diverts to come and see me, wagging her tail.

'This way, Frosty.' Poppy hauls on the lead with no effect whatsoever.

'Remember she's deaf. She can't hear you. Hold the lead a bit tighter. That's right. Go on Frosty.' I gesture at her to back off and she returns to the line of pets being shown off around the ring.

Emily looks at me, her face pink with maternal pride. 'If there was a prize for best-behaved child, Poppy would actually win it today.'

Maz and Fifi call the competitors into the middle of the ring in no particular order, and line them up before walking along the line where Maz, with a little interference from Fifi, strokes the pets, studies them and asks the handlers questions. I crane forwards to hear when she begins to interview Poppy.

'And what does Frosty have to eat?' she asks.

'She has dog food,' Poppy says, stroking Frosty at the same time.

'She's nervous,' Emily says.

'What do you think is so special about Frosty?'

'She's dead,' Poppy says matter-of-factly.

'Oh?' Fifi joins in. 'She looks very much alive to me.'

'She means deaf, don't you,' Maz says. 'Frosty can't hear a thing. She was a cruelty case.'

And I overhear someone in the crowd muttering that Frosty is bound to be the winner then, with a great back story like that.

'It's just like X Factor,' they grumble.

Emily winks at me and lifts Daisy, who's started to whinge, out of the pushchair. One side of her face is red and covered with beads of sweat from the heat.

'Oh, you're too hot, darling.' Emily adjusts Daisy's sunhat and removes her cardigan. 'I'm so sorry. I'm a terrible mother.'

'You're a great mum. I wish you wouldn't keep saying that.'

Fifi sends the pets off around the ring once more and, under Maz's direction, calls them back in reverse order from sixth to first place. Emily grips my arm as first the snake, then the cat, then the rabbit and the scruffy dog are called in, but not Frosty or the ferrets in the box. Mrs Dyer's Great Dane has been withdrawn – he had an attack of ring-shyness, I think it's called, and disappeared over the rope at the entrance with his handler and Mrs Dyer chasing off after him. Poppy marches round, appearing oblivious to the fact it's a competition, so when the ferrets are pulled into second place, she keeps walking even though Emily's shouting at her to attract her attention. Maz and Fifi have to ambush her and Frosty and direct them to the winner's podium, where they stand on top of the bale of straw, Poppy grinning and Frosty with her tongue hanging out.

'Hurray,' Emily cheers, making Daisy startle. 'Well done!'

I'm glowing, and not just because of the sun, when my sister puts her arm around me.

'We are two proud mothers, sis.'

Maz hands Poppy a red rosette and a silver trophy.

'I'd quite like a pink one.' Poppy's voice rings out loud and clear with an edge of complaint.

Emily groans. 'Poppy, please don't spoil it . . .'

'I think the red is best,' Fifi says quickly.

'I'm not keen on red.'

'But look how it matches your beautiful dress. Pink wouldn't do at all.'

Poppy looks down and smooths her skirt. Apparently satisfied with the match, she accepts the red rosette with good grace.

'Phew,' Emily says, as a photographer from the *Chronicle* enters the ring to take a photo. 'Crisis averted.'

'They are so cute,' I say, with a lump in my throat, as I watch Poppy attach the rosette to Frosty's collar. Frosty shakes herself and the rosette falls off. Poppy picks it up again and sticks it between her teeth for the lap of honour, like the showjumpers do in the main arena. Frosty looks sleek and shiny as she trots around with her, her ribs only just visible under her skin now. She is one very lucky dog.

Maz and Poppy bring Frosty back to us across the ring, as the crowd begins to disperse.

'Hi, Zara.' Maz does a double take when she sees my twin.

'This is my sister, Emily,' I say, introducing her.

'Oh, you're Murray's wife. Alex looks after your sheep.'

'That's right,' Emily says.

'I didn't put two and two together when I met you through Frosty,' Maz says. 'I've always been better at remembering animals than people, I'm afraid.'

'I don't envy you having to choose the best pet,' I say.

'It isn't easy.' She grimaces. 'I wanted our assistant to do this, but he planned his holiday deliberately for this week. Still, it's over now for another year and I can relax.' She pauses. 'Just one thing . . . It's always a touchy subject and I hope you don't mind me saying so, but you're going to have to be careful about the diet.'

'I am,' I say. 'I'm a member of a slimming club.'

'Not you, you idiot,' Emily chuckles. 'Maz is talking about the dog.'

'Oh yes, the dog. What's wrong with the dog?'

'She's beginning to lose her waist. It was good to feed her up, but now she's hit her target weight, you need to cut down on her food.'

'You'll have trouble persuading Gran not to feed her, Zara. She's always giving her titbits,' Emily says.

'I know, and she gives Frosty her breakfast, then forgets she's given it to her and gives her another one. I'll do my best, though. If I tell her it's for the sake of Frosty's health, Gran will come on board.'

'I'll see you later maybe,' Maz says. 'I need to relieve Alex of the childcare. He'll be on the bouncy castle with George or helping Seb and Lucie with the ponies.'

'Can I have a pet of my own, Mummy?' Poppy asks when Maz has gone.

'We'll see,' Emily responds.

'You always say that.' Poppy shows Daisy the rosette. Daisy grabs it and sucks on the ribbon. Poppy snatches it back, making Daisy cry.

'You can have one when you're old enough to look after it.' Emily rolls her eyes at me. 'Auntie Zara had to wait until she was a grown-up before she had a dog.'

'Everyone in my class at school has a pet,' Poppy argues. 'It's not fair.'

'I know, darling.'

'Why don't you give Frosty a drink for me?' I say, distracting Poppy, who pours the dog a drink from the container I've brought with me. I don't want her catching any germs!

'Where do you want to go next?' Emily asks as we prepare to move on.

'We could check on Gran's cake.'

'On the way to the shearing,' Emily adds.

'Will Lewis be there?'

She nods.

'Come on then.' Emily's right. I'm going to have to face him at some time. I might as well get it over and done with.

We take Frosty into the WI tent with us, where the judging of the cream teas has just finished and the Best Victoria Sponge competition is in full swing. Jennie from Jennie's Cakes is at the table, surrounded by eager WI members and an honorary man, who has entered the baking competition for the third year running. While Jennie, who's in her forties and wearing a straw hat, cream blouse and flowing floral skirt, looking very much the farmer's wife, gets to eat cake, I notice her elder son, Adam, pushing a pushchair back and forth, trying to soothe the baby sitting inside it. It must be eighteen months or more since I saw Jennie for her

221

postnatal visits at Uphill House, when she returned from giving birth to baby Reuben in hospital. She only just made it, having been on the verge of giving birth on a carnival float.

Reuben is Adam's half-brother and a late baby. Adam was not overly impressed at the time, but he seems to accept him now. Every so often, he leans down and tickles the baby's tummy – all he's wearing is a nappy – making him giggle.

I notice Rosie, too, the teen mum-to-be, dressed in the shortest of shorts and a vest top, her arms burned from the sun, with her mother, Michelle. Frances, the receptionist at Otter House vets, is also looking on, her brow furrowed and her fingers tight on her handbag.

'I thought this was supposed to be fun,' I whisper to Emily. 'Frances looks like she's about to be pushed off a cliff.'

'She gets really wound up about it,' Emily says. 'She's won every year since anyone can remember.'

'That one is Gran's,' I say, as Fifi slices a sliver of cake with a silver knife and places it on a doily for Jennie to taste.

'Mummy, I can't see,' Poppy says.

Emily struggles to lift her so she can have a look. 'Jennie has to eat an awful lot of cake. I wonder if she actually enjoys it any more.'

'I don't see how anyone could ever get bored with cake,' I observe as Jennie takes a mouthful of Gran's sponge. Does she like it? I watch with bated breath, looking for a sign to show she's impressed, but her eyebrows fly up, her nose wrinkles and the sinews of her neck jump out as she grimaces with disgust. Fifi offers her a tissue into which she discreetly spits it out.

'I'm sorry, I really want to like it, but that is unpleasant. There's salt in the mix. It's inedible.'

'So Rosemary's is out of the running,' Fifi says. 'It's such a shame when it looks so elegant. I thought Frances might lose her crown as Queen of the Victoria sponge this year.'

'It's unlike Gran to make a mistake – she's been baking for years.' Emily looks at me. 'She won't be able to stop laughing when she finds out what she's done. This will go down in family history.'

'She isn't going to find out,' I say quickly. 'We aren't going to tell her.'

'Why not? It's hysterical.'

'She'll be upset.'

'She'll be cross with herself at first, but you know what she's like. It doesn't take her long to find the funny side in most things.'

'Trust me. It really is better that she doesn't know.' I repeat one of her sayings for the second time recently. 'Out of sight, out of mind.'

My sister frowns. 'Is there something you aren't telling me? Is Gran all right?'

'She's been a little forgetful recently.'

'She's eighty – I think she's allowed the odd lapse of memory, or is it more than that, Zara?'

I'm spared the inquisition by a commotion coming from just inside the entrance of the marquee.

There are shouts of, 'She's fainted. Give her some

223

space. Is there a doctor in the tent?' and, 'What about the St John Ambulance?'

'Look after Frosty for me, Emily. Let me through – I'm medical.' I make my way through the silent crowd to find Rosie on the ground, cradled in her mum's arms. Her cheeks are flushed and clammy. I kneel beside her and check the pulse at her wrist. 'Rosie, it's me, Zara. Can you hear me?'

'What are you doing, young man? You can't just push in here like that.' Fifi's voice rings out from behind me as the chatter of voices begins to rise again. 'This has nothing to do with you.'

I glance up to see Adam, Jennie's son, forcing his way past Fifi and her handbag.

'I will have to call security,' Fifi threatens, by which I think she means one of the burly farmers.

'This has everything to do with me,' Adam argues. 'Rosie's pregnant.'

Everyone in the tent falls silent once more. It's so quiet you could hear a fly landing in the clotted cream.

'I can see that,' Fifi says. 'You might think I'm stupid, but I'm not blind. Please move away. Now!'

'No way. Rosie's pregnant and it's my baby!'

'Oh dear,' is Fifi's reaction, as Adam falls to his knees and reaches for Rosie's hand.

'What's wrong with her?' He bites his lip.

'She's fainted, that's all,' I reassure him. 'Come on, Rosie, wake up.'

'She doesn't want you here, Adam,' Michelle snaps. She sounds like she wants to hit him. 'After all the things you said about my daughter . . .'

'I didn't mean them,' he says hoarsely. 'You were pretty vile about me.'

'Which isn't surprising when you've ruined my daughter's life.'

'Let's concentrate on Rosie and the baby, shall we? This isn't the time or place for recriminations,' I interrupt. 'Rosie, are you okay with Adam being here?'

Please say yes, I think, aware from the tension in his body and the twitching of the muscle in his cheek of how much this means to him. It's sad when the prospect of a new baby is fraught with anxiety and accusation, and I wish that Michelle could see that life would actually be more straightforward with dad on board. 'Well?' I go on.

'Yes . . .' Rosie whispers, barely moving her lips.

'Thank you . . .' Adam says, his voice breaking. 'From now on I'm with you all the way, I promise.'

I glance towards Michelle, who shrugs in resignation.

'Right, let's sit you up, Rosie. Michelle, you stay where you are. Adam, come round to this side.'

'Zara, I had some bleeding this morning. It wasn't much, but . . .' Rosie murmurs as they sit her up.

'Why on earth didn't you say something, you silly girl?' Michelle interrupts.

'Because I don't want to think about losing it.' Rosie strokes her belly. 'It means everything to me.'

'I think it would be worth getting you to hospital for a scan to check on the baby,' I say. 'There's no need to panic.'

'That's good advice,' Fifi says, reminding me of

her presence. 'Keep calm and carry on. Move away, everyone.'

I suggest that Michelle fetches her car to drive her daughter to the hospital, because her condition doesn't warrant calling for an ambulance. Jennie appears with a glass of water for Rosie and an apology, it turns out, for Rosie's mother.

'We shouldn't have fallen out over this. It's wrong and I'm sorry if I said some hurtful things,' she says. 'I'm really very sorry, to you and Rosie, especially.'

'I said some terrible things too,' Michelle says eventually.

'You said you didn't want this baby,' Adam interrupts.

'I know, but now I've got used to the idea, I want it to be fit and healthy.' She lowers her voice. 'And to be loved.'

'By its mum and its dad,' Jennie adds for her. 'I know Rosie and Adam are no longer together, but that's no reason to deny him access to his baby. It isn't fair.'

'I've never said he can't see the baby,' Rosie interrupts. 'Mum, what have you been saying?'

'Nothing, apart from making it clear that we thought it was less upsetting all round if Adam had no contact,' Michelle says.

'For God's sake, Mum!' Rosie exclaims. 'Can't you stop interfering?'

'I'm sorry. I can see I was wrong, but I was trying to protect you.'

'What about the baby? It needs to know its dad.'

'Please don't upset yourself any more—'

'I'm not upsetting myself – you're upsetting me.'
Rosie looks close to tears.

'We'll talk about it later. Adam, would you like to come along with us to the hospital? I could do with you, in case she faints again.'

'I think she'll be fine.' I recheck her pulse as she sips some water. 'It looks like a touch of heatstroke to me.' Her pulse has settled to a slower rhythm and her skin has lost some of its clamminess. As for the baby, babies are pretty resilient, so fingers crossed.

'They've just announced the final of the shearing,' Emily says when Rosie is on her way to hospital. 'Come on, Zara. Hurry up.'

I walk with her, and Daisy who's in the buggy, and Poppy who refuses to relinquish Frosty. The greasy scent of chips and doughnuts combined with the thought of seeing Lewis again makes me feel slightly sick.

CHAPTER THIRTEEN

A Yard of Ale

Arriving at the shearing stand, which is rigged up with two stations supplied with machine clippers and a generator, I notice the pair of collies, Mick and Miley, lying in the shade of the platform at the bottom of the steps with their tongues lolling out. I follow the dogs' eyes to find their master, who is waiting with his arms folded across his chest, his muscles ripped. He's wearing a cap back to front, a torn vest and jeans. He's tanned and dirty, and any exposed skin is shining with sweat, a look that turns my stomach in the nicest possible way, even though I know it shouldn't. It's a visceral response and, for the sake of my sanity, I have to beat down the flicker of desire that reignites at the sight of him, because nothing has changed. If he didn't exactly lie to me, he was economical with the truth.

'He's in the final,' I say, trying not to sound too impressed. 'Wow.'

'Against Chris, Izzy's husband and champion shearer for many years,' Emily says.

'Murray didn't make it then,' I tease her.

'He's adjudicating. Look.'

Murray is talking to an old man with a flat cap and a shepherd's crook. Emily calls him over.

'How's it going, my lover?' he asks his wife.

'It's been an eventful show so far. I'll explain later.'

'Daddy,' Poppy says, 'look what I won.'

'What was that for, darling?'

'The best pet.' She shows off the red rosette.

'You're a pet?' Murray chuckles and Poppy bursts into giggles. 'I'm not a pet, Daddy. It was Frosty.'

'Come on, Pops. Come and help Daddy time the shearing.' Murray reaches down and sweeps her onto his shoulders. Poppy looks around from her vantage point and, suddenly overtaken by a wave of uncharacteristic shyness, wraps her arms around his forehead and hides her face in his curls.

'Zara.' I hear Lewis call my name and that's all it takes to make my heart beat faster and confirm what I already knew: that, like a shepherd watching his flock, I'm going to have to stand guard over my emotions to have any chance of peace of mind when he's around.

'Good luck!' I call back.

'This young upstart's going to need all the help he can get,' Chris says with a jovial smile on his weathered face. 'He's a beginner – he hasn't even got his own sheep.'

'I'll have more sheep than you can dream of one day,' Lewis banters.

229

'I'd be careful if I were you, Chris,' Murray says. 'I saw him in action last night and he's pretty quick. He can do one in less than a minute.'

'It's about stamina and skill as well as speed, though. Come on, Murray, what are you waiting for? Let's get this party started.'

'All in good time,' Murray says. 'Go and get yourselves ready, but wait until I give the order to start.'

I watch Lewis enter the pen at the rear of the platform, pick up one of the ewes and carry her to his station, striding along with ease, even though she must weigh all of ninety kilos.

'He's fitter than ever,' whispers Emily, who's perched on one of the steps giving Daisy a bottle. 'I'm putting my money on Lewis.'

Chris wipes one hand on the fleece as he and Lewis wait poised for Murray to start the competition with their sheep in front of them, caught between their legs so they're facing towards us.

'Three, two, one, go,' Murray says with a flourish, and they're off, the rays of the afternoon sun glancing off the clippers as Lewis shears the wool from the sheep's brisket, belly and front legs, before moving her so he can clear the hind leg and head of the tail. The fleece starts to fall away from the skin when he takes the ewe's head and swings his legs around her, moving the clippers along her neck to her chin.

I glance towards Chris. There's nothing between them. They're neck and neck, so to speak. People begin to cheer them on. I'm gripping my hands together, willing Lewis to win. He moves on to the second ewe and begins to advance on Chris, until the ewe starts to kick out and fidget, slowing him down again.

'Oh, that isn't fair,' I murmur.

'I expect she's ticklish,' Emily says as the ewe starts to quieten down. Lewis makes up lost time with the next one, overtaking Chris, and finally he finishes with ten seconds in hand to the applause of the crowd.

Chris is a gracious loser, stepping forwards to shake Lewis's hand.

Murray is smiling. 'You're beginning to show your age.'

'Maybe it's time to step aside and let the young ones win,' Chris says ruefully.

'I'll be back to defend my title next year. You can be sure of that.' Lewis jumps the rail down from the platform with one lithe movement and jogs up to me.

'Hello, Zara.' He smiles apprehensively. I don't know how to react, but Frosty has no inhibitions. She's all over him, squealing and barking with delight. He gives her a quick rub before turning back to me. 'What did you think?'

'That was sick,' I say, as in 'brilliant', like the spark in his eyes as he picks me up and hugs me.

'Hey, put me down.' I kick my legs and push against his arms. 'What are you doing?'

'Sweeping you off your feet, I hope . . .' He grins as he places me back on the ground. My knees are weak, my resolve like jelly. 'I'm young, free and single,' he whispers as he draws me away from the crowd and into the shadow of a giant combine harvester. 'I promise you that.'

'What about Jade?'

'We're finished.'

'I know – you said so. What I mean is, how can you be so cool about it? She must have been gutted.' I stare at him. Has he no heart?

'She wasn't all loved up. It wasn't like that. When I talked to her about how I felt about you, she admitted she'd been seeing someone else while I was away. Jade and I have hardly seen each other since before Christmas. I've been off working while, as I suspected, she's been otherwise engaged.' Lewis pauses. 'That makes her out to be the bad guy, but although I've won the shearing, I wouldn't win a prize for the best boyfriend in the world. I didn't look after her in the way I should have done. I didn't pay her enough attention.' He shrugs. 'I've been doing a lot of thinking while I've been milking cows and, ultimately, I've realised that Jade and I should never have got together.'

'So you make a habit of rushing into relationships that don't work out?'

'I wouldn't say that. I reckon you're allowed the odd mistake on the way to finding your soul-mate.' He bites his lip and steps closer. 'I've missed you.'

'I've missed you too, and not necessarily in a good way.' Lewis's face falls as I continue, 'I'm still furious with you.'

'I never meant to deceive or hurt you.' He takes my hand. 'I thought I was doing the honourable thing, but I got it wrong, badly wrong.' His grip on my fingers is chafing, but I like it. 'I thought that if I sorted things out with Jade, there'd be no need to bother you with it. I was taking the easy way out and it backfired . . . and I'm glad in a way because now it's all out in the open.'

I stare at him, watching the expression in his eyes flicker from hope to despair and back again. I watch the pulse throbbing at his throat, beating fast in time with mine. Can I forgive and forget? He moves towards me and touches his forehead to mine, just as he did when we were out training Frosty – before he went away; before everything went awry.

'Please, give me a chance to show you how grown-up I can be.'

'Go on, Zara,' I hear Emily call.

'Put the poor bugger out of his misery,' Murray joins in.

'He's a top bloke,' Chris says.

'Zara?' Lewis repeats, and the sound of his voice melts any remaining doubts away. Lewis made a mistake. We all make mistakes.

'Yes,' I say, 'yes, yes, yes.'

'Whoop-whoop!' Emily calls as Lewis kisses me.

'The winner gets the girl,' Chris jokes.

'Come on, everyone,' Murray cuts in. 'The beer tent beckons. Put her down – the winner has to drink a yard of ale to celebrate. It's tradition.'

'Are you coming with us, Zara?' Lewis says hesitantly. 'I won't drink more than a yard, I promise.'

'Of course I'm coming along, but what about the dogs?'

'Mick and Miley will stay with the sheep and I'll

pick them up on the way back. Poppy will look after Frosty, won't you, Poppy?'

Poppy gives Lewis a big smile and skips ahead with her dad, Frosty beside her on the lead. Lewis walks with me. I catch his scent of sheep, musk and oil.

'It's great to see you again,' he begins.

'It's good to see you too.' I smile to myself. I'm allowed to change my mind. As Gran would say, it's a woman's prerogative. I wonder briefly how she is, but then I find myself wanting to fill the silence between me and Lewis. I don't know what to say, so I start asking him questions about shearing, a topic I know very little about. 'That was an impressive . . .' What do you call it, I wonder, a shear? I settle for 'performance'.

'I've been practising.' Lewis shows me his hands. They are callused, cut and engrained with dirt. 'I could shear a sheep in my sleep.'

'I suppose you have to start all over again tomorrow.'

'That's what I'm here for.'

'I don't know how you do that without catching their skin. I've always wondered how you know where the wool ends and the sheep begins.'

'It's practice. The first few sheep I ever sheared at college were covered in plasters by the time I'd finished.'

'Really?' I say. 'Don't they stick to the wool?'

'I'm joking.' Lewis squeezes my hand.

'Since when have you been so interested in shearing?' Emily says, catching up with us, with Daisy's cross-country buggy bumping along across the grass.

'Go away, sis,' I tell her hotly as Lewis responds, 'It's second nature. You have to mind the ears and teats. I've seen someone take an ear off before. You have to be careful, but not too careful, if you know what I mean. When you faff around, you end up with extra cuts into the fleece and that makes the yarn no good if you want to go on to spin the wool.'

I know it's ridiculous, but I'm like a love-struck teenager, hanging on to his every word. Knowing he's beside me makes everything seem brighter, the candyfloss look pinker and fluffier, the fresh doughnuts smell sweeter, and the rainbow of sweets on the stalls appear more colourful, but for once I have no desire to eat them.

Lewis chuckles wryly as we reach the beer tent. 'So, now you're an expert on shearing, is there anything else you want to ask me about sheep? They're my specialist subject.' He raises one eyebrow and adds, 'We could do something else more interesting later, if you like—'

'Lewis,' Murray yells. 'Get yourself to the bar. This one's on me and Chris.'

'I'll see you later, Zara.' Lewis hesitates as if he's struggling to tear himself away. 'I mustn't let the side down.'

I watch him drink his yard of ale, egged on by the other farmers. Having spilled most of the beer down his front, he pulls off his vest, revealing a six-pack and a V of dark blond hair across his chest. He uses the vest to mop up before tucking it into the waistband of his jeans. Chris thumps him on the back and Murray half strangles him. Emily glances across to me and grins. Boys will be boys.

The celebrations continue at the family meal back at the farm. Mum and Dad call me to say they're giving Gran a lift so not to worry, and Rosie texts to let me know the baby is fine. Murray is pouring drinks while Emily cooks, and Poppy skips around the kitchen table with her rosette between her teeth. Frosty lies underneath, belly up and snoring lightly. I'm giving Daisy her bottle – at least, I'm trying to. Daisy is too occupied with staring at me and pulling the odd funny face to concentrate on drinking her milk. I touch the end of the teat to her mouth and the milk dribbles down her chin. When she's finished messing around, I hold her against my shoulder to wind her. She burps loudly and leans back, grabbing onto the silver chain I'm wearing around my neck and snapping it. I catch it, rolling it up and putting it discreetly into my pocket. It's a shame it's broken. I've had it for many years, but it isn't the end of the world.

'So where's my rosette?' Gran asks, greeting everyone as she comes in with Mum and Dad. She's wearing what she calls her glad rags – a white blouse, tartan skirt, tights and court shoes – and she brings a box of chocolates from the shop as her contribution to the evening.

'You can share mine,' Poppy offers.

'I'm sorry, Gran, but you didn't get one this year,' I say.

'Not for my cake? You did take it to the WI tent like I asked you to, Zara?' She looks at me, her expression a mixture of confusion and hurt. 'There was nothing wrong with that cake. It was the third one I made and it was perfect.'

'There was a lot of competition this year.' Against my effort to soften the blow, Emily goes on tactlessly, 'Jennie thought you'd put salt in instead of sugar.'

'Never!' Gran exclaims.

Emily opens the tin I brought back with me and leans down under the table to offer Frosty a sliver of cake. She turns her nose up.

'You see? Even the dog won't eat it.'

'That is sour grapes and sabotage,' Gran says. 'I knew I should have taken it to the show myself.'

'There's no way anyone could have tampered with it. Half of Talyton St George were in that marquee. There's no conspiracy.'

'Unless someone slipped indoors when I was baking . . .' Gran looks troubled. 'Frosty wouldn't have heard them, would she?'

'She would have seen them, though,' I insist, moving towards her. 'If I could I'd award you a rosette: first prize for being the best gran in the whole world.'

'You're always a winner to us.' Emily gives Gran a hug and glances at me over her shoulder, her forehead lined with concern. I shrug. I don't know what's going on. I wonder if I should have a word with Ben.

'Catch up later after the party?' Lewis says when he sits down at the table beside me, freshly showered and shaved, and slightly sunburned.

I know what he means – when there's no one else around. I can't wait for us to spend time alone together,

237

but I'm going to have to dream up a way of escaping discreetly from my family.

'Where's your necklace?' Lewis asks. 'You were wearing it earlier.'

'Oh, Daisy got hold of it – it snapped. I don't think it was designed to stand up to babies.'

'That's a shame. Do you want me to have a look at it, see if I can fix it?' he offers.

'No, don't worry, but thanks anyway.'

When the meal ends, Lewis thanks Emily and stands up.

'I hope you don't mind, but the dogs could do with a stroll.'

'Even though they've had a long day at the show?' Murray says.

'They're always up for a walk.' Lewis's cheeks grow flushed. 'Zara, do you want to bring Frosty along too?'

'I think I'll come along with you.' Murray makes to get up from the table.

'I don't think so,' Emily cuts in quickly. 'You, my darling, are in charge of the dishes.'

'I'd like some fresh air too,' Gran says with a wicked smile. She's on form, I think, the cake debacle apparently forgotten, but I notice she's been here all evening with the buttons on her blouse fastened on the wrong holes.

'You and Poppy can take a torch and go and pull some beetroot from the garden,' Emily says. 'I want some for a salad tomorrow.'

'At last,' Lewis says when we're walking across the fields in the darkness, our way lit up by his headlamp torch, and almost alone, apart from the three dogs and a pair of owls calling to each other, and the rustle of a rabbit or a fox from the hedge.

'I know. I'm sorry about my family.'

'Why? I love them. They're so chilled compared with mine.'

'You and Connor seem pretty relaxed.'

'That's because we're away from home. My dad's very strict. He once threatened to kick Connor out of the house when he found a girl in his room. He packed his bags for him and left them at the front door, but Mum persuaded him to give Connor a second chance.' We walk on a few paces before Lewis begins talking again. 'This thing about the drinking. We ought to discuss it.'

'Now? Do we have to?' I don't want anything to spoil the evening.

'It would be good to clear the air. I don't want anything else, no more misunderstandings and issues to come between us. I'm sorry for getting wasted. I didn't realise . . .'

'Realise what?'

'Emily told me about your granddad.'

'I see. He was a lovely man . . .' I stifle a memory of Granddad taking me and Emily swimming at the pool before the leisure centre was rebuilt. 'His liver packed up. That's what killed him. He might still be alive if it hadn't been for his addiction. He and Gran were planning their retirement when he died. I was sad – and angry at him, even though I don't think he could help it – but it was so much worse for Gran. I admire her for staying strong and getting through it. It's why she's held on to the shop for so long: to give her something to do and keep his memory alive.'

'Knowing about your grandfather puts a different perspective on the situation. You must think I'm very insensitive.'

'You aren't. It's me overreacting.'

'Or a bit of both.' I can hear the smile in his voice. 'I enjoy having a few drinks with Connor and the lads – although I don't always feel the same on the morning after.'

'And I don't drink because I've seen the consequences of heavy drinking, not just my grandfather, but as a midwife. Alcohol can have a devastating effect on babies and families. OMG, you must think I'm very boring.'

'Not at all,' he says. 'I find you . . . fascinating.'

'I can promise you I'll never lecture you on your choices. I just don't want to be there on your lads' nights out.'

'I've got it.' Lewis takes my hand and I link my fingers through his. He stops when we're under the spreading branches of one of the oak trees that grows from the hedgerow and pulls me close. I look up into his eyes, or rather straight into the searing light of the torch. I reach up and click it so it's aiming skywards.

'I'm sorry,' he chuckles. 'I meant to dazzle you with my witty banter, not my headlamp.' He gazes at me with a shy hunger in his eyes. I tilt my head to kiss his mouth, and he's holding me, his hands firmly on my back then straying down to my buttocks. I can hardly breathe, giddy with happiness and desire until . . .

'Is that your knee?' I ask, pulling away slightly.

'I think it's another part of my body,' he says with a wicked smile.

'No, there's something nudging my leg.' I glance down. 'Oh, it's Frosty.' She's butting her nose in between our shins in what appears to be an attempt to push us apart.

'Your command for "no" isn't going to be any use in the dark, is it?' Lewis observes. 'Shall we go back to the house? I can show you around the annexe, although, I warn you, I haven't put anything away yet.'

'I'm sorry,' I sigh. 'I'd love to stay longer, but Gran will be expecting me to take her home.' I force a smile, hoping he understands. 'It's past her bedtime.'

'Another time soon then?'

'Soon,' I echo.

When we return hand in hand to the farmyard, Lewis whistles for Mick and Miley who come flying out of the shadows. Miley skims past Frosty, growling as she passes. Frosty snaps back, but Miley's too quick for her.

'What was that about?' I exclaim, checking Frosty over.

'Miley's jealous. It's going to take her a while to get used to the idea that you and Frosty are in my life.'

'Not too long, I hope,' I say with a chuckle. 'Since when does a dog decide whom their owner can or can't see?'

'Miley's the possessive type. If she was a person,

she'd probably be the deranged-stalker type. Don't worry about it.' Smiling, Lewis kisses me once more. 'I'll be shearing all day tomorrow and Monday. How about Tuesday evening?'

'That's perfect.' I can't wait. For the first time in a while, I feel optimistic about the future. Who knows where this is going, but I'm enjoying the ride.

CHAPTER FOURTEEN

Home Alone

On Monday morning, I find Claire in the nurse's room at the surgery, where she's sorting out some equipment, including a kidney dish, a bottle of surgical spirit and some blood tubes, to take on a home visit to one of her elderly patients.

For once, the hot topic of conversation is not the wedding, but my love life.

'How was your day at the Country Show? What was it like seeing Lewis again?'

'He's asked me out.' My face aches from smiling. 'We're going on a date.'

'That's brilliant.' Claire's eyes shine, reflecting my happiness. 'Don't tell me. You're already thinking about following me and Kev up the aisle.'

I laugh. She's winding me up.

'I'm planning to take it slowly, one date at a time, not

243

rush into things like I did with Paul,' but I know as I say it, and think of Lewis, that it's going to be close to impossible because I'm already head over heels in love with him.

'So where's he taking you?' Claire asks.

'A sheepdog trial – you know, like *One Man and His Dog*.'

'Never heard of it,' Claire snorts.

'Gran told me about it. It was on the television regularly some years ago and, according to her, it was quite exciting and the highlight of her week. It's a competition to see who can get their dogs to move some sheep around a field in the fastest time.'

Claire's eyes shoot up towards her fringe.

'Are you taking Frosty?'

'No, she wouldn't have a clue, and I don't want her to distract Lewis's dogs.'

'It sounds like the world's worst date to me.'

'Lewis is really keen to introduce me to something different. I think it'll be fun. And anyway, Claire, I don't care where we go. I'm looking forward to spending time with him . . .'

'And his dogs and a load of sheep,' Claire finishes for me. 'It's hardly romantic, is it?'

'It is,' I insist. 'It's outdoors up at East Hill . . .'

'The wind will cause havoc with your hair – and how will you dress to look sexy and alluring?'

'I'm not going to go overboard. I want him to see the real me.'

'So soon? Are you sure?'

'Yes, and I want to see the real Lewis.'

'I'd be pretty miffed if Kev asked me to an event like that for a date.'

'I'm really looking forward to it. It's hard to find a time when we're both free, and I'd rather compromise and go out somewhere than be stuck on the farm, riding on the back of a tractor, digging ditches and pressure-hosing the sheep shed, like Emily used to when she was dating Murray.'

'I suppose so.' Claire smiles. 'Kev paid for a taxi, dinner and champagne, and bought me chocolates on our first date. Each to their own . . .'

I keep quiet. I get the impression Lewis is perpetually short of cash. I don't want to embarrass him and I certainly don't expect to be spoiled with material goods like Claire.

'I don't care where we go, as long as we can talk.'

'And snog,' Claire chuckles. 'How far would you go on a first date? Would you go all the way?'

'None of your business.'

'We didn't do it for ages. It took a long time for Kev to prove he was the man for me.'

I don't want to talk about the fact that Lewis and I have already slept together, so I return to the safer topic of my outfit. 'I've ordered a pair of cropped trousers online.'

'You've always maintained that crops didn't suit you.'

'They look great now I've lost weight, actually.'

'Do you think it would work out cheaper for me to keep a dog than pay a subscription to fat club?'

'I doubt it very much.' I'm thinking of the money I've

spent replacing the things Frosty has destroyed so far, and the vet's bills for her vaccinations and worming. 'And you really shouldn't take on a dog unless you've thought about it first.'

'Like you did, you mean?'

'That's right,' I say, grinning at the memory of how I acquired Frosty without any forethought at all. 'I wouldn't change it now, though, not for anything.'

'Kev and I might get a puppy after the honeymoon.'

'So many couples I meet have done that. If I were you, I'd go straight for the baby and miss out the dog.'

'You're probably right, except that we're planning to give ourselves at least a year to enjoy married life before we embark on trying for a family.'

I smile ruefully. I expect Claire's written the dates in her five-year diary: conceive baby, give birth to baby, start programme to return to pre-baby weight . . .

I'd bet that Rosie, my teen mum, who's due to see me this morning, wishes she'd planned her baby for some way into the future.

'Hello. How are you?' I close the door behind her as she joins me half an hour later. She has a neat bump beneath a short, skater-style dress.

'I'm good, thanks. A lot better than when I last saw you.'

'Thanks for letting me know how it went at the hospital.'

'It's me who should be thanking you for what you did.'

'I didn't do anything.'

'You got Mum and Adam talking to each other.' Rosie smiles. 'Anyway, everything's fine. We got to see the baby on the scan and I couldn't believe how much it's grown. Adam was made up.'

'I'm glad. Have you had any more bleeding, or anything else that worries you?'

'No, it's cool. Everything's cool.'

'How were the exams? Did you get to them all?'

'I did.' She grimaces. 'I'm waiting for the results now. I just hope they're good enough for me to do what I want at uni.'

'Which is?'

'Physiotherapy. I'm going to take a year out, then apply – at least, that's the plan, although –' she looks down at her stomach – 'the best-laid plans, and all that. Mum wanted me to have a career behind me, but I've told her I'll just have to have the baby first and the career second.'

'Your mum isn't here today?'

'I've come straight from work.' Rosie smiles. 'It's nice to have a break from serving tea and cake. I work at Nettlebed Farm.'

'I've never actually been there.'

'It's great if you're a little kid who likes to stroke the animals.'

'How many hours are you doing?'

'Five days a week.'

'How are you managing?' I ask.

'I do get very tired sometimes, but don't tell me to stop. I need the money to buy things for the baby. Adam's working too.'

'I don't like to sound as though I'm prying, Rosie, but where are you living at the moment?'

'With my parents. Dad has kind of come to terms with the fact I'm having a baby. In fact, I think he's quite excited about it. He took me out to test prams and buggies, which was really embarrassing because everyone thought he was the baby's dad.' She pauses. 'It's Mum who's the one who's most upset right now. She keeps saying she wishes she could have the baby for me, but I've told her I'm going to bring the baby up myself.'

I hope she isn't going to try to take over, I think. I've seen it before.

'What about Adam? What part is he going to play after the baby is born?'

Rosie's eyes glisten with tears.

'I'm sorry. You don't have to talk about it. It's just that you do have to think about who you want at the birth, because it's going to come up on us quicker than you expect.'

'Oh, he'll be at the birth,' Rosie says. I hand her a tissue. 'He's going to step up and be a dad. Adam has promised he'll be there for the baby. He'll be able to visit whenever he wants to and, when the baby's old enough, he's going to have him, or her, overnight at his mum's house . . . He's going to pay what he can, too, towards nappies and clothes.' Rosie's voice trails off. The subject is closed, but I feel very sorry for her because it's clear she still has feelings for him.

'Have you any worries, any questions you'd like to ask me? You know,' I go on when Rosie remains silent, 'it's okay to ask for advice. Remember that. It doesn't make you a bad mum. It's far better to talk to someone – me, Dr Mackie or Dr Nicci – than to sit and worry on your own.'

'Thanks, Zara. I do talk to Adam's mum quite a lot – she's great. She's given me some bits and pieces she had for her baby, Reuben.'

'That's good.' I'm glad Rosie has some support. It's going to be tough for her being a single mum. 'Have you anything to ask about labour, how you'll know when it starts, anything like that?'

Rosie shakes her head.

'You have my number and you know where to find me, anytime. Let's go and see Janet to make you another appointment, unless you'd like me to visit you at home?'

'I'd rather not. I don't like talking in front of my parents. Mum's always there, listening in and telling me what to do.'

'You wait – you'll soon find out that mums really do know best. You'll be exactly the same when your baby has a baby.' I frown. 'If that makes sense . . .'

As soon as Rosie has left the surgery, Janet catches me at reception.

'There's a call from one of your mums, Tessa. She wants to see you ASAP. She doesn't want to come to the surgery, though, and I didn't push it – she sounded very upset.'

'I'll go and see her after my appointments this morning. Can you call her back and let her know?'

'Of course.'

I know what it's about – I've been trying to get hold of her. Tessa had the anomaly, or twenty-week scan two days ago and saw the consultant yesterday.

I meet her at the Sanctuary where she's outside the kennel block, dressed in maternity leggings and an old sweatshirt, creating some construction of timber and chicken wire.

'Hi,' I say.

'Hi,' she says, looking up. Her fingers are raw and bleeding and her eyes are red-rimmed, as if she's done a lot of crying. 'A fox got hold of three of our rabbits last night and ripped them to shreds. I'm making repairs, but it isn't going well.'

I'm sorry for the rabbits, but the loss seems insignificant in the scheme of things, when I'm far more concerned for Tessa.

'Would you like to come indoors?' She drops her hammer and staples, abandoning them on the ground.

'That's a good idea. I'll make us some tea if you show me where everything is.' I follow her to the bungalow and indoors to a tiny kitchen, where she flicks the switch on the kettle and rinses two mugs in the sink. I can smell a faint scent of dog and baby bird overlain by fresh paint.

'How's Frosty?' Tessa always asks after her.

'She's fine, thanks.'

'Still being naughty?'

'She wouldn't be Frosty if she wasn't. She's such a handful.' Tessa smiles a small smile. 'More importantly though,' I continue, 'how are you?'

'I don't know, to be honest. I had my scan . . .'

'I know . . .'

'It isn't good news,' she says, breaking down. 'There's something wrong with the baby's heart. It hasn't formed properly.'

'Come and sit down.' I guide her to the sitting room. 'The tea can wait.'

There are pictures on the walls: photos of Jack and Tessa's wedding, her dad dressed as a pantomime dame, and an oil painting of a dog, a roan-coloured cocker spaniel with a sad, grey face. The name 'Tia' and a date in gold letters are etched on the frame.

There's a real dog, a live one, on the sofa.

'Buster, get down,' Tessa says wearily, and I can see, like Frosty, that Buster has no intention of taking any notice of his owner's wishes. He wags his tail and smiles, his big jaws wide open.

I hesitate. He's one scary-looking dog, a bull-terrier type, all black apart from a splash of white on his chest. His teeth are enormous.

'It's all right. He won't hurt you. I can lock him out if you're worried, though.'

'There's no need. There was a time when I wouldn't have been able to walk into the room, knowing a dog was in there, but Frosty's helped me overcome the worst of my fears. I'll be fine.'

Tessa sits down beside Buster, who rests his head on her lap. I take the armchair opposite. There is a tank containing a patterned snake on the bookshelf, and paint pots and paintbrushes in coffee jars on a table in the corner of the room, evidence of a job half done.

'Jack's been doing some decorating before the baby

251

comes . . .' Tessa stops abruptly, lowers her eyes and strokes the dog before resuming. 'Thanks for coming to see me, Zara. I could do with someone to talk to. I've tried to speak to Jack, but he was out late last night, walking the dog, and I haven't seen him since early this morning. He's avoiding the situation, whereas I tend to confront things head on.'

'Give him time,' I say. 'It must have been a shock to him too.'

'I understand that, but I don't think I'll ever forgive him for disappearing and leaving me to deal with this alone.' Tessa's fingers clench around Buster's collar. 'If he walked in through that door right now, I think I could kill him, and don't go telling me that people react in different ways and all that. He's my husband. He bloody well should be here at a time like this – otherwise, what's the point of being married?'

I can empathise with her. I nod and let her continue.

'I feel as if Jack blames me. Could it be my fault, something I've done? I had a few drinks before I knew I was pregnant.'

'Tessa, it's nothing you've done or not done. It's one of those things.'

'Poor baby, it's so unfair. We've seen the consultant, who's gone through some of the options, but it was all so sudden, I couldn't think straight and I didn't ask all the questions I wanted to. I suppose I'll have the chance to ask them when we see the specialist next week.'

'A paediatric cardiologist?'

She nods. 'They're going to do a special scan of the

baby's heart to see what can be done, if anything, either before or after he's born.'

There are no words that can adequately express how sorry I am, and I know from experience there are many questions that will remain unanswered.

'He – it's a boy. Jack wants me to have an abortion.'

'And?'

'I don't. I can't. What if I did get rid of him and the baby turned out to be . . . what's the word?'

'Viable,' I contribute.

'Thank you. I couldn't have that on my conscience. And there is a chance he'll be all right and able to live a full and normal life, play football on the Green with his dad and go to school and college.' Tessa's hands are shaking as she blows her nose into a crumpled tissue. 'Oh, I can't concentrate on anything at the moment. What if Jack's right? What if the baby's born dead or dies just after birth? What if he survives but he's brain damaged and can't ever walk and talk? Jack says it isn't fair to bring a child into the world when you know it will be in pain, but I'd care for him and make sure he was comfortable. I'd do anything. But Jack is being so selfish, putting himself and our lifestyle first. He has no . . . feelings.'

'You don't believe that. Jack's a caring person. He's scared too, and grieving, and it must be killing him to see you like this. I can speak to him if you think it would help.'

'I'd rather you didn't. I don't want him to know I've talked to you. He doesn't know you're here, but I had to call you because I need to get my head straight.'

'There are organisations, people who can help you talk things through.'

'What would you do if it was your baby, Zara? You have to help me here.'

'You know that's an impossible question to answer. I can run through the facts, the best- and worst-case scenarios, but I can't decide for you. All I can do is support you and Jack.'

'I'd feel so guilty if I decided not to keep going with the pregnancy.'

'If you did it for the right reasons, the right reasons for you personally, no one will judge you for that.'

'My dad would. He's an old softie, like me,' Tessa says bluntly. 'Please can you check the baby's heart's still beating? I haven't felt him move yet today.'

I set up the Doppler, wanting to reassure Tessa that her baby is okay for now and that she has plenty of time to make her decision.

'There we go,' I say, smiling as I find the heart with the probe, bumping along happily between 130 and 140 beats per minute.

'He likes music,' Tessa says. 'He always squirms when Rihanna comes on the radio and falls asleep to Ellie Goulding, so he must be able to hear or feel something, mustn't he?'

I've learned to trust a mum's instincts. They are almost always right.

'Let's see what the specialist says next week,' I suggest. 'In the meantime, if you have any concerns or you just want to talk, you know where I am. You're welcome to contact me day or night.' I reach out and touch her shoulder. 'Take care of yourself, won't you?'

'I'll try,' she says wanly.

'Don't get up. I'll see myself out.' I leave Tessa sitting with her arms around Buster's neck and her chin resting on the top of his head. How I wish things could be different.

The sheepdog trial isn't quite as Gran described it. There are a few whiskery old farmers in their tweeds and flat caps, but there are also plenty of younger competitors and spectators, and dogs. I've never seen so many collie-types in one place.

Lewis parks the pick-up and lets Mick and Miley out of the back while I survey the scene, the bowed trees and the sweep of gorse and heather falling towards the glittering sea. There's a burger van, ice-cream vendor and several caravans with awnings where families are drinking tea and coffee.

'What do you think?' Lewis asks, as he opens the door for me.

I gaze at him, hoping the answer is in my eyes. All I want to do is kiss him, but it isn't exactly private. He's wearing blue jeans, a T-shirt and a red cap turned back to front. A silver whistle hangs from his neck. He holds his crook in one hand and a rolled-up blanket under his arm. The dogs are at his heels, whining and trembling with excitement.

'They love it.' Lewis grins. 'Oh god, Zara. I hope I haven't made a mistake, dragging you out here and expecting you to enjoy hanging around in a field all day.' He touches my arm.

'Don't be silly. I can't wait to see what it's all about. And –' I lean up and whisper in his ear – 'I want to spend time with you, which is difficult when we're both so busy.'

'Perhaps I should have cancelled my entry and taken you out somewhere else.'

'I don't care where we go, as long as we have some fun together.'

'And what kind of fun might that be?'

'You know very well.'

'I hope Mick behaves himself. Sometimes he can get distracted.' Lewis pauses, a twinkle in his eye as he looks me up and down. 'A bit like me, really. Are you going to give me a good luck kiss?' he adds as I slide out of the passenger seat onto the peaty ground.

'Oh yes. Most definitely,' I say, kissing him on the lips.

In spite of Claire's gloomy prediction that it will rain, the sun comes out from behind the clouds and Lewis and I sit on a blanket on the wiry grass to watch the first few competitors, so that he can explain the intricacies of working with a pair of dogs before his turn comes. I get the gist of a couple of technical terms, but can't get to grips with the scoring.

'All you need to know is that you drop points for running the sheep too fast so they panic and miss the gates on the way back down the hill, for losing sheep en route, for failing to shed them properly . . .' Lewis waves his hand 'Don't worry about that one. It's a technical term.'

'I can't believe everyone's taking it so seriously.'

'It's very competitive, much like shearing.'

'I didn't realise you could have so much fun with sheep.'

Lewis chuckles and asks me again what I think.

'It's better than watching cricket,' I say, as I observe two dogs circling the sheep at the top of the hill and sending them down the course, backing off and coming in again to the sound of their master's whistle.

'I should hope so. Cricket's really dull.'

'I quite like watching cricket.'

'Oh, I see.' Lewis hesitates. 'I thought you were winding me up.'

His comment reminds me that it's very early days for our relationship, even though we've been intimate, and I really don't know him very well.

'I'm going for a quick warm-up to remind Mick to listen to me,' he goes on, making to stand up.

'Just a mo,' I say as he's on his hands and knees. 'Don't you want another kiss for luck?'

'Let's try it and see if it works,' he says, kissing me before he gets up.

'Good luck, Lewis.'

He reaches for his crook, checks he has his whistle and calls Mick and Miley to attention before walking away down towards the start of the course, where he introduces himself to the judges, one of the whiskery gentlemen and a woman of about my age, dressed in leather boots, jeans and a waistcoat. She smiles and tips her head and I wonder if she's flirting with him, but I don't worry because I'm with him now. Lewis's hair gleams in the sunshine, reminding me of the dark days when everything triggered memories of Paul and I didn't think I'd ever be happy again.

The sheep are penned at the top of the hill where they are released to graze in readiness for Lewis to send the two dogs on the outrun (I have learned something). Mick runs up to the left and Miley to the right to meet and pick up the sheep. Miley gets there first and Lewis has to whistle to drop her to let Mick catch up before the dogs work together sending the sheep steadily down the slope between the first set of gates to the shedding ring, a circle of mown grass, where Lewis keeps Mick standing still while using Miley to separate the sheep into two groups. Mick is impatient, sneaking forwards, but Lewis spots him and gestures to him to keep back.

'Lie down!' he growls at him. 'Mick, lie down!'

He drops just in time to avoid heading the sheep – which are back together as a small flock – off in the wrong direction. Lewis whistles and the dogs move the sheep on down the hill through the next set of gates and towards the pen. No mistakes as far as I can tell. I touch my chest, my heart hammering against my fingertips, as the dogs drop to their bellies once more and Lewis, holding the rope on the gate and tapping the ground with the end of his crook, guides the last sheep into the pen and closes the gate behind it, slipping the rope over the post. He's done it. I clap my hands and the dogs leap up at their master, competing with each other for the most praise.

Lewis strolls back with the dogs at his heels, their ears pricked and their tongues almost touching the ground.

I stand up. 'How good was that!' I say, hedging my bets because I really haven't a clue.

'It wasn't bad,' Lewis says. 'At least Mick didn't send the sheep off to the other side of the county like he did in the last one we entered, and Miley didn't go on strike like she did in the one before that.'

'You're making Frosty sound like the paragon of canine virtue. I was under the impression your dogs were perfectly trained.'

'Sometimes the training flies out of the window when they're out and about – the excitement of the competition goes to their heads – Mick's, anyway. I fancy a burger. How about you?'

It's one of the best dates I've ever been on. We eat greasy burgers with onions and ketchup, drink hot tea and cuddle up to admire the skills and teamwork of the shepherds and their dogs. Lewis comes second in his class and we take Mick and Miley back to the farm before going on to the pub. On the way back home, we hang out for a long while, talking and kissing in the pick-up before Lewis drops me off outside the shop.

'I'd like to see you again,' Lewis says quietly. 'Soon . . .'

'I'd like to see you too.'

'I'll call you.'

'Thank you for today. I really enjoyed it.' I catch hold of his hand. 'One thing, though . . .'

'Yes? What is it?' he says, a shadow of anxiety crossing his eyes.

'Just promise me you'll never turn up in tweeds with a flat cap and whiskers. It isn't a good look.'

259

He chuckles. 'I promise.'

'Goodnight.' I lean up and kiss him.

'Goodnight, Zara.'

I watch him go, torn between the sensation of wanting to part in order to have space to mull over the day and revisit every look, every touch, every kiss, and the feeling of not wanting to spend a moment apart. I let Frosty out without disturbing Gran, but she doesn't show the same consideration to me the following morning when she turns up in my room with tea and biscuits and perches on the end of my bed with the dog.

'What time did you roll in last night? You sounded like a herd of elephants.'

'I'm sorry. I tried to be quiet.' When I came back through the hall with Frosty, the cuckoo clock sounded once and I added ten more to take it to eleven. 'It wasn't late. I was home an hour before midnight.'

'You might think I'm old and losing my marbles, but you can't pull the wool over my eyes. You make a pretty useless cuckoo.' She pats my knee. 'Never mind, Zara. Love makes you a bit cuckoo at first.'

As it turns out, love makes the dogs behave quite oddly too. The next time, Lewis and I meet at the farm and walk through the fields. At first I have Frosty on the lead, but Lewis suggests I let her off to run with Mick and Miley. Mick and Frosty play in the long grass, rolling each other over, but the way Miley rounds them up like sheep, her head low to the ground and her lips drawn back as if she's hunting, makes me feel uneasy.

'You see, they're going to be all right.' Lewis squeezes

my hand affectionately as I look up at him, aching with lust and adoration. I slide my arm around his back and slip my fingers through the belt-loops of his jeans.

'We could go back to my place.' Lewis grins and bumps his hip against mine.

'This minute?'

'Why not?' He rests his hand on the curve of my waist and I find I can't think of any reason at all, so we head back, Lewis whistling for his dogs.

'Look at Mick,' I say. Whenever Lewis whistles, Mick brings Frosty back with him, chasing across the fields, as if he's acting as her ears. 'Miley's being left out, though. It isn't fair.'

'She's a bit of a loner. I got Mick from a farm where I was doing some work, but Miley came from a puppy farm. She was the last of the litter, and kept with her mum in a filthy old shed. I took her mum too and rehomed her to a friend of mine. Miley tolerates Mick, but doesn't interact with him, which is why he's so pleased to have someone to play with.'

I try to make it up to Miley but, like me, she only has eyes for Lewis.

CHAPTER FIFTEEN

One More Push

My mobile rings when I'm having a quick coffee in the office with Kelly one morning.

'It's Lewis,' I say, taking the call.

'You just had to point that out, didn't you?' Kelly says, grinning. 'Go on. Talk to lover boy.'

I pick up a pen and start doodling on a copy of *Midwifery News* as he invites me over to the farm after work tonight.

'I'll cook dinner,' he offers.

'I didn't have you down as a chef,' I smile. 'What's on the menu? Beans on toast?'

'I'm not saying. It's a surprise. Just bring yourself – and Frosty, of course.'

'I can leave her with Gran.'

'Because of Miley, you mean? I think we're going to have to let them get used to each other. If we keep them apart, they'll never learn to get along. We could take them out before dinner.'

'And after that . . .?' I glance across to Kelly, who's sticking her fingers down her throat.

'Please Zara, I'm married, we don't do that kind of thing any more.'

'Who's that?' Lewis asks.

'It's Kelly messing around.'

'Don't you two have anything better to do?'

'We have actually. I've got an antenatal class and Kelly has three visits. I'd love to come for dinner. I'll see you later, about seven.'

'This sounds like the start of something big,' Kelly observes.

'We're just getting to know each other and taking it slowly.'

'If you say so.' She doesn't believe me, I can tell, and of course she's right not to.

I'm happy to see that the mums-to-be start chatting and making friends as soon as they arrive in the meeting room where we run the antenatal classes. I catch sight of Rosie first of all.

'Hi, Zara,' she says, helping me get some chairs out.

'How are you today?' I ask.

'Mum took me to the hospital yesterday because I thought there was something wrong with the baby.' She smiles ruefully. 'It turns out it was trapped wind. It's so embarrassing.'

'Don't worry about it,' says one of the other mums-to-be. Gemma is twenty-eight and works in the baker's in Talyton St George. She freely admits that she eats far too many cakes, and when I first met her I assumed she was pregnant when she wasn't. Today she's wearing a long white summer maternity dress, which reminds me of the WI tent at the Country Show. 'You weren't to know. You're lucky, Zara,' she adds, turning to me. 'When you have your own children, you'll be an expert.'

I don't say anything. I just smile.

'Hey, what are your tips for bringing on labour?' asks Millie, the oldest person in the group at thirty-seven. She swallows from a bottle of antacid. She says it's for her reflux, but I can't help wondering if it's a psychological prop because she drinks it like water.

'There's raspberry leaf tea,' I say. 'Some women say that helps.'

'I've tried the curry – but that hasn't worked,' Gemma says.

'My cousin says sex is a good way of bringing on labour,' Millie joins in.

'No way,' Gemma giggles. 'Sex is what got me here in the first place.'

'I'm glad to see you're keeping your sense of humour,' I say, 'but can we get on now? I'm going to talk about the physical process of labour today and tips for keeping calm and focused.'

'I've already thought that one through,' Gemma says. 'I'm sending Dave off to the pub for the duration.'

'Surely you want him with you at the birth?' Millie exclaims. 'I want my husband there to support me and guide me through.'

'Watch you suffer, you mean?' Gemma says brightly.

I look towards Rosie, who's flinching.

'There's no need for anyone to suffer,' I say. 'We'll go through methods of pain relief next week.'

'My sister says that you can have all the pain relief available and it still bloody hurts,' Gemma says.

'A little discomfort is a natural part of the journey, soon forgotten once the baby arrives.' I'm not sure anyone in this group believes me. They've been watching too many TV programmes about midwives and labour, I reckon. Soon antenatal classes will be superfluous.

When we've all sat down in a circle to begin the class, I notice how Rosie is very quiet, stroking her bump and gazing out of the window. Now and again, she checks her mobile and types a text, presumably to keep in touch with her friends. I don't comment – she isn't being rude. She's a teenage girl trying to keep everything normal when it's anything but, which is what I do with Gran. Everything's normal, even when I return home briefly the same evening to find the milk in the oven and Norris in a strop over being given dog food instead of cat. When I take his bowl to give to Frosty, and offer him a saucer of cat biscuits, he lashes out at me.

'Don't blame me when it wasn't my fault,' I tell Norris as I watch the bobbles of blood well up along my arm. 'You really shouldn't bite – or scratch – the hand that feeds you.'

Having sorted out the mix-ups, I change and head to the farm with Frosty – I still find it strange going straight to the annexe to see Lewis, instead of calling on my sister.

Lewis's accommodation is in an extension to the main house; it is built from local red brick with a tiled roof and stable doors front and rear. As soon as Frosty and I approach, Mick and Miley come flying out barking, sending Frosty's hackles up.

'I'm here,' I call to Lewis, who appears in the doorway with a towel wrapped around his middle and an electric razor in his hand.

'I kind of guessed. You've caught me out.'

'I couldn't wait to see you,' I say, flushing at the sight of him. It is a very small towel.

'Come on in.' Lewis closes the door behind me and the dogs, and Mick and Miley trot into the kitchen, their claws pattering on the vinyl floor, while Frosty makes a beeline for the sofa bed in the living room.

'Frosty, off,' I say, gesticulating at her to get down. 'I'm sorry, Lewis. We're working on that one,' I go on when she ignores my command and settles down on the duvet, digging it up to make a nest in which she curls up with her nose resting on her tail.

'She isn't allowed up on the furniture at your gran's, is she?' Lewis pulls the duvet from underneath her and Frosty jumps down, her brow crinkled, as if to say, what did you do that for? She sits down and gazes up at Lewis, thumping her tail against the floor, and making him laugh. 'I think she's shown you up, Zara. Don't tell me she sleeps on your bed!'

'Occasionally, she jumps up and lies across my feet. I can't stop her.'

'You could shut her out of the bedroom,' Lewis says, amused.

'She gets upset and scratches the door. I don't want to hurt her feelings. It's the way she looks at you with those soft brown eyes . . .'

'I'd never have imagined you'd end up like one of those mad dog people, like Wendy,' Lewis says. 'When are you going to buy the scarf and the tweed skirt?'

'Maybe I already have,' I tease.

'Very funny,' he says. 'I'll get dressed then.' He looks me up and down, his appetite clearly not for food. 'Unless, you're offering yourself up as a starter,' he begins.

I hesitate. 'I'm sorely tempted, but shouldn't we save it for later in case Poppy decides to knock on the door?'

'I suppose we should get the dogs out before it gets dark, too.' Lewis smiles ruefully, grabbing some clothes from a box under the sofa bed and getting dressed. 'You aren't peeking, are you?'

'No,' I say quickly, but the giggle that escapes my throat reveals otherwise. He has a narrow waist and long muscular thighs. He's perfect.

'Right, I'm ready.' He fastens the buckle on the belt of his jeans and ruffles his hair. 'I'll stick the dinner in the oven – it can warm through while we're walking the dogs.'

'Did you cook that from scratch?' I ask as I follow him into the kitchen, where he takes a dish of some kind of pasta bake from the fridge and places it in the oven.'

'I wish you didn't sound quite so surprised – I am house-trained.'

'I'm impressed.'

'I went to the baker's for fresh bread and the sauce is from a jar. I boiled the pasta and tossed the salad leaves in an olive oil and herb dressing. Does that count?'

'I don't think it matters.'

Lewis sets the timer on the oven. 'Let's go.' He doesn't need to call his dogs; they're sniffing at his heels as soon as he starts putting his shoes on.

We stroll around the fields where the sheep are chewing the cud and a pair of buzzards, crying like babies, are being harassed by the rooks that are nesting in the trees in the covert. On our return, we eat, finishing our meal with the door wide open and the pink evening sunshine streaming through the windows in the annexe kitchen as the sun begins to set behind the wooded hills. Lewis's crook leans against the wall behind the door beside his boots, his keys lie on the worktop and the sink is piled up with dishes.

The dogs are sleeping. Mick and Miley are lying in their matching beds in the corner of the kitchen, while Frosty is stretched out on the mat Lewis has put down for her. Every so often, she sighs in protest at being made to be like the other dogs, but I try to ignore her because Lewis and I are together and she's going to have to get used to following his rules when we're at his house.

'The dogs seem settled,' Lewis observes.

'Perhaps they will be all right together in the end.'

'It's looking promising. I don't think Miley and Frosty will ever be best mates, though.'

'They seem to have decided to tolerate each other, which makes life a whole lot easier.'

Lewis's thigh bumps gently against mine. I slide my hand across the worktop and touch the tips of my fingers very gently to his.

'Well,' he says, 'would you give me a Michelin star?'

'Definitely,' I say. 'Though not necessarily for your cooking.'

His face falls. 'Was it that bad?'

'I'm teasing. That was lovely, thank you. You must come round to the flat so I can return the favour, although you might have to put up with Gran.' I stroke Lewis's hand, noting the curling blond hairs on his skin, the rough calluses and scabs.

'You don't have to rush off tonight?' he asks.

I gaze into his eyes. I couldn't leave now, even if I had somewhere else to be. My heart pounds, my knees grow weak and the core of my belly seems to melt. The attraction, like an invisible thread, closes the distance between us until his lips are on mine.

'Shall we move into the other room? It's more comfortable.' Lewis draws back slightly and tips his head to one side, adding, his voice rough with desire, 'If I can't have you soon, I'm going to spontaneously combust.'

I stand up and take his hand to lead him out from the kitchen, and I don't know what happens exactly, but there's a clattering sound behind us, followed by a growl, and Lewis and I turn to find the dogs – Miley and Frosty, to be precise – scrapping and snarling among scattering plate fragments over a crust of leftover garlic bread. Mick is standing barking, like a headmaster trying to break up a fight in the playground.

Frosty and Miley are having a tug of war over the crust, but when neither of them is prepared to give it up, Miley lets go and flies at Frosty, biting at her neck until she gets a firm grasp with her teeth and shakes her. Frosty is screaming. I'm screaming at the dogs. Lewis is trying to separate them.

'Get her off! She's going to kill her!' I look around for a weapon, finding Lewis's crook. I hook it around Miley's neck and haul at it. Still, she won't let go of poor Frosty. Lewis grabs the crook too and, between us, we manage to pull her off, choking, cold-eyed, and intent on returning to finish off what she started. Lewis drags her away and shuts her in the other room and I fall to my knees to help Frosty, but her eyes are filled with terror and, before I can hold onto her, she struggles to her feet and runs across the kitchen, out of the door and across the yard.

'Frosty!' I scramble up to chase after her, but I'm too slow, and the last I see is the white tip of her tail disappearing through the hedge across the drive. 'Frosty!' I glance down to find my fingers are wet with blood.

'Frosty's bleeding,' I say, turning to Lewis, who's right behind me with Mick at his heels.

'Which way did she go?' he says.

I show him and he takes Mick to the point in the hedge where she disappeared.

'Find her.' Lewis sends him through the gap. 'He isn't a sniffer dog, but it's worth a try.'

'Where are you going?' I say quickly when he heads back across the yard. 'That's my dog out there; she's petrified and she could be bleeding to death.'

'I know. I'm taking the pick-up. You go through the field. I'll see if I can head her off – if she's still running, that is. Go, Zara,' he adds with urgency. 'Go!'

I run across and climb the gate. I can see Mick searching the top of the field with his nose to the ground, tacking back and forth like the boats do on the estuary down at Talymouth. I jog across the grass, my legs heavy with apprehension at what I'm going to find – if we find her because, with her long legs, Frosty could be miles away by now. I notice how Mick pauses, raising his head in the ear-flipping breeze. Suddenly, he turns and disappears under the fence and into the covert beyond.

'Anything?' I hear Lewis calling from the gate that opens out onto the road.

'I think Mick's onto something,' I yell back.

I struggle over the fence – the posts are wobbly – and duck under the low branches of hazel and ash, catching my trousers on brambles as I follow the sound of Mick whining from somewhere in the undergrowth. I hear the sound of an engine cutting out, then Lewis's footsteps as he catches up with me, his breath harsh and rasping with the exertion.

'Where did Mick go?' he gasps.

'Sh,' I say sharply. 'Listen.' There's a whimper. 'That's her. That's Frosty.' I crawl further into the bushes and there, in a small clearing, is Mick, standing over my beautiful dog, licking at her neck. 'Frosty!' She's lying on her front, panting. I kneel beside her and grab hold, but she isn't going anywhere this time. She's too weak.

271

'How is she?' Lewis joins me with his mobile pressed to one ear. He hands me a tea-towel. 'I grabbed it from the kitchen,' he says in explanation. I fold it and press it hard against the wound in Frosty's neck to stem the steady flow of dark blood.

'It's coming from the jugular. Oh god, she's going to die.'

'Hold on, Frosty,' Lewis says. 'Thanks. We'll be on our way,' he finishes his call. 'Zara, let's get her into the pick-up. We'll take her straight to Otter House.'

'I can't let go of this,' I say, gesturing to the makeshift pressure pad, where a deep purple stain is seeping through. Lewis pulls off his T-shirt and I wrap that over the top.

'Which vet is it?' I ask abruptly when we're speeding far too fast down the lane towards Talyton St George with Frosty in the front and Mick in the back.

'Maz.'

'Good.'

'It's lucky there's no one else on the road,' Lewis comments. 'How's she doing?'

I shake my head. I can't speak. Frosty's barely conscious, her body heavy across my lap. My fingers are sticky with blood and my heart weighed down with guilt for having put her in this situation because I knew – Lewis and I both knew – of the potential for a proper bust-up. We should have kept the dogs apart, especially when there was food around.

At Otter House, Maz and Izzy admit Frosty straight away, telling Lewis and me to wait while they do what they can. Lewis sits in reception, staring at the toe of

272

his sock – he didn't even put his shoes on before we left the farm – while I pace the floor.

'Sit down,' he says, looking up.

'I can't.'

'I can't begin to say how sorry I am,' he begins after a long silence.

I put my hand up. 'Don't! Don't say anything.' The lights are down low and the heat has gone out of the day. The scent of dog and disinfectant and the sound of the drunks' happy laughter as they kick a tin can along the street make me feel nauseous.

Eventually, Maz appears, surrounded by a halo of light from the corridor beyond her.

'How is she?' I ask. 'How's Frosty?'

'Very poorly,' she says gently. 'She's lost a lot of blood. Izzy's on the phone trying to find a donor dog – she really needs a transfusion.'

It doesn't seem very promising to me. It's late. People will be turning in for the night.

'What about Mick . . . or Miley?' Lewis moves up beside me. 'They're working collies,' he adds. 'Mick is a good boy. If I could sit with him while you take the blood . . .'

'Can you bring him in right away?' Maz says.

'He's right here in the pick-up. I'll fetch him.'

'I'll check him over beforehand to make sure he's healthy,' Maz goes on, but Lewis is already at the door.

'Are you sure, Lewis?' I feel guilty offering up Mick – he's a very sensitive soul and he's already done enough by following Frosty's trail and finding her.

'It's now or never. It'll be too late in the morning.'

Maz invites me to sit with Frosty; she is lying on her side wrapped in blankets on the prep bench. She's on a drip and has a large bandage snug around her neck. Izzy is holding a mask over her nose to deliver oxygen.

'Oh, Frosty . . .' I'm close to tears as I reach out and stroke her head. 'Why's she shivering? She can't be cold.'

'She's in shock,' Maz says. 'Would you mind holding the mask so Izzy can get on with preparing for the transfusion in case we go ahead with it?'

I don't mind at all. I'd do anything for Frosty – she's my best friend, my confidante, my baby. I hold the mask. Her eyes are open, but I'm not sure she's aware of what's going on. She knows I'm here with her, though. At least, I hope so.

Within half an hour, Mick is sitting on a trolley alongside us. He has an IV line in and a collection bag gradually filling with blood. Lewis stands with him, reminding him now and again to stay. Mick looks resigned.

Maz monitors both dogs while Izzy gets theatre ready.

'I'm going to operate. I'll extend the wound and check for any damage to underlying structures in her neck before I suture it up – and I want to see how far the bite wounds on the left side of her chest extend. I can't see anything on the X-ray, but I'm still worried she could have punctured a lung. Are you okay with that?'

I nod. I have no choice.

Soon Frosty is on an anaesthetic machine, being transfused with Mick's blood. Mick is enjoying tea and biscuits, thanks to Izzy, who offers Lewis and me the same while we return to wait in reception.

'You can take Mick back to the farm,' I say to Lewis. 'There's no need for both of us to be here.'

'There's every need,' he responds. 'I feel responsible. It was my dog . . .'

'This isn't the time.' I sit with my legs, arms and fingers crossed, waiting for news, while Mick lies cuddled up on Lewis's knees. It's one of the longest waits of my life before Maz appears again.

'How is she?' I say, jumping up.

'She's holding her own. That's all I can say.'

'Can I see her?'

'You can see her in the morning. She's heavily sedated. She has a shaved area on her neck with stitches, a bandage around her ears, a chest drain because the bite wound to her chest has penetrated through the muscle, and the drip and transfusion still going in. She's on antibiotics too. Izzy is going to sit up with her through the night. If there's any alteration in her condition, the slightest change at all, we'll be in touch with you. Otherwise, ring at eight and we'll update you then.'

'I'll drop you home,' Lewis says, coming over and touching my shoulder.

'It's all right. It's just down the road.'

'I don't like the idea of you being alone.'

'I won't be. Gran will be there.' I could do with a hug, but not from Lewis right now. I don't blame him, but he's tied up with what's happened to Frosty and I can't quite break through that. I want my gran.

'Please, it's the least I can do.'

'I'll walk,' I say firmly. At the word 'walk', I fold up, distraught at the thought I might never walk Frosty again. I never thought I'd say this, but walking my troublesome dog is one of the best things in the world. When I'm holding her lead, she holds my heart.

CHAPTER SIXTEEN

Down to the River

Frosty's condition starts to improve during the next twenty-four hours and I'm not sure whether to be pleased or worried when I pick up a text from Maz on the way home from work.

Tried to call you. Can you pop into the surgery this evening, about 7? Maz

'How is she?' I ask as soon as I'm shown through to the consulting room. 'I spoke to Frances at reception, but she said I had to wait to see you.'

'Not good, I'm afraid,' Maz says. 'Her temperature is very high and the wound on her neck is starting to break down. I've sent a swab off to the lab and put her onto another antibiotic while we wait for the results.'

I clutch my throat. 'So the worst has happened? She has an infection.'

Maz nods. 'She's quite depressed and refuses to eat.'

There's a pause. 'I thought it best that you came to see her.'

I know what she means. This is my chance to say goodbye.

'Come with me.' As tears flood down my cheeks, Maz hands me a tissue from the box on the shelf, and takes me through to visit Frosty; she is in a cage under the stairs, lying on her belly and resting her head on her paws.

'We thought she was better off out of the way of the racket in kennels. Hey, Frosty, look who's here to see you?' Maz smiles wryly. 'I don't know why I talk to her all the time when I know full well she's deaf.'

'I do it too.' Frosty raises her eyes, but doesn't wag her tail. 'Is it all right to give her a treat?'

'You can try. Izzy's been offering her all sorts, but she's turned her nose up at everything so far.'

'I expect she's missing my gran's home cooking. I'll bring some in.'

'I'm not overly optimistic, but it's worth a try. We'll be here until at least eight.'

I check my watch. 'I'll go now. Gran had some lamb shanks in the fridge this morning.'

'Don't expect too much, will you, Zara?'

'I understand.' I need to do something, though, anything to keep busy, so I return to the practice with a small portion of lamb, gravy and mashed potato, and sit with Frosty. I offer her the dish, but she barely sniffs it.

'Frosty, you have to eat,' I murmur.

'Any interest?' Izzy asks, passing by with a pile of fresh laundry.

I shake my head. 'She's going to die, isn't she?' I don't know how that makes me feel about Miley and Lewis.

'No, she isn't. Here, give me that.' Balancing the laundry on one arm, Izzy reaches down for the dish and sticks her finger in it. 'Let me give that a blitz in the microwave.'

When she comes back, I put the dish in front of Frosty. Nose twitching and ears cocked forwards, she lifts her head just high enough to reach over the rim of the bowl and lap at the gravy.

'There you go,' Izzy says. 'Who wants to eat their dinner cold?'

Frosty swallows a piece of lamb whole before deciding she's had enough.

'That's a good start,' Izzy says.

'Let's hope that's a turning point,' Maz says, joining us again.

'I'll bring her a scrambled egg for breakfast – she loves that.'

'While you're at it, you can provide Meals on Wheels for the rest of us,' Izzy smiles.

'Thank you, both of you.'

'She's looking brighter. Let's see what tomorrow brings,' Maz says.

I call Lewis on my way back home.

'You should have let me know you were visiting her. I'd like to have come with you.'

I don't know how to respond. I don't want to hurt

his feelings by confessing that I wouldn't have wanted him there. I don't blame him personally for what Miley did. I'm afraid that when I see him again, I'll blame him by association, and I won't feel quite the same about him.

'Give Frosty a big hug from me tomorrow.'

'Will do,' I say. 'Bye, Lewis.'

'I missed my goodnight text last night.'

It is one of those conversations where there's more meaning in the silences than the words.

'I was asleep by nine. I'll speak to you tomorrow.' I cut the call. As I continue walking along the road, Mrs Dyer comes rushing up to me, towed along by her enormous dog. (Since I became a member of the dog-walking set, I've found out that he's called Nero and he's a Great Dane.)

'How is Frosty?' she asks. She is red-faced, and panting almost as much as the dog.

'She's in a bad way,' I say, and then I find I can't speak any more because I well up again.

'I'm so sorry. We're all rooting for her, you know. Everyone's missing her antics out on the Green.'

'Thank you,' I mutter. I'm missing her more than I ever imagined was possible.

The next day brings better news, though. Frosty has eaten scrambled egg for breakfast and, that evening, I am walking her home with her tugging on the lead, growling as she plays, trying to snatch it out of my hands. Apart from her war wounds, she's back to her normal self.

Gran greets her with a bowl of chicken stew.

'There's enough left for you and Lewis,' she says.

I thank her and explain that I haven't invited him.

'Well, you should. Poor man. He'll want to see you. You haven't seen him for a while. I'll make myself scarce this evening so you can . . . canoodle.'

'Gran! You don't have to hide in another room.'

'Your mum and dad are taking me out for a fish-and-chip supper and some sea air.'

'You don't have to go out with them on my account.'

'I know, but I rather fancy fish and chips, so I thought, why not? It's time we buried the hatchet.'

'That's great.' Not only does she have some time away from the shop, it gives me and Lewis the perfect opportunity to meet without worrying about whether our dogs are going to kill each other.

Within a couple of hours, the chicken stew is gone and Lewis and I are cuddled up on the sofa with Frosty. It's cosy, and I'm waiting for Lewis to make a remark about how dogs shouldn't be allowed on the furniture.

'You know,' he begins, 'the last thing I want is you blaming me because Miley went for Frosty.'

'I don't blame you. I blame myself.'

'You haven't been in touch much the past few days.'

'I'm sorry, but I keep seeing Miley with her jaws around Frosty's neck,' I say with a shudder. Lewis hugs me closer, his arm around my shoulder. I turn my head to face him.

'You still like me, though?' He bites his lip, waiting for my answer. I notice a pulse throbbing in his neck and let my eyes follow the angle of his jaw up to his cheekbone. It really wasn't his fault. He's kind and handsome, and I love every part of him.

'Of course I still like you.' I fling my arms around his neck and we kiss.

'That's better,' he says eventually.

'Don't stop,' I smile.

'I want to pay Frosty's vet's bill. At least let me do that.'

'It's all right – I've sorted it and I don't mind. Having her back here beside me is worth every penny.'

'I'll pay you back then. How much was it?'

'I'm not telling you.' I gaze at him. 'You have no money.'

'I have money,' he says quickly, his body stiffening. 'I've arranged a loan from my parents.'

'Frosty's my responsibility, although I wish I'd insured her for vet's fees.'

'You have to let me make some kind of contribution.'

'And I'm telling you, no.' I tilt my head and kiss him again and the subject is closed for now, at least. I lose all sense of time and place until the sound of the doorbell jangling cuts through the rush of blood in my ears.

'Yoo-hoo. I'm back.'

'It's Gran . . .' I hiss, and Lewis pulls back with a growl of frustration.

'Another time,' he whispers.

Once Lewis has gone, I ask Gran about her trip out with Mum and Dad. According to her, they had a stroll along the promenade and stopped for refreshments at the Seaview tea rooms, but she didn't enjoy it.

'That's a shame. Why was that?' I ask.

'It reminded me of how your granddad and I used to go to the beach with Nobby to dig up rag-worms to bait their hooks for catching mackerel.'

'Is there anything else? You seem . . . upset?'

'I wish I knew where that little red bucket was. You haven't seen it, have you, Sarah?'

'Sarah?' Gran isn't making sense. 'I'm Zara.'

'Oh yes,' she says slowly.

'I think it's time for you to go to bed,' I say, forcing a smile. That's the first time she's become confused between me and my mother. 'You must be tired after all that sea air.'

'I should find that bucket first.'

'Don't worry about that now. Let's leave it till morning.' Hopefully, she will have forgotten it by then.

The next day, she seems much better, up early to open up and serve customers, and I can breathe a sigh of relief, although I know the improvement in her condition will be temporary.

Mum drops by at ten for a quick chat, taking me out to the Copper Kettle for a coffee and cake.

'We need to talk about Gran,' she says when we settle down in the corner of the tea room, at a table covered with a plastic mat in a blue and yellow gingham pattern which matches the curtains. We share the space with a couple of baby buggies and three tartan trollies.

'It's like a rainforest in here,' I say, ducking one of the leaves of a giant cheese-plant.

'Please don't try to change the subject.' Mum drops three lumps of sugar into her mug and stirs them into her coffee – white coffee, not a latte, because Cheryl sees no necessity to move with the times, and who can blame her when she's always busy? It's a gold mine. 'Did Mother talk about her afternoon out?'

'She didn't say much, only that you'd been to the Seaview tea rooms. Have they reopened? Only I thought they closed years ago.'

'We took her to the café next to the lifeboat station. She can't have been to the other place since Dad . . .' Mum's voice cracks at the memory of her beloved father, before she continues. 'Since before your grand-dad passed away.'

'I expect she got a bit mixed up. I do too, after a double shift.'

'It isn't just that, though. When we took her to the seaside, she was wearing her blouse inside out and she didn't have her purse with her. Please tell me what's going on. She's always been so sharp.'

'Who doesn't have a wardrobe malfunction now and then?'

'The purse? She always carries her purse.'

'Does it matter? Were you expecting her to pay for the fish and chips?'

'Of course not.' Mum frowns. 'It was our treat.'

'Trick or treat?'

'I don't know what you mean. You're talking in riddles.' Mum sighs deeply. 'Zara, you and your grandmother are one of a kind.'

'What I mean is, was this trip a trick to persuade her

to look at retirement homes by any chance? She was quite upset when she came home – she didn't look as if she'd had a good time. Did you put pressure on her?'

'We did not, although we might have mentioned selling the shop again,' Mum concedes. 'And before you criticise, we are not being cruel or unreasonable. We all want the best for Gran. I'm afraid, though, that we have different ideas as to how to go about it.'

'What's best for her is that she stays in her own home with me, where she can continue to gossip with her friends and customers.'

'She clearly isn't coping.'

'I'm here with her. I'll keep a closer eye on her in future and make sure she dresses properly.'

'You have a demanding job, a career. You don't have time to look after an elderly lady who's losing her memory. Stop trying to tell me she's just tired. She's becoming extremely forgetful.'

'It's better for her brain if she stays active and busy, than be stuck in a nursing home with no mental stimulation apart from the telly,' I counter. 'I can't bear the thought of her being alone and unhappy.'

'She wouldn't be alone,' Mum says.

'What about poor Norris? No one else will want him.'

'Oh for goodness' sake, he's only a cat.'

'Gran loves him. She'd hate to be without him.'

'She'd get used to it. The stress of running the shop can't be good for her brain either. Please think about this very carefully. You're young. You have your own life to lead. Don't let that bloody shop tie you down.'

'Mum!'

'Yes, I swore. So what? I'm that serious about it. That shop is bad news. It's always felt like a millstone around my neck.'

'I didn't realise you felt like that,' I say, surprised. 'It's supported the family for years.'

'At what cost? I stayed at home for longer than I needed to, delivering papers and helping behind the counter; then after I got married I was obliged to continue to work there because it was the family business. If it had been successful, Dad would never have turned to drink. As it was, he and Mother were always bumping along, close to bankruptcy. When Dad passed away, your father and I propped it up with our savings so Gran could stay there.'

'I'm sorry. I didn't realise.' I feel guilty now. 'I didn't know it had been such a struggle.'

'Your dad still has to lug boxes back from the cash-and-carry. He has a bad back and he can't carry on with it much longer.' Mum pauses. 'Zara, we're thinking of you, our daughter. We don't want to see you throw away your career for the sake of Gran and the shop. We want you to be happy. Do you understand?'

I nod. 'I think so.'

'So please, will you use some of your influence with your grandmother to see if you can make her see sense.'

'Things aren't as bad as you're making out. We're managing.'

'But you'll speak to her?'

I bite into my slice of carrot cake. It's one of those

286

occasions when it's easier to say 'yes' and worry about it later.

The following Tuesday, a few days after I brought Frosty home from Otter House, I'm taking her for a walk down by the river. Baby the Chihuahua from dog training is out walking in what looks like a bikini top and hula skirt with her owner, coming towards us from the direction of the Talymill Inn, on the narrow path between the river itself and a curving channel alongside that is verging on becoming an oxbow lake. My immediate thought is to turn around and walk into the field to put some space between Frosty and the other dog, but it's too late and Baby is almost upon us. Trying to remain calm, I take a breath and give Frosty the hand signal to sit. To my amazement, she does as she's told and sits quietly as Baby's owner walks her hurriedly past. I notice how her eyes latch onto Frosty's wounds as if to say: she's got what she deserves, then.

I give Frosty not one, but three liver treats before walking on, only to have to stop again when I hear a voice behind me.

'Is that you, Zara?'

I turn to find Wendy with five dogs mooching along with her – they seem quieter than normal, probably because of the heat.

'That's never Frosty?' she says. 'I can't believe it.'

'I told you she was a good dog.'

'What have you done to her? Put her on drugs?'

'I had some help from a shepherd who has working collies.'

'I see. He must have the magic touch.'

I try not to giggle. Lewis certainly does have a magic touch, and not just with Frosty.

'How is Rosemary?' she asks. 'I popped in to pick up my dog magazines.' She subscribes to at least five. 'She got in a terrible muddle with my change.'

'I expect she's tired. She hasn't been sleeping well.' And neither have I, but I don't mention that part of it, where Gran's had me up at three almost every night for the past two weeks, all upset because she can't find her way back to bed. 'Don't worry. She'll be all right.'

'I hope so. I know we've had our differences over the dog training, but I don't bear grudges and I'd like to help if you need anything. Let me know, won't you?'

'Thank you, but we are managing perfectly well.' My mobile rings, rescuing me from Wendy's rather overwhelming concern for my grandmother's state of health. 'I've got to answer this – it's work.'

Wendy walks past me with all five dogs and Frosty sits, barely moving a muscle. I wonder if it's the result of her being stuck at the vet's, sitting in a cage as other dogs go by and realising that they aren't going to hurt her. Whatever the cause of her change in behaviour, I'm one proud mum.

Frosty has her nose down a rabbit hole along the bank while I'm talking to Kelly on my mobile. One of our mums-to-be has gone into labour and she is with her.

'How long do you think it will be before you need me? I'm free now if that helps.'

'I shouldn't hurry, if I were you,' Kelly sighs. 'She

told me she was ready to push so I dropped everything and came straight out.' She lowers her voice. 'She's only three centimetres dilated. Everything's looking fine, but I have a weird feeling she's going to end up in hospital.'

'Keep me in the loop then. Give me a call in an hour or so and let me know how she's getting on.'

'Will do. See you later.'

I continue walking along the path where the July sunshine is turning the grass yellow. Kelly's weird feelings, as she calls them, tend to turn out to be accurate, not so much premonitions as a result of her years of experience, so I contact Lewis to warn him that I might have to cancel our date tonight. It's fine because he knows I'm on call.

'What are you up to now?' he asks.

'Guess . . .'

'Walking the dog. What's new?' He chuckles. 'You're obsessed.'

'It's good for me,' I say, smiling. I feel so much better since I've been back to walking the dog every day. Frosty's looking so much better, too, where the hair on her neck and chest is beginning to hide the scars from her scrap with Miley. 'I'll see you . . . when I see you.'

'And when will you let me know when that will be?'

'I'll let you know –' I chuckle – 'when I know.'

'Catch you later.'

Grinning, I cut the call. I love that we're a couple. Although I learned to be happy being single, I actually feel normal again. 'Come on.' I give a gentle tug on

Frosty's lead to remove her from another rabbit hole. 'Let's walk.'

There's hardly anyone about, apart from Uncle Nobby, who is snoozing under an umbrella on the far side of the river, partially hidden by the reeds, with his fishing rod set up to make a catch, and a couple of teenage boys skulking under the hedge by the old railway line with a bag for life clanking with cans.

As we make our way around the curve of the river, I catch sight of a familiar figure striding towards me in waders and carrying a swan hook.

'Hi, Jack,' I say, shading my eyes from the sun.

'Oh, hello. I couldn't catch it,' he says in some kind of muttered explanation. 'There's a pair of swans nesting down here and I've had a report that one has a broken wing, but I can't get near either of them to check it out. I'll have to come back later and try again.'

'Better luck next time.' It occurs to me that I haven't seen Jack since before he and Tessa received the worrying news about their unborn baby. 'How are you?'

'Fine, thanks.' He looks as if he could do with a shave and a haircut.

'And Tessa?'

'Okay.' He shrugs. 'Oh, I don't know. The baby has what the doctors are calling a serious developmental abnormality, a hole in the heart. Of course Tessa isn't okay.' He stares towards the hills in the distance as if he's trying to collect himself. 'Neither of us is,' he goes on, his voice breaking. 'In fact, things aren't good between us at the moment.'

'Oh, I'm sorry.'

'No, I'm sorry. You don't want to hear any of this,' he says gruffly.

'I'm here, as a friend and Tessa's midwife, and I promise you, no one else will know anything about it. Anything you say is completely confidential.'

We sit down, perching side by side at the top of the river bank. Frosty insists on sitting between my legs, even though she's already panting with the heat. I dig around in my pocket, finding sweets and liver treats. I offer Jack a strawberry lace and watch the water flow clean and clear over the stones and the bright green, almost fluorescent weed on the riverbed. I send Frosty away, afraid she's going to succumb to heatstroke, and she trots down the bank and into the water, drinking and snapping at the flies at the same time.

Eventually, Jack speaks. 'We both want kids. We knew we'd have a family one day, and Tessa was ecstatic when she found out she was pregnant . . . It was exciting at first. I let my imagination run ahead, thinking about what the baby would be like and where we'd take him.' His voice trails off. 'Then the doubts set in. To be honest, they set in before this —' he swears, 'scan.'

I wait for him to carry on.

'I was scared at the thought of suddenly being responsible for a child, another human being, and knowing everything would be different, that me and Tessa would never be the same again.'

'That's rather dramatic.' But then, what do I know what effect a child has on a marriage? I've not had a baby. I know the theory and I've seen what happens in practice, but I have no personal experience of my own.

'It's true, though. Tessa wants to keep the baby and I don't, and she hates me for it.' He holds up one hand. 'Before you go telling me, like everyone else does – my in-laws included – to give it time, nothing will change the way I feel. I love Tess more than anything, but I think we'll end up divorcing over it. She has faith that everything will turn out for the best while I'm always looking on the dark side.

'How will she cope? Can you imagine going out every day to the supermarket, or the beach, having to protect your kid from other people's stares and comments if it ends up brain-damaged and in a wheelchair? She says she can deal with it, but I'm not so sure. She says she'll give up working at the Sanctuary, if that's what it takes.'

What can I say? 'This baby could be born perfectly healthy, or at least able to live a happy and fulfilling life.'

'Or it could die in the womb . . . or be born to suffer. It might need surgery immediately after the birth or later in life. It might require a heart transplant. Oh, we've been told so much stuff by the doctors, I don't know what to believe. Basically, nobody knows, and I don't see why we should take the risk. There's no doubt that something's wrong.' Jack's nose drips.

I hunt for a tissue, but all I can find is a poo bag.

'I've told Tess where I stand,' he goes on. 'She says I'm selfish for admitting I don't want to be tied down for the rest of my life, twenty-four/seven, looking after another human being who can't walk or talk or feed themselves, but I'm not. I'm thinking about her and the sacrifices she would make for that baby, and most of all I'm thinking of that child, the frustration of not being able to communicate, the suffering of another human being who's in chronic pain. What kind of a life is that?

'Maybe I'm being really non-PC when there are people out there trying to tell me that all life is precious, but how can they really know?'

'They can't, I suppose,' I say, but he doesn't appear to be listening to me. He's in his own world, in pain and suffering for himself, his wife and his unborn child. His face crumples and his shoulders quiver, his body and soul racked with grief. Even though I've seen it so many times, it doesn't get any easier.

'Oh, Jack . . .' I reach out and hold his hand. 'You can speak to one of the doctors at the practice if you need more support. There are organisations that can help you, too. You only have to ask.' My mobile rings just at the wrong moment. 'I'm sorry, I have to take this.' It's Kelly, asking me to join her.

'I'm really not sure about this,' she says. 'I think two midwives will be better than one.'

'It's work. I have to go,' I say, letting go of Jack's hand.

'I should be getting on my way too,' he says quietly.

Back on my feet, I wind Frosty in from where she's wallowing about in the river on the lead, and we walk back to the Green where the Animal Welfare van is parked. Jack hesitates as we reach the maypole that stands in the centre of the sweep of grass.

'Thank you, Zara.'

'That's okay. If you want to talk, anytime, you know where I am.'

He takes me by surprise, stepping forwards to give me a big bear hug.

'You don't realise how much it's helped, just having someone to talk to . . .'

'Any time.' I pause. 'I hope you catch that swan.'

'I'll get it in the end,' he says with a small smile, as he steps away and unlocks the van. 'Cheers.'

As Frosty and I walk onto the Centurion Bridge to cross the river on the way back into town, he drives past, and I can only hope that he and Tessa, and their baby, will become one happy family.

Back at the shop, I make Gran a late lunch because there's no sign of her having eaten anything since breakfast, and leave Frosty with one of her chews, before I join Kelly at the cottage between Talymouth and Talyton St George where Tori and Rob live. This is Tori's third labour, her fourth baby. The twins are seven and their sister is four, and they are staying with their grandparents for a couple of days. Rob is a craftsman, a thatcher, and Tori looks after their smallholding, rearing chickens and ducks and growing vegetables. Being what I'd call an 'earth' mother, with a garland tattoo around her ankle and loose brown hair halfway down her back, I'd have expected her to know her body and what it's telling her.

Rob is fifteen years Tori's senior, a jovial man who

seems too rotund to be climbing up and down ladders. He makes tea while I examine his wife in the playroom among the children's toys. She's very uncomfortable, but she says she doesn't want any pain relief.

'Are you thinking what I'm thinking?' Kelly asks me.

'Yes, I agree with you.' I turn to Tori. 'I know this isn't what you want to hear, but we're both of the opinion you should be in hospital for the birth.'

'I'm having a home birth,' she says quickly, and I realise she might be going to be difficult about the idea of a transfer. 'That's what I've planned for.'

'And when you wrote out your birth plan, you were aware that even the best-laid plans can change,' Kelly joins in.

'I don't want any medical interventions. It isn't right to interfere with nature.'

'Sometimes nature needs a helping hand,' Kelly says, and I begin to wonder if she's a little afraid of Tori. It's time to stop pussyfooting around though, I think. Like the principle of good cop, bad cop, I take on the role of 'bad' midwife.

'You feel as if you want to push, yet your cervix is only seven centimetres dilated. Because you've been pushing against it, it's developed a lip, which could be what is preventing it dilating further. At the moment, there's no way this baby is coming out through the route nature intended.'

'You mean, I'm going to have to have a section?'

'It will be up to the doctor.' I pause briefly. 'Have you got your bag packed?'

295

She shakes her head.

'I'll arrange the transfer and ask Rob to put some things together for you,' Kelly says.

'No, I'll do that,' Tori says. 'He hasn't a clue. When I wanted camomile ointment after Opal was born, he came back with camomile tea.'

Kelly and I have a quick discussion in private in the garden outside.

'I'll go with her,' she offers.

'Are you sure?' I say.

'I'm in no hurry to go home – the kids can have fish and chips from Mr Rock's tonight. The other half can babysit for a change. And you'll be free to spend time with the lovely Lewis or your gran.'

'Thanks, Kelly. I owe you one.'

It's a shame Tori didn't get her home birth, I think, when on my way back to Talyton, but at least she's in the right place to ensure her baby's delivered as safely as possible.

Arriving back at the shop, I find a police car parked outside with its wheels on the pavement.

'Gran?' I push the door open to discover her sitting on the chair we keep behind the counter with a cup of tea, and Kevin taking notes on some electronic device. 'Are you okay?'

'There's been a burglary.' Gran's cup rattles against the saucer.

'Mrs Witheridge alleges that some money has gone missing,' Kevin says. 'Hello, Zara. How are you?'

'Great, thanks. How about you?'

'I'm really looking forward to the wedding now.'

'I think it's sweet that a man is so enthusiastic about getting married,' I observe.

'When I say looking forward to the wedding, I really mean, to when it's over and done with. Claire's talked so much about it, I reckon I could set myself up as a wedding planner.'

'Maybe you'll have to, young man, if you don't catch my burglar,' Gran interrupts. 'All this talking isn't getting us anywhere . . .'

'I apologise,' Kevin says, blushing.

'I should think so too. Whoever it was will be miles away by now.'

'How much money's gone missing?' I ask.

'Twenty-five pounds from the till,' Gran says. 'They must have taken it while my back was turned. It's those grockles, not one of my regulars.'

'I don't see how that's possible when you always keep the till shut. Was anything else taken?'

'The china teapot, the one in the window has gone.' She turns to Kevin. 'Why aren't you checking for fingerprints?'

'The teapot's in the storeroom,' I point out. 'The lid broke when you were rearranging the display the other day. Don't you remember?'

She frowns and shakes her head. 'That can't be right. I reckon my granddaughter's making that up, Police Constable.'

'Why would I want to do that? No one would want to steal that thing anyway,' I say lightly. 'It's hideous.'

'So it's just the money, twenty-five pounds in five-pound notes?' Kevin says.

'Just a minute, Gran. Did you remember to take off the twenty-five pounds you paid James when you cashed up today?'

'Of course I did. What do you take me for? I'm not stupid.'

'Let me see the cash book.' I move around to the back of the counter and take the book out of the drawer. I open it up and check the totals for the day. 'I don't see any mention of the paper boy's wages.' I flick back through the pages. 'You haven't made a note of them this time.' I pass her the book to show her, but she refuses to look at it, keeping it firmly closed in her lap.

'So, Zara, have you solved the case to your grandmother's satisfaction?' Kevin asks.

'I think so. Case closed.' I'm aware Gran is giving me one of her looks. 'It seems that we should put this down to a simple mistake. Thank you, Kevin.'

'Any time,' he says, slipping his electronic notebook into his pocket. 'Don't worry – these things can happen to anyone.'

'Say hi to Claire for me.' I show him out and bolt the door behind him. 'Come on, Gran. Let's go upstairs.'

'I need to find that money first,' she says in all seriousness.

'We know where it went, don't we?' I take her hand and give it a gentle squeeze. 'You used it to pay the paper boy.'

'Did I? Did I really?' She sucks on her teeth. 'Well, if you say so . . .'

I hold out my arm.

'I feel terrible for wasting police time.' She clutches

my sleeve and I escort her to the flat. 'I've never done such a silly thing before. I have to be the maddest frog in the bag.'

'I don't think anything of the sort.' I try to check myself but the words, effectively a denial that there's anything wrong, come out anyway. It's easier than facing reality.

In the kitchen, Gran and I sit at the table, the scent of brandy rising from her tea. Norris is eating his dinner while Frosty looks on drooling, having finished hers in two seconds flat. She lies on her belly and gradually wriggles closer to the dish until the cat can't take any more. He explodes into a yowling bundle of spiky fur and launches himself onto the top of Frosty's head, at which she turns tail and runs for it, flinging him off on her way through the kitchen doorway. Norris lands on his feet with a thud and strolls nonchalantly back to his food as if nothing's happened, while Frosty lies down on the landing.

'I don't understand why she doesn't give up – she knows what he's like. It's like she forgets . . .'

'What was that, dear?' Gran says.

'I said it's like Frosty forgets how fierce Norris is. She really doesn't speak "cat".'

'Neither do you. You're more of a dog person.' Gran pauses. 'You know, I'm sure I heard voices today. Someone did come into the shop.'

'I hope they did,' I say. 'You need your customers.'

'They didn't buy anything. They walked about – I heard their footsteps while I was upstairs fetching my glasses – and then they left without buying anything.'

'So they were having a look around. People do.'

'They moved the jigsaw puzzles from the top shelf to the middle. Now, why would they do that, unless I disturbed them before they had a chance to take them away?'

I'm convinced she's imagining this scenario. I wonder if she nodded off at the counter – she has done it before – and then woke up, confused. Either way, I'm not sure I can leave her here alone tonight, which means either taking her on a date with Lewis or cancelling completely. The latter seems the safer option and I've already warned him I'll probably be working.

'I'll cook some bacon and eggs.'

'Aren't you going out tonight?'

'Not tonight.'

'That's nice. We can have a quiet night in,' she says with a small smile.

'I could do your nails if you like.'

'That would be fun. You know, I feel safe when you're here.'

I take Frosty out to the garden and return Kelly's text telling me that Tori's baby arrived safely by C-section before I call Lewis.

'Hi, darling,' he says. 'Are you free later?'

'I'm sorry . . .'

'You're catching a baby.' I hear the disappointment in his voice. 'Never mind. Tomorrow?'

'Tomorrow should be fine.' It crosses my mind that I should really explain that I'm staying at home with my grandmother, but it seems too complicated and I'm not sure he'll understand why I feel I should be with her tonight and not with him, and Gran's calling me because she can't find the frying pan. 'I have to go. I'll speak to you tomorrow.'

'Don't drop it,' he says.

'Don't drop what?'

'The baby,' he chuckles. 'I'll miss you.'

'Me too. I'll see you soon.'

'Tomorrow night?'

'Yes, tomorrow.' I gaze up at the stars in the night sky. I should be free to see Lewis, but what am I going to do about Gran? Am I going to have to start looking for a granny-sitter so I can go out?

We have a fun evening together – when I say, 'fun', it's pretty low-key. I paint her nails, cook her dinner and pour her a small sherry, and we watch a medical drama together before I send her to bed, taking the opportunity to cuddle up with Frosty and call my sister.

'Hello, stranger,' she says lightly. 'I haven't heard from you for a while.'

'I'm sorry,' I tell Emily. 'I've been rushed off my feet.'

'It's all right,' she says, chuckling. 'You've been leading our shepherd astray.'

'How are you and the girls, and Murray?'

'We're all well, thank you. How is Gran? I spoke to her the other day and she sounded as if she'd been on the sherry.'

'She's okay,' I say.

'Come on.'

'All right, she's been getting in more of a muddle recently, but it's fine.' I explain about the visit from

301

the police. 'It was a misunderstanding – a funny one at that.'

'Where are you, Zara?' Emily asks. 'I saw Lewis and he said you were working tonight. You haven't left Gran on her own? You really shouldn't have, not tonight.'

'Don't worry, she's tucked up in bed.' I breathe a sigh of relief because I don't have to lie exactly to my twin. 'I won't be back late.'

'Well, if you ever want me to spend an evening with her, you know where I am – at least, that is as long as your memory's intact. It's been a while.'

'I know. I'll be over soon, I promise.'

Unfortunately, Gran wakes at three in the morning again. I hear her wandering around the landing, asking where her room is. I get up to escort her back to her bedroom, but I don't get back to sleep for worrying. She's still asleep when James arrives to deliver the papers. I wake her, but she's confused, mistaking me for my mother, and when she does manage to get out of bed, she's unsteady on her feet. I can't leave her and I'm supposed to be going to work.

I call Kelly from the kitchen where I'm multitasking, preparing breakfast and feeding Frosty and Norris at the same time.

'Hi, I wouldn't normally ask, but is there any chance you could cover for me this morning?'

'Oh, I don't think so . . .' She sighs.

How many times have I covered for her when she's had something on, like the children's doctor's appointments, Nativity plays and sports days? And now, when I need this one tiny favour, she's going to make a fuss about it.

'Just for a couple of hours,' I go on. 'If you could just run the antenatal class . . .'

'What for?'

'It's my gran – she isn't well this morning.'

Kelly says more gently, 'You seem to have been under a lot of strain recently. I'll cover for you today, but don't make a habit of it. It's my fault the managers have their eyes on us – I took advantage once too often.'

'You didn't tell me that . . .' I'm more worried now.

'It's okay. I'll make sure they don't hear of it.'

'Perhaps I should go off sick for the day.'

'No, you've covered plenty of times for me in the past. I'll do it. I'm just saying, don't make a habit of it. The last thing either of us needs is to lose our jobs.'

'I'll see you later, I promise. Thanks.' I cut the call and gaze at the array of bowls on the kitchen worktop. Why is life so complicated? I've managed to pour cornflakes into Frosty's bowl and put Frosty's biscuits into mine.

CHAPTER SEVENTEEN

One Man and His Dogs

'Hi,' Lewis says, dropping by to the shop one morning a week after I had to ask Kelly to cover for me. 'Where's Rosemary today?'

I lean across the counter, knocking over a box of football cards with my elbow, aiming to kiss him on the cheek, but finding his lips instead and his arms around my back, lifting me off my feet.

'Hey, put her down. Get a room, will you?'

Lewis lowers me gently.

'Paul?' I say, looking past Lewis's shoulder.

'Good morning,' he says. 'I've come in to see if Katie's magazine's been delivered – I ordered it last week.'

'Can I finish serving Lewis first?'

'Yes, go ahead.' Paul hovers at the counter while Lewis buys mints from a jar and a bottle of water.

'Oh, and I'll have some chocolate too,' he says.

'Some of us have work to go to.' Paul fidgets.

'Be patient,' I smile as much to be friendly as to acknowledge my ease at being in the presence of both my current man and ex-husband. Life is good. I'm secure again. I give Lewis a flirty glance.

'I could have ordered it off the Internet,' Paul says, reminding me of his presence, 'but I wanted to keep our local shops open by buying it from you.'

'That's very considerate of you.' I try to catch one of the mints that bounces out of the scales as I pour them out of the jar. 'We are struggling at the moment.'

'Why aren't you at work today, Zara?' Paul asks. 'Have you given up on midwifery? Only you always seem to be here, behind the counter.'

'I'm helping out,' I say, not wanting to reveal to Lewis the extent of my role as my grandmother's shop assistant, at which Gran appears at the door, struggling to get through it with two bags of shopping. Lewis is there first, with Paul close behind him.

'Thank you, my dears,' Gran says, as they each take a bag and bring it to the counter. One bag falls over, sending several oranges tumbling onto the floor.

'How are you going to make a pie with those? Where are the apples? And the bread?' I check inside the second bag, finding five, no six, bars of lavender soap from the pharmacy. 'Gran!' I try to make a joke of it. 'You just can't get the staff nowadays. I should have given you a list of what we needed, or done it myself.' However, she seems oblivious to what I'm

305

saying, looking at Lewis and Paul who are gathering up the oranges.

'It's Paul and the shepherd.' She beams at me. 'All these lovely men coming to call on you.'

I smile to myself. It's like living in a sweet shop – I am living in a sweet shop.

'Uncle Nobby saw you canoodling on the Green with Jack Miller the other day,' Gran continues.

'Where did he get that from?' I say, aware of the way Lewis freezes, his fingers tightening around one of the oranges. 'He must have been mistaken.'

'You told me you'd seen Jack.'

My heart shrinks at the sound of her big mouth. Why can she remember that, yet forget what I asked her to buy less than an hour ago?

'I'm sure it was Jack,' she goes on, frowning.

'I ran into him when I was walking Frosty,' I say, aware that Lewis is staring at me.

'Uncle Nobby was fishing when he noticed you. He said he waved, but you were all caught up chatting. I remember it was last Wednesday because that's the day we had omelette for tea and watched Corrie and that hospital drama together. You said it was a proper girls' night in.'

'Shall I take this stuff upstairs?' I say, trying to divert her.

'Jack caught that swan, by the way,' Gran continues, oblivious.

'Paul wants to know if his magazine has come in. Perhaps you can have a look.' I'm about to take the bags, but Lewis gets hold of them first.

'Allow me,' he says, his tone ominously flat, and he follows me upstairs where he puts the bags on the kitchen table with a thud.

'Would you like a coffee?' I check through the shopping. 'Gran's forgotten to buy any teabags.'

'Coffee's fine.'

'Sit down then. I'll make it.'

Lewis remains silent while I boil the kettle and make two coffees.

'I'll take one down to Gran later,' I say, leaning against the worktop.

He looks up. 'Why didn't you mention you'd seen Jack?'

'Because it isn't important.' I sip at my coffee, flinching a little at its bitter taste. 'It's no big deal.'

'Why would Rosemary say you were – how did she put it – canoodling then?'

'We were talking, that's all. I don't know where Uncle Nobby got that from. I did see him but he was on the far side of the bank, sleeping off his lager or cider or whatever he'd been drinking. Either he or Gran has got the wrong end of the stick,' I add, assuming that this is the end of it. 'Are you free for lunch?'

Lewis shakes his head. 'I should be getting back to the farm.' I notice how he bites his lip, as if deep in thought. 'Are you sure you're telling me the truth?'

'How can you say that?'

'Because you're very secretive sometimes.'

'I shouldn't have to explain where I am and what I'm doing every hour of every day.' My neck grows hot with annoyance at him, and shame at myself for

307

putting myself into an awkward situation, but he should trust me, shouldn't he? The trouble is, though, I have been economical with the truth about the evening I spent with my grandmother when I said I was at work.

'I thought you'd always be totally honest with me. I'd never lie to you.'

'I know that,' I say, suddenly afraid that Lewis is slipping away from me.

'I knew you weren't out catching a baby the other night. Your car was in its parking spot.'

'So you're stalking me now?'

'I happened to be passing,' he says. 'I'm confused. Why pretend you were out when you were at home with your gran? Unless she's covering for you and you were out with Jack or some other bloke?'

'That's ridiculous.'

'Is it?' I read the hurt and anger in his eyes and my chest grows tight with pain and regret.

'Gran wasn't feeling very well.'

'You could have said so.'

'I didn't want you to feel bad. I thought it was a lame excuse for turning you down that night. When you assumed I was working, I thought it was easier to leave it that way.'

'You're treating me like an idiot.' Lewis runs his hands through his hair. 'I've never felt this way about anyone before, but you're behaving as if you don't care for me at all.'

'I'm sorry.' I walk over and rub his shoulder, but he shrugs me off.

'What for?' he asks. 'For lying, or being found out?'

'Look, I admit I should have told you where I was the other night, but this thing about Jack . . . well, it's nothing. I don't expect you to list every female you come across each day.' Lewis looks at me blankly. 'Why can't you take my word for it that nothing happened?'

'Does Tessa know about this?' he says, his tone hardening.

'No, she doesn't,' I say quickly, 'and it has to stay that way.'

'So something did happen!' He stands up. 'I knew it!'

'I was consoling him.' I grab onto his arm. 'Please let me explain as far as I can.'

'Ha ha,' Lewis says with sarcasm. 'Very original. Jack was upset so I gave him a hug and snogged his face off.'

'I hugged him, but it was for a good reason.'

'Yeah, this one – you're cheating on me.' To my alarm, his lip begins to tremble.

'Of course I'm not. I can't tell you why. It's confidential.'

'And I suppose the reason your ex-husband is always hanging around in the shop is confidential too?' He hugs his chest.

'Look, I shouldn't say any more, but since you clearly won't believe me unless I do – it's to do with work. As you know, Tessa is pregnant.'

'And?'

'Please don't ask me any more.'

'Come on, you can tell me.'

'I can't, and if you're unable to respect that then . . .'

'Then what? Go on,' he says. 'I knew you were going to dump me. I knew I wasn't good enough for you.'

'Oh for God's sake, I'm really fond of you, but . . .' I pinch myself to stop the tears that threaten to overflow. 'It's you I want to be with, not Jack, not Paul, not anyone else, but I can't be in a relationship with someone who doesn't trust me.'

'And I can't be with someone who gives me reason to be suspicious.'

I take a step back, put my hands behind my back and take a grip on the edge of the worktop.

'What are we going to do? I can't be dealing with all this drama – I have enough of it at work.' I bite my lip as he gazes at me. I don't flinch. I have nothing to hide and nothing to feel guilty about. 'If our relationship is like this now, what will it be like in six months, a year? I'm sorry for not being completely straight with you. I regret that. I should have known it would come back to bite me on the bum.' I shrug. 'As far as I can see, we have a choice. If you decide you can't bring yourself to forgive me . . .'

'Oh dear . . .' His expression softens. 'I'm being a bit of a prat, aren't I?'

'I've been stupid too.' I should have guessed Lewis would be slightly paranoid about me seeing other men. His reaction is only natural.

He steps towards me and sweeps me into his arms.

'I can see you're telling the truth. I don't want to lose you over some silly misunderstanding.'

I look up, letting my fingers play with the collar of his polo shirt, and give him a small smile of relief. 'I think that was our first row,' I murmur. Which is good, because it means our relationship is genuine and means just as much to him as it does to me.

When we finally return downstairs, Paul has gone and Gran is behind the counter, talking to Granddad's photo as if nothing has happened.

We spend the next evening making up and, afterwards, Lewis suggests I bring Frosty up to the farm.

'Are you sure?' I say.

'It's time we tried to sort the dog issue out. Neither of us has much time off – at least, not at the same time, and not being able to walk the dogs together or having to keep driving back to the farm to let the collies out is a pain in the neck.'

'Sometimes it feels as if Frosty's running my life,' I admit, 'but I'd rather keep them apart.'

'We can't do that for ever. She could go on for another twelve years yet. That's a lot of inconvenience.'

'If we should stay together that long,' I point out.

Lewis grins. 'You're such an old pessimist. Who knows what will happen?'

'I thought owning a dog was supposed to be fun, not an ordeal. What you're saying makes sense, though. We can't go on like this, but I'm scared of what Miley and Frosty might do to each other.' My lip quivers as I picture them tearing each other apart. 'Frosty's been better with other dogs since she came back from

Otter House, but that doesn't mean she'll be any less offensive to Miley.'

'We'll supervise, and make sure there's no food involved,' Lewis continues. 'If there's any sign of aggression between the two girls, we'll separate them again.'

He's convinced me to give it a try, but it is with some trepidation that I take Frosty up to the farm the following evening. When I pull into the farmyard, Lewis comes out of the annexe to greet me.

'Anyone would think you'd been waiting for me,' I say, smiling, as I get out of the car.

'I've been waiting all day,' he says, reaching out and pulling me close. I throw my arms around his neck and we kiss passionately until Frosty utters a whine of impatience.

'Are you sure about this?' I ask him.

'This,' he murmurs, holding me tighter against his long, lithe body, 'or the dogs?'

I take some time to answer, enjoying the contact. 'What do you think?'

'I'll make sure I keep Miley under control,' he says. 'I can't say the same for myself, though . . .'

'Later,' I say, giving him a gentle shove. 'Come on, let's go for a stroll before it rains.'

We walk the dogs with Miley and Frosty on leads, taking them into one of the fields so they have plenty of space not to feel threatened. Lewis and I sit down on the grass a few feet apart and let the dogs choose whether or not to make an approach. In the end it's Frosty who goes first – a good sign, I think, because it suggests she isn't completely terrified of Miley, who freezes as she sniffs at her nose.

'Chill, Zara,' Lewis says quietly.

Miley moves along Frosty's side, arching her back and holding her tail upright. The fur on her scruff stands up on end, as do the hairs on the back of my neck. Frosty bows and wags her tail, and Miley bows in return, uttering a yap as if to say, 'Let's play.'

'They'll be okay,' Lewis says, getting up to let both dogs off their leads.

I sit back, breathing a sigh of relief as the two girls chase around at speed, Frosty's long legs soon overtaking Miley. Mick joins in, another potential flashpoint, but he can't keep up with them, dropping back to sit with Lewis while waiting for their return.

'That couldn't have gone any better,' Lewis says when we're back in the annexe. 'They cleared the air with that fight they had before. I know it will take a long time to trust them when there's food around, but we can at least walk them together and have them in the same room.' He sits down on the sofa and I sink down beside him.

'Do you realise this has been my first full day off in four weeks?' Lewis says.

'I do – I've hardly seen you.' It's all very well finding a man at last, but it isn't so great when you can't actually spend time with him because you're both so busy.

'I'm sorry,' he says ruefully. 'Your brother-in-law is a slave-driver and I need the money. The shearing's done, I've moved sheep, vaccinated sheep, trimmed

313

hundreds of sheep feet . . .' He sighs as he rests his arm around my shoulder. 'I even count sheep in my sleep.'

'What are you going to do next?'

He kisses me. 'I don't know. I had a call back about the position in Wiltshire.'

'The permanent one?' I wish he was permanently in my life. I wish I had a thousand sheep so I could give him a job.

'Yes, that one. They turned me down,' he says flatly.

'You're disappointed?'

'Of course I am – they said they didn't think I'd fit in, that I was too young. It was perfect for me, except for it being a hundred miles away from Talyton St George – and you. So I guess it's for the best in a way.'

'You lead a precarious existence. I'm glad I have a steady job – I can't imagine not knowing what I'll be doing or where I'll be from week to week.' I don't say it, but I'm also very happy he isn't making a permanent move. I'm not sure about a long-distance relationship. 'What are you going to do?'

'Keep looking. Something will come up.'

'Where will you live?'

'I don't know. I could move back in with Mum and Dad for a while – if they'll have me. I could come and see you, if you'd like me to.'

I turn my body towards him and slide my hands up around his neck. 'Of course I want you to. I don't want you to go away.'

Having spent two evenings in succession with Lewis,

I'm hoping we're both free on the third one, although we're going to confirm later. In the meantime, I have a long shift at work. At the surgery, I have a booking-in appointment and three others before a home antenatal visit and a clinic down at Talymouth. Claire catches me before I start.

'How are you?' she says brightly.

'Good, thanks. You?'

'I'm a bit frazzled, as usual. I need to speak to you before you see your first one.'

'Can I catch up with you in a sec?' I say, because Ben is waving me into his consulting room for a planned update about one of my young mums-to-be who came in to see him with gestational diabetes a couple of days before.

'Yes, but promise me you'll come and find me before you call in your first appointment.'

'All right. I will,' I say, but as it turns out, by the time I've spoken to Ben, Claire is already tied up redressing a leg ulcer. Too late, I think, as I scan the waiting room for women of child-bearing age. There is only one, and I can see now why Claire was so keen to give me advance warning, because my heart misses a beat as I register that she's sitting holding hands with Paul, which can mean only one thing. OMG! Is this for real? I clear my throat.

'Katie,' I say. 'I'm Zara. Come through.'

'I'll come in with you, darling,' Paul says, making a show of being the perfect boyfriend. 'I'm glad it's you, Zara. Katie, she's the best you can have.'

Katie appears a little embarrassed at being seen

by her boyfriend's ex-wife, and so she should be, I think. I'm devastated and furious at being put in this situation, and I can't understand why she allowed Paul to recommend she booked an appointment with me when she could so easily have had one with Kelly.

Paul shows Katie to a chair, his arm on her waist, as if she can't possibly identify a chair by herself. 'Let me have your bag,' he adds, taking it from her.

She's much younger than he is – twenty-one, according to her notes, so I don't know why I've been worrying about the age gap between me and Lewis. She's about the same height as Paul, slim and gorgeous in a supermodel kind of way, with long, lustrous dark hair and immaculate nails. I can deal with that, and the fact that Paul is clearly besotted with her, but I can hardly bring myself to look at the tiny baby bump that sits neatly beneath her light summer top.

I take a deep breath and go through my list of questions as I normally do.

I ask about Katie's occupation, my inner bitch hoping she's going to say she's unemployed, but she isn't. She's a beauty therapist and masseuse and works at a local spa – she and Paul met when she called an ambulance for one of her clients who'd fallen off a treatment table, dislocating their shoulder.

'It was love at first sight,' Paul smiles.

'Have you been pregnant before, Katie?' I continue.

'I had a termination when I was eighteen,' she says without a flicker of emotion, which I find hard to forgive.

316

'This baby wasn't planned,' Paul says proudly. 'It just happened.'

Look at me, look at what a stud I am, is what he's really saying, with that stupid grin on his face. I'm struggling not to tell him what I think. He could have at least given me some warning, time to prepare myself, or even asked me whether or not I was happy to be his girlfriend's midwife.

'I'm pleased for you both,' I say, but I really don't mean it. 'Now, Katie, I'd like you to pop on the scales to check your weight before I measure your bump.'

When I check her weight, Paul comments rather critically that she's put on a few pounds recently. It's what he used to do to me, and I'm so glad we're not together any more.

'That's what tends to happen when you're pregnant,' I say in her defence, 'although you shouldn't start eating for two just yet.' I write some notes in her pregnancy record book. 'You'll have a scan in two weeks' time and another appointment with me after that. Do you have any questions?'

'I'm going to have the baby in hospital, because I prefer the idea of having the baby by Caesarean rather than naturally,' she says. 'Can you add that to my notes?'

'We don't just say, yes, have a C-section. There are risks involved with surgery, just as there are with a natural birth. Have you really thought this through?' I don't think Katie sounds too posh too push. She thinks she's too pretty.

'My friend had one; she said it was the best thing she'd ever done.'

'You have to go through an operation.' I look to Paul for support – surely, he can't condone her attitude with his background?

'Lots of women have them,' is all he says.

'I can be awake though, can't I?'

'You'd have an epidural so you can't feel anything . . .'

'Perfect,' she says.

'And you wouldn't be able to get up and look after your baby straight away.' Are you putting your baby or yourself first? I want to ask her. Some people are so selfish. Why have a baby in the first place if you aren't prepared to put it ahead of your own interests?

'It won't change my life,' Katie says. 'I won't let it.'

I bite my tongue.

'You're looking well, Zara,' Paul says in an aside to me as he leaves the surgery. 'How's the shepherd?'

'He's fine, thank you.'

Paul's eyes narrow. 'I don't think he's right for you.'

'It's none of your business.'

'He doesn't have a permanent job and he doesn't have any money.'

'Money doesn't matter. I'm independent. I look after myself,' I say, annoyed.

'I don't want to see you get hurt.'

'Well, thank you for your concern,' I say with sarcasm. 'If you cared that much about my feelings, you wouldn't have let your girlfriend book in with me. Or you would have – at the very least – asked me how I'd feel about it first.'

'I'm sorry, you're right. I should have told you about the baby, not sprung it on you like this,' he says. 'We didn't have much luck, did we?'

I shake my head. 'Go and look after Katie and your baby, will you? Don't worry about me any more. This is hard, but I think we should stop trying to remain friends.'

'But it's what we agreed after the divorce. I don't want to cut all ties.'

'It isn't working for me. I need to move on.' By keeping in contact with Paul, I'm only fuelling Lewis's suspicions that we still have feelings for each other. It sounds as if I'm letting him control who my friends are, but it isn't like that. Claire has made me wonder about Paul's motives for keeping in touch – I thought he was trying to support me and make sure I was all right, but I can't help thinking now if he's deliberately setting out to unsettle Lewis and wreck our relationship.

Back at home after work, I munch my way through a bag of pick-and-mix, and suffer the pain and pleasure of eating a whole packet of flying saucers that are sweet and sharp at the same time. I don't want to see Paul again. It should have been me pregnant with his baby, not this woman he's been with for all of five minutes. Even worse, this proof of his virility has shown that our failure to conceive really was all my fault. I haven't even got the comfort of not being certain to cling on to any more. I know I can get through this, but the feelings of inadequacy and loss remain like the bitter sherbet tang in my mouth.

In fact, it's as if Lewis knows how I'm feeling, because at six he rolls up at the shop. I hear his voice as I'm putting Frosty on the lead and slipping into my sexy (I'm joking) trainers, ready to go out for a walk after work.

'Hi, Rosemary, how are you?'

'Yoo-hoo. Your young man is here for you,' calls Gran.

'I'll be with you in a sec.' I stuff a few treats into my pocket and walk along the corridor with Frosty. She squeals with delight. In fact, I'm not sure which of us is most pleased to see him. 'I wasn't expecting you,' I go on, moving in to touch my lips to his.

'I thought I'd see if you wanted to go out tonight,' he says, kissing me before turning his attention to Frosty.

'Hey, sometimes I think you'd prefer me if I had furry ears and a waggly tail.' I give him a playful nudge. 'I was just about to walk the dog.'

'I'll come with you.' He nudges me back. 'We could stop at the pub for something to eat.'

'How lovely,' Gran sighs. 'Zara could do with cheering up. She's been like a bear with a sore head since she came home.'

'Have I really? I'm sorry.' I pause. 'Gran, you don't mind?'

'If you go out? Of course I don't. You don't have to ask my permission.'

'I'll see you later then.' I grab a bag and we are on our way with Frosty. Lewis takes my hand and swings my arm as we stride along through town.

'Hello,' calls Mrs Dyer, who's walking towards us on the other side of the road with her hand on Nero's collar. I tighten my grip on Frosty's lead and hurry along.

'What are you doing, the one hundred metres or something?' Lewis chuckles.

'I really don't want to have to stop and talk right now.'

'Oh dear, you did have a bad day then.'

'It wasn't the best. How about you?'

'It was interesting,' he says, growing serious as we reach the Dog and Duck at the bottom of town where we cross the road. 'Murray and I dug out the ground for the new barn – he's hoping it'll be big enough to take one of the tractors and some of the winter hay and straw so there's more room for lambing the ewes in the spring, but I think he's being optimistic. Oh, and we went to look at a ram. Murray isn't sure, but he thinks it would be worth sourcing rams from different bloodlines this year to see if it prevents the problems we had lambing some of the ewes. He's trying to cut down on the rate of Caesareans.'

'I suppose it reflects badly on the shepherd if it's too high.'

'Luckily, Murray knows it isn't me. He couldn't deliver some of them either.'

We walk across the Green, and reach the stile and kissing gate into the field that runs alongside the river. Usually, I clamber over the stile and let Frosty jump it, but Lewis opens the gate and goes through, stopping to close it behind him.

'You have to pay me with a kiss before I'll let you through.' He tips his head to one side, like a dog trying to look appealing. We kiss and he pulls away slightly. 'The price has gone up since you've been standing there,' he teases. 'It's three kisses now.'

'Lewis,' I say, laughing as I catch sight of Aurora walking her dog towards us, 'we'll cause a traffic jam.'

He lets me through the gate and we start out along the path beside the river.

'It's a shame you couldn't bring Mick and Miley with you. They'll be fed up, won't they, missing out on a walk?'

'They're all right. They've been running around on the farm and playing with Poppy all day. I left them crashed out in their beds.'

'Ah, sweet,' I say, as we walk on hand in hand along the path beside the river.

'So, tell me about your bad day. Did you catch any babies?'

'Not today. No,' I hesitate, a little apprehensive about opening up old wounds, and Lewis's insecurities and jealousies, by mentioning Paul, but I remember how I promised to be open with him. No more secrets, no more lies, apart from a little economy with the truth over Gran because I don't want him to feel constrained to avoid the subject, or let it slip when he's chatting with Murray and Emily. I really don't want to worry my sister with it.

'I saw Paul – at the surgery,' I hasten to add.

Immediately, I sense the tension in Lewis's fingers.

'It was work. His new girlfriend is pregnant.' I bite my lip.

'And?' he says. 'Something's upset you. What is it?'

'Oh, Lewis, it made me feel so sad,' I go on, recalling the way Paul held his arm protectively around Katie's waist, and stifling an instantaneous sob of distress.

Lewis swears. 'I knew it.' He drops my hand and turns to face me. 'I knew you were still in love with him.'

'I'm not,' I say, tears streaming down my face.

'You're crying. Why else would you feel like this? I can't believe you're such a hypocrite, having a go at me for questioning you about Jack when you're clearly jealous of your ex's new girlfriend.'

'It isn't like that.' I shake my head, wondering how I'm going to make him understand. I know he's young, but I'm surprised at the immaturity of his reaction. I mention Paul and he assumes I still have feelings for him, when the only man I'm interested in is Lewis.

'What is it like, then?' His tone is hot with resentment. 'I'm trying to trust you, but it's almost impossible when you're standing in front of me, broken-hearted. I know from experience that it's tough letting go sometimes, but I wish you could switch off your feelings for Paul once and for all. It makes me feel that you don't really like me, that I'm second best, when I want to be the first person you turn to when you're feeling unhappy—'

'And that's what I'm doing now, turning to you,' I cut in, but Lewis blunders on.

'If you don't think you can get over him, then perhaps—'

'Lewis, no, you have to listen to me. Please . . .'

'Go on,' he says grudgingly.

'I'm upset, yes. I'm devastated, but it wasn't about Paul, as such. It was seeing his girlfriend pregnant . . .'

'And? People have babies all the time. You of all people know that.'

'But I can't,' I sob. 'I can't have a baby.'

'You what?' says Lewis, his voice rasping.

'It's never going to happen.'

He stares at the curve in the river where the water is orange and mixed with iron-rich sediment from the bank above, and I can feel doubt and fear settling in my heart at the thought that this could very well be a deal-breaker. What man will want me, knowing I can't have children?

'I remember you said you and Paul tried to conceive and failed, that it was part of the reason why you divorced,' he says eventually.

'It was the reason we got divorced. I thought Paul and I could get through anything, but our marriage wasn't strong enough.'

'Come here.' Lewis pulls me close and holds me, gently massaging my back. 'I'm so sorry, darling, I didn't realise.' He tilts his head and rubs his nose against mine. 'You never know how things will work out, but you'll be all right. You've got a great job, friends and family, and you have me,' he goes on, as I begin to feel slightly better.

'Thank you.' I lean up to kiss him, just as Frosty spots another dog, strolling along on the other side of the river. She drags me towards the riverbank, barking, not in readiness to attack as she used to, but in a friendly greeting.

'Calm down, Frosty!' I do my grimace as the signal for 'no', but it's impossible to get the message across when her attention is elsewhere, her intention being to slide down the bank and swim to the other side. I manage to haul her back, winding her in on the lead to the top of the bank where she gives herself a good shake, showering me and Lewis with water. 'Thanks for that,' I mutter, as Lewis squats down beside her and asks her to sit.

'Treat, Zara,' he says, when Frosty obeys him first time.

'Is that for you or the dog?' I say, feeling rather foolish being able to control neither my dog nor my emotions when it comes to Paul becoming a dad. I thought I'd begun to accept that I'd never be a mum, but this wave of grief has taken me completely by surprise. I hand Lewis a liver treat. Frosty takes it very gently from his fingers.

'Good girl.' Lewis strokes Frosty as he looks up at me. 'Shall we go and get some food? I'm starving.'

'Okay,' I say, although I'm not hungry and we walk to the Talymill Inn where we sit outside at one of the picnic benches, eating chicken salad and chips. Frosty sits at my feet drooling.

'That dog has too many titbits,' Lewis says, grinning.

'That's Gran's fault. She forgets.' I push the rest of my chips aside. 'I need to talk to you about what I said earlier.'

'Go on.'

I gaze at the table, running one fingernail along the grooves in the wood. 'It's rather a sensitive subject, but it's important.'

'What is it?' I'm aware that Lewis sits back, holding on to his pint. 'You're worrying me.'

'When I said Paul and I couldn't have a child, I didn't know for sure which of us had the problem. The tests indicated that it was me, and the consultant said the chances were Paul could father a child, but today proves he was right. It's my fault we didn't conceive. I'm infertile.'

'Did you have fertility treatment then?'

'We had two rounds of IVF. We didn't have a single embryo.'

'I'm sorry,' Lewis says quietly, his voice hardly audible over the sound of the water that rushes through the mill race nearby.

'I did everything I was advised to do to maximise our chances. Paul kept on at me about losing more weight – I tried, but it didn't exactly fall off me – and then I grew angry with him. I used to shout and yell at him not to keep blaming me.'

'I'm not surprised. That's very unfair,' Lewis says as I take a breath.

'I didn't feel feminine any more. I even wondered in the darkest moments whether I was some kind of freak of nature, whether I wasn't female at all.'

'You're all woman to me.' Lewis leans closer and slides his arm around my back.

'Seeing Paul today brought it all back. It's a wound at the very heart of who I am, and now I feel stuck.'

'Stuck?' Lewis frowns.

I force a smile. 'At the risk of sounding like an old woman, I'm of an age where I can see that the natural progression of life is to fall in love, marry and have kids, and live happily ever after, but I'll never have the fairytale ending.'

'All fairytales are different,' Lewis observes. 'At least the ones Murray reads to Poppy are.'

'No, they aren't. Everyone except the baddies lives happily ever after.'

'And the boy and the girl get together in the end, but they don't always have a baby.'

'That's because it's part of the happy-ever-after.'

'You know what I mean,' Lewis sighs in mock frustration at my stubborn pretence of not under-standing. 'Why haven't you talked about this before?'

'Because it seemed too soon to talk about babies with you. If I'd just met you and gone on about my fertility problems, what would you have thought? That I was immediately thinking long-term and serious? That's a great way to keep a guy interested,' I say ironically.

'I see.' He rubs the bridge of his nose.

'Maybe I should have told you straight off, but then before today . . .' I take a deep breath before continuing, 'The tests Paul and I had showed that it was me who had the problem, but I've always clung on to the hope they were wrong. Now I know for certain it was me, not Paul.'

'It's certainly a big thing.'

'So now you know.' I wipe my face with a tissue.

'I'll understand completely if you want to push off and find someone else.'

'Why would I want to do that?' he says, sounding hurt.

'Because . . .' Does he need me to spell it out?

'Listen, Zara. I'm not going to disappear. You are the most beautiful,' he whispers in my ear, 'sexy woman in the world and I don't care about the baby stuff. It doesn't matter to me.'

'But what about—' I go on.

'Sh.' He runs his hand through my hair and down to the nape of my neck. 'I don't know how you do your job, helping all those babies into the world, when you know you can't have one yourself.'

'Some days are easier than others,' I say, thinking of Adam and Rosie and their accidental pregnancy, and another mum-to-be who burst into tears because she didn't want twins. 'I wouldn't have it any other way. I love my job.'

Later, when we've finished eating and watching the world go by with the sun setting behind the trees, I invite Lewis back for a coffee.

'Or do you have to get back for the dogs?' I add with a smile.

'They'll be fine for a bit longer,' he says quickly. 'Your gran won't mind?'

It turns out that she's waiting up for me, dressed in a tatty pink dressing gown and fluffy slippers, and cleaning out one of the kitchen cupboards.

'I'll make the coffee,' she says when she realises Lewis is here.

'I'll do it. Lewis is my guest.'

'It's no trouble,' she says, filling the kettle.

'I didn't think you'd still be up,' I say, slightly irritated with her for not taking the hint and retiring quietly and tactfully to her room.

'I can't sleep anyway.' She flicks the switch at the socket, turning it off rather than on.

'That kettle won't boil like that, will it? Here, let me.' She looks at me much as Frosty does when I've told her off.

'I wish you wouldn't keep doing things for me. I'm perfectly capable.'

'I know. Why don't you go to bed and I'll bring your drink in for you?' I pause, waiting for this to sink in, and wishing I could rewind the clock because there was a time when she would have made herself scarce without me having to spell it out for her.

'It's always nice to have company.'

'Yes, but two's company and three's a crowd. And it's very late. You have to do the papers in the morning.'

'I suppose I do need my beauty sleep. Goodnight, dear.' With a sigh of resignation, she shuffles away, without waiting for her drink or saying goodnight to Lewis, which in a way is a relief, but also a worry.

'I thought your gran would have been up for a chat,' Lewis says when we're curled up on the sofa later. 'Is she all right?'

'Why do you say that?' I say abruptly. 'She seems fine to me.'

'No reason.' He shrugs then rests his head against

329

my shoulder, closing his eyes. I can hear his breathing deepen and my heartbeat quicken.

'How long can you stay?' I whisper.

He opens one eye and grins. 'As long as you like.'

CHAPTER EIGHTEEN

When Needs Must

As Lewis has become part of my circle of friends, Kev invites him to join the stag party a couple of weeks before the wedding. Claire insists on seeing them off in taxis heading to the nearest city, Exeter, to hit the bars and clubs. She gives the boys a list of rules: no laxatives, no waxing, no permanent markers or tattoos. Murray folds it into a paper dart and aims it out of the window of his taxi while Lewis blows me a kiss.

'You might as well have added "no fun" at the end,' I point out when she explains what she's done. 'They won't take any notice anyway.'

'They'd better,' she says. 'I don't want anything to ruin the wedding photos. I don't want to have to do it all again because the boys have mucked them up, shaving Kev's eyebrows off or doing something equally disfiguring. Come on, let's go down to the Talymill Inn for something to eat.'

We've already had the hen do – it was very sophisticated: afternoon tea at a posh hotel in Talymouth – and tonight is an opportunity to clear up any last-minute arrangements for the wedding. While we eat chicken and chips, she makes a list of people who haven't replied to their invites yet and writes a note in my diary to keep me available for an evening of making favours.

'I'm not sure I'll be free,' I say.

'Lewis will have to put up with it for one night,' Claire says, sounding slightly miffed. 'Or he can come and help too.'

'I don't think it's his scene.' I smile at the thought of him counting out sugared almonds and tying ribbons. 'I'll see what I can do. Did you have the final dress fitting yesterday? You haven't mentioned it.'

'I did – I took my mum with me.'

'And?'

'It's perfect. I thought they'd need to let the waist out just a little, but it's fine.' She sighs. 'All we need now is for the boys to behave.'

'Oh, they will. You worry too much. I thought we'd all agreed that what goes on on the stag, stays on the stag.' I stand up. 'Can I get you another drink? I'm driving – as usual.'

A couple of hours later, just before eleven, when the landlord is ringing last orders, we head outside to find my car. A bat swoops down from the roof of the old mill and disappears into the darkness, making me jump, and then my mobile vibrates in my jacket pocket. I pull it out and check the caller ID, half expecting it to be one of my colleagues or mums-to-be, but it's Lewis. Glancing towards Claire, I take the call.

'What's up?' I ask.

'We've lost the groom,' he says anxiously. 'I was hoping he might have made his way to find Claire.'

'Well, he hasn't,' I say, slightly annoyed.

'What's happened?' Claire cuts in, trying to take my phone from me. I hang on so we're both listening in at the same time. 'Lewis, what the —' she swears, 'have you done with him? You can't just lose my fiancé.'

'Don't panic. We're organising a search party – this place is crawling with police since Kev brought so many of his mates with him.'

'This isn't a joke,' I say, seeing how upset Claire is. 'How drunk are you?'

'We've had a few. Kev must have had a couple of pints and a few shots – I haven't been counting.'

It's fair enough, I suppose. I don't like it, but it seems that you can't have a stag do without copious amounts of alcohol.

'You were supposed to be looking after him,' I groan.

'I know – one minute he was with us, the next he'd gone. Hang on a minute. Someone's seen him.' There's the sound of muffled conversation and a clunk, as if Lewis has dropped his mobile before he returns. 'Some woman's just said she saw a man fitting Kev's description heading out along the bypass.'

'Okay, I'll come and see if I can find him,' I say. 'Claire's with me – she can come too.'

'You'll be able to spot him fairly easily – he's wearing a dress.'

'He wasn't when you left.'

'We helped him get changed . . . into a wedding dress.'

'Oh, very original,' I say, although I can't help smiling. 'I'll see you later.'

We pick Kev up on the inner bypass in the city, where he's slumped at the foot of a lamppost in a veil, an ivory gown and torn stockings. His face is covered in pink lipstick. I jump out of the car, but Claire is with him first and I'm expecting her to yell and scream at him, but she stands there in front of him, leans down and touches his cheek, and bursts out laughing.

'You silly sod. You can't even get through your own stag party.'

'I'm sorry, darling,' he mumbles. 'I wanted to come and see you.'

She holds out her hand and helps him up and into the car.

'Let's get you home to bed, then tomorrow, nice and early, I'll set you up with a big greasy fry-up.' Claire flashes me a smile. 'Thank you for this, Zara. Thank you for picking up the runaway bride.'

'Yeah, except I can't run,' Kev says. 'I'm bloody legless.'

'You said it.'

'I've been getting some funny looks,' he goes on.

'Shut up, Kev,' Claire says. 'I don't want to know. I'm just glad you're still alive, no thanks to the rest of the lads,' she adds, which reminds me to let Lewis know we've retrieved the lost groom when we arrive back at Talyton St George.

Fortunately, the other members of the party return safe and sound, although they suffer from mega-hangovers the next day, and Lewis apologises to both me and Claire. He also arranges to take me out for my birthday at the end of August, a week away.

Lewis whistles through his teeth when he comes to pick me up.

'Hey, I'm not one of your dogs,' I say lightly, as this stranger in a white shirt, tie and dark trousers opens the door for me.

'You look amazing,' he breathes.

'Thank you.' I'm wearing a new dress with a wrap-around top, which reveals just enough cleavage, and a fitted skirt which flatters my curves, and he can hardly keep his eyes off me as I settle in the seat beside him in the pick-up. 'I hope you're going to concentrate on the road,' I say, flirting with him.

He kisses me and presses a small package into my hand. 'Happy birthday, Zara.'

'What is it?'

'Open it and you'll find out.' His lips curve into a smile as I open the gift bag and pull out a small box, inside which I find a delicate silver chain. 'I remembered that Daisy broke yours.'

'Thank you, that's such a lovely present.' I'm touched, especially as it must have been worth at least a couple of ewes for his flock. I take the necklace out and hold it up to my neck.

'Let me do that.' He takes over from me as I fumble with the catch. 'There.' He lays the links of the chain flat against my skin, stroking my collarbone and touching my throat at the same time, while I look into his eyes. They are soft with the shadows of the evening sun, and I can't resist kissing him, at which a horn sounds close by, making me jump.

'Oops, I hit it by mistake,' Lewis laughs. 'Come on, we'd better go before we make a spectacle of ourselves. People will talk. I hope you're hungry.'

I am now, I think, but not for food.

'Emily recommended this place,' Lewis says, pulling up outside the Barnscote about fifteen minutes later. It's a well-renowned country hotel, centred around a medieval Devon longhouse built from cob and thatch, with climbing plants around the door.

'This is where Claire's having her wedding,' I say.

'Have you eaten here before?'

'I had lunch with Claire when she was trying it out. It was lovely – but Lewis, are you sure? Dinner here costs an arm and a leg.'

His response is to get out of the pick-up and hold the door open for me. I shouldn't have raised the subject of money. It was tactless of me.

Elsa, the proprietor who breeds Happy Pigs as a sideline, welcomes us with non-alcoholic cocktails and shows us to a table in an alcove by a window in the dining room, where flowers cascade from a vase on the sill and a candle flickers in a cranberry glass.

'I hope you have a wonderful evening,' she says after she's introduced us to our waiter for the night.

'Hello, Adam,' I say, not giving anything away.

'Hi.' His face reddens as he hands out the menus. 'I'll be back to take your order.'

'Adam's a hardworking young man,' Elsa says. 'He's just done a shift for his stepdad on the farm, haven't you?'

He nods. I'm impressed because I suspect he's working all hours to support his baby when he or she arrives. He takes our orders and brings bread rolls and drinks while we're waiting for our starters.

Lewis's glass chinks against mine. 'Happy birthday, Zara,' he repeats. 'And, just so you know, I love being with you, and I have every intention of staying around a whole lot longer. Here's to the future.'

'The future,' I murmur, as butterflies start fluttering in my throat at the thought that we're getting serious here.

'What are we going to buy Claire and Kev for a wedding present?' Lewis asks. 'I'll pay my share.'

I explain about the flying owl. 'Claire left a wedding magazine at the surgery the other day, and I was having a flick through when I saw an article about having an owl to fly the rings down the aisle to the best man. It looked amazing and very romantic.'

'I've got a mate from uni who's a falconer.'

'I had my heart set on an owl.'

Lewis smiles. 'He has a couple of owls. I'll ask him if he'd do it for a few drinks and a piece of wedding cake.'

'That's great – if you think he'll do it.'

'Will Claire appreciate this alteration in her plans for the dream wedding?'

'I hope so. I've spoken to Kev and he's cool with it. He said he couldn't speak for his fiancée because she usually speaks for herself, but he thought it was a safe bet. I just want to do something really special for my best friend.' I correct myself. 'For my best girlfriend.'

Once we've eaten, Adam brings the bill and chocolate mints.

'Let's go halves,' I say. 'It's only fair.'

'No,' Lewis says rather sharply. 'This is my treat.'

'I'm more than happy to pay my way.' I'm glad I didn't offer to pay the full amount – he's really miffed about it. 'I don't see why men should be expected to pay for everything.'

'I know but, as I said, this is mine.' Lewis hands the plate with his card to Adam when he next comes by. 'I wouldn't have done this if I didn't think I could afford it.'

I touch the chain at my neck. It's too much. I earn more than he does and will do for the foreseeable future.

The following morning we are in bed – strictly speaking the rather uncomfortable sofa bed in the annexe at the farm – with mugs of coffee on the side table. Lewis's dogs have been out for a quick run and now they're back snoozing in their beds. I gaze across to where Lewis is lying on his back, exposing the smattering of honey-gold curls across his chest. His lips are curved into a small smile and my heart tightens with happiness at the sight of him, my toy-boy . . .

Lewis opens one eye, turns his head and grins. 'What are you looking at?'

'You, of course,' I say, as he props himself up on one elbow and reaches out to stroke the curve of my waist.

'How long can you stay?'

'I'll have to take Frosty for a walk later.'

'I'd like to find a way for us to spend more time together.' Lewis leans across and kisses me gently. 'I don't want to carry on like this. Zara, I want you to move in with me.'

'I'm sorry?' I'm so taken aback, I sit up, clasping the duvet across my breasts.

'I love falling asleep and waking up with my arms around you.'

'I love it too.'

I reach out and touch his shoulder as he continues, 'And I'd like you to be here much more. I want us to be together – sometimes I feel as if we hardly see each other.'

My heart leaps, then falls back again. 'Oh, Lewis. I'm flattered that you asked, but—'

'But?' His expression darkens slightly as a cloud passes across the morning sun. 'Is this about the stag?'

'No, it isn't,' I exclaim. 'Look, this isn't personal.' I love him to pieces. 'It's Gran. I can't move out. She needs me.'

'You can't be there for ever,' he says, frowning. 'Come on, I want to wake up beside you every morning – not once or twice a week, if we're lucky. And if I do have to move away for work, I want to make the most of the time we have.'

'I can't really move in here – this belongs to Murray and my sister.'

'It's a temporary measure. I've been looking at places to rent. There's a cottage in Talyford – we could share the bills.'

'It's silly to commit yourself to a six-month rental agreement when you might find a job at any moment,' I point out.

'I'll have to settle down one day. I have plans, as I've said before, to rent or buy some land where I can keep sheep, breed them and rear them, and be a full-time shepherd. That way I can make some serious money.'

'How can you cope with sending the lambs you bring into the world off for meat?'

'I love sheep, but I also like a roast leg of lamb with gravy and crispy potatoes – don't you?'

'I'm afraid I've stopped eating lamb since I saw you carrying that one into Emily's kitchen. It was too cute. I feel guilty when Gran serves up lamb shanks and I have to decline.'

'You can't go on like that,' Lewis says. 'It's my job, my income, my life.'

'I know,' I sigh.

'You've gone all ethical on me. What about Murray? He lives off his sheep.'

'Yeah. I suppose it's a necessary evil. I can see you rear them kindly and they have a good life while it lasts.'

'So will you move in with me if I can find the right place?'

I smile ruefully. 'I can't move in with you right now. It's impossible.'

'Are you saying this because you don't want to live with me?'

'No, I've said. It isn't personal. I'd love to move in with you, but I want it to be right.'

'In the perfect world we'd move into a place of our own with the dogs, but that isn't going to be any time soon.' Lewis takes my hand. 'Zara, I live for the moment. Life's too short for anything else.'

'I'm the practical one, then, and you're the romantic,' I say as I run through the options. 'There isn't room at Gran's for you and the dogs. Norris would go ballistic or expire from the shock.'

'I don't want to live with Rosemary. She can be good fun, but I want to be with you, not your grandmother.'

'I've been giving Gran a hand with the papers and behind the counter when I can.'

'That's fair enough, but you don't have to live with her to help her out.' I don't respond as Lewis continues, 'I wish you were a bit more of a pink fluffy romantic. I'd pretty much moved you in.' He lies back, his hands behind his head, staring at the ceiling.

'Gran relies on me, and I've promised her that I'll be there for her, as she was for me when I was in bits when my marriage ended.'

'So what are you saying?'

'That it's a lovely idea because there's nothing I love more than curling up with you in bed at night and waking up with you in the morning, but I can't move in with you at the moment. I need time to talk to Gran and see how I can organise things so I know she's all right.' I feel sick with regret. I so want to move in and

341

for us to be together, but I can't let her down. I just can't. Boyfriend or grandmother? My loyalty is torn in two.

'You're always so busy,' Lewis goes on. 'Is it for real or is it an excuse? Sometimes I get the impression you don't want to hang out with me, that you'll do anything to avoid it.' He looks so downcast that I'm seized with guilt. He holds my hand and runs his fingertips up and down my forearm, grazing my skin. 'I want to be your best friend and lover. Zara, I want to be your hero.'

My mouth runs dry. 'You are my hero,' I stammer.

'Can't we try – say you stay here three or four nights a week to begin with?' Lewis tries again.

I've all but run out of excuses. 'I'm sorry, I can't. It's worse than you think. Gran isn't coping.' To my chagrin, hot tears come rolling down my cheeks, and along with them comes the truth – about the forgetfulness, the accusations and my promise to Gran that I won't let her go into a home. 'It's pretty awful to see her going downhill. It's like losing a tiny piece of her every day.'

Lewis cuddles me.

'I knew there was something wrong – you should have told me before.'

'I know. I've been in denial about how bad things are, and I suppose I was hoping that if I didn't speak about it, it would go away. Now I've had to face up to it.'

'I can help. She could move in with us at a push.'

I look up. 'The last thing I want is for you to feel obliged to take on the two of us.'

'Obliged? That's a horrible word.'

'I realise that, but I can foresee a time when I'm going to have to give up everything to care for her full time.'

'You mean your job?'

'I'd take on the shop as an alternative.'

'But you're trained to deliver babies, not newspapers. No, you can't!' Lewis exclaims.

'Gran has a saying: when needs must.'

'She has too many bloody sayings,' he says. 'I can top that – a problem aired is a problem shared. Can't Emily and your parents help out with the shop? It must be their turn by now.'

'My parents have already decided which home Gran will go to – and, let's face it, with two children and the farm, Emily has her hands full.'

'What about an assistant for the shop, a full-timer?'

'I've been looking into the accounts and what she's entitled to, and there isn't enough money coming in. She won't countenance selling the property and she gets so confused sometimes, I really don't think she'd cope living anywhere else.'

'That's so sad. I can't imagine my grandparents being in that situation – they're all very healthy for now. Listen, you must promise me you won't jack in your job.'

'I can't do that. My mind's been going around in circles and I can't see any other way.'

'There has to be,' Lewis says. 'I know you don't want to, but I reckon you have to speak to the rest of the family. They might be able to come up with a solution.'

'Sometimes you sound so old,' I tell him with a smile.

'Do you know what's wrong with Rosemary? Has she seen a doctor?'

I shake my head.

'You really must get this sorted. Promise me you'll make her an appointment – it can't be that difficult when you work from the surgery.'

'Oh, I don't know. I don't want to upset her. She's very frail, mentally, I mean.'

'I understand that you're afraid of getting a diagnosis, but what if there's some treatment she can have to improve her health, at least for a while? All the time you're covering for her, she could be missing out.'

'I see what you mean. If I did arrange for her to be checked out, you wouldn't let on to Emily, would you?'

'I'd leave that to you, but remember you can't protect her for ever.'

'Thank you, Lewis.'

'It's nothing,' he says, but it means everything to me. 'You know, I understand why you can't commit to moving in with me at the moment, although I'm disappointed, but I won't push it until you feel ready.'

I give him a hug. I can't believe how lucky I am.

I talk to Claire at the surgery later, when I drop in to make an appointment for Gran, saying how sometimes I wish I could be completely irresponsible and do my own thing. Claire says perhaps I should, because Gran wouldn't want me to put my life on hold for her, but I know I can't. I'm not like that.

In the evening, a few days after my birthday, I turn the sign on the shop door to 'Closed' and slide the bolts across. I did the shopping the day before, and dealt with the papers in advance of going out to work this morning, so all that's left to do is cash up and cook dinner. I don't know how my grandmother kept it all together over the years. I smile ruefully as Frosty comes trotting in to remind me she could do with feeding too. I'm sure she'd like a walk as well, but I can't face it. I've been on my feet all day and I'm shattered.

'I'll take you out in the morning, I promise.' I wander upstairs with the dog behind me to find Gran who is asleep in her chair with the television on – it's a repeat of *Come Dine with Me*, I think. She has her mouth open and her tea cup emptied into her lap. With a sigh of frustration, I turn the volume down.

'Hey, I'm watching that.' Her voice is croaky and thick with sleep.

'You'd nodded off,' I say, gently removing the cup from her grasp. 'You've spilt your tea again.'

'Oh dear.' She seems remarkably unconcerned as I fetch some kitchen roll to mop up.

'Would you like a fresh one?'

'No, thank you.' She strokes her crinkled forehead with her fingertips. 'What is the time?'

'Teatime. I thought we'd have cod and parsley sauce, one of your favourites.' I remind myself not to keep talking to her as I would to Poppy. 'I've made you an appointment with Dr Mackie.' I spoke to him at the surgery today. 'He's making a house call tomorrow.'

'There's no need for that. I'm not ill.'

'We talked about this yesterday and you agreed it

was a good idea to have a checkup to make sure. Like an MOT,' I add encouragingly.

She frowns. She's lost, I can tell, and I feel terrible: sorry for her, angry at her too for not being able to remember something we only discussed a short time ago.

'Like an MOT on a car,' I repeat, and she smiles and nods.

'Oh yes, your granddad used to have a car.'

'I'm talking about you seeing the doctor,' I interrupt. 'He's coming at eleven and I'm going to sit in with you because, as you've always said, two heads are better than one.'

'What am I going to say to him?' she asks.

'It's all right. Leave it with Ben, I mean Dr Mackie. He'll ask you some questions, that's all.' I smile to reassure her. 'We can have a nice chat with him.'

When Ben comes the next day, he asks her what day it is and what she had for breakfast. She looks confused, but to be honest there are times, depending on how busy I am, when I wouldn't have a clue either.

'Gran, it's Tuesday and you had toast for breakfast,' I say.

'Ah, Zara, your grandmother is supposed to be answering for herself,' Ben says with a smile. 'These questions do have a purpose.'

'Oh, I'm sorry. Of course.' I feel like a complete idiot.

'Why are you asking me these questions? You're here because . . . because . . . ?' Gran turns to me, frowning, 'Why is he here?'

'It's for a checkup,' I say firmly.

346

'I can tell you, young man,' she addresses Dr Mackie, 'I don't need one.'

'We might as well make sure while I'm here.' He asks her more questions, and every so often she looks to me for help and I have to force myself to remain silent. At the end, Ben asks her again what day it is. She gets the date right and the year wrong. According to her, it is 1965, and I'm beginning to feel like I'm taking part in an episode of *Ashes to Ashes*.

'How old are you, Rosemary?' Dr Mackie says without a flicker of his expression.

'Oh, you must never ask a lady her age,' she says coquettishly to cover the fact, I believe, that she really doesn't remember. Dr Mackie glances at me. He knows that too.

'You're having some difficulties with your short-term memory, Rosemary,' he says. 'I'm going to refer you to a consultant who will do some more checks to see how we can best help you.'

I could cry because he's confirming my worst fears, but Gran, if she is frightened, doesn't show it. She's happy in the here and now, stroking Frosty who sits at her feet.

'I'll show you out,' I say to Ben, and on the way downstairs, he talks.

'Don't worry. There are things we can do. I'm going to send Claire over to take some blood and ask her for a urine sample to make sure she hasn't got an infection somewhere, which might be affecting her cognitive capacity; although I'm afraid it's more likely that she's showing early signs of dementia.'

'How will it go on?' I ask tentatively, because I can't help feeling I don't want to know.

'There are different types and they can progress in various ways, depending on the individual.' Ben shrugs. 'I'm afraid I haven't got a crystal ball, but she will eventually need full-time care. And, as for running the shop – which is what this is really about, isn't it?, because she doesn't want to give it up – I can't see how she can do it for much longer. Your family is going to have to make some tough decisions on her behalf.'

'She seems quite paranoid sometimes, blaming people for stealing things she's mislaid herself,' I say. 'Is that part of it?'

'Denial? Insecurity? She can't remember, she might be having delusions, or filling the gaps in her memory with false information. It's hard to tell.'

'It's sad, so very sad.' I wrap my arms across my chest. 'She was always so sharp.'

'Some people like to create a kind of memory bank of photos and anecdotes with their relatives. Sometimes it helps.' Ben pauses. 'Anyway, Claire will be over later to take the blood. If you want to talk any time, you know where I am.'

'Thank you.' As I see Ben out, I can hear Gran shuffling about upstairs, heading for the bathroom, but I remain in the shop, needing some time alone to think. Like Gran, I've been in denial, but Ben has changed that. My grandmother isn't merely getting old, she's in decline and it's time I faced up to it.

I grab the biggest bar of milk chocolate I can find, strip the wrapper and peel the foil away, releasing the gorgeous aroma of cocoa and sugar. I bite into it, feeling the texture strain against my teeth until it breaks and floats across my tongue, melting to a smooth, sweet silkiness. I'm in heaven, but it's only a temporary fix because soon Claire turns up to take the blood, reminding me of Gran's fragility all over again.

'Thanks for saving us a trip to the surgery.' I show her up to the flat where Gran is in the living room, sitting gazing at the television again. 'Claire's here.' I pick up the remote and turn the TV off.

'What did you do that for?' she says.

'Because I can't hear myself think.'

'Oh, hello.' Gran turns slowly to face Claire. 'What are you doing here, dear?'

'She's come to take some blood for that test Dr Mackie asked for.' I start to wonder if she's deaf, like Frosty.

'It shouldn't take long.' Claire unpacks her bag on the side table. She applies a tourniquet to Gran's arm, taps at the vein and slides the needle in, making Gran wince.

'Oh dear, you don't seem to have any blood today.' Claire tries again.

'The last time Dr Mackie had a go, he said it was like getting blood out of a stone,' Gran says, and Claire rolls her eyes and says, in that case, she knows why he sent her instead of doing it himself.

'Dr Mackie is a busy man,' Gran says, excusing him.

'Here we go.' Claire loosens the tourniquet from Gran's arm, and asks her to hold a cotton-wool ball over the site of the injection while she rolls the containers to mix the blood. 'I'll take these back to the surgery now and we should have a result by tomorrow lunchtime. Dr Mackie will phone you.'

'I do like Dr Mackie,' Gran says wistfully.

'He might make another house-call if you're very lucky,' Claire teases, but she looks at me, her expression serious. I turn the television back on, sneaking the volume up a little more than normal.

'What's wrong?' Claire asks me on her way back downstairs.

'Ben thinks she has some kind of dementia, not that I really needed him to confirm it.'

'Oh, I'm sorry.' She gives me a one-armed hug. 'It isn't the end of the world, you know.'

'You've seen enough patients to realise that it isn't great, though,' I point out.

'You'll have to tell your mum and dad now, and Emily,' Claire says. 'You can't keep struggling along on your own.'

'I can't . . .'

'You can't not. She's their family, too. You can't keep this to yourself any longer. You've been covering up for her, protecting her for ages now. It can't go on. You have your own life, career, gorgeous boyfriend . . . Oh, and a dog. You're putting everything at risk. Look at you, you're shattered.'

'I'm a bit tired,' I admit, 'but that's work.'

'And doing the papers first thing in the morning?'

'When I can, not every day.'

'Promise me you'll speak to your parents. There's only so much you can do.' Claire hesitates. 'I can tell

350

you that caring for someone with dementia is all-consuming. I know you want to do the right thing by your grandmother, but you have to think of yourself too. She wouldn't want you to lose everything because of her.'

'I can't abandon her, not after all she's done. When Paul and I split up, she was there for me.' I lower my voice. 'You all were, but in the darkest of times, when I thought I was going mad, Gran kept me going. I owe her.' I bite back sudden tears. 'It's going to be tough, though, I know that. I just hope that Lewis understands.'

'He will,' she says reassuringly, 'if he loves you.'

'He hasn't said so exactly, but I'm pretty sure he loves me. The question is, Claire, does he love me enough?'

CHAPTER NINETEEN

Here Comes the Bride

After the doctor's visit, a week passes and I still haven't told my parents about it, but I make the excuse that I haven't had time to see them because I'm helping Claire with the final preparations for her wedding at the weekend.

If she could have planned the weather, she couldn't have done any better. When I open the curtains on her big day, I discover that it's a magnificent September morning, bright, breezy and unseasonably warm, and perfect for dog walking. I throw on my trackies and head downstairs to pack the newspaper boy's bag before sending him on his way.

'Is Mrs Witheridge all right?' James asks, hesitating at the door with the bag over his shoulder.

'She didn't sleep very well last night.' I found her wandering about in the shop, eating pear drops at three in the morning. 'Thanks for asking.' My mobile rings.

'I'll see you later, James,' I say, answering it without looking at the caller ID. 'Hi, Lewis.'

'It's Claire, you muppet. When are you going to get here?'

'Don't panic. According to the schedule you gave me, I have another half an hour before I'm supposed to be at your mum and dad's.'

'Which one are you looking at? Which schedule?'

'I don't know.' I stick my hand in my pocket and pull it out. 'It's dated last week.'

'Not that one, the one I dropped into the shop yesterday – I gave it to your gran.'

'That wasn't wise. You should have just emailed it.'

'I'll do that right now.'

'No, don't bother. Just let me know what time you want me.'

'Now, Zara. I need you here now.'

I smile to myself. 'I need to take Frosty for a very quick walk and make sure Gran's up and dressed before I leave. I'll be with you as soon as I can.'

'Can't you miss walking the dog just this once?' Claire grumbles.

'Mrs Dyer's coming in to let her out now and again during the day, and I'd like to be sure she's settled. If I don't keep her routine, she'll probably start wrecking the place again. Look, I'll be with you shortly. I promise.'

Three hours later, Leanne and I are helping Claire and the dress out of a white limo decorated with ribbons and flowers. Leanne is Claire's younger sister. She's a teacher at a secondary school in South London and, since her last relationship ended a few months ago, she's been trying to find a permanent position closer to home. She's petite and quiet, but her hair is loud, pink with a coppery sheen which clashes with the blue bridesmaids' dresses.

'My shoe,' Claire exclaims as she tries to step out onto the pavement outside the church. 'It's caught in the hem.'

'Don't move,' I say, diving down to hunt through the acres of ivory satin and lace of her skirts and unsnag the heel of her shoe from the stitching, while Leanne holds her arm to steady her. 'That's it. You can relax now.'

'I can't,' she says. 'I'm so nervous.'

'I don't know why. You look amazing,' Leanne reassures her.

'Is my hair all right? Is my veil straight?'

'It's beautiful. You're beautiful,' Leanne says. 'Now come on. Kev will be waiting.'

Claire's dad takes her hand and leads her towards the church where a crowd are waiting: shoppers here for Talyton St George's Saturday market, residents, patients and passers-by. Janet, having taken a break from morning surgery, wishes Claire all the best, but I notice that Ben has been hijacked by Fifi Green who, although not invited to the wedding, is dressed for one. I spot Lewis with Gran on his arm and they join me briefly as the crowd applauds the bride and gasps at the dress and the bouquet.

'I thought I'd make sure your gran turned up. I persuaded her to shut up shop for the rest of the day – I've left a sign on the door.'

354

'Oh, thank you. You're a star. By the way, is every-thing sorted?' I ask. 'Is Rob here?'

'He's waiting around the back of the church. Harry's given him the rings. You look unbelievable, by the way.' He smiles and kisses me on the cheek, and adds, with a wink, 'Unbelievably blue.'

I glance down at my gown. 'The colour's growing on me.'

'I thought you said it didn't suit you, but it brings out the colour of your eyes . . . and it really shows off your figure.'

'Oh, he's such a charmer,' Gran cuts in, reminding me of her presence. 'Don't you think he looks handsome too, Zara?'

'I do.' Lewis looks more gorgeous than ever, clean-shaven and older somehow in a suit and tie, and the thought crosses my mind that I wouldn't mind walking down the aisle to meet him at the altar, which is odd when I have no intention of getting married again.

'I'll catch you later.' Lewis turns away and walks Gran down the path to the entrance to the church, where they disappear into the shadows as the best man, hot and shiny in his morning suit, comes jogging towards us with his top hat in his hand. It's Harry, Kev's brother.

'Kev's shitting himself.' Harry smiles ruefully. 'I don't know why. I've told him Claire has everything under control. All he's got to do is remember his lines and put the ring on her finger.' He clicks his tongue. 'Simples.'

'Has Nobby turned up?'

'Your uncle, the organist?' Harry nods. 'I dosed him up with black coffee and sat him in front of the organ. Thanks for the tip about bringing a flask.'

'Come over here,' Claire calls to me. 'I want a photo of you, me, Dad and Leanne and the little girls before we go into the church.'

By the little girls, she's referring to Kev's nieces, who are bridesmaids too.

'I'll let the groom know you're here.' Harry dashes off back through the churchyard, while we stand in the sunshine for photos before following Claire and her father inside the church, where the air is cool and fragrant with the scent of lilies and roses. The bride's train brushes along the ancient stone floor between the oak pews, which are filled with her and Kev's families and friends. I catch sight of Emily, Murray and Lewis, who is holding Poppy's hand as she stares at Claire with wide eyes.

Uncle Nobby's drunken version of 'Here Comes the Bride' comes to a stumbling halt as Claire reaches the altar, where a rainbow of light streams through the stained-glass window above. She turns and hands me her bouquet to hold until the ceremony is over, and Leanne and I step aside to take our places in the front of the pews beside Claire's mum, Irene, who's weeping into a tissue.

'I'm going to miss my wonderful daughter,' she sobs quietly.

'Think of it less as losing a daughter and more about gaining a son-in-law,' Leanne says cheerfully.

'Kevin?' Irene continues to cry, taking no notice when the vicar raises one hand for silence.

'Why is Claire's princess dress too long for her, Mummy?' pipes up a familiar voice.

'It's called a train,' Emily says in a whisper that seems to ring out throughout the echoing chambers of the church.

'It's a dress, not a train, silly Mummy.'

I look towards Claire to gauge her reaction but she only has eyes for her groom, whom I take it isn't her mother's first choice of husband for her elder daughter. I know she and Kevin have had their differences over a speeding ticket.

'Any more, and you'll have to wait outside. Got that!' Emily hisses.

'Ouch, you're hurting me,' Poppy wails.

'I'm not touching you . . .'

'You're pinching me.'

'Poppy!' Murray picks his daughter up and hoists her onto his shoulders, ensuring quiet as the bride and groom make their vows.

The vicar asks Harry for the rings, at which he makes a show of searching for them, patting his pockets and shaking his head, and I can see Claire is waiting and she's just about to open her mouth to give him a good rollocking for losing them, when Rob the falconer appears in a brown jerkin and breeches from behind one of the stone pillars at the end of the aisle. A white barn owl is perched on his outstretched arm.

'Oh, what's this?' Claire exclaims. 'There must be some mistake. You've got the wrong wedding.'

'Hush,' Kev says, going on to whisper in her ear. Claire turns to me, one eyebrow raised. I nod and cross my fingers behind my back, hoping she's going to like Lewis's and my gift.

Harry stands to one side of the happy couple and nods towards Rob, who releases the owl. There's a collective gasp from the wedding guests when it soars silently along the centre of the aisle like something out of a fairytale. Harry gives the owl his cue as planned before the ceremony, but instead of swooping onto his arm, it gives him a second look and flies a circle above the altar before flying up into the tower and perching on a ledge, from which it stares down, its face like a pale disc.

'What am I supposed to do now?' Harry asks, looking towards Rob, who comes scurrying along the aisle, arm outstretched and gazing anxiously up into the arches of the tower.

'Don't worry. I'll get him down.' Rob whistles. 'Come on, Merlin.'

Merlin refuses to budge.

'I think he's enjoying the attention,' Leanne whispers to me.

'What are we going to do if he doesn't come down?' I respond. 'Claire's going to be so upset.'

'What's the phrase? Never work with children or animals?' Leanne says with a half-smile.

'Merlin, get yourself down here, you little bugger,' Rob mutters.

'Mummy, that man sweared,' Poppy says out loud.

'Sh, you'll frighten the owl,' Emily says.

'He won't come down. He's a naughty monkey, isn't he?' Poppy goes on.

'He's an owl actually,' Murray says dryly.

My neck is beginning to ache as I stare upwards, willing, praying even, for the owl to fly down, but all he does is shuffle to the end of the ledge.

'Don't go to sleep,' Rob calls. 'Please, don't . . .'

'How long do owls sleep for?' I hear Claire asking. 'Aren't they nocturnal? He'll be up there all day.'

I want to run from the church in tears for letting my best friend down and ruining her big day, but I glance towards Lewis who is gazing up at the owl with an expression of shock. Apparently aware that I'm looking at him, he turns and mouths with a wry smile, 'Owl be with you, or maybe I won't.' I suppress a giggle, suddenly able to see the funny side of the situation.

'You think you're such a hoot,' I mouth back, before turning my attention back to the reluctant ring-bearer. Merlin cocks his head one way and then the other, and finally launches himself from the ledge, swooping down to Rob's arm to a collective sigh of relief, laughter and applause.

'He's come back down.' Poppy squeals with delight while Claire embraces Kev, dislodging her tiara and veil, which Leanne rushes forwards to put back in place.

Harry unclips the rings with trembling fingers and places them on a velvet cloth for the vicar, before Rob carries the owl back along the aisle, allowing the wedding to continue, the only further hitch being the hitching together of Claire and Kevin as husband and wife. When Kev kisses his bride, Lewis winks at me and I blow him a kiss back. It's strange, but I feel as if we've been together for ever and Paul and I never happened.

Claire and Kev hold hands as they walk down the aisle, nodding and smiling. Leanne and I follow, along with Harry and Kev's twin nieces in blue dresses with flowers in their hair. Outside, in the sunshine, we shower the bride and groom with a swirling confetti of rose petals before the photographer runs through Claire's list of required poses. When it's the turn of the groom's family, I take a break, joining Murray and Emily.

'I want an owl,' Poppy says, tugging on her mum's sleeve.

'An owl wouldn't make a good pet,' Emily says. 'They don't always do as they're told for a start.'

Poppy puts her hands on her hips and tosses her ringlets. 'I want an owl,' she repeats belligerently.

'We have owls on the farm,' Murray says.

'When can I have a kitten?' Poppy tries a different approach.

'One day,' Emily says, and for this occasion the response is enough. Poppy runs away with Lewis for a brief game of hide and seek amongst the gravestones, with the other little bridesmaids who are growing bored with proceedings.

'It's a shame you couldn't bring Daisy with you,' I say.

'I understand where Claire's coming from – she doesn't want a crying baby ruining her day. I'm quite

360

surprised she invited Poppy, although I'm pleased
she did. It's good to give her some time away from
her little sister and vice versa – I turned my back for
a second yesterday and she'd half choked Daisy on a
grape. A whole grape? She's six months old.' Emily's
voice sounds strained.

'Would having a pet distract her attentions from the
baby?' I suggest.

'I'd be afraid she'd kill the pet instead. I don't think
she's old enough to bear the responsibility, and Murray
and I, we haven't got time for anything else. It would
be too much. We're both completely frazzled by all
the broken nights.' Emily sighs. 'I know this sounds
terrible when you . . . There are days when I wish we'd
never had Poppy.'

'You don't mean that.'

'There are times when I do.'

'It will get better, I promise.' I want to add that one
day she'll look back and smile at the naughty things
Poppy has done, but I don't think that will help at the
moment. 'I can see you're struggling. Just tell me what
I can do.'

Emily opens her mouth to respond, but I cut her
off.

'Don't try to convince me you're coping when it's
clear you're not, and don't feel that you're imposing
on me. You're my sister and I want you to be happy.
Let me have Poppy for a day.' I hold up my hand. 'No
arguments.'

'Thank you,' Emily says.

The wedding party decamps to the Barnscote Hotel

for the reception; when we arrive, Claire decides she needs a visit to the Ladies.

'If I ever do this again, remind me to allow for the owl,' she says, laughing. 'That was genius, Zara. I've never seen a ring-bearing owl at a wedding. I hope someone took a picture of it when it was flying down the aisle.'

'I don't think they did – flash photography puts him off. You had some photos taken with him outside the church, didn't you?'

'He's so beautiful. I half expected Harry Potter to turn up. Thank you, it was the best wedding present we could have had.' Claire hands Leanne her bouquet as we reach the toilets. 'How do you expect me to get in there with the dress?'

'With difficulty,' Leanne giggles. 'Here comes the bride, all fat and wide.'

'Are you going in forwards or in reverse?' I ask.

'It'll have to be reverse. I'll never turn round in there.'

'You might do it as a four- or five-point turn.'

'This is ridiculous. I didn't think about it when I chose the dress.' Claire is laughing as she turns to me. 'Don't let the train drag on the floor.'

'I won't.' I gather it up tightly in my arms. 'Let's drape it over your shoulder and see if you can manage, otherwise I'll have to join you in there.'

I push the door up as far as it will go and wait outside, holding it semi-closed.

'Has everyone turned up?' Claire asks.

'Gran came along with Lewis.'

'That's good. I hoped she would.'

362

'The only guests who couldn't make it are Tessa and Jack. Tessa isn't well.' I worry about them, wondering if they're trying to avoid questions about the baby, because I can't imagine they can answer with any joy. I make a mental note to call Tessa on Monday for a chat. 'Are you okay? You're taking a very long time in there.'

'I'm done,' Claire says.

'Let's go and get this party started then,' Leanne says. 'I'm starving.'

'So am I. I feel a bit light-headed and I haven't had that much champagne.' Claire emerges clutching the train and looking pale beneath the fake tan. She has that delicate, almost translucent appearance that I've seen many times before and I can't help wondering . . .

'Come on. Stop dreaming about the hot shepherd and come and catch this bouquet,' Claire says, handing me the train once she's washed her hands and taken the flowers from her sister.

'I'm all right, thank you,' I respond. 'I've had my chance at marriage. Let someone who hasn't have a go – not that I believe there's any truth in it.'

'Don't spoil my day,' she says brightly as we join the rest of the wedding guests in the dining room. 'Humour me.'

Kev escorts his new wife up to the mezzanine gallery and introduces her before she turns to throw the bouquet over her shoulder. She puts so much energy into it that the flowers hit the ceiling above and drop straight down into my hands when I couldn't have tried any harder to avoid them.

'Yay!' Claire cheers from above. 'Zara, you're next!'

'Oh no, I don't think so.' I hold the flowers as far from my body as possible, as if they're infectious, while Claire runs down the steps, holding up her skirt, comes over and hugs me. 'It'll be my turn to laugh at you when you're planning your wedding.'

'I've told you before. I'm not going to marry again. I've been there before, remember?'

Claire nods towards where Lewis is chatting with my gran, Emily and Murray. 'I have a premonition that someone will change your mind. Now, I'm going to catch up with my mum who's having a nervous breakdown before we sit down for the meal. Have you got the seating plan?'

'I gave it to Elsa to put up on the board outside.'

'Would you mind making a couple of changes?' She whispers in my ear.

'Will do.' I catch the silken fragrance of roses from the bouquet. There has to be some matchmaking to make a wedding complete. 'What shall I do with the flowers?'

'I don't know – leave them on the top table?'

'Isn't it on the plan?' I tease.

'Oh, sod that. I've lost the plot.' Claire laughs. 'Let's just relax and enjoy it.'

Lewis joins me with a glass of champagne in one hand and his other hand on my bottom. I lean up and kiss him on the lips, then step away, or at least, I attempt to, but I appear to be stuck to the floor. I glance down.

'Lewis, you're standing on my dress.' I give him a gentle push and, chuckling, he moves aside. 'I'm just going to rescue those people over there from Rosemary. The sherry has gone to her head.'

'Thank you,' I say, smiling as he walks across the room to take my grandmother by the arm and guide her back towards us.

After the meal, Harry makes the best man's speech. There are a couple of stories about Kevin which shed an entirely different light on what I thought of him, and from Claire's expression are revelations to her too, followed by a list of thank yous.

'Finally,' Harry looks relieved that he's about to reach the end of his ordeal, 'last but not least, the bridesmaids who are all, I have to say, looking absolutely beautiful today, not that they don't always, I'm sure. Zara and Leanne, I'd like to spank you for all you've done today.' He stops abruptly as those who are still listening, a fair few, burst out laughing. 'Did I say what I think I said?'

'You have such a dirty mind, Harry,' Kev exclaims.

'I'm sorry, I didn't mean it. I meant to say thank, not spank. Definitely not spank,' Harry blusters, reddening to the roots of his hair.

'I'm not sure I'd say no,' Leanne whispers aside to me as Lewis calls out, 'Hey, hands off my girlfriend. If anyone's doing any spanking, it's me.'

When the next round of laughter subsides, Poppy comes up to the top table and gazes at Harry in awe as she asks him if her auntie Zara has been very naughty.

'I don't know,' Harry says. 'You'll have to ask Lewis that.'

'No, please don't.' I cover my face.

'Yes, spare my bridesmaid's blushes,' Claire joins in.

'It's too late!' I exclaim.

'You could melt a marshmallow on your cheeks right now, Zara,' Claire grins.

Distracted, I dig around in my bra for Claire's wedding day spreadsheet, and open it up. 'Harry, nowhere on here does it say, embarrass the bridesmaids.'

'Hey, give that to me.' Claire reaches across and snatches it from my hands.

'What are you doing?'

'Celebrating my freedom. I've been ruled by this piece of paper, this plan, for over a year.' She holds the corner in the flame of one the candles in the floral centrepiece on the top table.

'You rebel, you,' I say, watching it catch and burn, at which Kev pours a glass of water over the top.

'If you persist, wife of mine, I'm going to have to arrest you for criminal damage.'

'Do I get the full treatment, the uniform and the cuffs?' Claire giggles.

'That's too much information,' Leanne squeals. 'Really!'

The bride and groom cut the cake with its nurse and policeman topper and we drink a toast while the band sets up in the next room, ready for the dancing. Claire and Kev take to the floor for their very first dance together before everyone else joins in.

Towards the end of the evening, I begin to lose myself, dancing to the slow numbers in Lewis's arms. Emily brings me back to earth, tapping me on the shoulder. I stop with Lewis's arm around my waist.

'I'm sorry for cutting in, but we're off home. Poppy's in a strop and Gran seems very muddled. We'll drop her at the flat. Don't worry, I'll make sure she's tucked up in bed with her cocoa or whatever she has before we leave.'

'I don't wanna go home,' Poppy wails as the band pauses between numbers. 'I wanna stay here.' Her voice is drowned out by the sound of drums and a bass guitar.

'I'll come and say goodbye outside,' I suggest as Lewis's hand slips down to my buttock.

'Is Lewis coming to say goodbye?' Poppy asks.

'Yes, please,' Emily says, answering for him. 'And if he could just come back and read a bedtime story. Only joking . . . I really should have taken you on as our full-time nanny. Lewis is the only person, apart from Grandma, that Poppy takes any notice of.'

We head outside into the cool evening air and send Poppy on a search for the family car, but she doesn't want to have anything to do with it. She folds her arms and stamps her foot on the gravel as Lewis and I, Emily and Murray look on somewhat helplessly.

'Poppy, it's dark and it's way past your bedtime,' Murray says.

'It's not dark. Look.' Poppy points to the lanterns that are dotted around the car park.

'It's still past your bedtime,' Murray insists.

'It's past *your* bedtime, silly Daddy.' Poppy scampers off towards the line of vehicles nearest the exit, and I can almost hear Emily's sigh of relief that she's decided to go along with the idea of looking for their car.

'She's a nightmare sometimes. Who'd have children?' Emily stops abruptly. 'I'm sorry, sis, that was—'

'It's fine,' I say quickly, determined that nothing will spoil the day.

The scent of buddleia is heavy in the air and the shadows of several pigs snuffle about and snort in the dark, the light of the moon catching their backs and the metal curves of the roofs of their arks in the paddock behind the gate. There's the sound of footsteps and someone swearing lightly as they trip into a flowerbed.

'Who is that?' Murray says.

'It's all right.' I recognise Leanne's voice. 'It's just us.'

'The bar's back that way,' Murray chuckles.

'I don't think they were looking for the bar,' Emily says.

'Is that you, Harry?' I say, catching sight of the best man's face as he moves into the light, his shirt undone and looking worse for the wear.

'We thought we'd get some fresh air,' he says.

'Sure,' I say.

'We believe you. Thousands wouldn't,' Murray says ironically.

'Oh, leave them alone,' Emily sighs as he sings the first few lines of 'Love Is in the Air'. 'Goodnight, Zara.' She gives me a hug. 'Goodnight, Lewis.'

'Goodnight, Emily.'

'Where's Poppy?' Lewis asks.

'She was right here just now,' Murray says.

'Poppy, come here!' Emily calls, her voice strained. 'Where are you? We're going home.'

'I'm not going home!'

I follow the sound of Poppy's protestation, catching sight of her running towards the road. My heart misses a beat, but it's all right because it's late and there's no traffic, except I can hear the distant hum of a car heading this way.

'Poppy!' Emily screams, as Lewis and Murray start to run after her. 'Stop right there!'

Poppy hesitates and, for a moment, I think she's going to turn back.

'No!' she screams back, and sets off again, straight into the road. All I can see are headlamps illuminating a tiny girl, suddenly turned to shadow as somebody throws themselves at her. All I can hear is the car skidding to a screeching halt some way down the road before a scream, a thud, then nothing apart from what feels like an endless, empty silence before Emily runs forwards, crying out, 'Poppy! Oh no, Poppy!'

I will never forget my sister's screams as Murray intercepts her and holds her back. He looks at me, his eyes crazed with fear.

'You look. I can't,' he says, his voice breaking.

I bite my lip, afraid of what I'm going to find because it's obvious now that Lewis is involved. Both the men ran after Poppy, but he was the one who got to her.

My heart is pounding as my feet scrunch across the stones to where the driver of the car is already out, shining a torch onto the far side of the road, where a figure is struggling to get up. Lewis is still with us, but what about Poppy? Where is she?

'Stay there, sir,' the driver orders. 'Let me have a look at you and the child before anyone moves.'

I recognise the voice. It's Ben, Dr Mackie. I catch sight of gleaming ringlets of hair draped across Lewis's arm while, behind me, Emily is still screaming for her baby. I cross the road, forcing myself to look, and at that moment, Poppy opens her mouth and cries. My body floods with relief. She's alive, at least.

I call for Emily and Murray who come rushing over.

'Poppy, darling, Mummy's here.'

'And Daddy,' Murray says gruffly.

'You're all right,' Lewis tells her. 'You're safe, Pops.' He makes to stand up again.

'I said, stay there, sir.'

'Lewis, thank god,' I breathe, kneeling beside him. 'I thought . . . Never mind. Do as the doctor tells you.'

'Zara?' Ben exclaims. 'It's Claire's wedding do, isn't it?'

'It is.' I extricate Poppy from Lewis's arms. 'Are you okay, darling? Does anything hurt?'

She thinks for a moment, pressing her finger to her lips and looking up at the stars before shaking her head.

'Murray, take her inside,' Ben says. 'If you could put the hazards on my car, Zara, I'll sort it out later. I think I ran it into the bank.'

'What about Lewis?' I ask.

'I'm fine, really.' He gives me his hand to pull him up.

'Let me be the judge of that,' Ben says sternly. 'You've had a nasty bump on the head.'

'Have I?' Lewis touches his forehead, winces and checks his fingers. 'Oh, I'm bleeding.' In the light of the torch, he looks pale and dazed, and dark blood trickles down the side of his face. His shirtsleeve is ripped from top to bottom, revealing a graze all the way up his forearm.

'Do we need an ambulance?' Murray comes running back, accompanied by Kev. 'Elsa's asking if she should call 999. Emily's looking after Poppy.'

'Give it a minute, or two,' Ben says quietly, and he asks Lewis a few questions and taps his chest, deciding that it's safe to move him indoors. 'We don't need an ambulance, but we'll have to call the police to report the accident.'

'I've called it in,' Kev says. 'Someone will be out to take the details.'

Murray and I help Lewis back into the hotel where he's treated as a hero. Elsa wants to give him a brandy. Ben says no, but he'll have one, thank you.

'I didn't see her. She appeared in front of me, like a ghost. I don't know how I stopped in time. Where is Poppy?'

'She's inside with Emily and her great-grandma,' Elsa replies.

'I should clean those wounds up.' I touch Lewis's shoulder.

'Ouch!' He holds out his hand. He's shaking.

'I'm sorry.'

'I hope you're going to be gentle with me,' he says cheekily.

'I'll fetch the first-aid kit,' Elsa says.

'It's all right,' Ben says. 'I'll fetch my bag from the car. I reckon that's going to need two or three Steri-Strips.'

'Do you think that will be enough to keep my brain in?' Lewis says. 'It's throbbing a bit.'

'No more dancing tonight,' Ben says. 'Take a couple of paracetamol – that should do the trick. And you shouldn't be left on your own for the next twenty-four hours. You could be concussed.'

'I'll stay with him,' I say, smiling. 'It's no trouble!'

I clean up Lewis's head wound and Ben applies the butterfly strips.

I help him out of his shirt, unfastening the buttons down the front one by one, and sliding the material off each shoulder, taking every opportunity to touch his warm skin and feel the hardness of the muscle underneath. I know it's naughty, but he is so yummy, I could eat him. Elsa brings him a clean, short-sleeved shirt – it's a fraction tight across the shoulders but it will do for now.

I pick out the gravel from the grazes on his arm, using the tweezers from Ben's visit bag, before cleaning the wounds with antiseptic.

'You are a cruel woman,' Lewis says.

'I'm sorry. I know it hurts.' I pause. 'What do you think, Ben?'

'You've done an excellent job,' he says, peering through his reading glasses. 'Lewis, I'd like you to pop into the surgery on Monday so I can check up on you. I can prescribe you antibiotics if it's necessary.'

Emily and Gran turn up with Murray, who's holding his wide-eyed and weary daughter in his arms.

'Poppy, what did you want to say to Lewis?' Emily says.

'Thank you.' She takes her thumb out of her mouth for just long enough to speak.

'I want to give you a hug, but it looks as if it could be too painful. I want – we both want to say that we can't thank you enough. There are no words . . .' Emily's eyes well up with tears

'We're for ever in your debt,' Murray finishes for her.

Lewis blushes as Murray clears his throat. 'I happened to be in the right place at the right time. Anyone would have done the same thing.'

'You can run bloody fast,' Murray goes on. 'You should start training for the Olympics.'

'It was the adrenaline,' Lewis says, reaching out for my hand. I squeeze his fingers.

'I think I should take you home,' I say. 'Emily, could you drop the three of us at Gran's?'

'Of course,' she says. 'We'll see to Mick and Miley tonight.'

'Their biscuits are in a tin in the cupboard under the sink,' Lewis says. 'They have two each when they go to bed.'

'I'll go and say goodbye to Claire,' I say, smiling. Lewis has remembered the dogs, so he can't be feeling too bad, although I won't stop worrying about him for the next twenty-four hours. There are occasions when I wish I didn't have a medical background, and this is one of them. I can't help imagining the worst!

Luckily, the bride has no idea of how serious the situation could have been.

'Kev told me Lewis walked into a door. Is he okay?'

she asks. 'Silly bugger, that's what comes of having too much to drink.'

'He's fine, but I'm going to take him home now. Carry on. Don't stop the party!'

CHAPTER TWENTY

Shepherd's Warning

Lewis stays overnight in the flat, sharing my single bed, and I can't take my eyes off him or stop listening for his breathing. I have to keep telling Frosty not to get on the bed because there isn't room, but it is impossible to do successful signing in the dark.

'I'm sorry,' I whisper, gently pushing her down again.

I check the clock on my mobile. Is Lewis sleeping or slipping into a coma? I stroke his cheek, feeling the rough stubble against my skin. He stirs and mumbles something in his sleep. An hour later, I check on him again. When there's no response, I switch on the bedside lamp and squeeze his hand. He opens his eyes.

'Zara, what's up?'

'How many fingers can you see?' I hold up two.

'Um, four.'

'Four?' I can't disguise the panic in my voice. 'Are you sure?'

He smiles. 'Only joking. Did you have to wake me up?'

'Doctor's orders.'

'What's the time?'

'Three o'clock.'

He groans. 'I won't get back to sleep now.'

'If I had my way, you'd stay awake for the whole twenty-four hours.'

'It seems a bit pointless for both of us to have to suffer from sleep deprivation. Thank you. I'm sorry if I sound ungrateful.' Lewis shifts onto his elbow, wincing as he raises his body. 'I have a terrible headache.'

'I'll get you some more painkillers,' I say, jumping up.

'Please . . .'

I fetch paracetamol and water and stand over him like a nurse on the ward as he takes it, and then I curl up beside him with the duvet wrapped around us, when the shock of what happened the night before finally hits me. Poppy, running away across the gravel, the sound of brakes and the terrible thud in the darkness followed by my sister's screams. I shudder at the memory.

'I thought I'd lost you.' I start to cry.

'You softie. I have no intention of reaching my expiry date yet. There's too much to experience, too much living to do yet – and preferably with you.' He reaches over, turns out the light and holds me closer until I can feel his breath warm and damp against my hair.

'I love you,' I murmur, but I'm not sure he hears me because, in spite of his protestations that he won't get back to sleep, within seconds of his head hitting the pillow, he's snoring lightly. Frosty is on the end of the bed, lying across our feet, and I don't have the heart to turf her off again.

The next morning, Lewis and I have breakfast together with the Sunday papers.

'When we move in together, we'll be able to do this every Sunday,' he says, looking up from the sports pages.

'I'd love to, but—'

'I know. I can wait,' Lewis cuts in.

'Thank you.'

'You're worth waiting for,' he says with a glint in his eye, and I picture us making a home together: me, Lewis and the dogs.

'I didn't know you liked football,' I say, changing the subject.

'I have an interest in it. I'm not fanatical, though.'

'I'm taking Claire and Kevin to the airport this morning. I assume you're coming with me?'

'So you can keep an eye on me?' he says with a small smile.

'Well, yes. The twenty-four hours isn't up yet. It's the perfect excuse for us to spend a whole day together.'

'Actually, I feel fine, and I'd really like to go back to the farm to check on the dogs and Poppy.'

'We can do that on the way, if we leave in the next half an hour or so.'

'I mean, I'd like to have a shower and . . . have a bit of space.'

'I'm sorry. I've been suffocating you . . . ?'

'It isn't you, Zara. You've been amazing. I'm not sure I'm up to listening to Claire and her plans for the honeymoon just now.'

'That's okay, but you really should have someone with you,' I try again.

'I'll be all right. I can knock on Emily's door or phone you if I feel squiffy.'

'You'll ring me later?'

'I promise, as long as you promise to stop nagging me.' With a rueful smile, Lewis stands up and clears the table before we get ready to leave.

'Where are you going?' Gran says as I pick up my keys from the counter where I left them the night before.

'I'm taking Lewis back to the farm so we can see Poppy, and then I promised Claire and Kevin I'd take them to the airport, remember? They stayed at the Barnscote for their first night as husband and wife.'

'How romantic,' Gran sighs. 'I remember my first night as a married woman. We stayed at the King's Head – when it was a pub, that is. We had stout for a nightcap and porridge for breakfast.'

'I think Claire and Kevin were planning champagne and a fry-up.'

'Where are they going for the honeymoon?'

'Las Vegas.' I'm sure I've told her several times before. 'Gran, much as I love our little chats, I have to go. I don't want them missing their flight. I won't be too long.'

'You two have a lovely day,' she says. 'Goodbye.' I notice how she doesn't mention Lewis saving Poppy's life the night before, a sign of a further change in her condition. I swallow hard, composing myself before I turn back to her to wish her a happy day too.

On the way through Talyton St George, I make a quick stop at the pharmacy – it isn't open on a Sunday, but I called to ask a favour – before driving up to Greenwood Farm, where Lewis and I find Emily, Daisy and Poppy in the farmhouse kitchen. Daisy is in her high chair, almost asleep in a bowl of pureed carrot, as if she's had one lullaby too many.

Murray joins us from upstairs, fastening the buttons on his check shirt.

'I overslept,' he says with a grimace. 'My fault – I have a sore head. Probably not as painful as yours is, mate,' he adds to Lewis. 'You have quite a bruise.'

Lewis grimaces. 'I've had worse.'

'I'd really rather someone kept an eye on you today,' I say, worrying that I'm sounding too clingy. 'I know about these things.'

'She's right, Lewis,' Emily says. 'Trust me, I'm a nurse.'

'I need to sleep. Zara kept waking me up to check I was still alive last night and I'm completely shattered. I promise you that if I feel sick or faint, I'll come straight over and find you. How about that?'

It seems like a good compromise.

Emily offers us a second breakfast, which Lewis accepts before turning to Poppy.

'How are you, Pops?'

'I don't know,' she says, her hands on her hips.

I glance towards Emily. 'She sounds just like Mum.'

'Sometimes I think she spends too much time with her.' Emily takes a plate of sausages from the range and puts it on the top before pouring four coffees and turning to her husband. 'Murray, now would be a good time.'

'Time for what?' he says.

'You know very well.' She gives him a dig in the ribs.

'Hey, don't do that. I'm feeling delicate.'

'You need to man up,' she says, chuckling.

'Emily and I have been talking about last night,' Murray begins, 'and as we've said, we can't thank you enough, and we've been thinking what we could do in return.'

'You don't have to do anything,' Lewis says.

'We do.' Emily sips at her coffee.

'We'd like you to stay on at Greenwood Farm. You can live in the annexe rent-free for the foreseeable future. In return, you can help us out now and again, while being free to work elsewhere the rest of the time.'

'Really? Do you mean it? That's too much,' Lewis says, frowning.

'We can't afford to keep you here working full-time for us. There isn't the money, but you might as well use the annexe – it'll only stay empty for months.'

'Don't you want to rent it out?' Lewis asks.

Emily shakes her head. 'I'm not keen to have people

we don't know living here on the farm.' She gives me a look and I know exactly what she means, that she has an ulterior motive for letting him stay. 'What do you think?'

'It's a very kind offer,' he says. 'Are you sure?'

Murray thumps him on the back. 'Of course we are. You're more than welcome.'

'I'll say yes, then,' he responds. 'Oh, that's great. I'm made up.' He reaches his arm around my waist and I lean into him. 'You've saved my life. I thought I was going to have to go back to live with my parents for a while. Thank you.'

Reluctantly, I check my watch. 'I'd better go. I don't want to be responsible for Claire missing her flight. I'll see you later, Lewis. And I'm glad you're all right, Poppy.'

Lewis kisses me briefly on the cheek and I head over to meet Claire and Kevin at the hotel; they're packed and ready waiting in the snug alongside reception.

'Hi.' Claire yawns.

'It was a good night, was it?' I say.

'She was asleep within five seconds of going to bed.' Kevin smiles wryly.

'That's marriage for you,' Elsa interjects from the desk. 'You'll have to get used to it.'

'How are Poppy and Lewis? I only found out this morning,' Claire says.

'They're fine, thank goodness.'

'I wonder how Ben is, too. He seemed pretty shocked.'

'His car's a write-off,' Kevin says. 'It hit the bank so

hard it damaged the chassis beyond repair. It's lucky no one was seriously hurt.'

'It was an eventful day,' I muse.

'Lovely, though,' Claire says. 'It didn't go to plan, but it couldn't have gone any better – the rest of it, I mean, not the part with Poppy running out into the road.'

'It's a hard lesson for her, but I don't think she'll do it again.'

'I should hope not.' She pauses. 'I thought Lewis might have come along with you this morning.'

'I dropped him at the farm – his head hurts, but he's okay.'

'He is such a hero,' Claire says.

'My hero,' I say, smiling. 'I'm so lucky.'

'I'm sure that one day you'll walk up the aisle with him. I'm pretty sure that by the time we get back from our honeymoon, you'll be engaged,' Claire giggles.

'Please don't. We've been together for three months, that's all. We've talked further about moving in together, making a commitment.' I can feel the heat radiating from my cheeks. 'You know how I feel about marriage.'

'I do,' Claire sighs. 'It's a shame you're such a cynic, but I do understand.'

'Are you all right?' I ask her. 'You're looking a little pale.'

'I hardly had any champagne yesterday. It's weird. It's like as soon as I stop, I get sick. I'm always unwell when I'm on holiday.'

'Ah, darling, it's the stress of planning the wedding, which was wonderful by the way.' Kevin holds his arm around Claire's waist.

'It was a beautiful day.' I think of Lewis laughing as I caught the bouquet. The flowers will be drying now, pressed between sheets of absorbent paper in preparation for being rearranged into a two-dimensional picture for posterity.

'Is it time to go or do I have a minute or two for another coffee?' Kevin says. 'I think I need one.'

'I reckon we should leave by ten, so you can have up to twenty minutes.'

'Would you two like a drink?' he goes on.

'No, thank you, but before you go, I have something to give you – a belated wedding present.' I take my most recent purchase from my bag and place it on the table.

'What's that?' Claire picks it up, tears open the top and peers inside. She looks back at me, eyebrows raised in question. 'Zara, it's impossible.'

'Are you sure about that?'

'I can't be.'

Claire shows Kevin the kit still inside the bag.

'You're pregnant?' Kevin exclaims.

'You know I can't understand why you haven't made chief detective by now,' I tease. 'Go and do the test please. I'm on tenterhooks.'

'What, now?'

'Yes, now!'

'Will you come to the Ladies with me? Kev, I would ask you, but it looks a bit odd.'

'I'll wait here,' he says, his face paler than ever. 'I can't face coffee now. How did this happen?'

'We don't know if it has yet,' she smiles weakly.

'Come on, hurry up.' I link my arm through hers and drag her along the corridor to the toilets. I have to unwrap the kit for her and read her the instructions before I virtually push her into a cubicle. I wait outside, checking my hair in the mirror. I look like a complete wreck: no make-up, and bags like hold luggage beneath my eyes.

'Oh-mi-god, oh-mi-god, oh-mi-god. There's a line already.' The cubicle door flies open. 'I can't look. Look at it for me, will you?' Claire holds out the wand, turning her head away so she can't see it.

'It is as I thought. It's positive.' A mix of emotions swirls into my heart. How are you supposed to feel when your best friend falls pregnant without even trying? It is tough right now, but I know from experience that the pain will fade eventually, just as it did each time Emily told me she was expecting. 'Congratulations.' I give Claire a hug, but she appears frozen.

'I'm sorry, this sounds awful, but I'm not sure I'm ready for this.'

'You're going to have to get used to it. Let's go and give Kev the good news.' I gaze at her. I thought she'd be excited, but she's tearful. 'You've always said you'd have a family.'

'Yes, but not so soon.'

'At least you'll be married,' I say lightly.

'I suppose so.'

'Shall we go?'

'Give me a minute.' Claire leans over the sink and splashes her face with water. 'I look terrible.' She grabs a paper towel and dries herself. 'You're the midwife. Why aren't I glowing?'

'Because it's early days. Give it another month or so and you'll be looking and feeling great.'

'Thank you, Zara. For everything.'

'I haven't done anything,' I say bashfully.

'You've been amazing. You supported me through the last year, helping me through when I was going to give up. Most people would have left me to it. You didn't. And I must have been so boring, going on and on about invites and favours and seating plans, and forcing you to go to fat club.'

'You didn't force me. I needed to do something about my weight.'

'Frosty did more for that than I did. You're a fantastic bridesmaid and the best "best friend" anyone could have.' Claire wipes her eyes and swears. 'Why am I crying? I'm going on honeymoon with my lovely husband and I'm having a baby.'

'So you're okay?' I ask.

'I'm fine,' she sniffs. 'I've never felt better.' But as soon as she announces her happy state of mind, she dashes off into the cubicle to throw up. I follow her, touching her shoulder as she leans over the bowl.

'You poor thing.' I hand her a tissue. 'Have you had breakfast?'

'I couldn't face it. It was the smell of the coffee.'

'You need to eat something. When you feel better,

385

go back to Kev while I ask Elsa for some hot water and lemon, and a biscuit.'

'It can only be a few weeks – I put the tiredness down to stress and planning the wedding and losing weight.' She touches her stomach, gazing down in disbelief as we sit in the snug sharing a plate of ginger biscuits. 'I can't believe there's a baby in there. OMG, you know what this means? I'm going to have to start planning the nursery.'

'Please, can we enjoy the honeymoon first?' Kevin says, but I can tell he's over the moon too. He turns to me. 'It is all right to fly and everything?'

'Yes, of course it is. You just need to make sure your wife has plenty of rest and a healthy diet. I have to remind her of that because she's a nurse and, from my experience, nurses are the worst people in the world, apart from doctors, for looking after themselves.

'Book an appointment with me or Kelly when you get back,' I continue, addressing Claire. 'I won't tell anyone. I'll let you do that.'

'You can tell Lewis, but perhaps not your gran,' Claire says. 'She's no good at keeping secrets.'

'I don't think she'd be able to remember for long enough to spread the gossip, even if I did tell her.'

'I'm sorry. Remember, if there's anything I can do to help, you know where I am.'

'Yes, in Vegas, hopefully,' I say, changing the subject. 'Can you do me a favour while I'm away – only I've tried to get hold of Tessa and Jack to find out why they didn't make it to the wedding? I wondered if they were okay.'

'I'll see if I can catch up with them,' I say. 'Let's go or you'll miss that plane.'

I call Tessa the next day to ask her how she is. 'I haven't heard from you for a while and you didn't come to the wedding. Someone said you were ill,' I say tentatively.

'I'm all right,' she says, sounding anything but. 'I've been seeing my consultant.'

'I know, but I thought it would be good to catch up.' I pause. 'Can I drop by some time? I've got a bunch of old newspapers if they're of any use to you.'

'We can always find a home for them. How's Frosty?'

'She's good, thanks. Did you know she had a fight with one of Lewis's collies and came off worse?'

'I did hear via Jack and the vets. He's always popping in there with something. Come over at lunchtime if you're free.'

I meet Tessa at the Sanctuary where she's mucking out this time.

'Where's the horse?' I say, looking into the empty stable.

'He's been rehomed.' Tessa forks dirty straw into a wheelbarrow. 'He was with us a week, a young carthorse called Teddy.' She stops to rub at her back.

'Are you sure you should be doing that?' I ask her. 'You don't look terribly comfortable.'

'I have to keep busy. It stops me driving myself mad.'

'It's all very well keeping fit and active, but equally you must be careful not to overdo it.'

'I know.' Sighing, Tessa rests the fork across the barrow. 'I'd better empty this. Oh, what am I thinking of? This isn't a social call. Come on over to the house and I'll put the kettle on.'

'Don't worry about the kettle. I can't face any more tea when I've already got a sea of it squelching about in my stomach. It's one of the hazards of the job.'

'Thanks for getting in touch, Zara,' Tessa says when I've checked her and the baby, measuring Tessa's blood pressure and the size of her bump, and listening for the heartbeat.

'As far as I can see from the outside, all is well.'

'Is the baby growing?' Tessa alternately chews on her lip and nibbles at her fingernails.

'You're the right size for your dates. There's no sign that this is a small baby.'

Tessa sits down on the sofa and strokes her belly.

'The consultant wants me to have an elective C-section at 37 weeks. What do you think?' She shakes her head, her eyes gleaming. 'It isn't what I'd hoped for . . .'

'It's the best option for both you and the baby in this situation.'

'I suppose so. I know it's less stressful for the baby than going through a natural birth, and the doctors can intervene quickly if he needs to go on life support straight away. If he makes it that far . . . They can see the hole in his heart on the scans and they think it's fifty-fifty whether or not he'll need surgery to close it, but there's still a chance there are other problems they can't see within the heart muscle.'

'He's doing well at the moment,' I reassure her.

'Is there any chance you could be there?' she begins.

'I know it's a lot to ask because you work in the community, not at the hospital, but I'd really appreciate your support.'

'What about Jack? What does he think?'

'I'm not sure he'll be there. We've been rowing a lot when it's supposed to be a special time for us – well, it is special, but for all the wrong reasons.'

'Is there anyone else you can ask?'

'Dad's going to be there. He's in denial that there's anything wrong and can't wait to meet his grandchild.' Tessa smiles ruefully. 'I just hope he doesn't have another heart attack, he's so excited.'

'I'll do my very best to be there. When you get a date, let me know straight away and I'll put it in the diary.' I smile again. 'I want to meet this baby too.'

CHAPTER TWENTY-ONE

Red Sky in the Morning

Fortunately, Lewis suffers no lasting damage from his knock on the head and life goes on, but something has changed for me. Even though we haven't been together that long in the scheme of things, I love him more and more, but the image of Lewis carrying Poppy in his arms and the tenderness in his eyes as he handed her over to Murray sticks in my mind, bringing back the pain I felt when I discovered I couldn't have children. Seeing Kev's delight and pride in the idea of becoming a dad hasn't helped either, and even though Jack is finding impending fatherhood an understandably frightening prospect, whatever happens with the baby, he will always be a father, whereas if Lewis and I continue and take the next step eventually to move in together, he will never have that opportunity. I know he's said he doesn't mind, but is it really fair to let him give up his dream of having a family for me?

I decide to talk about my worries with my sister, the next time we're free to chat face to face without Murray or Poppy listening in. A couple of weeks after the wedding, I leave Frosty at the farm and Emily drives up to the Sanctuary with me.

'I wonder if we were too hasty promising Poppy a pet,' she says. 'I'm not sure I want the extra responsibility.'

'You can't back out now. She'd never forgive you!' I exclaim.

'I know.'

'You haven't told me when you'd like me to have her for a day.'

'Actually, it's hard for us to let her out of our sight at the moment, after what happened at Claire's wedding reception.'

'The offer's open any time.'

'Thank you, but it's going to take a while.'

'I understand.'

'How are you and Lewis?'

'Fine,' I say quickly. 'Why do you ask?'

'You don't seem to have seen much of each other, that's all, so I wondered . . .' her voice fades. 'Oh, tell me it's none of my business. I expect you've been at work.'

'I've done some extra on-call. A member of one of the other teams has been off sick.'

'What about Gran?'

'What about her?'

'Has she been giving you the run-around? You can be honest with me.'

'I've been doing the odd shift in the shop,' I admit. 'We're coping, though. It isn't a problem. Everything's cool. Really.'

'You would tell me if there was something wrong?'

I stare out of the window. The trees are losing their leaves, their crowns orange and yellow against a metallic grey sky.

'Actually, there is, but it's me, not Gran or Lewis,' I say eventually. 'It's the baby thing. I'm surrounded by couples having babies, men becoming dads, and I can't get my head round the idea that if Lewis and I stay together, he'll never be a father.'

'Isn't that rather jumping ahead?' Emily says. 'I thought you two were having fun, taking one day at a time and all that.'

'It is and we are, but it is getting serious.'

'I think it's lovely,' Emily sighs. 'You two seem so good together. He's been great for you, really brought you out of your shell, while you're a steadying influence on him.' She turns up the lane to the Sanctuary.

'He says he doesn't mind that I can't have children.'

'There you go, then. Lewis is cool with it, so why are you worrying about it?'

'He says he's fine with it now, but he's young and his feelings may well change.'

'He knows his own mind.' Emily pulls into a space in the car park outside the bungalow at the rescue centre. 'Zara, why don't you just go with the flow?'

'It doesn't feel right, forcing him to choose between me and having a family. I feel like I'm being selfish.'

Emily stares at me, giving me one of the looks she usually reserves for Poppy.

'Does Lewis love you?' she asks impatiently.

I nod.

'And do you love him?'

'Yes, more than anything.' I bite my lip.

'So there's no problem.' Emily reaches behind her and grabs her bag. 'Let's go.'

I get out of the car, unconvinced by my sister's theory that love can conquer all obstacles. Isn't the fact I love him all the more reason for me to let him go?

'Why didn't you bring Poppy with you?' I ask.

'Because I don't want her falling in love with an unsuitable creature. I'd like her to have a pet much like Frosty, but on a smaller scale. Murray wants a proper dog, as he calls it, one at least the size of a Labrador; but, as I pointed out to him, she wouldn't be able to take it out for walks. She'd end up being towed about like Mrs Dyer.'

Emily and I meet Tessa at the Sanctuary. She waddles out from the bungalow, dressed in what looks like one of Jack's old coats and maternity jeans.

'Hi,' she says. 'Thanks for thinking of us. Let's hope we can match you with the dog of your dreams.'

'It's Zara who dreams about dogs, not me,' Emily says, laughing. 'A particular person's dogs.'

'You mean the shepherd,' Tessa says, turning to me. 'You're still going out with him? I'm a bit out of the loop at the moment.'

'For obvious reasons,' Emily says. 'How are you? You look enormous. I bet you can't wait.'

'I'm dreading it actually,' she says. 'I was on the computer just now, writing a blog for our website, and I was thinking how much easier it would be if birth was fully automated and you could just press a button to download. I'm booked in for a C-section tomorrow. Are you still free, Zara?'

'I'll be there, don't you worry. Have you packed your bag?'

'Ten times over. Jack says I'll have to pay a supplement for excess baggage.'

'Have you got the big knickers?' Emily teases. 'I had to go out and buy some specially.'

'I had to get a couple of baggy nightshirts.' Tessa slips her hand inside her coat and strokes her bump. 'I worry about missing out on a natural labour, but I'm also glad I have a set date. By this time in forty-eight hours, Sprogget – as I call him – will be here.' She changes the subject and I wonder how it feels when there is so much uncertainty about the baby's health. At least her mention of Jack suggests he's coming round to the idea of being present at the birth. 'Let me show you the dogs we have up for rehoming.'

'Are you sure you should be doing this?' Emily asks. 'Shouldn't you be resting?'

'This is my favourite part of the job. I warn you there's a litter of puppies that are exceptionally cute, but they won't be ready for another three weeks.'

'I don't want a puppy,' Emily says. 'I'd like something older – not too old, but preferably house-trained. I'll be responsible for it, but it's supposed to be a pet for Poppy.'

Entering the kennel block reminds me of the time I brought Frosty to the Sanctuary. I recall the little old sausage dog with sad eyes in the corner of the first pen, and how I felt then. Now I feel ten times worse, especially when I see that he or she is still here and I have to force myself to walk past to the next pen.

'Oh, I want to take them all home,' I say, squatting down to stroke a black Labrador-type dog through the bars of the gate.

'He's lovely, but he's too big,' Emily comments. 'What about the Jack Russell?'

'She isn't suitable for a home with small children,' Tessa explains. 'She's too reactive.'

'Does that mean she bites?' Emily says wryly.

'As far as we know she hasn't ever bitten anyone, but she has the potential to be a bit snappy. She growled at Maz when we had her checked over at the vet's.'

'She reminds me too much of Uncle Nobby's dog,' I observe, moving on to the next kennel where there are two lurchers, mum and daughter, who need to be rehomed together.

'They've never been apart,' Tessa says. 'It seems a shame to separate them.'

'I can't take two,' Emily says. 'Murray would kill me.'

We look at the puppies, four bundles of fluff, rolling around with each other while their mum, a scruffy cream dog with patches of fur clipped from her skin, looks on.

'They are gorgeous,' Emily sighs, 'but no . . .'

'That's pretty well it then,' Tessa says.

'What about the sausage dog?' I ask.

'He's very sweet – all he wants is food and cuddles – but he's a little older.'

'How old?'

'He's nine. Of course, he could go on until he's thirteen or fourteen, but there are no guarantees.' Tessa returns to the first pen and opens the door. 'Sherbet,' she calls softly. Immediately, the dog's expression changes and he's up on his paws, trotting over to us, wagging his whip-like tail so fast it's a blur. He has big brown eyes, a long pointed nose, and even longer body, short bow legs and a shiny tan coat that reminds me of the skin of a fried sausage. He sniffs at my knees.

'He can smell Frosty,' I say. 'How did he end up here?'

'His elderly owner had to give him up because she was moving into a retirement home after her husband died – Sherbet couldn't go with her. It was heartbreaking.'

I bite my lip. I hate the thought of poor Sherbet being wrenched from his owner's arms, especially if they had a bond as strong as mine and Frosty's. I can hardly bear it.

Emily bends down to stroke him. 'I think he's too old.'

'You're being ageist. You wouldn't say that about a person,' I point out.

Emily looks up at me, grinning. 'I can't believe how much you've changed.'

'Can we take him for a walk?' I ask Tessa.

'There's a circular stroll around the copse that takes

about twenty minutes. That will give you some idea if he's for you and you're for him.' She fastens a lead to his collar and, with a wink at me, hands the end to Emily. I smile. Tessa and I want the same thing. Let's hope that Emily can be persuaded that she does too.

My sister and I wander up through Longdogs Copse with Sherbet trotting along with us, stopping now and again to investigate a scent in the peaty leaf litter along the path, or to dive into the damp undergrowth and reappear a few seconds later, shaking water from his back.

'Poppy's favourite food is sausages,' I say, thinking of all the reasons why Emily should pick Sherbet. 'And his name – it reminds me of the flying saucers Gran sells in the shop.'

'All right, I know what you're up to. I'm just worried about what Murray will say.'

'Will say? You said "will" not "would"?'

'I feel like Sherbet's chosen us. He's friendly and, with those little legs, he won't need hours and hours of exercise, will he? Do you think he'll get on with Frosty?'

'Who knows? She gets on better with dogs than bitches.

The main question here is: will Poppy like him?'

And I know when Emily says that, that we're going to find out.

When we arrive at the farm, I have a shivering Sherbet in my arms.

'Where are we?' I murmur, at which he pricks his ears and stares out of the window.

Murray is at home with the girls, waiting for us.

He greets us at the door with Daisy swamped in an enormous bib in one arm, and a bottle in the other. She holds out her hands and squeals with excitement at seeing Emily.

'I reckon I'm feeling even more pleased to see your mummy than you are,' Murray tells her, handing her straight over to Emily. 'She's been a complete widget since you left.' He runs his hands through his hair and Emily laughs.

'Now you know how I feel sometimes, frazzled daddy. Where's Poppy? I thought she'd be here.'

'I'm here, Mummy.' Poppy pushes past her father's legs and stops in front of me. 'Oh, Auntie Zara,' she breathes, her eyes latching onto the dog.

'This is Sherbet,' I say. 'Come with me.' In the kitchen, I sit down with a wriggling sausage dog in my arms, and he's so long it's almost impossible to keep both his front and back end on my lap at the same time, so I let him gently onto the floor.

'Kneel down, Poppy, then let him sniff your hand.'

Sherbet, under my supervision because I'd hate my niece to feel the same way about dogs as I did, licks her fingers, sending her into a fit of giggles.

'That tickles.'

Sherbet wags his tail, again so fast you can hardly see it, and then he plonks his front paws on Poppy's knees and plants a soppy lick on her nose. She throws her arms around his neck.

'Be gentle with him, won't you? Just like you are with Frosty.' I pause, a lump in my throat as I watch the two of them. I don't need to ask if she likes him.

'Ah,' Emily says, standing behind me. 'He's lovely, isn't he?'

'He's my pet.' Poppy beams. 'He's the best pet in the whole wild world.'

'What do you think, Murray?' I ask as he steps up behind my sister and places his hands on her waist.

'That is so not a man's dog. I'm not sure it's even a dog. It's a sausage!' he exclaims.

'It's a dog, silly daddy,' says Poppy, putting him straight.

'It looks like it's come straight out of the frying pan.'

'And into the fire so to speak,' Emily adds. 'I hope he's going to survive all the attention Poppy's going to give him.'

'Don't expect me to walk it,' Murray says lightly.

'I wanna show Lewis,' Poppy says.

'Is he in?' Emily asks.

'I think so.' I noticed that his pick-up was outside when I drove up to the farm this morning, but it turned out he was out with the dogs, so I missed him. He must be back by now, though.

'Let's go then,' I say. 'Poppy, we'll have to put Sherbet on the lead. We don't want him to run away.'

She insists on attaching the lead, sticking her tongue out as she struggles with the clip, before we pop across to the annexe, where I knock on Lewis's door, sending the collies on the other side into a flurry of barking. Lewis opens the door, yawning and rubbing the back of his neck. He gives me a heart-stopping smile and a kiss on the lips before dismissing Mick and Miley to

399

the kitchen and turning to Poppy. 'What a sh-amazing dog. What's his name?'

'Sherbet,' she says, wrapping the lead around her waist. 'Sh-amazing Sherbet. Do you want to come for a walk with us?'

'Okay, but we won't go too far – we don't want to wear him out on his first day.'

'Are Mick and Miley coming too?'

'I think it would be wise to leave them behind,' Lewis says, and we walk together around the field alongside the drive. I slip my arm through his and follow behind Poppy and Sherbet, whose front legs seem to trot along, while his back legs skip.

'You and Emily didn't think this through, did you?' Lewis says. 'You went with your hearts not your heads.'

'Sherbet was in the kennels when we took Frosty in that day. I couldn't bear the idea of leaving him there any longer. What's the problem?'

'As soon as it rains, he'll disappear in a puddle. I've never seen a dog with such ridiculous legs. Mind you, he is cute.'

'Poppy's fallen for him.'

'I reckon he's fallen for her too.' He holds my gaze as he continues, 'Love at first sight – that doesn't happen very often,' and I know he's talking about us. I'm consumed by a rush of guilt for talking about the future of our relationship with my sister, not with him.

'I bet Poppy will refuse to go to big school now,' I say.

400

'Yeah, she'll want to stay at home with Sherbet. Ugh, what a silly name.' Lewis wrinkles his nose.

'She won't change it. Murray's already tried to persuade her to call it something macho like Rocky or Arnie.'

'That's so wrong,' Lewis says. 'The way he minces along, he looks like a girl.'

'What, Murray?' I say, teasing.

'No, the dog.' Lewis glances towards me. 'You're winding me up.'

'Maybe a little.' I let go of his arm and run after Poppy. Lewis chases behind me and overtakes, reaching my niece just before I do.

'Shall we put your new pet through his paces, Pops?' he asks, squatting so he's at her level. She frowns, and sticks her thumb in her mouth while still holding the lead. 'Let's pretend he's at dog big school and find out what he knows.'

'How?' she murmurs.

'Ask him to sit, like you do with Mick and Miley.'

'Sit!' she says, gazing at the dog; he looks up, his brown eyes showing a crescent of white beneath them. 'Sit,' she repeats, at which Sherbet plonks his bottom straight down. 'Good boy,' she says excitedly.

'He knows that command,' Lewis says. 'How about "down"?'

'Down,' Poppy says, holding out her hand.

Sherbet throws himself down and rolls over, exposing his naked belly.

'He's a star, isn't he?' I observe, feeling a little

inadequate on Frosty's behalf. Why can't my dog do that? 'I wonder what other tricks he can do.'

He can bark to order and offer his paw.

'He should join Mensa,' Lewis says. 'He's almost as smart as Mick and Miley.'

'Do I detect the voice of a competitive dad?' I say, amused, until almost immediately I realise what I've said. Inwardly, I cringe. How can I deny him the chance of being a proper father when he's clearly made to be one? I only have to see him with Poppy to realise that he's a natural. Knowing that I can never provide him with a child is acutely painful – in fact, right now it's killing me.

Apparently unaware of my inner turmoil, Lewis smiles and changes the subject. 'How's Rosemary?'

'Gran's okay. At least, she was when I left her this afternoon. It's all right. James did a shift in the shop after school – it's his mum's birthday soon and he's keen to have the money.'

'It's a help, but it isn't really the answer, is it?'

'I know . . .'

'I understand your loyalty, but you are wrong about what's best for her.'

'Have you been talking to Emily?' I say suspiciously.

'The subject has come up, but that's irrelevant. Your grandmother needs care in a professional setting. It's like you asking me to deliver a baby. I'd have an idea of what I'm doing, but it wouldn't be the same as having a qualified midwife present.'

Inside, my stomach is churning, but I let my expression go blank as he continues, 'You can't be with her full time. It isn't practical. You can't afford to give up your job—'

'I will if I have to,' I interrupt.

'Trust me, if you were stuck indoors twenty-four/seven, having to watch over someone all the time in case they leave the gas on or put the cat through a hot wash, you'd crack up sooner or later. You know she's going to get worse. She's gone downhill since I first met her.'

'What you say makes sense, but—'

'All I'm saying – borrowing one of Rosemary's phrases to summarise – is don't let your heart rule your head.' He looks ahead to where Poppy is trying to drag Sherbet away from a tuft of grass where he's having a good sniff.

'Let's take Sherbet back to the house,' Lewis says when we catch up with my niece and the dog. 'I expect he'll want his dinner. You did buy him some food, didn't you, Zara?'

'Actually, we haven't got that far yet.'

'It's all right,' Lewis says quickly, as Poppy's face starts to crumple at the thought of her pet being half starved. 'I have plenty of dog food and dog biscuits and chews.'

That's my man, I think. Lewis always saves the day.

Later, we feed all four dogs, separately, of course. Although Frosty and Miley tolerate each other now, there's no point in taking a risk. After that, Emily invites me and Lewis to join her, Murray and the girls for tea before we return to the annexe together.

'Are you staying over tonight?' Lewis asks as he turns the lights on.

'I won't,' I say reluctantly. 'I'm going to the hospital for a delivery first thing tomorrow morning.'

'Why? I thought you did home deliveries.'

'I do attend hospital births sometimes. It's nice to be able to be there, especially when you've met the mum-to-be on several occasions throughout the pregnancy, or she's a friend. You get pretty close.'

'I see.' He smiles wryly.

'It's Tessa,' I explain. 'That part's common knowledge, that her baby's being delivered, but I can't go into detail.'

'I hope it goes well,' Lewis says.

'By this time tomorrow, they'll be a proper family.'

'There are many different kinds of families . . .' I look up at him, but he's looking over my shoulder as he speaks. 'Couples like us with dogs instead of kids, for example.'

The wistful tone of his voice chokes me. I step up close to him and spread my palm across his chest, rumpling the material across the hard, slab-like muscle of his pectorals, keeping my eyes averted to hide my distress. I want him so much, yet how can I let him sacrifice his future happiness for me? It isn't right, but he's being so sweet and loving that I can't bring myself to talk about the decision that is crystallising from the confusion in my mind. It's breaking my heart.

Lewis grasps my wrist and leans in for a kiss. 'Hey, let's make the most of the next hour or so.'

'Actually, I think I'd better be going.'

'Are you sure?' He sounds disappointed. 'Are you okay? You've gone very quiet.'

'I have a lot on my mind.' I know it isn't fair, but I'm not ready to tell him. I'm not strong enough.

'Tessa's baby – it's all right, I know you can't tell me, but there's obviously something very wrong. You go and get some sleep. I'll be fine here with a beer and a couple of old episodes of *Top Gear*.' He accompanies me and Frosty to my car where we kiss goodbye.

'I'll see you tomorrow night,' he calls, waving as I drive past him.

'I'll be in touch,' I call back guiltily.

It's lucky I return home when I do, because I find Gran wandering about in the kitchen, dressed in her nightie and carrying the watering can from the garden. The hob is immaculate and the breadbin is firmly shut, just as I left them. Norris is prowling up and down on the kitchen table, mewling for his dinner.

'What are you doing with that?' I ask her as Frosty greets her by licking her bony knees.

'I don't think your granddad watered the begonias so I thought I'd do it and now I can't find them.'

'That's because we don't have any begonias,' I point out gently, 'and, if we had, they'd be outside in the tubs.' I'm not sure I'd recognise a begonia anyway – I'm not good at flowers.

'Granddad grows them every year. He'll be very upset if he finds out I haven't looked after them. He's very ill, you know.' My grandmother touches her chest. 'It's his heart.'

I am puzzled.

'Granddad isn't ill. He's . . .' I can't bring myself to say it, which is a mistake because Gran misinterprets the situation and her eyes light up.

'You mean, he's getting better?'

'No, I'm so sorry, he's dead.' My heart tears in two as I watch how her expression changes, flicking through distress, recognition and a sudden lack of interest.

'Of course, he's dead. What did you think I meant?'

'You said he was ill,' I say gently.

'He was. Before he died, he was very unwell. Dr Mackie said so.' Gran hesitates. 'Where have you been, you dirty stop-out?'

'I've been out with Emily today to choose a pet for Poppy. We've got her a sausage dog. You'll love him when you see him.'

'What time is it?'

'Eight thirty. Have you had anything to eat today?'

'I had some bubble and squeak with an egg for tea,' she says, but I don't believe her. I think she's covering for herself. If she can't remember to eat, how on earth can she manage the shop? 'James came round after school – he gave me a hand with the reckoning up.'

'With the till, you mean?'

'Yes,' she sighs. 'Are you being awkward? All these questions are making my head hurt.'

'Never mind, I expect you're tired. Let me have the watering can. I'll feed the cat and make us cheese on toast.' I ate at Emily's so I don't need food, but I'm hungry and sad and I could do with some comfort slathered with tomato ketchup.

That night, I dream – thanks to the slabs of molten cheddar on toast, I suspect – of dogs and Gran, of babies and Lewis, but the next morning I wake, focused on being present to support Tessa and Jack when they welcome their son into the world.

I am there when Tessa is given an epidural in preparation for the C-section. I stand at one side of her, holding her hand, while Jack holds the other.

'That's it,' I tell her. 'Keep very still.'

'All done,' the anaesthetist says eventually. 'You can lie down on your side now.'

Tessa groans as she changes position. 'That feels so weird.'

Jack moves aside and stands with his arms crossed, staring at the floor.

'You'll be able to go to theatre soon,' I say. 'You'll be awake throughout the procedure and, as soon as the baby's delivered, you can have skin-to-skin contact, depending on his condition.'

The corners of Tessa's mouth turn down and she begins to shiver. She's petrified. I stroke her shoulder, looking for Jack.

'Even the healthiest babies can have a slow start,' I go on. 'Sometimes they take a while to take their first breath. We know your baby has a hole in his heart, so everyone's prepared and knows exactly what to do when he arrives. We know he could be absolutely fine, or he might need to be stabilised and admitted straight to the neonatal intensive care unit. Whatever happens, I'll keep you up to date so you know what's going on, and I'll make sure you can hold him if it's at all possible.' I hear the sound of doors swinging closed. 'Jack?'

'He's scared,' Tessa says.

'Wait there. I'll go after him.'

'I don't think I have a choice, do I?' she says ruefully. 'I'm not going anywhere.'

'Not now,' I smile, in spite of the tension. Where is Jack off to, without saying anything, when his baby will be born within the next hour? I push the doors aside and turn right up the corridor, hoping he's heading that way. Partway down, I catch sight of him, stopping and slamming his forearms against the wall, burying his head and clenching his fists, and I don't know whether to be sorry for him or furious.

I march down to join him. Fury wins.

'Jack, you have to man up,' I say sharply. 'Tessa and the baby need you.'

'I can't do it,' he exclaims. 'You don't know how it feels, knowing your life is about to change.'

'For goodness' sake, your life changed from the moment you decided to try for this baby. Don't let yourself – or Tessa – down.' Jack ignores me, too caught up in the emotion of the moment. 'Look at me. You can do this. I know you can.' I wait for him to respond and, slowly, he turns to me, red-eyed. 'That's better. Now, come on. If you miss the birth, you'll always regret it.'

'Okay,' he says, taking a deep breath. 'Let's do this.'

In theatre, the screens are up and the surgeon is good to go – we make it back just in time.

'Your husband is here,' I say breezily, as though

nothing's happened. 'Jack, I'd stay this end if I were you . . . hold her hand.'

From when the surgeon makes the incision, I provide a running commentary for Tessa's benefit.

'You'll feel a dragging sensation as the baby's coming out.' I watch the surgeon pull the baby, a scrawny and limp scrap of a creature with bluish-purple skin and a tonsure of dark hair, from her womb. 'He's out now.'

An eerie silence follows as the baby is placed on a towel in the arms of one of the team of specialists standing by, and bundled across to the trolley on the other side of theatre, where he is surrounded by a crowd of doctors and nurses. There are mutterings of Apgar scores and orders to intubate and administer drugs, but no baby's cry.

'Is he alive? Is he breathing?' Tessa asks tearfully as Jack stands with her, grim-faced.

'We don't know yet. They're giving him oxygen and drugs to stimulate his breathing.' The expressions on everyone's faces are beginning to worry me deeply. Even the surgeon looks grim as she stitches and staples Tessa's Caesarean wound closed.

'Please, let me see my baby,' she begs, but I know as the paediatrician approaches us that any hope of that in the immediate future is impossible. He addresses Jack and Tessa.

'Your baby's made it this far, but he isn't breathing for himself, so we're having to do it for him. We're taking him straight to intensive care, which is one of the options that we talked about before.'

'How is his heart . . .?' Jack asks, his voice quavering. 'Is he going to live?'

'I can't give you any answers just yet. I'll see you both later.'

Jack is on his knees with his arms around Tessa's shoulders. They are both sobbing. I can hardly bear it. After a while, when the surgery's over and the screens have been removed, Tessa glances up at me.

'What happens now?' she murmurs, her face pale and her eyes ringed with dark shadows. 'I want my baby.'

'I know, but I'm afraid it'll be a few hours yet. You'll be on the ward for a while to recover from the epidural. Jack can go and see the baby, take some pictures and bring them back for you.' I hand her some tissues to mop up her tears. 'It's horrible being apart like this, but he's in the best place.' I don't say it, but I realise from experience that no news is probably good news at this point. If there was no hope for the baby, the team on the unit would be doing their utmost to bring mum, dad and baby together to spend the last precious moments together and say goodbye. 'Why don't I ask your mum and dad to come and sit with you while Jack goes to the unit?'

'The last time we heard, they were in the coffee shop,' Jack says.

'I'll find them.' I fetch Tessa's parents, Steve and Annie, leaving them with their daughter while I accompany Jack to intensive care, where we find the baby in an incubator. He's wearing a light blue woolly hat and he's surrounded by tubes and leads and monitors. His eyes are closed, his skin mottled, and although a machine is breathing for him, his chest seems to collapse and expand much more than it should with each breath. The nurse with him explains that he's in a critical but stable condition. He's had a scan and the doctor is talking to the paediatric cardiologist about the possibility of surgery to close the hole in his heart. He will need surgery, but it's whether it has to be done now, or can be left until he's older and his condition's improved.

It's a relief that the baby is alive and that everything is being done that can be to help him, even though there could be months, or years, of worry ahead. I look towards Jack, but I don't think he's taking in the information. His eyes are on his baby, his expression a mixture of deep anxiety, love and adoration.

The sight of father and son sends a sharp pain knifing through my belly. The bond – even though Jack tried to resist it – is there, a natural instinct, and once again I think of Lewis and how unfair of me it would be to deprive him of the chance of fatherhood.

'Are you okay?' I ask him.

'Yeah,' he responds. 'I'll take some photos on my mobile – if you wouldn't mind taking them to show Tessa, I'll stay here for a while.'

'Of course I don't mind.' I smile to myself. What happened to the man who didn't want Tessa to have this baby when there was so much uncertainty surrounding his health? I watch him take several snaps before I take his mobile to show Tessa and her parents. I repeat what the nurse said and then make my excuses and leave, but not before Steve Wilde ambushes me with a friendly bear hug, squeezing all the air out of my lungs.

'Thank you,' he says. 'You've been wonderful.'

'I haven't really been able to do very much,' I stammer as he releases me.

'I know that if you could have done, you would have waved a magic wand and all would have been well with my beautiful grandson, but as it is, you've been a marvellous support to my daughter and, if he'd only admit it, my son-in-law as well.'

'I'll pop in tomorrow to catch up with Tessa and the baby,' I say. 'I'm sure they'll both be staying for a few days at least. Go on. Go back to your daughter.'

I go on to do my visits, knowing that this is a day that Tessa and Jack will never forget. I'll never forget it either, and that's what makes being a midwife more than a job. You become part of people's lives.

When I finish my shift, I decide to meet Lewis, the man who's become such a big part of my life to the extent that I can't bear to think of going on without him. To think it has come to this when I started out with all good intentions to keep our relationship on a casual basis, just for fun. I thought I could deal with it, but my attraction to Lewis was too strong, too powerful to resist, and now it's all the more agonising that it has to come to an end.

I find him out in the barn with the new ram.

'Hi,' he says, moving across to kiss me. I turn slightly, offering my cheek. 'Good timing. I was just about ready to stop for tea. How was your day?'

'Okay.' I shrug.

'I heard Tessa's baby's in intensive care. Murray told me – the news is out.' Lewis reaches out his hand. 'I'm sorry. It must be hard sometimes. Let me give you a hug.'

There's nothing I want more than to fall into his arms, but I know I can't. The longer I drag this out, the worse it will be for both of us. I take a step back.

'Lewis, we need to talk,' I say, more sharply than intended.

'Sounds ominous?' He cocks one eyebrow. 'Is there something wrong? There is, isn't there?' he challenges when I don't respond. 'You've been . . . I can only describe it as a bit cool towards me. I got the impression when you didn't want to stay last night that it was because you were going off me.'

'It isn't that,' I say.

'So there is something wrong.' His voice is husky with concern. 'What is it? You're scaring me. Are you trying to say what I think you are? I thought everything was great between us. We're so good together. I've never met anyone like you before.' Lewis runs his hands through his hair. 'When we first met, I didn't think we'd have much in common—'

'I know,' I interrupt, but he continues, 'I feel like you're part of me, Zara. Please don't tell me it's over.'

'I'm sorry.' My brow is tight, my chest aching.

'So who is it?'

'There's no one else, I assure you.'

'Is it Paul?'

413

'No . . . Why should this have anything to do with him?'

'Because he's always trying to stir up trouble between us. The last time I saw him I was with Murray at the pub. He came over, bought me a beer and started talking about how you left him because you were all screwed up about not being able to have a baby. He said you'd do the same to me.'

'That's a lie,' I exclaim. 'What did he think he was doing?'

'Trying to break us up. He's a devious little man who for some reason known only to himself doesn't want you to be happy. It's all right. I told him to f*** off. Was I right not to believe him?'

'You certainly were. To think I've tried to be nice to him and keep some kind of friendship going, and all this time he's been stabbing me in the back!'

'So what is it?' Lewis says, returning to the original subject.

'I've been thinking and I can't . . .' I frown. 'Don't say anything. Let me speak. You told me when we first met that you wanted kids, and when I see you with Poppy and Daisy, I can see you're going to be a fantastic dad one day. I can't let you sacrifice the chance of having children and a family of your own for me. You're young and you have plenty of time to find someone else.'

'But I don't want anybody else. I want you. I love you,' Lewis says.

'I know you love me,' I say in a low voice. 'You don't just say it, you show it in every way, the little things you say and do; but eventually you'll come to resent me for not being able to give you a child.'

'This is because of Paul, isn't it? He's poisoned you.' Lewis grabs my shoulders and presses his fingers into my flesh. 'I'm not like your ex-husband. I would never come to resent you.' He relaxes his grip and runs his hands up and down my arms. 'I would never tire of you.'

'Sh!' I touch my fingertip to his lips. 'It's easy to say you aren't bothered now but, trust me, I've seen the way childlessness can eat away at a relationship.' It's true: I've seen how it can devour love and destroy a couple.

'We could always adopt. There are other ways of having a family.'

'I know.' I see it all the time. During my experience as a midwife, I've seen babies given up for adoption or taken into care for fostering, and I've met pregnant women acting as surrogates. I've seen couples go through the stresses of IVF as Paul and I did, and fall apart after the arrival of a much-wanted baby. 'You see, you say you don't mind, but you're already thinking of the options,' I point out. 'You can't put your hand on your heart and tell me honestly that you'll never yearn to be a father.'

'I might regret it from time to time,' he admits, 'but that's only natural. It wouldn't be the be-all and end-all to me. Zara, I wouldn't expect you to go through any treatments or procedures if you didn't want to. I want you, not a baby.' He hesitates, his voice choked. 'We can be a ready-made family – you, me and the dogs.'

'It isn't the same,' I insist. I am crying. Lewis is crying. I love him, adore him, because he's perfect, funny, warm and energetic, but I have to let him go so he can be free to move on. I steel myself. 'It's over. I'm sorry. I hope you find what you're looking for.' I tear myself away and run across the yard to my car, jump in and drive off with Lewis running alongside, banging on the window with his fist.

'Zara, please listen to me.'

I pull away at speed, bumping down the farm track through the puddles. When I glance back, Lewis is standing staring after me, his shoulders slumped and his face and sweater plastered in mud. Our romance is over and I'm utterly devastated. I need to talk to someone and all I can think of is my sister, but I can't go back to the farm for fear of increasing my torment by running into Lewis again, so I pull in further down the lane and call her on my mobile, but she isn't answering her phone and it's Murray who pulls in alongside the car in his tractor and jumps out.

He knocks on the window. Reluctantly, I open it, blowing my nose at the same time.

'Can I help you?' he asks with a goofy smile. 'Are you all right?'

'I'm fine,' I say, choking.

'You aren't. What on earth's happened?' My shoulder is clamped by Murray's vice-like grip – his way of comforting me, I think.

'Lewis and I are finished. It's over.'

'The bastard.' Murray presses a grubby finger to his lips. 'I didn't have him down as one of those.'

'He isn't.'

'I could thump him one for making you cry. In fact, I'm going to set him straight.'

'No, don't make things any worse.'

'It might make him see sense and, if not, I'll make sure he sees stars, at least. After all he's said about you and what Emily and I have done for him. He's an ungrateful sod.'

'Really, don't . . .' I take a deep breath. 'It was me. I finished with him.'

'You did!'

'Yes, I did,' I say miserably. 'I've made up my mind and there's nothing anyone can do or say to change it.'

'Why don't you come back to the house? We'll put the kettle on.'

'That's very kind, but I can't face anyone right now.'

'Well, what are you going to do? You can't sit here all night.'

'You're right . . . I should go home.'

'I can drive you if you like.'

'I'll be fine,' I sigh. 'Thanks, Murray. Tell Emily I'll be in touch.'

Murray reaches through and pats my hand on the wheel.

'You know where we are if you need us. Don't worry, I'll see Lewis is all right. We'll have a few beers.'

Once Murray's gone on his way in the tractor, I head back into Talyton, my head spinning, my heart in turmoil. I don't tell Gran and I have the briefest conversation on the phone with my sister just to let her know I'm all right. I can't eat and I don't sleep.

Tonight, Frosty lies heavily on my feet, matching my sighs with hers. She knows I'm unhappy, and I'm not the only person around here who's going to miss Lewis. He's part of Frosty's life too, or was . . . A lump catches in my throat. I stuff the corner of the duvet into my mouth to stifle my sobs. I still love him and always will.

When I wake there are three missed calls from Lewis. While I'm walking Frosty before breakfast, he calls again. This time, I answer.

'Zara, I had the worst night ever, thinking about what you said,' he begins. 'You're wrong, you know. You can't impose your perception of how I might feel in three or four years' time on our situation. You can't possibly guess the future. Now, I'm a happy-go-lucky kind of person who takes one day at a time, and all I want is to go back to how we were and do that with you, not worrying about what might or might not happen. I understand you feel more secure knowing you have things planned out as far as you can, but life isn't like that. It has twists and turns, and ups and downs, and I want to go through them with you at my side. Please, meet with me later so we can talk. I miss you so much.'

'I'm sorry,' I say softly. 'It's better we don't see each other. There's no point. It will only make things worse.'

'So you do have feelings for me still?' he says, sounding more optimistic. 'The baby thing wasn't just an excuse?'

'Of course I have feelings for you, but that doesn't

418

mean there's any chance of getting back together. Nothing's changed.'

He sighs deeply and I feel as if I have a knife through my chest. 'If you're sure then.'

'I'm sure. I'm sorry,' I repeat.

'I'm sorry too.' He clears his throat before he continues. 'As you've made your mind up, I'm going to go and stay with my parents. I don't think I can bear to remain at the farm.' His voice breaks. 'There are too many memories . . . Goodbye, Zara.'

I cut the call, unable to speak.

The next morning, although it's the last thing I want to do, I crawl out of bed, shower and dress and, having made sure Gran has a cup of tea and breakfast, I drive to the hospital to visit Tessa. I find her on the neonatal unit with Jack and the baby, who is still in an incubator and surrounded by wires and monitors. It's good news, though. Although he's having oxygen through a tube in his nose, I can see that he's breathing for himself.

Jack notices me first. 'Zara. It's great to see you.'

Tessa looks up from where she's sitting in a chair in a white robe. There's a blue teddy bear in her lap.

'I brought you these from me and Frosty,' I say, handing her a box of Maltesers. 'You're looking well,' I go on after she thanks me. 'How's he doing?'

'He's doing much better now. In fact, the doctors think that they can delay surgery on his heart until he's bigger and stronger. He will need to have an operation, but there will be less risk of complications.'

'Have you been able to hold him?' I ask.

'Show Zara the pictures,' Tessa says, and Jack hands me his phone.

'He's gorgeous,' I say, a lump in my throat as I study the look on Jack's face as he looks down at his wife and their baby son.

'I'm sorry. Jack took hundreds. He's so excited, he's told everyone.' Tessa smiles. 'We're so lucky.'

'It could have been very different,' Jack says quietly, 'and there's a long way to go.'

'I know.' Tessa touches her husband's hand. 'We'll get there, though. We will.'

'What have you called him?' I ask.

'Oliver Jack Steven Wilde,' Tessa says.

'I won't lie and say that it suits him because I can't tell. You can hardly see him under that hat,' I say, amused. 'Can I get you a coffee?'

'No, thank you. Jack can go and get something to eat from the shop later. You get on. I'm sure you have plenty of other things to do.'

'I'll catch up with you all soon,' I say. 'All the best.' I leave the new family to continue to bond, knowing that they have many challenges ahead. I have challenges of my own today, not least coping with the aftermath of my break-up with Lewis, as well as Gran and the shop, and my everyday work with my mums and their babies.

CHAPTER TWENTY-TWO

The Fun of the Fair

Exercise is supposed to make you feel better when you're feeling down, and it's true, because when I return from delivering the papers with Frosty on a cool October morning as the sun is beginning to warm through the mist, revealing a hint of blue sky and a bright day to come, I feel more positive than I have done for a while.

I push the shop door open and let Frosty off the lead just inside. She trots away leaving damp paw-prints across the floor as she heads towards the counter where Gran and Mrs Dyer are talking.

'How much did you say that comes to, Rosemary?' Mrs Dyer asks. 'There's a magazine, a bar of milk chocolate and a witch's hat for Hallowe'en – I like to dress up when the children come trick or treating.'

'That'll be five shillings and six.' Gran frowns as she stares into the till. 'I've run out of half-crowns.'

'Here, let me sort it out,' Mrs Dyer says gently.

'It's all right. I'll do it,' I say, moving behind the counter to join Gran. 'Let's start again.' I ring up the prices, which add up to a sensible total in decimal, before taking Mrs Dyer's money and giving her the change.

'Well I never,' Gran mumbles. 'Who'd have thought it?'

'I think you must have had a flashback,' I tell her. 'You were working it out in old money – it all changed in the 1970s way before I was born. Gran, can I ask you a favour? Would you mind giving Frosty her breakfast?' With tears in my eyes, I glance towards Mrs Dyer. 'I think she's having one of those days.'

'I have them all the time,' she says, trying to make light of the issue. 'Zara, is everything okay? Only Rosemary wasn't having a very good day the last time I came in. She gave me the wrong change. I gave it back, of course, but there may be people who aren't so honest.'

'Actually, she's becoming a little forgetful,' I admit.

'I know what that's like. My old mum, bless her heart, went the same way.'

'I'm going to have to call in sick. I'm supposed to be at work.'

Mrs Dyer takes off her coat. 'I can help out for the morning.'

'Oh no, I couldn't possibly—'

'You go. We're neighbours, part of the community, and we help each other out. Rosemary and I can have a nice chat about the old days.'

'Thank you so much. I'll find someone to cover the afternoon. I'll be back at lunchtime.' I run upstairs, change without showering and grab my keys.

I call Emily, but she isn't well. She's been throwing up for a couple of days and doesn't feel up to doing anything, so I brace myself and phone my parents. It's Mum who answers.

'I hate to do this, but could you look after the shop this afternoon? Gran's in a bit of a pickle and I can't ask James because he's on holiday. It's half-term. Please, I'm desperate.'

'I'll be straight over,' she says after a pause.

'I won't be here. Mrs Dyer's holding the fort. You've saved my life.'

As I cut the call, my mobile rings. It's Claire at the surgery and she's in a flap.

'I don't know where you are this morning, or if you can help, but we have a baby emergency here. It's Rosie. She's in labour. I've called for an ambulance, but I think it'll be too late.'

'I'll be right there.' I run faster than I've ever run before, reaching the surgery in a record two minutes. Janet opens the door for me.

'She's in there.' She points to the nurse's room. 'Ben—'

I don't stop to hear any more, rushing straight through to find Claire's sanctuary rather overcrowded, with Rosie lying on the trolley and Ben, Claire and Adam surrounding her. Ben looks up from where he's examining the mum-to-be, maintaining her modesty with a judiciously placed sheet.

'Am I glad to see you?' he says, moving over to speak to me. 'I haven't delivered a baby for years, and mum is very anxious. I think this is your department, but I'll be right back if you need me. Mum is fully dilated and ready to push.'

'Thank you,' I say, as Rosie utters a scream.

'That hurts sooooo much!'

Adam, his face pale and his teeth gritted, stands holding her hand.

'All right,' I say as the contraction passes. 'There isn't time to get you to hospital. You're going to deliver your baby very soon.' Rosie's crying and shaking. 'I need you to calm down and focus now.' I glance towards Claire and give her a list of the basic kit that we need, such as towels, clamps and scissors.

'I'm onto it,' she says.

'Rosie, with this next contraction, I want you to push as hard as you can into your bottom.'

Claire hands Adam a piece of damp paper towel. He wipes his face.

'That was for Rosie, but never mind,' she smiles. 'Hang on in there, Adam,' she adds. 'It won't be long.'

'Push,' I say. 'Keep pushing. That's great. I can see the baby's head. Now, pant – that's it. With the next contraction, your baby will be born. Ready?'

'Noooo,' she bellows as the next pain builds.

'That's good. Now push!' It doesn't take much effort. The baby's shoulders pop out like a cork from a champagne bottle. I catch it under the arms and lift it onto the towel that Claire spreads across Rosie's chest, at which the baby cries and kicks its legs.

'This one is a feisty little thing,' I comment.

'What is it?' Adam asks.

'It's a girl,' I say, checking. 'Congratulations.' I clamp the cord in two places and let Adam cut it while Rosie gazes at her baby daughter.

'She's amazing,' she whispers. 'I don't believe it.'

I look towards Claire, who has tears streaming down her face.

'Don't – you'll set me off.' I smile. 'Well done, team.'

'OMG, I'm so emotional,' Claire says as the room starts to flash with blue light.

'The ambulance is here,' Adam says.

'Too late,' Rosie says.

'Has baby got a name?' I ask.

'We're going to call her Isla,' Adam says. 'Isla Jamelia.'

'That's beautiful,' I say, having been slightly concerned they were going to choose something much more way out, as my last teenage parents did, naming their daughter Porsche and son Aston. They were also the couple who couldn't comprehend how they could be having twins when they'd allegedly had sex only once.

'Thank you, Zara, and Claire,' Adam begins. 'I'm sorry we barged in on you like this, but I couldn't think of anywhere else we could go, and I really didn't want our baby to be born in the butcher's or the baker's.'

'I'm glad you were with me, Adam,' Rosie says. 'You were sick. You didn't faint or throw up.'

'You were great.' Blushing, he leans down and plants a kiss on her lips. I smile to myself. They're going to be okay.

Later, I call Kelly to explain why I haven't made it to Talymouth.

'I have been working,' I say, going on to explain about the surprise arrival.

'It sounds like it,' she says, sounding less miffed now she knows I'm not skiving – not that I would. She does occasionally! 'Do you want to go straight from Talyton to see Lucia and her new baby rather than come here first? She was discharged yesterday.'

'Yes, good idea,' I say, thinking I can have a quick catch-up with Claire over a much-needed coffee and biscuits and drop into the shop to check Mum's arrived before flying off on the visit.

Claire and I sit outside in the sunshine.

'That was an eventful morning,' she sighs.

'In more ways than one,' I agree, telling her of my woes with Gran and the shop.

'You aren't having a good time at the moment, are you? You're still going around like a shepherd who's lost their sheep.' She gazes at me, one eyebrow raised. 'Or should that be a sheep that's lost its shepherd? Have you heard from him at all?'

I shake my head. 'I had the odd text from him at first, but it was too hard. I told him it was better all round to have a clean break. I haven't heard from him since.'

'I'm sorry for raking it up again, Zara. I was hoping . . .' Claire bites her lip. 'It's such a shame. You seemed to be so perfect for each other.'

'Never mind about me. How are you? I haven't seen much of you since you came back from the honeymoon.'

'I'm feeling much better, at least I was until I saw Rosie in labour. I'm dreading that part.' She grimaces. 'I've changed my mind about the drug-free homebirth. I want the epidural, pethidine, everything.'

'Have you finished the nursery?' I'm teasing, but she in all seriousness goes on to tell me how she's washed the walls and chosen the paint. We finish our coffee and Claire takes the mugs inside, while I return to the shop to find Mum in the window with a cardboard box, rubber gloves and a bucket of soapy water, obliterating all trace of my grandmother's display of patriotism.

'Where's Gran?' I ask.

'I've packed her off to bed.' Mum pauses with her hands on her hips. 'We need to talk.'

No. It's on the tip of my tongue, but the look on my mother's face makes me hesitate. She isn't angry with me. She's concerned.

'You can't go on like this.' She holds up her palm. 'Let me finish. I know Mum hasn't been her normal self for a while, but today . . .' She turns away, her shoulders slumped, and pretends to wipe down one of the empty shelves.

'Oh . . .' Choking back a sob, I reach out and rub her back. 'I'm sorry.'

'I feel as if I've lost her.' Mum swivels round to face me. 'The person I knew, the funny, capable, sometimes difficult mother I loved . . .' Her face crumples, reminding me of Poppy, 'She's gone.'

'She hasn't. There are times when she comes back,' I insist. In the background, I hear a single 'Cuckoo'. It's twelve o'clock and even the cuckoo clock is giving up. 'She can still have a giggle. She can still be very stubborn.'

'I'm sorry, but you really have to snap out of this denial and accept the situation for what it is.' Mum's voice softens. 'I know it's hard, but we have to work together to find a solution that works for Gran and the rest of the family.'

'Put her in a home, you mean?'

'Not necessarily,' she says. 'Let's talk about this another time.'

'Yes, I'd better go. Thank you.' I'm not looking forward to that conversation. It will only lead to an impasse because, although life is getting harder for both of us, it isn't at the stage where I'd be prepared to break my promise to my grandmother.

In fact, her condition appears to stabilise over the next three weeks, and I find myself able to concentrate on work, with James doing the odd shift after school and Mrs Dyer popping in now and again to check that Gran is coping. It's a relief – with the distraction of busy clinics, tricky deliveries and some happy postnatal checks, I find I have to push thoughts of Lewis to the back of my mind for a significant part of every day, even if those thoughts return with a vengeance during the rest of my waking hours.

Eventually, I decide to stop torturing myself and look forward not back. Lewis maintains a presence in my life that is unhealthy, like a jam sandwich or a great big chocolate éclair. I can make a start by deleting his number and his texts, all of them, including the locked messages that have been tormenting me for the past weeks, their presence on my mobile tempting me to relive the good times, the best days of my life, but although it's simple enough to erase the history from my SIM with a touch of a button, it's harder, maybe impossible, to erase all traces of him from my heart. I take a deep breath and, fighting the palpitations of doubt in my chest, press delete.

Immediately, my heart breaks all over again and I can't get enough oxygen into my lungs, but Frosty's here to comfort me in her own way, bringing me one of my shoes. She sits at my feet and pushes it onto my lap. If it wasn't for her, I wouldn't want to get up in the mornings, especially when I dream during the night that I have a baby of my own; except, when I pick it up, it weighs nothing, and when I unwrap the blanket from its face, there's nobody there, no one to love.

Emily and I meet to walk the dogs on another sunny October afternoon in what is turning out to be an Indian summer.

'Where's Sherbet?' I ask, noticing that he doesn't come scampering out of the house to greet us as he normally does.

'He's on his way,' she says. 'Look, here he is.'

I turn to see Murray driving the tractor into the yard with Sherbet on his knee in the cab.

'What the . . .?' I say. 'I thought he wasn't going to have anything to do with the dog.'

'That's what he said,' Emily chuckles. 'The trouble is that Sherbet has a way of turning the emotional screw, sitting in his basket looking all dejected, and Murray's decided he can't bear to leave him alone while Poppy's at school and I'm out and about. It's "take your dog to work day" every day down on the farm, you know.'

'Daddy, give me my pet back,' Poppy calls. 'We're going for a walk with Frosty.'

'All right. Give us a chance.' Murray climbs out of the cab with the dog tucked awkwardly under one arm. He kisses Sherbet on the top of his head and lets him down, when he comes trotting up to Poppy and Frosty, squeaking with excitement.

'Come on, sausage,' Poppy says.

I watch Sherbet trying to play with Frosty. He wants her to bow and bark at him, but she thinks it's more fun to run back and forth jumping over him with her long legs. I believe she's missing Mick almost as much as I miss Lewis. I expect Miley's happy now, too, having her master back almost to herself, unless he's moved on and found someone new.

Emily and I walk on, keeping clear of the sheep that are nibbling at the short grass on the hill, while Poppy is distracted collecting the conkers from amongst the fallen leaves of the horse-chestnut tree. Daisy is sitting up in the pushchair, cooing and gurgling as if she's part of our conversation.

Emily stops at the top of the slope and looks back towards the farmhouse.

'Zara, I have a confession to make. Two, actually.'

'Oh? That sounds ominous. Go on. What are they?'

'Lewis is coming back!' Poppy calls, holding the front of her dress up as a container for conkers, which spill out as she trots towards us. 'He'll be here for the Tar Barrels.'

430

Lewis? The blood seems to drain from my body, sending me into shock.

Emily groans. 'I'm sorry, sis. I should have known Big Ears was listening.'

'I'm not Big Ears, Mummy.'

'Go and fetch Sherbet,' Emily says. 'Look, he's got himself stuck in the hedge. All I can see is his tail sticking out from the bushes. Hurry.'

Poppy runs off to extricate her pet and Emily turns back to me.

'Why?' I say. 'Did you and Murray invite him back? Why on earth would you do that? Didn't you think for one moment how I'd feel about it?'

'Listen, it's complicated and, believe me, Murray and I didn't do it without a lot of thought.'

'You know, there isn't a day that goes by without me thinking of him. I'm not sure I can bear the idea of seeing him again, either here at the farm, or running into him in Talyton. It's too painful.'

'I'm so sorry, Zara.'

'Why?' I repeat.

'The sickness I had a couple of weeks ago, well . . .' Emily stares at me. 'Do I have to spell it out?'

I brace myself. 'You're pregnant!'

'It was an accident.'

'Don't you ever listen? What did I say to you about contraception after Daisy was born?'

'I know, but it isn't the end of the world. Murray's over the moon. He's always wanted a big family.'

'There was a time recently when you said you wished Poppy—'

'Stop! That's enough. I didn't mean it – I was having a bad day. I'm sorry. I couldn't bring myself to tell you before, but I can't keep it secret for long, I'm already starting to show.'

'It doesn't matter. I've steeled myself against other people's good news so many times . . . Emily, I'm really pleased for you, and I'm made up because I'm going to be an auntie three times over. I hope Poppy will be all right about it this time.'

'She's so besotted with Sherbet, she probably won't notice,' Emily says with a fond smile. She grows serious again. 'I'm sorry about bringing the subject of Lewis up. I didn't realise it was going to hit you quite so hard.'

'It isn't me I'm worried about. It's Lewis. I hurt him badly.' I know it was for the best, but I'll never forget the hurt in his eyes when I rejected him.

'It isn't for me to say whether you did the right thing, or not, but there are couples who, for various reasons, don't have kids. When Murray spoke to Lewis on the phone the other day, he was still really cut up about it, but he wanted to come back.'

'I hope he isn't thinking of this as an opportunity to rekindle our relationship.'

'I think you made it pretty clear when he left that there was no chance of that happening. No, I reckon he's being pragmatic – he needs the money and he and Murray have a bit of a laugh working together.' She leans down and pops Daisy's soother back into her mouth before giving me a hug. 'I could say we've changed our minds and find someone else.'

'Don't. I know he's the best shepherd for the job.'
It's a double whammy: Lewis and the baby. I try to
stay strong but inside I'm devastated all over again.
Unlike with my ex-husband, I don't think I'll ever
get over my ex-boyfriend.

Poppy comes running back with Frosty and Sherbet.

'Where are the conkers?' I ask, glad to have the
opportunity to change the subject.

'Over there. I'm going to let Daisy carry them.'

'We can put them in the pocket at the back of the
pushchair, as long as you remember to take them out
when we get back to the house,' Emily says. 'Come on,
Pops. Zara can give us a hand.'

'I hope you don't mind, but when Lewis does come
back, I can't see myself spending much time at the
farm.'

'That's okay. I understand why you don't want to
see him. I won't take it personally,' she says. 'Although
I'm not sure you'll be able to avoid him in such a small
town.'

The night of the Tar Barrels, an annual event in Talyton
St George, draws closer, and the signs go up around
town: Flaming Tar Barrels; enter at your own risk.
There is an air of excitement and anticipation. Spare
rooms are tidied up for guests, the bonfire is being built
on the Green, the equipment for the funfair is arriving
in convoy, and there are extra deliveries of beer to the
local pubs.

For some of us, life goes on as normal, and I have
plenty of work the day before the event, including

a few appointments at the surgery, one of which is a routine antenatal check at twenty-five weeks for Katie, Paul's girlfriend. I'm delighted for all the wrong reasons when he turns up with her. I invite them into the nurse's room and check through the notes. She's had her twenty-week scan and all is well.

'Good morning,' Paul says, as if I'm his best mate. 'How are you doing?'

I turn away and focus on Katie and their baby. I really don't care about Paul any more. I run through the process, asking questions, checking Katie's blood pressure and the baby's heart.

'Have you brought a urine sample?' I ask.

'I forgot. I'm sorry.'

'Oh dear, how many times did I remind you?' Paul sighs. 'You are so ditsy, I despair.'

'Never mind,' I say, handing her a pot. 'You can provide one now.'

I wait until Katie leaves for the toilet before I turn on Paul, who's looking at me with the usual annoying smirk on his lips.

'You didn't answer my question, Zara,' he says quietly. 'How are you doing? Really? You know you can be straight with me.'

'It's none of your business,' I snap.

'You're a bit touchy today. I heard you and Lewis had split up.'

'Didn't you hear what I just said? What I do, who I'm with, how I'm feeling – they have absolutely nothing to do with you, you cold bastard. I know what you tried to do, planting ideas about me in Lewis's head, but I'm so sorry to disappoint you – your sneaky lies had no influence on our break-up.'

'My god, you're in a right strop today,' Paul says without wavering. 'It must be your hormones.'

'Listen to me – I want nothing more to do with you. I'm transferring Katie's care to another member of my team.'

'You can't do that.'

'Oh, I can.'

'But what will I tell Katie when I've been going on about how you're the best?' Paul blusters.

'I'm sure you can make something up – you're pretty good at that. Now, go and sit in the waiting room while I test this urine sample. Go on. Piss off . . . and while you're at it, go somewhere else to buy your chocolates and magazines.' As soon as Katie walks back into the room, I transform from furious ex-wife to reassuring professional midwife.

'I'll wait outside,' Paul says quietly.

'Are you sure?' Katie says.

'I'm feeling a bit faint,' he goes on, excusing himself.

Pleased that I've managed to have it out with Paul at last, I return from work to find my father boarding up the windows. The butcher's and greengrocer's are already obscured by sheets of plywood.

'At least Frosty won't worry about the fireworks,' I say, giving Dad a hug. 'Gran can stay and dog-sit tomorrow night. I'll pop in now and again to make sure she's all right.'

435

'She can't stay here much longer,' Dad says.

'I know. I'll talk to her.'

'When?'

'Soon,' I say stubbornly. 'Thanks for doing this.'

'I've done it every year since your granddad died and your gran still hates me.' He grins. 'She won't change now. Are you going to watch the barrels tomorrow night, or have you got better things to do?'

'Emily's bringing the girls here so Poppy can watch from the window upstairs. Murray wants them to stay safe.' I sound nonchalant, but I love the tar barrels, the bonfire being lit on the Green, the smell of smoke, the fireworks, and the surging crowds that carry you back and forth through Talyton's streets like a cork in the sea.

Gran sits at the kitchen table while I prepare jacket potatoes, sausages and chocolate cake, decorated with sweets to make it look like a bonfire, before the family turn up. My grandmother talks about Tar Barrel nights gone by, repeating the same stories over and over again, but I don't mind. I'm happy to see her so animated and looking forward to the evening. I take her out with Emily, Poppy and Daisy to see the first barrel being lit and watch the children carrying it past the shop, but by ten thirty, she takes herself off to bed, leaving me and Emily to catch up.

'I saw Tessa the other day,' Emily says. 'We met up for coffee at the garden centre.'

'How is she?' I ask my sister, who's sitting up with a sleepy Poppy in her arms, and Daisy snoozing in her travel cot in the flat.

'She seems a bit stressed out. It's hard enough looking after a new baby, let alone one who has a heart defect.'

'Oliver's okay, though?' I saw Tessa when she brought the baby to the doctor's recently to see Ben about various minor ailments, sniffles and rashes. According to her, Oliver is doing well, although he might still need surgery to close the hole in his heart.

'He seems fine to me – he's about six weeks old and already smiling at everyone. He loves Daisy.'

I'm glad the baby's thriving. It's early days, but hopefully he'll be one of the lucky ones and the hole will close on its own within the first couple of years of his life.

'Do you mind if I go and watch the midnight barrel?' I say after a while. 'I'll wave.'

'That's okay with me.' Emily gazes out of the window. 'I don't like the feeling of being crushed among all those people – I'd rather watch from a distance. Wish Murray luck if you get close to him. He and Lewis were somewhere by the Dog and Duck the last time I heard from them. What's the time?'

I check my watch. 'Eleven thirty. I'd better grab my coat.'

'Have fun.'

'I'll try to,' I say, a little concerned now that I might run into Lewis, whom I've avoided so far.

'Have you seen Gran?' Emily says suddenly.

'She was here when I came back in from the last barrel. She said she was going to bed, or, more accurately, I suggested she should go. I'll check on her on my way out.'

However, when I knock on her door and push it ajar, her bed is empty, the duvet on the floor. 'Gran? Where are you?' I turn the light on. Her handbag isn't in its usual place on her bedside chair. A pulse of doubt begins to beat at my temple. 'I can't find her.'

'What do you mean?' Emily says, joining me on the landing.

'She isn't in her room.' I run downstairs. Her coat is gone and her shoes. 'She's gone out.'

'Out?' Emily frowns as Daisy begins to cry upstairs where she left her. 'How can she go out on a night like this? It's cold and she's too fragile to stay on her feet in that crowd of people. What does she think she's doing?'

'She doesn't think – that's the problem. Oh god, this is all my fault.'

'Of course it isn't.'

'She wanders off all the time – I forgot to lock the door.'

'Are you saying what I think you're saying?' Emily exclaims.

I nod. 'It's the only way . . .'

'We'll talk about this later. First, we must find her,' Emily says. 'If only Frosty could talk.'

'You must have heard something.'

'Nothing at all. It's been pretty noisy,' she says, looking hurt. 'She can't have travelled very far on a night like this.'

'She could have gone down to the river, or she could

438

be halfway to Talymouth by now. I wish you'd kept an eye on her.'

'Is this what it's like, Zara? When you said "keep an eye", I didn't realise I had to watch her like a hawk. I didn't imagine she'd wander off like that.'

'Let's not fight. Let's concentrate on finding her. You stay here in case she comes home.' I run down the stairs and outside into the street, jogging up through the crowds and pushing my way to outside King's Head House, where Murray, wearing a ragged old sweatshirt full of holes from last year's tar barrel and covered in smuts, stands beside a giant barrel that's been soaked in tar. His hands are wrapped with layers of rags to protect his skin from the heat. Lewis is beside him, his hair gleaming in the light of the streetlamp. My chest tightens because, as I feared, seeing him brings the feelings I had for him flooding back, the pang of love and the pain of loss, but I dismiss them quickly. I have to find Gran.

'Murray,' I yell, but he doesn't hear me over the sound of shouting and cheering.

'All set,' he bellows, and one of the other local farmers – Chris, I think – lights the final and heaviest barrel of the night and helps hoist it onto Murray's shoulders, where it burns, spitting sparks and a tongue of fire.

'Lewis!' I yell at the top of my voice. I push in closer as Murray starts to run the barrel down the street, until I can feel the flames lick at my skin as the barrel passes too close for comfort.

'Zara, what the hell are you doing?' Lewis says, whisking me out of the way.

'Trying to find Gran. I need help. She's gone missing.'

'I saw Kev not so long ago,' he shouts in my ear. 'He was outside the flower shop chatting to a group of tourists who hadn't realised what they'd let themselves in for when they decided to see one of Talyton's local traditions.' He takes my hand and pulls me through the crowd, jostling people aside as we push against the flow of people. 'There he is.' Lewis waves and, within five minutes, Kev is doing his best to alert his colleagues to look out for an elderly woman of Gran's description, although I've struggled with what she's wearing because I'm really not sure, apart from her coat. Lewis and I make our way towards King's Head House, hoping to spot my errant grandmother.

'Do your parents know?' Lewis asks.

'I'll try them now.' I call my mum, who is safely ensconced at a friend's house on the new estate, having watched the earlier barrels for the children and teenagers. 'Gran's gone missing,' I say abruptly. 'Lewis and I and the police are searching for her. I thought you should know.'

I'm not sure of my mother's reaction because my father takes over the conversation.

'Where are you, Zara?'

'At the top of Market Square.' I watch as Lewis starts asking the onlookers who remain, milling around, if they've seen a lost OAP. 'I thought I'd walk around the one-way system first.'

440

'I'll take your mum down to the river,' Dad says. 'Keep in touch, won't you?'

'It's a plan,' Lewis says, as I cut the call, 'but forgive me when I say I don't think you'll find her there. Rosemary likes bright lights and company. She isn't going to wander off along the river by herself.'

'So where would you look, seeing you know her so well?' I say, trying not to sound sarcastic when Lewis is, after all, being helpful. He could be watching Murray and the other barrel rollers, jostling for possession of the barrel and lost in a plume of smoke.

'The funfair,' he says. 'I bet you any money that's where she's gone.'

I hope he's right, I think, as we jog down towards the Centurion Bridge and the Green, following the flashing lights and the cacophony of music and screams of fear and delight.

'This really is like looking for the proverbial needle in the haystack,' Lewis observes as we step into the magical world of the fairground.

'Should we split?' I ask tentatively.

'Good idea. You take the centre while I do the stalls on the perimeter. We'll meet back here at the Hoopla. Don't worry. We'll find her.'

I make my way past the Wild West shooting range and the Lucky Dip, spooked by the enormous fluffy toys: tigers, bright yellow lions and puffins. Where is she? Am I going to find her before she freezes to death or falls and breaks her hip? I look across to the Haunted House ride, a conveyor-belt trip through a garish pink castle, and back towards the Teacup ride where a single

441

grey-haired woman, dressed in a flowing nightie, is spinning around with one hand in the air and the other holding onto the bar in front of her.

'Gran?' It's definitely my grandmother and I give the attendant a good telling off, I'm ashamed to say, to assuage my anger and guilt at myself for not locking her indoors.

'What were you thinking of? She's eighty.'

'She had the right money. I don't need to ask for proof of age,' the attendant grumbles, letting her off the ride. I step forwards and take her arm, noticing how her eyes are flicking back and forth as she tries to steady herself.

'Oh, that's such fun,' she chuckles. 'Sarah, you must have a turn.'

'I'm good, thank you. And I'm Zara, not Sarah – not that it matters.' I'm just glad to find her alive and well. 'Where's your coat? And your purse?'

'I gave them to a nice young man to look after while I was on the ride.'

'Oh, great.' My heart sinks again. 'I don't suppose he's hung around to give them back to you.'

'I have no reason to doubt him,' Gran says.

'Who was it?'

'His name escapes me, but he was very kind, although he did make me miss my turn on the Big Wheel.'

How naïve is that, when Talyton St George is filled with strangers tonight. I swear under my breath. 'You do realise we'll have to go and cancel your bank cards,' I say crossly.

'I left them at home. I'm only carrying cash.'

'How much?' I ask.

She smirks. 'I raided the till. I'll go to the bank tomorrow.'

I'm lost for words, and my grandmother's hands are turning bluish-purple in the lights along the walkway as I rest my jacket around her shoulders and lead her back towards the Hoopla.

'Come on, Gran.'

'I don't want to go home.'

'It's getting late. It must be past your bedtime.' I change the subject. 'Look, there's Lewis. Do you remember him?'

Lewis comes over to greet her. 'Hello, Rosemary.'

'Hello, young man. You're Zara's husband,' she says brightly. As I attempt to correct her misconception, she continues, 'Have you come to take me home?'

'Yes, I have,' he says gently. 'You look as if you've been having fun.'

'I've been on all the rides,' she says, smiling as she takes his arm. 'I feel quite giddy.'

'And cold, I should imagine.' Lewis places his hand over hers as though to warm it up.

'It's all right,' I say, meaning, don't worry, she's my problem, but he seems keen to accompany us back to the shop, weaving through the crowds that are beginning to disperse now that the final barrel has been run. It lies burning in the street, a smoking skeleton of charred wood and incandescent white metal, watched over by the rollers who will rescue the hoops to sell to the highest bidder as souvenirs.

I catch Kev on our way to let him know the good news. He's at the foot of a lamppost, trying to talk a drunk down from the top.

'The show's over,' he calls. 'Come on down, matey.'

'Good luck with that,' I say. 'I don't envy you your job.'

'It has its moments.' Kev smiles. 'I'm glad Rosemary's turned up safe and well.'

I let Lewis and Gran into the shop where the rest of the family, apart from Murray, is waiting anxiously.

'Thank goodness,' Mum says, taking my grand-mother's hand. 'What did you think you were doing, you silly old fool? You worried us sick.'

'She went to the fair, didn't you, Gran?' I say in explanation. 'She's okay, a bit cold, that's all.'

'Should we call the doctor?' Emily asks when we join her upstairs with the girls.

'No,' I say. 'All she needs is a hot drink, some warm clothes and a seat by the fire. There's no harm done, apart from the fact she's lost her coat and a purse full of cash. She says she gave it to someone to hold onto for her, but she can't recall who it was.'

Mum smiles ruefully. 'They'll be miles away by now.'

'There's no use crying over spilt milk,' Gran says, joining in, and I have to agree. There are bigger things to worry about, as my mother reminds me a while later, having asked me to join her downstairs in the shop on the pretence of checking the till. The others are drinking tea and eating honey on toast, including Murray, who's joined us to have Emily attend to the inevitable burns on his head, neck and hands. Poppy is awake now, too, playing with Frosty and wishing aloud that she was at home with Sherbet.

I open the till with Mum looking on. It's empty apart from a few pennies and ten-pence pieces.

'There's a place in the old people's home that Dad and I looked at earlier this year. I rang them last week.'

It's a statement of fact and I have no stomach to argue. The till snaps shut.

'You were right. I was wrong,' I say eventually. 'I'm sorry.'

'You can see this can't go on. Someone, probably Gran, is going to get hurt, or worse.'

'I know. I'll speak to her tomorrow.'

'Thank you, darling.' Mum embraces me. 'Let's forget any unpleasantness that there's been over the past few months and start again without blame and recriminations. We all want what's best for Gran, for you, and for the family as a whole.'

Tears prick my eyes and the bitter taste of resentment towards my parents for what I've perceived as a lack of empathy for my grandmother dissolves like a fruit sour.

'What about Norris?' I ask.

'I'll take Norris.'

'You don't like cats.'

'You didn't like dogs, but it didn't stop you. It will be one less thing for Gran to fret about, knowing Norris is being looked after.' Mum smiles wanly. 'It's been quite a night. Dad and I are going home, but we'll be back in the morning to open up.'

'I can do that.'

'We have to share the responsibility between us, both looking out for Gran and keeping the shop running while we decide what has to be done with it. It's only fair. Let me know how it goes.'

'If she'll talk,' I say ruefully. 'I feel as if I lost Gran tonight.'

'Well, you did.'

'I don't mean it in that way. What I mean is, it's like she's gone, the person she was has walked out into the darkness, leaving this person who's vaguely familiar, but not the same. Everything has changed.'

My mind runs ahead. It isn't just my grandmother, I'm about to lose my home, and so soon after the blow of letting Lewis go. Life's a . . . I recall how Gran once described it, not as a bitch, but as a beach filled with pebbles, each pebble an experience that you might pick up either to keep in your hand or throw into the sea.

'It's going to be a tough time, but we'll get through it.' Mum gazes at me as I struggle to contain my emotions. 'Are you going to be all right tonight, love, or would you like me to stay?'

'Would you mind?' I leap at the offer.

'I'm offering, aren't I?' Mum gives me a half-smile as I thank her, and soon after, Dad leaves, along with Emily and the others. I'm aware of Lewis looking at me, as if he's trying to tell me something. I'm eternally grateful that he helped look for my grandmother, but I don't want to open old wounds.

Mum and I stay up for a while, washing up and tidying the kitchen.

'Your mobile went ping just then,' she says.

'Did it?' I say, trying to ignore it.

'Aren't you going to see who that's from? It might be Emily.'

I hunt around in my pocket – Gran left my jacket on the back of a kitchen chair. If she'd been her normal self, she would have joked about how cool she looked in it.

'Who is it?'

'No one,' I say, checking the message.

'Well, it must be from somebody.'

'All right, it's from Lewis, asking if I'd meet him for a walk with the dogs.'

'You aren't going to go, are you?' I'm not sure how much Mum knows, probably as much as Emily does, I suspect. I let my phone power down. I have more than enough to contend with, without Lewis. Seeing him again this evening has reminded me – as if I really needed a reminder – that I still love him and probably always will.

My heart remains broken and, the next morning, I break my grandmother's heart as well.

CHAPTER TWENTY-THREE

Someone to Love

It's like the film, *Groundhog Day*. Mum is looking after the shop while I talk to Gran upstairs.

'I'm so sorry. You've done so much for me and I wanted to look after you in return, but it's become impossible.'

She frowns. She's had a shower and washed her hair, which is still wet, like grey mouse tails stuck to her scalp.

'Can you remember what happened last night?' I continue. 'You took yourself off to the fair.'

'Did I? Did you come with me?'

'I came and found you.'

'Oh dear. I don't like to cause trouble.'

'You didn't. You haven't.' I feel the familiar sense of exasperation rising inside me at being unable to penetrate the wall of incomprehension that the dementia has thrown up between us. There's absolutely

448

no way of getting through to her. I try another tack. 'I know I promised I'd always be here for you . . .'

'You are here,' Gran says brightly. 'Look at you. You're right here in front of me. Unless you're a ghost.'

'I've tried really hard to make sure you can stay here and keep the shop going, but it's become apparent – no, obvious, that we can't carry on like this. You need someone to look after you full time, and I can't do that because I have to go out to work with my ladies and their babies. Do you understand?'

'Oh yes.' She nods vaguely. 'You have a lovely day. I'll cook us something special for tea. I think there's a nice piece of beef in the fridge.'

'There isn't,' I say. 'I had to throw it out.'

'I thought you knew better: waste not, want not.'

'It was off. I found it in the oven along with the butter and eggs.'

'I didn't put it there,' Gran says, immediately defensive, and I wish I hadn't mentioned the fate of the beef.

'Well, I don't know who did, unless it was Mr Nobody,' I say, referring to the imaginary culprit that Emily and I grew up with at home with Mum and Dad.

'Granddad, you mean. He's always putting things away in the wrong places so I can't find them.'

I run my hands through my hair, take a deep breath and try again.

'I'm sorry to upset you, but you are going to have to move out of the flat and into a home.' I don't intend to be quite so abrupt, but I don't know how else I can get the message across.

'I'm not going into a home. This is my home!' Gran exclaims, suddenly animated, as if I've flicked a switch. 'Zara, you promised . . .' Her lip trembles and my heart twists with pain at hurting her.

'I know . . .' I swallow past the tightening in my throat. 'I didn't foresee what was coming.' I lower my voice and add, 'And I don't think you did either . . .'

'What was that? What did you say?' Gran cranes towards me.

'Zara, there's someone to see you and your grand-mother,' Mum calls, interrupting our conversation. 'Shall I send them up?'

'All right,' I call back, wondering if it's Emily who's dropped in to make sure everything's okay after the night before. It crosses my mind that it might be Lewis, but it isn't. It's Adam, Rosie and baby Isla. Rosie, dressed in skinny jeans and a padded jacket with a fur hood, carries her daughter in her arms, while Adam follows behind.

'Hello. This is a lovely surprise,' I say, reminding Gran of the identity of our visitors in case she's forgotten them since they last came into the shop. It was a week or so ago; they came in to pick up some chocolate and update the ads in the window for Uphill Farm cider, which Adam's stepdad makes, and for Jennie's Cakes.

'What a lovely baby,' Gran beams. 'Does she belong to you, young man – only you seem far too young to be making babies?'

'Please don't be embarrassing,' I say. 'Is this a social call, Rosie?'

450

'I thought you'd like to see Isla,' she says. 'She's growing so fast, I can't believe it.'

I reach out and touch Isla's outstretched fingers. She gives me a tiny smile, yawns and closes her eyes.

'I'm sorry, I'm boring you,' I smile, looking back at Rosie. 'You're looking great.' Motherhood suits her.

'Adam's brought your gran's stuff back,' she goes on, nodding towards him.

He hands me a coat and purse. 'Rosemary asked me to look after these last night, but I lost her in the crowd and I had to run up to the King's Head for the last barrel to cheer for Guy.'

'Oh, thank you.' I'm touched and relieved. 'That's really kind of you. I thought she'd lost them. Why don't you stop for a cup of tea with us?'

The young couple glance at each other.

'No, thank you,' Rosie says. 'I'd like to get Isla home in time for her next feed.'

I escort them back downstairs, making sure they have some sweets as a gift before they leave the shop, and then return to Gran and our unfinished conversation.

'Now, where were we?' I begin, and smile to myself; if I can't remember, what hope is there for my grandmother? 'We were talking about you moving to a place where you can be looked after properly, where you can be safe.'

'Are you suggesting I go into an old people's home?' she says, looking affronted this time. 'Oh no. I will only leave here in a cardboard box.'

'I don't think you mean that.'

'I certainly do. I shan't leave until I'm carried out

451

in my coffin.' She grasps the edge of the table with both hands. 'You can't make me, Sarah.' A tear forms, glinting from the corner of her eye.

'I'm Zara. Sarah is your daughter.'

'Why do you want to put me away?' she asks.

'I don't want to.'

'Then why are you telling me this?'

'Because I've tried really hard to make sure you can stay here, but it isn't working for either of us. You need someone to look after you full time, and I can't do that because I have to go out to work with my ladies and their babies. Do you understand?' I repeat.

'Oh yes.' Gran nods vaguely. 'You have a lovely day. Will you be wanting tea tonight?'

'No, thank you. We've been through this already.'

'Aren't you going to work then?'

'Not till tomorrow morning.'

'I think I shall go back to bed,' Gran announces. 'Goodnight, Zara.'

'Goodnight,' I sigh. 'I mean, good morning. It's ten o'clock in the daytime.'

'What did she say?' Mum asks when I go back downstairs.

'I thought she'd be heartbroken, but I'm not sure what she thinks, whether she even understands what I've been saying.' It's me who's devastated, not my grandmother. 'You know, I think she'll be all right about it in the end. At the moment, she can't remember what we're talking about from one minute to the next.'

'I'll make sure we have her place confirmed and

paid for,' Mum says. 'Dad's looking into putting the shop on the market.'

'It would be a shame if it became a charity shop, or ended up being converted into a house. I'd like to see it stay as the local newsagent's.'

'So would I, but who will take it on? It needs a lot of work to update it. Anyone who comes in will want to modernise the flat.' Mum marks down reductions on some packets of chocolate buttons close to their best-before date. 'It could be difficult to find a buyer, but as Gran would say, we'll cross that bridge when we come to it.'

The next morning, my father looks after the shop, and I'm glad to get out and about because my grandmother insists on being there with him to make sure he gets it right. As I leave, Dad comments that it's going to be a very long day.

I visit one of my ladies, Charley, in Talymouth. Her husband, Ian, is a builder, and her house is an example of his work, set on top of the cliff looking out to sea, and extended in all directions. I wouldn't choose to live here if someone paid me, because when you look down the garden, you can see the new fence that Ian put up to replace the one that fell onto the beach last winter after a prolonged spell of heavy rain. In another ten or twenty years, the house will be gone too.

Charley isn't as far on as she hoped, and I have to explain that I'll come back in a couple of hours to see if she's progressing.

'I feel a bit of an idiot now,' she says.

'This is your first baby – it's often difficult to tell when labour starts, but these are Braxton Hicks contractions, not the real thing.'

'Is there any benefit in having an induction, a stretch and sweep, for example?' she asks.

'Why are you so keen to get this going? It's only a day past your due date.'

'It's the football. Ian has an important match tomorrow.'

'Does he play then?'

'Not for Arsenal.' Charley chuckles. 'No, he's got tickets to watch a match with some of his mates.'

'I'm not inducing you for a football match. Ian can surely be here for this one-off occasion? I mean, you don't have a baby every day.'

'And Ian doesn't get tickets to Arsenal every day either.'

What can I say? I'd be annoyed if my partner told me he couldn't make it to the birth of our child because he was going to a football match.

Charley rings me later to say nothing has changed, so I don't see her again until midday the following day when labour has definitely started and the baby is on her way.

'Ian's at the match,' she announces. 'He's texted me to let me know he's there.'

'Okay, let's see. How long will it take him to get back?'

'Several hours. The match hasn't begun yet.'

'Tell him to turn around and come straight back, otherwise he's in danger of missing out on the birth.'

As it turns out, Charley does everything she can to

454

slow the process down, but nature cannot be stopped. When you're in labour, you have no choice but to go with the flow, but Ian is lucky because, having threatened him with instant divorce if he arrives home too late, he turns up in his Arsenal shirt and slightly the worse for wear, with several of his mates, five minutes before his daughter is born.

'You are so going to have to make this up to me,' Charley says, cuddling her baby to her breast.

'It's all right, darling. It worked out. Lee drove down the motorway at eighty, I made it home in time and the Gunners won.' He grins, revealing a gold crown on a front tooth. 'It's the best day of my life.' He opens the bedroom door and calls down the stairs. 'Come and see the baby, and bring me a beer – there's plenty in the fridge.' I pack up my kit and make an attempt at clearing up in the presence of seven inebriated football supporters who are intent on wetting the baby's head.

'Thank you,' Charley says, when I'm ready to leave.

'Make sure you kick them out in the next half-hour,' I smile. 'You need to rest. Kelly will be back tomorrow. Any worries, let me know.'

It's been a long day and, when I reach home, I find three missed calls from Lewis, but I don't return them. There's also a message from Emily asking me to ring her, which I do. She wants me to meet Lewis.

'He keeps going on about it,' she says. 'He's driving Murray mad.'

'I don't want to see him,' I say. 'Don't you understand?'

'All he's asking is if you'll go out for a walk with the dogs.'

'And how do you think that makes me feel?'

'You could just catch up with him this once. It'll break the ice before you next come over to the farm for Sunday lunch. It wouldn't kill you, would it? And anyway, I think you owe him for helping you find Gran. He's a lovely guy and you two could still be great friends.'

'I don't think I can be just mates with Lewis. It wouldn't work.' I pause. 'I've got more important things to deal with – Gran, for example.'

'You're going to let Mum and Dad help you?'

'Yes. I can't go through this any more. The other night, she scared me witless, going missing like that.' I can't help picturing her on the Teacup ride at the fair, spinning around without a care in the world. It seems doubly cruel to take away her home, her way of life, and deny her that freedom to do whatever she likes, but gradually her loss of independence is encroaching on my freedom and, although it sounds selfish, I can't let it go on.

'Zara? You've gone quiet. Are you okay?'

'I feel so mean.'

'I know, but it's the right thing to do. No one will blame you – except Gran,' Emily goes on ruefully.

'Thanks for that. That's what I'm afraid of. She's going to hate me after this.'

'She isn't well. If she was her normal self, she'd understand.'

I bite my lip.

'It's easy to say . . .'

456

'I know,' my sister agrees quietly.

I wish her goodnight.

'Night, Zara.'

I have a shower and go to bed, falling asleep as soon as my head hits the pillow.

Having parked the car at the foot of the escarpment, I keep Frosty on the lead, walking along the steep path between the coppiced beech and hazel, the branches arching overhead and the sunshine casting dappled shadows through the autumn leaves, until I reach the plateau that looks out towards the sea. I stroll among the bracken, yellow gorse and purple heather to the wooden signpost, where I turn left and take a seat on the bench to take in the view and wait for Lewis and his dogs.

How do I feel? A little annoyed with myself for giving in and agreeing to meet him after all. Nervous too. But in the end I thought, why not? Maybe it's easier to clear the air when it's just the two of us, rather than wait until my whole family is watching.

A cold wind stings my cheeks and ruffles Lewis's hair as he strides towards me. Frosty tugs on the lead, twists her body and wrenches it from my grasp, tearing up to Lewis, barking with excitement. She leaps up into his open arms, leaps out again, jumps up and sticks her nose into the pocket of his trousers, and pulls out what looks like a banknote before tearing it up into shreds.

'That was twenty quid,' he says, looking down ruefully. 'What did you go and do that for, Frosty?'

'I'm sorry. She's pleased to see you.' And so am I, I want to say, if I'm being honest with myself. If I were a dog, I'd be wagging my tail too.

'She has an expensive way of showing it.' Lewis pauses without making any comment on the progress of Frosty's training. 'It's good to see you, Zara.'

'You too,' I say, even more nervous now because I feel too much for him ever to be just friends.

'Thanks for agreeing to meet.'

'Half an hour,' I remind him. 'That's all.' I relent a little, feeling more cheerful. 'You've had two minutes already.' I stand up and catch Frosty while Lewis whistles for the collies, which greet me calmly. I bend down and stroke Mick and then Miley. I've missed them. It's as if Lewis and I had our own little family that fell apart when I broke up with him.

'You can let her off, can't you?' he says. 'Mick is here to act as Frosty's ears.'

'She's missed that,' I say, unclipping her lead.

'Let's walk.'

We stroll closer to the edge of the slope and pause by a clump of trees to gaze out at the water. I lean against one of the trunks, glancing up at the fungi that emerge from the tree's core like giant dinner plates. Lewis places his palm against the bark and stands so close to me that I can feel the warmth of his breath on my skin.

'I haven't stopped thinking about you,' he says, so quietly that I can hardly hear him over the sound of my thundering heart. It is as though he is shepherding my emotions, rounding up the good ones and driving the bad away.

'Please, let's not go there.' I force myself to take back control before I'm swept up by a wave of lust and desire.

'How would you feel if I asked you again to take me back?' Lewis scrapes his fingernail across the trunk and chips off a fragment of bark. 'I've talked to Mick and Miley and, although they're good listeners, they aren't brilliant at dishing out advice. If they could have an opinion, they would probably tell me I'm on a hiding to nothing? Am I, Zara?' He drops his hand and gently touches my fingers. I draw back, burying my hands in my coat pockets as my heart pounds a familiar rhythm.

I shake my head. I didn't come here for this.

'I don't want to think about it.' I hear my voice grow harsh. 'I'm going back to the car – your time is up.'

'You agreed to meet me, so you might as well listen,' he says, blocking my path.

'I only came because you and Emily wouldn't give up, and you were kind helping look for Gran. Don't read any more into it.'

'Do you hate me that much?'

'Of course I don't hate you, but I can't take you back. It isn't that straightforward.'

'It seems very simple to me.'

When he stands in front of me like this, the old feelings come rushing back, but the underlying reason for my decision to break up with him remains the same. It's a physical pain, raw, throbbing and unrelenting. I'm barren, empty, infertile and incomplete. I can't have Lewis's children.

'I mean it when I say I love you more than anyone in the world,' he goes on. 'I've had time to think, to reflect on what I really want out of life, when I've never taken it all that seriously before. I've missed you more than anything. I told you, I can live without a child, but I can't live without you. I'll never let you down. I promise.'

I stare out to sea, my mind an ocean of uncertainty. My head is telling me to stay back and keep life simple, while my heart is telling me to go for it. I gaze back at him, his eyes glinting with that animal passion that I cannot resist. I want him. He wants me. Isn't that enough?

I stumble forwards, straight into his arms, and somehow his lips land on my mouth, or my mouth lands on his lips, I'm not sure which, and we're kissing like we've never kissed before.

Lewis pulls away slightly. I can hear his breathing, ragged and matching mine.

'Does this mean . . .?' he whispers.

I nod, at the same time as a dog, no, three dogs, start barking.

'Look at that,' Lewis says, stepping aside so I can see Frosty, Mick and Miley standing in a row, staring at us, open-mouthed, ready to bark again.

'I think they're telling us it's time to move on,' Lewis says, taking my hand.

'Let's go,' I add, happy to start again and see where it takes us.

'When we said we'd see where it goes, I didn't imagine we'd end up down here,' I say, staring out through the windscreen of the pick-up and trying to work out what Lewis is so excited about. We've been back together for over a month now, and it's a Saturday afternoon in early December, the day of Lewis's twenty-fourth birthday. The trees are bare of leaves, their branches dark against a pale wintry sky, and we're parked on the edge of Talyton's industrial estate, not far from Overdown Farmers and the garage where I have my car serviced.

'This seems a strange place to choose to celebrate your birthday. What am I supposed to be looking at?' I ask.

'The vista ahead.' Lewis drums his fingers against the steering wheel. 'Tell me what you see.'

'A desolate landscape,' I respond.

'Look more closely.'

'Okay, I can see a rusty five-bar gate locked with an even rustier padlock and chain with a kind of wasteland behind it. Isn't this the place where Frank Maddocks used to live, the father of the guy who abandoned Frosty?'

'That's what I've been told. It's come up for rent and I'm first in the queue. It isn't much, just a couple of acres, but it's a start.' Lewis smiles. 'It's for the sheep.'

The mention of sheep reminds me. I was going to give him his birthday card later with the meal I'm supposed to be cooking for him, a romantic evening with candles and a DVD, but it seems more appropriate now. I pull the envelope from my bag.

'You'd better have this,' I say, leaning across to kiss his cheek. 'Happy birthday, my darling.'

461

'Thank you.' I watch him open the card and pick up the piece of paper that slips out. 'What's this?'

'It's an IOU, as in "ewe".' I spell it out for him. 'I want to buy you your very first sheep, but I couldn't exactly go to the market to pick one up, and keep it in the annexe.'

'Oh, that's brilliant. You are a genius.' Lewis hugs me. 'I can buy several sheep, if I go ahead and rent this place.'

'Are you sure it's suitable? It's full of rubbish.'

'Come on, let your imagination run riot.'

'I'm sorry, but I'm struggling. The only things running riot are the weeds.'

'It needs a bit of work – that's why it's cheap. I've spoken to Murray and he's offered to give me a hand.'

'I wouldn't touch it. It's a terrible mess. It'll take years to clear up.'

'You have no vision, Zara.'

'You have no sense of reality.' I stop winding him up, not wanting to hurt his feelings because he's clearly sold on the idea of starting his farming enterprise here.

'We have to start somewhere.'

'We?'

'I was hoping it could be a joint venture. Why don't you come and have a look?'

I glance down at my feet.

'No excuses. I've put your wellies in the back.'

'You came prepared.'

Lewis reaches across the back of the seat and rests his arm around my shoulders. With his other hand, he strokes the inside of my wrist, sending thrills of anticipation across my skin.

'I want your opinion.'

'What do I know about land and sheep?' I chuckle.

'I thought I'd taught you quite a lot over the past few months.'

We walk to the gate and I climb over after Lewis, who turns and takes my hand to help me over a piece of discarded corrugated iron which lies between us and a clump of small trees. Beyond these lies a clearing of concrete hard-standing.

'There used to be mobile home on here. I thought I'd build a barn where I can store a trailer and tractor, and see if I can get hold of a caravan.'

'Not to live in,' I say quickly. 'That sounds too much like roughing it to me.'

'No, for somewhere to keep warm and boil a kettle when the weather's bad.' He tips his head to one side. 'A love nest, and then the rest of the time we can live just down the road in Talyton. There's a house for rent opposite the church, if you're interested.' He pauses. 'We can't stay at your sister's for ever. There'll be work at Greenwood Farm for the lambing season, and I expect Murray will keep me on for the shearing, but after that, Emily will be back after her maternity break. Not only that, it would be good to have a home that's more like our own.'

He's right, I think. I moved into the annexe at the farm with Lewis, more by accident than design, when Ally Jackson signed the rental agreement on the shop, which effectively made me homeless. (My parents decided to hang on to the freehold for now.)

'I'd love to get a place together,' I say, leaning against him.

He slides his arms around my waist and gazes into my eyes.

'I know you've said you'd never marry again, but is there any chance . . .?' he begins.

'No,' I say quickly. 'I'm sorry. That doesn't mean I don't want to spend the rest of my life with you. I just don't want the fuss, the ring and the piece of paper. It doesn't mean anything to me. I want us to stay just as we are.'

'That's okay,' he says, touching his nose to mine. 'I don't mind as long as we're together.'

'You won't expect me to do the farmer's wife stuff like Emily does, getting up in the middle of the night?'

'Maybe. You'll be better at delivering lambs than I am – you have smaller hands.' He holds my hand, turns it over in his and strokes my fingers. Sensing his desire, I look straight into his eyes.

'I think I'd like you to take me back to bed,' I whisper.

'You are insatiable . . .' He kisses my ear.

'It is your birthday,' I tease.

'It feels like it's my birthday every day.' He hesitates. 'I thought we were going to visit Rosemary.'

'We can do that on the way back to the farm – if you're sure.' I try to get there at least twice a week. 'She can be pretty peculiar. She doesn't always remember family now, let alone anyone else.' I bite my lip.

'I won't be offended.'

I link my arm through his and we return to the

pick-up. Lewis drives to the nursing home, stopping at the shop on the way to buy Gran some sweets.

I choose mint humbugs, sherbet lemons and jellybeans. Ally, James's mum, serves me, struggling to balance the scales as she pours the sweets into a paper bag. It doesn't seem right seeing someone else behind the counter. The name of the shop – the Village News – hasn't changed, but everything else about it feels as though it has.

'How's it going?' I ask her.

'It's been fun so far. Mind you, I thought it was going to be a whole lot easier to make money from newspapers, by selling and delivering them, than it is writing articles for the *Chronicle*. James is already threatening to strike over his pay.' She smiles wryly. 'I love my customers, though. They're great, very loyal to your grandmother, and the shop. Wish Rosemary all the best from me, won't you?'

'I will,' I say.

On my way out, I notice the headline on the *Chronicle*: 'Sentenced for Assault on Ex-Girlfriend', and a photo of Frank Maddocks's son. So, he hasn't been charged with animal cruelty, but he's going to be locked up for some considerable time. I'm not sure it's enough, but at least he's being punished. His girlfriend and baby appear to have had a lucky escape.

Gran is looking physically well, sitting in her room at the old people's home with the radio on and a book of crosswords that falls from her lap when I walk in to see her. I pick it up and flick through it. All the puzzles are blank. It's too late to expect that solving clues and playing word-games can improve her memory. She has the photo of Granddad on the shelf above her commode and John's letters in the drawer. I did get in touch with his family, but it wasn't good news – he died a few months after his holiday in Talyton St George and I decided to let sleeping dogs lie, as Gran would have said. Some romances are best left in the past. The cuckoo clock is on the wall beside the bed, but the cuckoo is silent now, as if it's retired to a quieter life behind its doors. I did suggest that we had it repaired, but my grandmother didn't seem interested in the idea. I think even that was beyond her, her life having shrunk, contained and confined within these four walls.

Does she ever think about her family unless we are here in person? I don't know. I don't like to think about it too deeply.

'Gran, do you remember Lewis, the shepherd?' I ask as she peers into the bag of sweets and chooses a mint humbug, meaning that her capacity for speech is somewhat inhibited for a while. She nods.

'We're going to rent a house in Talyton St George along with some land.'

'You're a handsome young man,' Gran says, and there's the briefest flash of that wicked twinkle in her eye, and for that instant I can almost imagine she's her old self.

I perch on the edge of the bed, giving Lewis a warning glance as he's about to sit on the commode. 'I'm not sure that will take your weight,' I say, amused.

'I'll stand,' he says. 'Thank you for the compliment,

Rosemary. You're looking pretty gorgeous yourself today.'

Gran's attention returns to the sweets.

'I reckon she's locked us out,' I say, looking up at Lewis. 'That will be it for today.' I steel myself to say farewell to this stranger, who looks like my grandmother, yet continues to grow less like her every time I see her. I stand up and kiss her on the cheek.

'Goodbye,' I mutter, not wanting her to see that I'm choked up with grief.

'Goodbye, dear,' she says, apparently unconcerned. 'It must be teatime soon.'

'Don't ruin your appetite then,' Lewis says, but I don't think she gets it.

'Thank you for coming with me,' I say on the way home. 'I'm glad we went. I feel better about it now. It was the right thing to do for both of us.'

'She seems well looked after,' Lewis agrees. 'And you seem a lot less stressed. It was a tough decision, but the right one. Can you forgive yourself now?' My forehead tightens when he continues, 'It seems to me that you don't have to beat yourself up about it any longer. As your gran might have said at one time, it's all worked out for the best.'

On the way back, the landscape doesn't appear quite so desolate beneath a flaming orange sky. Lewis stops the pick-up outside the rusted gate at the perimeter of the industrial estate to let the dogs out.

'Are you sure about taking that on?' I ask.

'I'm sure. I can borrow a tractor and trailer from Murray to start clearing it over the winter, then I can plough and seed it so there's grass for the summer. I have it all planned out.' He reaches out for my hand and raises it to his lips. 'You know, I'm beginning to wonder if it's all a dream. You'll have to pinch me.'

I pinch the spare fold of flesh at his waist.

'Ouch, not that hard,' he gasps, laughing. 'Maybe I'm not dreaming after all.'

'If you are, we're living the same dream,' I point out, looking towards the horizon, where the sun is sinking behind the hills, leaving the sky streaked with pink and grey clouds. 'Red sky at night, shepherd's delight.'

Lewis wraps his arms around me and pulls me close.

'I know this sounds a bit cheesy, but you're this shepherd's delight,' he says with a chuckle in his throat. 'I love you and I want to live the same dreams with you for the rest of our lives.'

'I love you too.' I lean up to kiss him. 'Now,' I add as seductively as I can, 'hurry up and take me home to bed.'

**Do you want to find out what happened
with Tessa and Jack?**

**Don't miss Cathy's exclusive short story
The Three of Us, only available as an ebook.**

The Three of Us

Tessa and Jack live at the Animal Sanctuary in Talyton St George. They had been friends for years, but it wasn't until Jack interrupted Tessa's wedding that she discovered his feelings for her were stronger than she ever knew.

Now, a year on, they could not be happier. And when Tessa discovers she's pregnant, it's as if all their dreams have come true.

But a scan shows that there are complications, and suddenly Tessa discovers that Jack has always had doubts about having a baby. Supported throughout by Zara, the village midwife, Tessa and Jack have some tough decisions to make.

However, as the baby's birth draws closer, Tessa and Jack grow further apart. Will he feel differently when the baby is born? Or will having her wonderful child mean losing the man she adores?

**If you'd like to see how
Tessa and Jack got together, then read**

The Village Vet

**In Talyton St George, vet nurse Tessa Wilde is on
the way to her wedding...**

It should be the happiest day of her life. But then her car hits a
dog, and though the dog is saved thanks to the Otter House vets,
her wedding is not.

Animal welfare officer and part time fire-fighter Jack Miller spends
his life saving animals and people. As one of Tessa's oldest
friends, he feels he has the right to interrupt her wedding and
rescue her from a marriage that can only end in tears.

But does he? Tessa is sure she doesn't need rescuing, least of
all by Jack.

When they begin to work together at the Animal Sanctuary,
however, Tessa begins to wonder whether being rescued by Jack
might not be such a bad thing after all.

Praise for The Village Vet

'A wonderful story about rescued animals and romance.
I loved it.' Katie Fforde

arrow books

Remember teen-dad Adam's mother Jennie –
the woman who bakes amazing cakes?
Read how she came to Talyton St George in

The Sweetest Thing

If only everything in life was as simple as baking a cake...

Jennie Copeland thought she knew the recipe for a happy life:
marriage to her university sweetheart, a nice house in the suburbs
and three beautiful children. But when her husband leaves her,
she is forced to find a different recipe. And she thinks she's
found just what she needs: a ramshackle house on the outskirts
of rural Talyton St George, a new cake-baking business, a dog, a
horse, chickens...

But life in the country is not quite as idyllic as she'd hoped, and
Jennie can't help wondering whether neighbouring farmer Guy
Barnes was right when he told her she wouldn't last the year.

Or perhaps the problem is that she's missing one vital ingredient
to make her new life a success. Could Guy be the person to
provide it?

Praise for Cathy Woodman:

'Funny, truthful and original . . . I loved this book' Jill Mansell

'Woodman's warmth and wit are set to make her the next big
thing in rural romance.' *Daily Record*

arrow books